PR

"*Fiery Star* was beautiful. I ... Company. I was kept guessing through all the twists and turns of the plot, and was moved by its characters, especially the storyteller, young Emma Lightfoot, whose courage will stay with you long after you finish *Fiery Star.*"
—Kelley Weir, actress, director and teacher

"Hopeful, rich in history, and shining with Emma Lightfoot's fierce and often wry voice, *Fiery Star* shares a world both lost and familiar, dangerous and beautiful. It caught hold of my heart and didn't let go."
—Kim Culbertson, award winning author of *Catch a Falling Star* and *Songs for a Teenage Nomad*

"The glow of *Fiery Star* lingers long after the last page. What better way to be immersed in the drama of an 1856 Gold Rush acting troupe than through the words of young Emma Lightfoot's journal? Finding the exact turn of phrase, Emma's descriptions enliven the interplay of haunting characters, California Gold Rush towns, and the mysterious fires that shadow the troupe's departures." —Shirley DicKard, Editor, *The Camptonville Courier*

"A colorful world of actors and outlaws comes to life in a debut historical novel from Rivers. Sixteen-year-old Emma Lightfoot lives in 1856 Placerville, California, one of many towns spawned by the Gold Rush. Her mother and siblings are dead, but she adores her father and closest companion, C.E. "Emmett" Lightfoot. They write and print the local newspaper, the Placerville Rattler, and at the book's opening, they both look forward to attending and reviewing the touring Star Troupe's play featuring Edwin "Ted" Booth, son of renowned actor Junius. But tragedy strikes when Emmett gets a splinter that becomes infected. Within a matter of days, Emma is the sole living Lightfoot. Saddled with her father's secret debts, Emma tries to turn a one-day gig as the theater company's washerwoman into a season-long engagement, and the troupe's iron-willed but kind co-manager, Hattie Burnham, brings her on after a strange fire destroys much of Placerville. Emma's new theatrical "family" includes brooding and handsome Booth; Hattie and her loutish husband, Ben; charming and privileged Harry; coquettish teen actress Sophie; 7-year-old "Fairy Star" Louise; and other eccentrics. The troupe tours the camps

and towns of the Sierra Nevada foothills, experiencing great triumphs—largely thanks to Booth's creative brilliance—and enormous setbacks. Most troublingly of all, a string of destructive fires points to a possible "firebug" in the troupe's ranks. The novel's large, colorful supporting cast demands readers' engagement. Each character is distinct and troubled in his or her own way, such as Emma's resilient best friend, Evangeline, turning to prostitution after her parents' death; Hattie's battling about finances with her gambling husband; or Booth's struggling with the shadow of his famous father...scenes and plotlines stand out for their tension and intrigue—a section describing a rescue attempt during a massive, town-consuming fire is knuckle-whitening...shines thanks to its compelling...cast and vividly constructed world."
—*Kirkus Reviews*

"Rich in historical detail and full of adventure, *Fiery Star* and its sixteen-year-old protagonist enchanted me. Orphaned Emma Rose Lightfoot and the family she discovers in the world of theater as she carves out her own, unique place in the world are such believable, fascinating characters that I felt as if I were saying goodbye to beloved friends when the last page was turned." —Tanya Egan Gibson, author of *How to Buy a Love of Reading*

"Reading *Fiery Star* is like being lifted back in time. You quickly find yourself dashing through the streets of Nevada City with young Emma Lightfoot, hailing the colorful characters who lived there in the rugged days of the Gold Rush." —Alaria Z. Bliss, author of *The Young Centaur*

"How refreshing to read Leslie Rivers's riveting novel of dauntless courage during the California Gold Rush, when "family" meant everything. Packed with illuminating historical details, *Fiery Star* takes you on a journey to 1850's California through the eyes of a plucky, orphaned 16-year-old girl earnestly searching for what makes life honorable and right. Rivers's descriptions of the countryside, towns, and theatrical performances sing. A seasoned theater artist herself, her knowledge of theater is boldly evident in her sparkling, humorous dialogue and central characters, actors in a touring troupe. Based in intriguing historical fact, *Fiery Star* is stunningly visual and emotionally moving." —Karen Ingenthron Lewis is author of the memoir, *I Married a Munster, an Epic Love Story*, and several plays. Former radio host of WBAI-NY's Al Lewis Lives, Karen regularly conducted listener-guided book reviews. She is a writer, actor, teacher, and owner of Ham 'n Cheese on Wry, a small press book development company.

"Leslie Rivers presents a deliciously descriptive, deeply felt, and authentically articulated journey to California's roots through the eyes of a young heroine, Emma Rose Lightfoot. Rivers offers marvelous behind-the-scenes glimpses into California Gold Rush era theater, mixed with great humor, rich sensitivity, and her own powerful theatre arts acumen. Rivers's characters and relationships are palpable, and her story-telling is impeccable." —Virginia Drake, actress and director

"*Fiery Star* is packed with adventure, comedy, tragedy, romance- - -and most thrillingly, at its heart is an original new heroine, Emma Lightfoot. It is Emma, a girl of 16, whose diary draws us in and leads us on an incredible journey! Emma captured my heart and imagination. *Fiery Star* is full of life because Emma Lightfoot breathes life in so deeply!

"*Fiery Star* has ranked among my "constellations" of favorites. I wait anxiously for the further adventures of the thespians, desperadoes, lovers, true friends, true villains and, of course, Emma Lightfoot. Emma has taken her place in the gallery of great American fictional (but oh, so true) characters."
—Michael Wells-Oakes, author of *A Cold December*, *Breath to Breath*, *Grace*

Fiery Star

The Journals of Emma Rose Lightfoot

by

Leslie Rivers

This book is a work of fiction. References to real people, events, establishments, organizations or locales are intended to provide a sense of authenticity and are used fictitiously. All other characters, and all incidents and dialogue, are drawn from the author's imagination and are not to be construed as real.

Book Cover & Interior Design by Julie Valin,
Self to Shelf Publishing Services,
www.SelftoShelfPublishing.com

Map by Jennifer Bliss

ISBN 978-0-9998514-0-1
Copyright Registration Number TXu 1-871-204, 2012

Author website:
www.leslieannrivers.com

Nevada City,
California

For Miranda,
who makes me proud

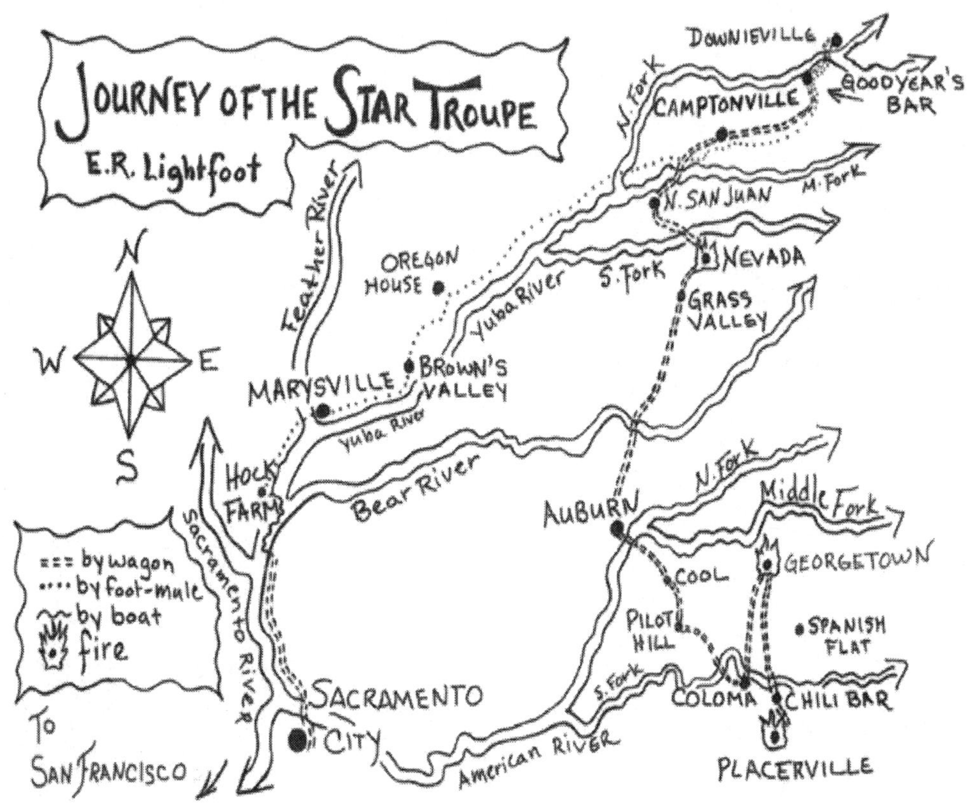

JOURNEY OF THE STAR TROUPE
E.R. Lightfoot
N
W
E
S
Feather River
OREGON HOUSE
MARYSVILLE
BROWN'S VALLEY
Yuba River
HOCK FARM
Bear River
Sacramento River
SACRAMENTO CITY
TO SAN FRANCISCO
American River
DOWNIEVILLE
GOODYEAR'S BAR
CAMPTONVILLE
N. Fork
M. Fork
N. SAN JUAN
NEVADA
S. Fork
GRASS VALLEY
AUBURN
N. Fork
Middle Fork
GEORGETOWN
COOL
PILOT HILL
SPANISH FLAT
S. Fork
COLOMA
CHILI BAR
PLACERVILLE
=== by wagon
.... by foot-mule
by boat
fire

FIERY STAR

CAST OF CHARACTERS

THE STAR TROUPE:

Miss Emma Lightfoot............................ *The Girl Who Does The Wash*
Mr. Edwin Booth, "Ted".. *Company Star*
Mrs. Harriet Burnham, "Hattie" .... *Actress/Manager*
Mr. Ben Burnham ....*Actor/Manager, Former Stagecoach Driver*
Mr. Augustus Thayer, "Gus" .... *Character Actor*
Ulysses... *Canine Extraordinaire*
Mr. Sumner Moone .... *Comedian, Song and Dance Man*
Miss Sophie Griffith.......................................*Soubrette, Singer, Dancer*
Mr. Harry Brown. ....*Juvenile Leading Man*
Frank Mayo... *Leading Man*
Mr. Jeriah Leach .... *Stage Manager, Character Actor*
Buck & Jimmy Bliss ....*Musicians, Wranglers, Bit Players*
Lem Mule.. *A Sweet Old Creature*
Mrs. Clarissa La Rue...*Character Actress*
La Petite Louise La Rue........................*Child Performer, a "Fairy Star"*

SUPPORTING CHARACTERS:

C.E. Lightfoot, "Emmett"........................*Editor, The Placerville Rattler*
Evangeline, "Evie" ....*Emma's Best Friend*
Mrs. Gee.. *Owner Of The Lucky Wash House*
Captain Avery Smith .... *Livery Stable Owner*
The Frisbie Family..*Theatre Owners*
Mr. James Hamlin. ....*Bookstore Proprietor*
Mr. S. E. Fletcher.. *District Attorney, Stargazer*
Mr. Eben Card .... *Dandy*
Tom Bell .... *Outlaw*
Miss Lola Montez...*Grass Valley's Superstar*

ALSO: Townspeople, Bandits, Fellow Artists, Circus Folk and Travelers Upon the Road

WHERE: California's Sierra Nevada Foothills and Sacramento Valley

WHEN: The Summer of 1856

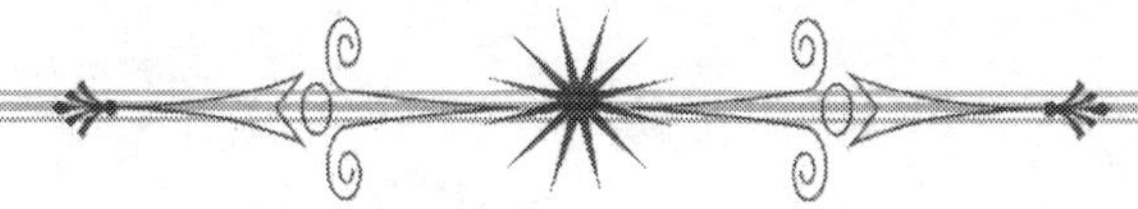

JOURNAL 1
The Girl on the Prairie

MAY 20 TO JULY 18,
1856

May 20, 1856

For my dear daughter Emma,
on the occasion of her sixteenth birthday,
this journal,
in the hope that she will put her thoughts to paper.
I am confident success awaits her
at every bend in the road.

Affectionately,

C. E. Lightfoot, Editor

"Emmett"

TUESDAY, JUNE 17, 1856. *Our rooms above the office of* The Placerville Rattler. *Past midnight—*

A Booth is coming to town!

As soon as I read the theatre bill, freshly tacked on the clapboards of the Greyhound Saloon, I hitched up my skirt and ran!

Emmett and I had been gadding about town, sniffing out last-minute news for Thursday's edition of *The Rattler*. He'd sent me off for details of next week's Ladies' Aid meeting, but news of a Booth trumps the ladies any day. The theatre is close to my heart, and it is dear to my father's heart, too.

Main Street is plagued with dust and potholes and was crowded despite the midday heat. I dodged miners' mules and dray wagons as I hastened in search of my father. Emmett is easy to spy—he is one of a kind—but I checked his usual haunts to little avail. He'd already departed the Round Tent Store, and his bench beneath the bell tower in the plaza was empty. I poked my head inside the newsstand and called out, "Seen my father, Mr. Davis?"

Davis chuckled. "Miss Emma, you're just a shake behind him. Try the Courthouse!"

The Courthouse is a piece up Main, and I was short of breath by the time I spotted the turkey feather on Emmett's wide hat. He was perched on the steps, in lively conversation with the litigants waiting in the shade, and scribbling furiously on the pad he keeps in his right coat pocket. The topic was the Vigilance Committees that have sprung up across California.

"I say, hang the devils, and rid the state of vermin," growled a leathery miner, spluttering tobacco juice onto the planks at his feet.

Emmett leaned in toward the man. "Without the law's say-so?"

I know Emmett has convictions about those Committees—"Nothing but lynch mobs!"—and is working up an editorial on them, but I couldn't hold back.

"Emmett! Emmett!" I dashed up the steps. "Come see! A Booth is booked into Placerville!"

Emmett halted, his pencil poised in the air. "A Booth, Emma? But Booth is dead."

"Oh, it's not the old Booth. His name is Edwin. 'Heir to the mantle' the bill says. Take a look for yourself!"

Emmett hesitated only a second, then shoved his pad and pencil back into his pocket. "Excuse me, friends." He tipped his hat to the gents on the steps. "My daughter has brought me delightful news!"

He tucked his arm in mine, and together we hustled back to the Greyhound. Emmett is not a man to move down Main Street in a straight line—he's often detoured by greetings to friends and acquaintances or by popping into an establishment to chat up an ad with a proprietor. But today he made good progress, and soon we stood, side by side, perusing the bill. It read like so:

PLACER THEATRE!

THE MANAGEMENT TAKES GREAT PLEASURE IN ANNOUNCING THEY HAVE EFFECTED AN ENGAGEMENT FOR TWO NIGHTS ONLY, WITH THE STAR TROUPE, AND THE YOUNG AMERICAN TRAGEDIAN,

MR. EDWIN BOOTH,

HEIR TO THE MANTLE OF HIS ILLUSTRIOUS PREDECESSOR,

JUNIUS BRUTUS BOOTH THE ELDER.

FRIDAY EVENING, JULY 4,

WILL BE PRESENTED COLMAN'S TRAGEDY OF

THE IRON CHEST

Sir Edward Mortimer .... MR. EDWIN BOOTH
Helen .... Mrs. Burnham

There was more on the bill, of course—musical and variety acts, and the promise of *The Taming of the Shrew* on the following night—but our eyes were riveted by the name of Booth!

"So," mused Emmett, "the old lion's cub will grace our stage. I'd heard Junius had a passel of sons, but I can't say as I've seen them. This Edwin will have some big shoes to fill."

"Perhaps he'll be wonderful," I said.

"There's only one way to find out. Let's hunt up Dunlap!"

We scurried around the back of the building and up the staircase to the Placer Theatre. The doors were open, but the manager's cubby behind the stage was vacant.

"Hmm," said Emmett, rubbing his chin. "Now, where should we look for a fellow like Dunlap?"

And we both exclaimed at once, "In the saloon!"

We hurried back down to the street. I waited by the door while Emmett peered into the Greyhound. Sure enough, he spied Dunlap's bright, checkered coat at one of the tables in the rear and quickly fetched the man out.

"Dunlap." Emmett smiled, charming as can be. "You've met my lovely daughter, Emma. Emma, you know Mr. Dunlap."

Dunlap gave me a pleasant enough nod, even if he did smell of beer.

"We would like to review *The Iron Chest* for *The Rattler,*" Emmett said. "I can guarantee you a prominent place on the 'Amusements' page and multiple mentions of your establishment."

"Lightfoot," Dunlap replied, "you don't have to sell me. Of course. I'll save you a seat."

"Two seats, if you don't mind." Emmett grinned. He pulled a cigar from his waistcoat pocket and offered it to Dunlap.

"Yes, indeed," said Dunlap, tucking the cigar away. "Two seats! A pleasure to do business, Lightfoot!"

When Emmett reviews a play for *The Rattler*, he always angles for two free seats instead of one. When I was small, it was cheaper to take me along than to hire someone to care for me, and I was happy there by his side. I still am. I love the smell of burning oil in the footlights and the shadows on the drops. I can't wait for that moment when an actor first walks out on the stage and anything can happen. And I can't wait to witness the Young American Tragedian!

Dunlap is never without a pocketful of tickets. He selected two and borrowed Emmett's pencil to scrawl "Complimentary!" across their backsides, and then to sign them "W. Dunlap, Mgr." We bid the gentleman a hearty thanks and started off in a high mood.

"Shall we celebrate over dinner, dear girl?" asked Emmett. "We have two choices—the Union Hotel, or the Union Hotel. Which do you prefer?"

"I'd say the Union Hotel!"

Emmett trades advertising to the Union's restaurant in return for credit. Its kitchen's bounty is the source of most of our hot meals. Tom, the waiter, greeted us with a bright, "Hello, Lightfoots!" and swiftly had us seated and served at "Emmett's Table" in the corner by the window.

As we sipped our soup, I said, "Emmett, there was a man posting the bill when I first passed by the Greyhound, a stranger. Do you think he could have been Edwin Booth?"

"I doubt if the star of the show would be posting his own bill. What did he look like?"

"Tall, light hair, a beaded hat band. He spotted me standing behind him and smiled at me. I think his eyes were blue, and his tooth was chipped."

"Did he speak to you?"

"Oh, no—as soon as he caught my eye, I got bashful and ran for you!"

Emmett laughed and wiped the soup from his mustache. "Old Booth was dark and on the short side. Although he was larger than life in front of the footlights. I saw him as Macbeth in Philadelphia and King Lear in Boston. He had such power, Emma. And that voice! When he roared, the rafters shook!"

Tom set our pork and potatoes before us, but Emmett paid them no mind.

"Even in '52, when he played Sacramento, the man was a sight to see. He was in his sunset, true—he was bowlegged, and his nose had been flattened in a bar fight—but no one could have matched him. I saw his Richard III four times! Why, he played that old villain as Fortune's fool, drowning in the sorrow of his sins."

I spied a tear in Emmett's eye. He brushed it away with his napkin. Emmett is stoic about much of life, but beauty makes him weep.

"You've teared up over Booth before," I said.

Emmett gave a somber nod. "Yes, indeed, when he met his end on that Mississippi riverboat. The man was trying to get home, and instead, he died alone, upon the water. Hardly fitting. He was a fine actor. Crazy as a loon, but very fine." Emmett shook his head and dug into his dinner.

For a time, we ate in silence in the comfort of each other's company. Only when Tom had brought our pie to the table, did I gather the nerve to ask, "Emmett, am I a good help to you with *The Rattler*?"

He looked up from his plate in surprise. "Of course you are, Emma. You're the best printer's devil an editor could wish for. You set type quicker than I do."

"And I'm a passable writer."

"You're a very good writer."

"Then I'd like to do more than the Ladies' News and digging up quotes for filler. Please Emmett, let me write the review for *The Iron Chest.*"

He frowned and took a long sip of his coffee. He loves to pen the theatre reviews.

"I'm sixteen now, Emmett."

"Have you been writing in the journal I gave you?"

"I'm starting it today. Please. I know I can make you proud."

He lifted an eyebrow at me, but then he put his hand on mine. "You go to it, dear girl."

I whooped, right in the middle of the restaurant. I would have hugged the man but for the pot of coffee between us. Once we were on the street, I broke into song, "A penny for a spool of thread, a penny for a needle!" Emmett whistled accompaniment, and, marching in step, we made our way cheerfully toward the *Rattler* office.

We were barely two doors from home when we came face to face with Clarence McPhee. Our song died right there. Emmett didn't snub McPhee—he nodded politely—but as McPhee shuffled awkwardly aside, we strode on with purpose until we were in the privacy of our own rooms.

Clarence McPhee showed up at the *Rattler* a week ago with a "proposition" for Emmett, that he would "take me off" my father's hands. He even offered to toss fifty dollars into the deal. Once Emmett realized that this proposition was a proposal—of sorts—he let McPhee know, in frank terms, that he didn't believe I was a liability, and that he reckoned he'd keep me about for a while. McPhee was taken aback. He has a pile of dirt that passes for a claim and he thinks himself a catch, although his clothes are rarely clean and his neck is scabby.

Later, Emmett laughed at the conversation. "I told him no, Emma, but I expect I could still hunt him up if you have a mind to walk down the aisle."

"I'd sooner walk on hot coals!"

"You sure? I might be able to bargain him up to sixty dollars. Maybe even a hog thrown in."

"Emmett!"

He put an arm about my shoulders. "Don't you worry, dear girl. Your home is here, until the day your heart says otherwise."

A woman in the camps can be a magnet for lonely miners. My best friend Evangeline lost her parents this spring and turned for a living to the Red House, where she must tolerate all sorts of men. Most of them are decent enough, but some have gotten desperate and hangdog, and they have lost their soul's compass. It makes me grateful to have my father at my side.

Once we were back in the newspaper office, Emmett deposited our tickets under a jar of chewed pencils on his desk, and we went happily to work on Thursday's edition. We had plenty to keep us busy, sorting the news we'd gleaned from the day and arranging the advertisements on the back pages. At long last, I looked up from the piles of paper before me. The wall clock announced it was past midnight. I neatened the stacks, took up a candle and our new volume of Dickens's *Little Dorrit*, and started for the stairs. Emmett was at his desk in the lamplight, still scribbling away on the front page news.

"Emmett? How's it coming?"

"Not bad. A few minutes more." I didn't want to keep him from it, so I headed upstairs. But his chuckle floated up behind me, "Seventy dollars and a goat?"

I should have tossed my book at him, but I was overtaken by giggles.

"Goodnight, Emma," he called.

"Goodnight, Emmett!" And I laughed all the way up to my bed.

Wednesday, June 18. *Our rooms. Very late on a summer's night—*

This is my favorite day of the week--the day we put *The Placerville Rattler* to bed! Around noon, while Emmett was still writing, I donned my printer's apron and long black sleeves and claimed my spot on the stool before the type case. I am the printer's devil, and I have the privilege of sorting the foolscap bearing my father's scrawled notes into the neat lines and columns of the printed word!

When I was small, Emmett spelled out my name backwards with bits of type and proceeded to print it on a sheet of paper, where it elegantly reversed itself and read, "Emma Rose." After that, I couldn't wait to learn the secret of setting type. I struggled to the verge of tears to make sense of it, until one day, my brain simply turned around! At school, I became the girl who could spell my classmates' names backwards on their slates, then hold them up to the piece of mirror in the cloakroom where they would magically read aright! Now my fingers fly as I compose the type.

My first task was to take on *The Rattler's* "Amusements" section. I laid out a fine announcement of Edwin Booth in *The Iron Chest*, with a starburst above the text. Dunlap will be pleased.

Then I turned to the large formes, where each of *The Rattler*'s pages takes shape. Letters become sentences, then paragraphs and whole stories. It is my hope to make *The Rattler* both correct and pleasing to the eye, with borders and embellishments of art upon the pages. Sometimes, though, I come upon a spot at the bottom of a column where the words simply will not stretch. This day, I called out, "Emmett?"

"Umm-hmm."

"Might you add a line or two to that article on the outlaw in Nevada? It's short."

He barely looked up. "I doubt if I can, dear girl. Our deadline is upon us."

"A few more words would do the trick--"

"And rob the reader of a jewel of wisdom? This is a job for filler!"

"Oh, fine," I said. "What shall it be? 'A stitch in time--?'"

"No. Overdone. Shakespeare? 'Brevity is the soul of wit?'"

"Too brief! We need more words." I grinned at him. 'It is a wise father that knows his own child?'"

Emmett snorted and raised an eyebrow, but he went right on. "I have it! 'Knowledge is the wing--'"

And we sang out together, "'wherewith we fly to heaven!'"

My father smiled and dipped his pen into the inkwell. "A fine sentiment!"

I agreed. "And it fits on the page to the letter!"

As the afternoon slipped into evening, we lit the lamps and carried on, Emmett with his editorial on the Vigilance Committees. When it was going well, he whistled merrily; when he labored, he let slip the occasional oath. Writing comes easily to Emmett, except when he cares deeply--then he struggles and scratches out line after line.

My father has never allowed me at hangings, although he is a regular attendee on behalf of *The Rattler*. He is outraged at those citizens who call themselves Vigilance Committees. He terms their doings "necktie parties dressed up in respectability," and returns from such goings-on pale and quiet, except to say, "A hanging is a dreadful thing, one I hope to never see again." Yet lynch law is the order of the day in California, now that the Gold Rush is tapped out. From San Francisco to the High Sierra, no one is safe from the noose, not even women. The Mexicana, Josepha, was hanged from a bridge up in Downieville just a few years back.

By nine o'clock, I had finished the formes for all the *Rattler*'s pages, save for Emmett's editorial. Emmett tied on his apron, and we turned to the printing press. Years ago, when the press was freed from its shipping crate to fill its place of honor in the office, Emmett had stood back in admiration and exclaimed, "A fantastical machine!" Young as I was, I understood. We couldn't help but run our hands over its elegant frame of black iron and the embossed serpents twined about its curves; we sighed in delight at the gilded eagle perched upon the top. Today, it is still a thing of wonder, for it turns tiny bits of lead and sheets of newsprint into ideas that fly off the page and give the whole town something to talk about.

Emmett and I locked a forme into the press's bed and began to print. Printing is a dance with its own music. When we work, we are in perfect rhythm with the squeal of the roller inking the type, the clinks and whirrs of the levers, the thunk of the wooden bar as the platen meets the paper. The printed sheets are lifted from the press with a gentle whoosh and hung to dry, filling the office with the smell of ink and the promise of a new edition.

We had just run the back page when there was a hearty knock on the office door. I wiped my inky hands on a rag and hastened over. It was Captain Avery Smith, from the livery stable. He had a bottle of cognac in his hand.

"Miss Emma," he said, his voice deep as a hard rock mine, "a pleasure! Might that reprobate father of yours be about?"

Emmett appeared from behind the pages hanging on their lines.

"Lightfoot!" exclaimed the Captain, hefting the bottle. "I've come by good fortune—a wine merchant desperate for a bay mare—and I thought of you, sacrificing yourself over here on the altar of journalism. Is it too late to lighten your labor with a quick refreshment?"

Emmett brightened. "Absolutely not! We haven't even taken the time to sup!" He untied his apron and ushered the Captain in.

Avery Smith is an old friend of Emmett's, a tall fellow with a fine profile, grey just beginning to show in his beard. He was a Captain in the war with Mexico and claims an acquaintance with Davy Crockett. This may be true, although he is fond of a good story. Emmett and he have spent many a happy evening swapping tales over a whiskey or two.

The office being warm, we pulled chairs out to a barrel in the back yard. Emmett lit a lantern as the Captain poured cognac for the gents and I brought out slices of yesterday's ginger cake. Then the Captain and Emmett puffed at their pipes, whilst we relished the night's coolness and the glow of the stars above. Emmett took an approving sip of the cognac. "Very fine, Smith."

The Captain nodded. "Could be the best deal I'll make all year."

"An old horse trader like you?"

"Times are not what they used to be, Lightfoot. How's *The Rattler* doing?"

Emmett shrugged. "As well as can be expected, given we're Placerville's smallest newspaper."

"Small but mighty," I chipped in.

"True," said Emmett. "The size of a paper does not define its quality. A diamond is tiny, but when pure and finely cut, it has no equal."

I could no longer hold back the news. "Captain," I blurted, "Emmett has given me a promotion! Edwin Booth is playing Placerville, and I shall write the review!"

"Edwin who?" said the Captain.

"The son of my deceased favorite," said Emmett, filling their glasses once more. "Old Junius Brutus Booth. Edwin will be at the Placer on Independence Day, and Emma shall be *The Rattler*'s critic!"

"Emmett has promised me a byline," I said. "My name in print!"

"In big bold letters," Emmett grinned.

"Captain, come with us," I said. "They'll play *The Iron Chest*, it's very dramatic."

The Captain shook his head. "I don't know, Emma. That may be a bit heavy for me."

Emmett chuckled. "Smith here is a fan of musical entertainments, Emma, especially ones with attractive young ladies decorating the stage."

"I appreciate the musical muse, Lightfoot." The Captain laughed, a low rumble.

"He does indeed," Emmett said, giving me a wink. "The last time Lola Montez played in these parts, he was at the stage door every night, 'appreciating' her Spider Dance!"

"The Countess is a fine ambassador for the cultural arts of Spain," the Captain replied. "And you, Miss Emma! You shall make a splendid reviewer. I congratulate and I salute you!"

He lifted his glass. Emmett followed suit, and they toasted me, "To Miss Emma Rose Lightfoot, Dramatic Critic!" My cheeks warmed at the pleasure of it.

At that moment, a streak of silver fire blazed across the velvet sky, flared, and vanished. "Oh, my!" I gasped, as Emmett and the Captain commended the sight with expletives of approval.

Emmett put a hand on my shoulder. "Make a wish, dear girl! But keep it a secret, or it won't come true!"

I closed my eyes and sought a wish that was strange and wonderful, worthy of a jewel hurtling through the night. But, in the end, my heart's desire was a modest one—that we may simply go on, from day to day, as happy as we are now.

THURSDAY, JUNE 19. *At the table in the office. A warm afternoon—*

The Captain did not linger last night--he knew we still had work to do. He left the rest of the cognac on the barrel and made a gracious exit. I tidied the used type into its case, and Emmett turned back to his editorial, although he stared into the distance, his pen quiet. I could see that he was tired.

"Emmett," I said, "it's late. Suppose we finish up in the morning? We've done it before."

He nodded. "You're right. I'll turn in soon." I kissed his cheek, and he patted my hand. "Goodnight, dear girl."

I went to my room and donned my nightgown, then lit the candle by my bed and began to write in my journal. I heard Emmett's steps on the stairs a few minutes later. His door closed, and he was quiet.

Just before dawn, I was pulled out of a fitful sleep by my father's voice drifting up the stairwell. I crept out of bed and peered down into the office. Emmett was pacing about in his nightshirt, reading from his notes and pausing only to scratch out one word and write another. He was wide awake and making lively progress on his editorial. I stumbled back to bed and fell into my dreams, until I was startled from my pillow by a yelp. Was it one of the coyotes who run the streets in the night? When I heard a muttered "Jehosaphat's cat," I knew it was Emmett. I hurried downstairs. He was leaning against the press, clutching a bloody foot.

"What's happened?" I said.

"I'm fine. I picked up a splinter from the floor. It's nothing."

"Shall I take a look at it?"

"No. It isn't much." He hopped to his desk and rummaged a handkerchief from a drawer, then tied it around his foot.

"I can help you clean it--"

"Don't worry, Emma. I'll doctor the dang thing. Go back upstairs. I'm almost finished here." He smiled through his pain and picked up his pen. I didn't argue--I climbed back into bed and pulled my blanket over my head.

By the time I awoke, Emmett had already printed *The Rattler*'s final page. We folded and bundled our new edition and borrowed a horse and wagon from the Captain to deliver it. Emmett is limping, favoring his right foot, but he's in good spirits. His editorial, "Vigilance or Violence?" is the buzz of the town.

Saturday, June 21—

The night has worn itself out, and the gray of dawn seeps like silt into our rooms above the *Rattler*. Emmett has fallen asleep—at long last silent and, I hope, resting. A fever has overtaken him with the swiftness of a hawk swooping on a rabbit. For two days, he has babbled, sweat soaking his bedclothes. I have been at his side, keeping cool rags on his forehead and clasping his hand to steady him as best I can. He does not resemble my father. He has lost his quick smile and the twinkle in his eye and is a pale stranger, the bones of his nose and cheeks as fine as china.

Always the newspaperman, he has been hard at work on his obituary. When he first took to his bed, his swollen foot propped on a pillow, he demanded his pad and pencil and scribbled with abandon. As the fever flared and his thoughts whirled about, he insisted I take notes for him. I have struggled to do his bidding. I regard an obituary as premature—I have every hope of saving my father, despite his claim that Death is just around the corner. I tried to argue him out of it. "Emmett, this is untimely. Obituaries are written after a body's decease!"

"That's right, dear girl," he replied, "when there's a limited likelihood of one's talking back—in fact, none at all. But if we pen my obit now, I shall get my two cents in print before it's too late. Help me out, Emma love, and quote me correctly."

I did so, if only to give him peace. Peace means rest, and—please, God—healing.

At first, as he dictated, I simply listened and scrawled a careless note or two. As the heat of his fever rose, so did his fancies—he repeated himself and brought in strange tales and characters. Soon, I was hard put to sort the truth from the delirium. But when he turned to me, eyes wide, and murmured, "Phoebe!" I knew of whom he spoke.

"I'm not Phoebe, Emmett. Phoebe was my mama."

"Phoebe, don't fret, I'll be with you soon. And the little ones, too—"

I could imagine all those young Lightfoots on the other side, whispering my father's name, but I was determined to anchor him in this world. "Emmett," I said, "you can't go. You still have work to do. Perhaps we should get back to this obit. I won't complain, I know what it means to you."

He squinted up at me and, with a nod, pulled himself back into the here and now. He frowned at the rafters. "It was a spring day," he sighed, "in my childhood."

I reached for the pad and pencil. "What was, Emmett?"

"The day when I was happiest."

"Was it a birthday?"

"Oh, no. I had simply been good, for some reason or other. My father was so delighted by this uncharacteristic behavior that he gave me the gift of a day of my own."

He closed his eyes and put all his strength into each word's utterance.

"My mother packed a lunch of bread and butter, and I set out on our plow horse, Calla. I was free—free of chores, free of brothers and sisters, free to explore the far corners of our farm. The old horse was as happy as I was to be turned loose. Her step was light, and her broad back rolled gently beneath me. We wandered through the sweet, new grass. We splashed in a stream and lazed in the meadow amongst a rainbow of wildflowers. I did not return home until dark, after we had witnessed the orange globe of the sunset on the one hand and the silver disc of the moonrise on the other."

I squeezed his hand. "I did not know of that day, Emmett. I am so glad that I do."

"It was a day that burned into my heart with all the brightness of a child's vision. It has lifted me through my darkest times."

Why had he never told me? Why does it take a fever to loosen the tongues of parents and children and open their hearts?

"Perhaps I'll see Calla when I cross over," he went on, with a ghost of a smile. "Ride with her through the Elysian Fields. And I'll look up old Shakespeare, too."

"Shakespeare's in the Elysian Fields?"

"No, no. He's loitering just beyond the Pearly Gates. If I can slip past the angels, I'll buy the man a drink and strike up a conversation."

"Emmett, you'll be holding court in the Greyhound Saloon in a few days, scaring up the news for the next *Rattler*—" But my voice caught in my throat. I turned to fetch a fresh rag for his brow.

A bell tinkled as hoofbeats sounded beneath the open window. In the shadows below, I made out a donkey cart halting by the *Rattler's* door. Painted across the tailgate were the words, "Lucky Wash House." A woman stepped out, moonlight gleaming on her silks. Old Mr. Yip, the driver, handed her a sizable basket as she delivered him a few words in Chinese.

"Mrs. Gee," I called. "Please come on up."

While she ascended, her step light upon the stairs, I tidied around Emmett, as if a neat sickbed might make him appear well. Mrs. Gee hurried through the bedroom door. Emmett turned bright eyes to her, but he said nothing. She took one look and sighed, "Oh, Lightfoot! Why you wait so long?" Although, in truth, it had only been a couple of days since his foot had purpled.

"Thank you for looking in, Mrs. Gee," I said. I was glad for the company.

"Has the doctor been here?"

"Yes. Runkler came twice. It's sepsis, he says. He left lye soap and a bottle of laudanum. I've done everything the man told me to do—"

Something behind my ribs gave way, and I couldn't gather the breath to go on.

Mrs. Gee took my arm. "Miss Emma, come here." She helped me to my chair by the bedside. I sank into it. "Okay?"

"I reckon," I managed.

"Anyone else come help?"

"My friend Evangeline stopped by. She brought some supper, but, Mrs. Gee, I can't eat, and my father turns away from the spoon."

Mrs. Gee gestured to the basket, which was filled with mysterious bottles and strange bundles. "Want I try?"

"Please."

"All right." She turned to Emmett. "Come now, Lightfoot, let's see what's up."

Gently, she unwrapped the bandage on Emmett's foot. It pained him, but he didn't protest. The doctor had lanced his heel and removed the offending remnants of splinter, to little avail. The skin was tight and the inflammation was streaking up his leg.

"Emma, you help me." Swiftly, Mrs. Gee rummaged through her basket and pulled out bunches of herbs and small round pellets of pills. For the next hour, we brewed tea and urged my father to sip, to swallow, to slow his tumbling, shallow breath. Mrs. Gee made a poultice and carefully redressed the wound.

A knock sounded on the office door, and I hastened downstairs. Mr. Seitz, the butcher, stood in the doorway. He is a large, shambling man, twice the heft of Emmett. He is also our landlord. Under his greasy coat, his nightshirt was tucked haphazardly into his trousers. "Miss Lightfoot, I want to speak to your father."

"My father's ill, Mr. Seitz."

"I heard he doesn't do so good."

"Can you come back tomorrow?"

"No. It's about a debt."

"We've paid our rent--"

Seitz scowled. "No. No, you have not."

"And given advertising, too, I believe."

"A pittance. You owe me three months rent--"

My stomach tightened at the news. "My father never mentioned it--"

"He's put me off for weeks. I want payment, now. He can't skip out by dying."

"Mr. Seitz, my father can't see you." I reached for the door to shut the man out, but Seitz stopped it with a huge, hairy hand. "Please go!" I said.

Mrs. Gee called down from the window above, "Seitz, go away. You got no business here tonight!"

"This is my property."

The donkey shifted in its harness. Mr. Yip disappeared into the cart.

Mrs. Gee leaned out over the sill. "Don't you bedevil Miss Emma. You go!"

Seitz took a step back onto the sidewalk and shouted up at her, "I don't take no orders from a Chinawoman!"

Mrs. Gee breathed down a fire of curses upon the butcher's head, all in her native tongue. When he shouted, "Shut the hell up!" and started once more for the door, Mrs. Gee sang out, "Stand back, Miss Emma!"

Seitz roared like a wounded buffalo as the water from our steaming kettle rained down upon his scalp. I slammed the door shut and drew the latch, for what good it would do. Seitz could have smashed the door with little trouble, but after a moment, I heard him groan and hurry away. Perhaps he'd chosen not to damage his own property.

I made my way up to Emmett's room. Mrs. Gee calmly replaced the cool rag on his brow. "I hope I don't cause trouble," she said.

"No, ma'am. I'm grateful to have you at my back. How did you know to come by?"

"The Captain sent word. Said your father's in a fix."

Emmett opened his eyes. "Inattention to detail," he mumbled.

"To what?" asked Mrs. Gee.

"To detail," I replied. "Emmett was too busy with an editorial to tend to a splinter."

"Such oversights can bring down empires," he sighed. "Certainly, it has laid me low."

"Here, Lightfoot, you take this now." Mrs. Gee held a small porcelain cup to his lips. He obeyed and presently grew drowsy. But before he nodded off, he whispered my name, and this time, he knew me. I settled beside him on the bed.

"You're a good girl, Emma," he said. "My finest accomplishment. Think well of me in time to come."

"Emmett, I think well of you every day. You don't need to ask me."

"*The Rattler* is for you."

I didn't know what to make of that. I simply nodded.

His voice had become so hollow, I had to put my ear close to his mouth to make out his meanderings. "Don't let the grass grow under your feet—we're only here for the blink of an eye. Chase your dreams. Never apologize for love. And, dear girl, have courage, and believe that I'm always with you." He dropped his head onto the pillow, exhausted.

A moment later, he rasped out a few more words. "Be kind to others?" I wondered to Mrs. Gee.

"No. A drink of water."

She poured Emmett a glass from the pitcher on the nightstand, lifted his head, and touched it to his lips. He drank, gratefully. Mrs. Gee helped him settle back, caressed the damp forelock off his brow, and spoke to him tenderly in Chinese. Emmett doesn't know Chinese—at least I never thought so—but her words gave him comfort. He gazed up at her with the faintest smile before his pale lids dropped, and he sank into a slumber.

Sometimes a tiny gesture hits like lightning and illuminates a whole new world of possibility.

I have always known the Gees as friends of Emmett's. He had a great liking for Mr. Gee, an enterprising and distinctive man. He grieved deeply when Mr. Gee met his demise at the sharp end of an associate's hatchet. He also admired Mrs. Gee's spunk in her widowhood. Mr. Gee had left a number of undertakings behind—Mrs. Gee swiftly took charge and showed herself a savvy businesswoman.

But the way Mrs. Gee's delicate fingers brushed across Emmett's forehead spoke of more than spunk. She is very pretty in her gowns and combs, and she has a smile that charms friends and disarms enemies. I know Emmett has made a point of stopping by the Lucky Wash House long after Gee's demise, and he often gives Mrs. Gee advertising, free of charge, in *The Rattler*. But, because he is my father, I have never thought of Mrs. Gee beyond the simple role of "family friend," and Emmett has never volunteered the secrets of his affections. As I watch him struggle in his sleep, I wonder what else lies hidden in his heart.

Mrs. Gee stayed on through the evening, tending to both father and daughter. She never spoke of her bond to Emmett, and I was too grateful for her presence to risk the rudeness of pressing her on it. Past midnight, she dosed my father once more, touched his cheek, and packed up her medicines.

"Will he be all right?" I asked, my heart thumping, afraid of the reply.

She shrugged. "I don't know, Emma. I hope so."

"He has to be."

"Yes. I be back in the morning, early."

"Thank you, Mrs. Gee."

"You manage till then?"

"I believe so." I am as worn as a bone in a sandstorm, but I am my father's sentinel, and, if Death is indeed around the corner, I cannot—will not—let down my guard.

"You need anything, Emma, you send for me."

"I will."

She gave me a quick bow, hoisted her basket, and descended to the donkey cart. I heard her wake Mr. Yip, asleep on the driver's seat. The cart's bell echoed down Main Street.

I stayed close by Emmett's side for a piece. I watched his chest rise and fall to make sure he was breathing, but I frightened myself a time or two.

I decided to write to stay awake and to jot down some of his obituary notes. Hopefully, in a day or two, we'll be tossing them into the back of the newspaper's "reject file," to lie unused for the next few decades. In the meantime, an obit is what he hopes for, and I can give my father that much.

MONDAY, JUNE 23, *a stifling evening—*

We buried Emmett at seven o'clock this morning, up on Sacramento Hill. He wouldn't have liked the hour if he'd been alive, but since he was sleeping in for good, I don't suppose it mattered much. It is hot, even for June, and the cool of morning made the occasion more bearable for the living.

The turnout was meager for a man as sociable as Emmett. He was fond of his friends, but few of them gathered at the graveside. Some were lured away by news of a strike over in Bedbug. Others were caught off guard by the swiftness of his demise.

I was grateful for the souls who did show, trudging up the road in the wake of the undertaker's wagon. Captain Smith, in his buckskin coat, lent a comforting bass to the psalm. Mrs. Gee was there, too, with her little daughters. They carried bunches of poppies and lupines. Amongst the handful of other mourners were Davis & Roy of the newsstand, and the proprietors of the *American* and the *Democrat*—rivals, but fellow newspapermen, nonetheless, come to pay their respects to one of their own. They brought a bottle of whiskey and hoisted Emmett a toast.

I was most thankful for my dear friend, Evangeline. Monday morning is slow at the Red House, and Miss Alice let her off. She'd changed to a simple dress, her Sunday best from a few years back, and her small dog Sparky wore a black ribbon about his neck. He seemed to know it was a somber occasion and sat quietly at the grave's edge, a worried look in his eyes. Evangeline came to my side and slipped her hand in mine.

The Reverend Tennant, of the Methodist Episcopal, is a kind man who offered his services gratis, but he is not an inspiring speaker. He referred to Emmett as "Emmett Charles," instead of "Charles Emmett," and he droned over the few facts he did have straight. Perhaps he was at a loss for words, as my father rarely appeared in any church. Still, I half expected to hear "Jehosaphat's cat!" ring from the coffin and witness Emmett rise, out of desperation, to deliver his own eulogy.

The Reverend wrapped up the obsequies with a shovelful of earth dropped into the grave. The clods sounded mournfully on the pine coffin. Emmett was truly to be left alone in that rocky hole. He'd always hated "bone orchards," and Sacramento Hill is a rough place, where a scrap of board suffices for those lucky enough to have a marker. It is a far cry from the green grass and neat stones of the family plot in Vermont.

Tears stung my eyes, but then Evangeline squeezed my hand. Her sweetness gave me the strength to remember that Emmett wasn't truly in the ground. He was free in the clouds, no matter where his bones were buried.

When the service ended, and the others drifted back toward town, the Captain joined Evie and me in the shade of a pine. "Now, Miss Emma, if I can be of any assistance, you let me know."

Mrs. Gee hastened over, her little girls in hand. "Me too, Emma Lightfoot! You need help, you say so."

"Yes. Thank you."

"Good! I send old Yip with supper! Lily? May?" The two girls handed me their bouquets, and the Gees and the Captain departed down the hill. Evie and I lingered, side by side on a broad stump. I thought of the tears my friend had shed when she'd lost her own parents to dysentery a few months back.

"Now we're both orphans, Evie," I said.

"What will you do?"

I could only shake my head.

"If you stay in town, Emma, I'll do everything I can for you."

"I know you will."

She put an arm about me, and we sat in silence, wondering how our childhoods could have died so quickly, until Evie said, "Shall I?" She took the bouquets from my hands and carried them to the head of Emmett's grave. Evie knows all the hymns, and as she adorned the red earth with lupines, she sang in her sweet soprano, "Heaven's morning breaks, and earth's vain shadows flee/ In life, in death, O Lord, abide with me." Sparky followed her about, taking in her every move.

At last, we spied the gravediggers, leaning on their shovels as they waited to put Emmett in the dark for good. I stood by my father's plot and searched for the right words to bid him farewell. I should have left him with a poem or some bit of wisdom to light him on his way, but, in the end, the best I could come up with was, "Good night, Emmett"—

although the sun was already high in the heavens.

Now I am home, in our rooms above the *Rattler* office. The beloved press is silent. Emmett's pipe is perched by his bedside, right where he left it.

Tuesday, June 24—

Too melancholy to write. I do not wish to remember these days.

Thursday, June 26—

I opened a window in the *Rattler* office this morning and sniffed wild roses warming in the sun. I fought to stifle the sob rising in my throat. That rose bush was one of Emmett's greatest pleasures—he kept his desk near the window to be close to its beauty. "A damn sight sweeter than tobacco or whiskey," he'd say, although the man had a fondness for those things, too.

I cannot surrender to weeping. I live within the thinnest shell of pretended well-being. If I allow it to crack, the darkness in my heart will flood out and drown me.

Friday, June 27. *An indifferent day—*

I am hard put to keep this journal. It's a stretch to see the point of it, except that Emmett had the wish for me to do so. These days, I write for a readership of one. Myself. And perhaps I write for Posterity, although the odds in this family of having a Posterity are dreary. I am, for now, "the last of my line."

Still, one can hope.

There have been visitors to the *Rattler* office, but they are mostly looking to collect on Emmett's debts. A very few have been condolence callers, including Clarence McPhee, who appeared, in muddy boots, to offer his sentiments and a fistful of flowers. I thanked him, but he did not depart, and I spent the next half hour averting my eyes as he scratched himself like a nervous hound.

I came upon our tickets for *The Iron Chest* this morning, the ends sticking out from under the pencil jar where Emmett left them. I can't yet throw them in the stove, but I've buried them in the back of his drawer, as far from my sight as if they'd been interred on Sacramento Hill.

SATURDAY, JUNE 28. *A suffocating afternoon, windows thrown wide—*

I must find direction and some kind of work, or I shall end up like one of those pitiful, destitute orphans in Mr. Dickens's novels. But where does one strike out to, to make one's fortune--Sacramento? San Francisco? I must be resourceful and conjure a plan.

This afternoon, as I was upstairs tidying the chaos left by my father's passing, there was a bang on the office door. I peeked from the window--it was Seitz, the landlord. I had nothing to offer the man. I tiptoed away and huddled on the top step of the staircase. "Miss Lightfoot!" he shouted, and pounded louder. I pressed my fingers into my ears and waited him out. At long last, I heard him depart and dropped my head into my hands.

Shortly, there was a rattle at the rear door, then the rasp of a key in the lock. Of course, Seitz would have a key. The door swung wide, and the butcher shuffled in. I made myself as small as possible up on my step. Seitz surveyed the office, then lifted a pad and pencil from Emmett's desk. He wandered about, scribbling down what could only have been an inventory of our possessions.

When he ran a big hand over our beautiful press with the golden eagle on the top, I could bear it no longer. "Mr. Seitz!" I exclaimed. "That belongs to my father!"

Seitz whirled about. His forehead still bore an angry red splotch, no doubt Mrs. Gee's doing. "Miss Lightfoot. I am here for my rent."

"I'm sorry about the other night," I said. "My father was in a bad way."

"I need the rent, Miss Lightfoot, and I need you out. My cousin is in the hardware trade, he wants to let the place. You have until the first. If I don't get the money, I take what's here--the press, the desk, the books, whatever you got."

"They're mine, Mr. Seitz. My father made some of that furniture--"

Seitz delivered me a cold glance. "You want them, you pay up." He ripped off his list and slapped the pad onto the desk. "Tuesday. Bring the money to my store." He stalked out and shut the door crisply behind him.

By Tuesday? Emmett has barely left me a pittance. His love was always *The Rattler* itself, not the business of it. His ledgers are sketchy at best. I've spent hours searching for the envelopes and bits of paper he has written IOU's and receipts upon--I have found them tucked into books, in a jar of biscuits, and stashed in his tobacco tin. I've turned up a few dollars and cents about his desk and in the pockets of his trousers still hanging in the wardrobe upstairs, but I can't get by on pocket change.

I spent the rest of the afternoon gathering my father's books. I shall find a safe haven for them, for I cannot abandon them to Seitz. The butcher is an uncouth man and more likely to wrap meat in the pages than to read them.

High on a shelf, I discovered a big Bible with gilt trim, our "family" Bible. I opened it gingerly, and at once I knew why I felt such trepidation. Ghosts rose from the page. Loving ones, of course, but bittersweet. They surrounded and settled by me, even the ones whose faces and names had blurred in my memory. Just inside the cover was Emmett's elegant hand, paired with my mother's simple penmanship. The delicate scent of a pressed rose from her garden mingled with smells of paper and ink. A list of entries filled the page--my parents' marriage date, and their children's names, with the days they were born and the days they were lost. Last of all was my mother's name, "Phoebe Elizabeth, died December 12, 1844. Flights of angels sing thee to thy rest!"

I have not been able to write Emmett's obituary--perhaps I dread what it means to see it in print. But a notation was a task that I could do for him. I took pen in hand and wrote a final entry on the Bible's page, "C. E. Lightfoot, Editor, died June 21, 1856. We are such stuff as dreams are made of."

Now, all are accounted for. Except for me.

SUNDAY, JUNE 29, 2 P.M. *A bright sky with a wisp of cloud. Behind the Rattler office—*

Yesterday morning, I was awakened by my dear friend Evangeline calling my name from the street. I hastened downstairs. "Good Lord, Emma," she said, giving me a hug. "I've missed you so! Are you all right?"

"I doubt it," I said, tugging my nightgown about me. "Just when I think I've pulled myself together, I go almost to pieces."

"I know." She did know. She'd lost both her parents in the same week.

She had only a minute, as she was running errands for Miss Alice, and Miss Alice keeps her girls on a tight leash. "But come by my place for a visit," Evie said.

"Oh, I'm not sure, Evie," I replied.

"Emma Lightfoot, you cannot hide in here like a badger in a hole. Come by! I'll be terribly sad if you don't." Evie turned soulful eyes on me, and I knew she meant it.

So, on this Sunday morning, I found myself headed for the Red House. Emmett never objected to my friendship with Evangeline—he was very fond of her—but he did not like the idea of my being seen about that place. I walked boldly most of the way up Main Street, but as I neared Cedar Ravine, I headed down to Hangtown Creek and followed its course until I was behind the house. Then I slipped up through a gap in the blackberry bushes toward a row of small shacks in the rear of the yard. I expected to find Evie idle, but when I spied Sparky, curled in his basket by the door, I knew she had a customer. The little dog bore the forlorn look of the banished. I settled on the step beside him. He waggled his stubby tail, and we kept our vigil together.

The yard was peaceful, sun glinting through the pines, and the music of the creek drifting up from the ravine. Striped butterflies busied themselves in the bushes about the little shacks. I can see why Evie prefers it out back rather than up at the Red House, where Miss Alice keeps her "first string." Those girls are a tough bunch, and Evie knows she's not in the same league—at fourteen, she's too young and skinny, and her teeth are a mite gappy, although she has lovely eyes and a good heart that shines through them. But she likes it out by the creek with the second string girls—she can have her little dog and steer clear of the cat fights up at the big house. She can also dodge Miss Alice better out there and slip away on occasion before she's missed.

Sparky and I didn't have to linger long. Soon the door creaked open, and a rumpled miner—one of the Cole brothers—stumbled out, Evie at his side. Sparky jumped for joy at the sight of her. "See you around, Bob—" she began, but when she spotted me, she rushed to throw her arms about my neck. "Oh, Emma, I'm so glad you came!" she exclaimed, and Mr. Cole wandered off across the yard, forgotten.

"Oh, my"—Evie pushed her brown curls off her face—"I'm only in my shift. Give me a minute, Emma, and let me tidy up a bit." She ducked inside, Sparky at her heels. I leaned against the door frame long enough to witness a drunken Bob Cole trip into the berry bushes, and, from somewhere amongst the thorny vines, grumble, "Ow, ow, owww--

goddammmmmmit!" Emmett used to joke that without Bob and his brother Elton to prop up business, the Red House would have collapsed long ago.

Presently, Evie sang out, "Come on in, Emma!" She had thrown on a pretty flowered wrapper, brushed her hair back, and washed away what was left of last night's paint. She pulled the oilcloth off the bottom of the bed—"That Bob Cole's a sweet fella, but he never takes his dang boots off"—and brought her mother's quilt out from a chest in the corner. She spread it across the straw tick. "There! Just like home!" In truth, the shack was as homey as Evie could make it. Wildflowers bloomed in a medicine bottle. The walls were adorned with pictures cut from *Godey's Lady's Book,* and over the chest hung a copy of *The Rattler.*

"I have a surprise! I'm glad you finally got here, 'cause I couldn't have held off on it much longer!" She pulled a fancy tin out from under the bed. "Candy for breakfast, Emma!" We huddled on the quilt, Sparky squeezed between us, and pried the lid off the finest box of sugarplums I have ever seen. They were topped with squiggles and rosebuds and bore a heavenly smell. "One of my customers brought them all the way from San Francisco!"

"He must be fond of you, Evie."

"Oh, he's a pleasant old gent. He certainly knows his sugarplums!"

We didn't wait a second more. We dived into those candies and had the loveliest time nibbling off the squiggles and making trades. Finally, I glanced over at Evie, at the smears of sugar at the corners of her mouth, and I couldn't help but smile. She must have seen the same thing on me, because she smiled, too, and then she giggled. Next thing I knew, we were flopped back on the quilt, laughing. "Oh, Emma, I'm so happy you're here," Evie said.

"Me, too, Evie." But then my stomach tightened, and my laughter died.

"Emma?"

"I don't feel right," I said, pushing myself up. "Here with sugarplums and happy times, while Emmett is in the ground."

Evie took my hand. "I am so sorry about your father, Emma. He was a fine, fine man. He was always so kind to me."

I could only nod.

"I know you miss him terribly. But he loved you. He wouldn't begrudge you a smile."

I knew she was right. She's younger than I am in years, but she's sometimes more wise. Emmett would only wish the best for me.

Evie also knows more about men than I do, or maybe ever will, so I ventured to bring up to her the dilemma of Clarence McPhee. At his name, she shook her head and exclaimed, "Oh, poor, poor Emma!"

"I reckon you know him. Is he a customer of yours?"

"No, not mine, thank heaven. He tries for the first string girls, but they find him plain old unpleasant. And though he likes to boast of his means, he never thinks to bring a girl a little gift, or even offer a kind word."

"The other day, he brought me a gift. A ham. He wouldn't leave until I sliced off a chunk and fried it up for him. Then he called me 'Puddin,' and his hands got presumptuous."

"You need to put your foot down, Emma. You tell him straight out to get away from your place. And it wouldn't hurt to aim a shotgun at his head. Do you have one?"

"No, I don't. Oh, Evie, I've tried to discourage him—"

"Try harder." There was a toughness in Evie's voice that surprised me, that was not the sweet Evie I knew as my friend. "Do you want to end up a miner's wife?"

"Oh, dear Lord, no—it's a terrible way to get by."

"Then don't let yourself get hitched to it. I have to deal with their muddy boots, but at least I can throw them out after twenty minutes. And I don't have to cook for them."

I sighed. "Where are all those fine, upstanding young men when you need them?"

Neither of us had a clue. We sat in sober silence, until at last Evie rose and said, "All right, now, Sparky and I have another surprise for you. We have prepared a show!" She crossed to a shelf and brought down a jar of pork rind bits. The little dog knew what was up and wiggled so that he nearly tumbled off the bed. Evie lifted him down. "Come on, Sparky," she said, and she put him through his paces. He reared up and danced in a circle, and even offered a paw to "shake hands." In the end, he jumped into Evie's arms for a bit of rind. She murmured to him, "Oh, Sparky, I believe we forgot something," and lowered him back to the plank floor. "Fetch, Sparky." He disappeared under the bed, and, in a trice, came out with a little parcel in his mouth. "Take it to Emma." And the dog delivered it to me, holding it by the ribbon so cunningly that it barely got wet.

"Open it, Emma!" said Evie.

I did, saving the ribbon and the bright paper. I lifted the lid off the box to find an elegant little ring, formed in strands of braided gold. It fit my finger perfectly. "It's a friendship ring," said Evie. "It ain't pure gold, but the jeweler said it's quality. Do you like it?" For a moment, I could not speak. "What's the matter, Emma?"

"Nothing," I replied, "it's beautiful." It was, and I knew how much it had truly cost her. I did not want to mar the moment with dark thoughts, but I couldn't help remembering that, not long ago, we were school friends, side by side at our desks, parsing grammar and passing notes, with families to go home to at the end of the day. Sparky turned on me his worried look. "It's okay, pup," I patted him, and then I took Evie in my arms and gave her a squeeze. "Thank you so much."

"What will you do now?"

"Oh, I don't know. It hasn't quite come to me, yet. I don't think I can keep *The Rattler* going. Perhaps I'll leave these parts for a piece."

That thought simply slipped out of my mouth, but Evie stared at me as if I had struck her with a plank. I couldn't bear to see her so.

"Well, maybe not right away," I said. "And only for a short time."

"Emma, don't go—"

"I don't know for certain yet that I will."

She didn't reply; she just looked down at her hands.

"I won't do anything without letting you know, Evie."

"I'm sure you won't, Emma," she whispered. "You're my best friend."

"You're mine, too."

Evie looked up at me. "If you stay, I expect Miss Alice would take you on. She's been like a mother to me."

I wouldn't peg Miss Alice as the maternal sort. She is a large woman with a lantern jaw and broad biceps. Evie's kind words aside, Miss Alice does not hesitate to keep her girls on their backs day and night—although she can beat off the bums with a stick like no one you ever knew.

Evie took my hand. "You could be out here by me, Emma, in the back of the yard—"

This put me in a delicate position. I have made a point not to judge Evie for her choices, but I do not see the same fate for myself. I struggled to find a way to make this clear without hurting my dear friend. I was saved by a loud knock on the door, and a bellow of, "Sweeeet-heart!"

"Oh, no. I'm sorry, Emma. Some of them fellas just don't have anything better to do. Quick, help me hide this candy—I ain't wasting it on a customer." We shoved what was left of it under the bed. "Just a minute!" Evie hollered. We folded up her mother's quilt and pulled out the oilcloth. Then she delivered me a quick hug. "I hope we see each other again soon," she said.

"We will," I replied. "My ring is so wonderful. Thank you!"

Sparky and I hastened out the door past Olin Linnet, a teamster from the lumber yard—not a bad-looking sort, except for an ear he'd lost in a fight. Linnet slammed Evie's door behind him, and Sparky took up his post in his basket.

"Goodbye, little one," I whispered to him. "Be good." And I headed back along the creek, turning the ring on my finger to make it shine in the sun.

Monday, June 30—

I have found, amongst the piles in the *Rattler* office, Emmett's theatre scrapbook. Artfully glued to its pages are reviews of dozens of plays that my father attended--many penned by Emmett himself. There is a section near the front filled with press for Junius Brutus Booth, plus pictures of him in his famous roles. He looks to have been a dark, handsome man, with a flashing eye. Does his son, Edwin, resemble him? In heaven, Emmett must be grieving that he will miss the latest Booth production.

As I thumbed through the scrapbook's pages, I caught a glimpse of Clarence McPhee lurking outside the *Rattler* office. I remembered Evie's advice, and, after the man had finally slunk away, went to visit Captain Smith at his livery stable on Coloma Street.

He was pleased to welcome me into his office next to the stalls. It smelled pleasantly of hay and horse sweat. "How have you been, Miss Emma?" he asked. "Are you still living over the *Rattler*?"

"Yes, sir," I replied. "For the time being."

"Will we be seeing another edition of the newspaper?"

"I doubt it."

"It's a fine little publication."

"Thank you, Captain. I know Emmett hoped I'd carry on with it. I wish with all my heart I could. But my father made it work because his opinions were so lively. People liked to hear the rattler's tail shake."

The Captain chuckled. "Yes. He could stir up quite a racket."

"And, Captain, even though my father trained me well, I can't get the low-down dirty news that feeds the front page and all those editorials.

Emmett knew the barrooms and the midnight card games. He could loosen the tongues of the folks there with cigars and tall tales."

"He had a talent for it, I must say."

"But I'm young, Captain, and I'm a girl. How many barkeeps will invite me in for a smoke and a hand of stud?"

"None, I hope, Emma. But I'm surely sorry to see *The Rattler* go."

His condolence brought a sting to my throat. "Sometimes, when my father's dreams were at stake, he just didn't think things through. He was badly in debt, Captain. Did you know?"

The Captain leaned back in his chair. "I did. This is a small town. People talk."

"I'm his daughter. Why am I the last one to get the news?"

"Your regard mattered to him, Miss Emma. Perhaps he didn't want to appear a failure in your eyes. Or perhaps he thought he could turn things around. C. E. Lightfoot was a dogged optimist."

"I could have handled the truth." We sat in silence for a moment, save for the nickers of horses rustling in their stalls.

"Is there any way I can help you, Emma?"

"Yes, Captain. I'd like a shotgun, please. On loan, of course—I'll return it presently."

He looked at me askance, but when I explained I was being harried by Clarence McPhee, he wasted no time in presenting me not a shotgun ("Don't want you blasting off a foot, Miss Emma") but a fine, lightweight rifle and a lesson in how to use it.

Afterwards, as he slipped the rifle into its sheath, he said, "Miss Emma, you've worried me. Perhaps there's a safer place for you to light than in your rooms. We could get you settled with a family in town—or better yet, what about Miss Ford's?"

I know the Captain means well, but the thought of Miss Ford's makes me cringe. She advertised every week in *The Rattler*:

MISS FLORA FORD'S BOARDING SCHOOL FOR YOUNG LADIES

ON BEDFORD STREET HAS OPENINGS FOR THE CURRENT SESSION.

TUITION, 75 CENTS A WEEK, NOT INCLUDING PIANO.

BOARD, $25.00 A MONTH.

Miss Ford's school occupies a whitewashed house with a pointy window on the top floor. Once, in passing, I looked up and saw faces staring down at me from behind the window, as if a girl on the loose was an oddity. Perhaps Miss Ford's pupils are pleased to be there, but they strike me as prisoners of propriety.

I did not speak my mind to Captain Smith, as he is a well-intentioned man. I thanked him and assured him I'd be careful. When I returned home and unwrapped the rifle, I found a buckskin pouch of gold dust tucked into the ammunition bag, at least thirty dollars' worth. I am grateful, although the Captain shall be the first of our creditors that I repay.

As evening drew on, I heard heavy footsteps approaching the *Rattler* office. Through the open window, I spied Clarence McPhee, toting a jug of molasses. I locked the office door and fetched the Captain's rifle, then settled myself in a chair. McPhee pounded on the door, bawling for me. Finally, he peered in the window. "Puddin'???"

I hate the name "Puddin'." I lifted my weapon, aimed it at his head, and deliberately cocked the hammer with a crisp "click." The molasses jug clunked to earth, and Clarence crashed away down the wooden walk. I hope that is the last I see of the man.

TUESDAY, JULY 1, *midafternoon. Too warm to be outdoors—*

I awoke this morning sprawled at the bottom of the stairs, half in a dream and half in a hard reality. Emmett had been calling to me, and I had been running to save him. But there was naught in the *Rattler* office but the pale morning light falling upon his empty desk. I rose slowly to my feet, grateful that no bones were broken, and limped back upstairs to my bed.

My family has been traveling around with me of late, whispering to me. I am angry with Emmett, so I whisper right back at him. How many times had he told me to wear shoes and an apron in the *Rattler* office? And there he was, wandering around down there by lantern light, in his night shirt and bare feet, because he had an editorial that couldn't wait until morning. When that nasty splinter found his heel, he didn't even have the sense to throw a little whiskey on his wound, and now, here I am in this mess. I know it's not right to think ill of the dead, but there it is.

I also think of my mother, and all those little brothers and sisters lying in rows back in Vermont, under the linden tree. They are not quiet.

Perhaps if I could remember them, give them back the colors of their eyes and the sounds of their laughter, they'd lie down in those graves a while longer. Or come closer to my heart. Emmett is still waiting for his obituary; no doubt the others long for the same. But how do I eulogize a family I miss but don't really know? How do I mourn them? I look at the family Bible, and I can only put faces to a few of the names.

I do have one strong memory:

When I was small, and my mother and I were shopping in the general store, I overheard one woman whisper to another, "She's lost all her other children." I gripped my mother's hand tighter. How could you lose your children? What would happen to me if I was lost? I worried about this until one day we visited the family plot with all its small stones, and I realized where they had gone. There was Bessie, who was taken by measles, Charlotte, who perished of diphtheria, Gilbert, who died in his sleep. The child Emmett used to speak of most was Charley, his eldest. Charley drowned in the well, tossing in pebbles to see how far it might be to the bottom. "Charley always was our scientist," Emmett would say. "The dear boy threw himself into his studies headfirst." This jest was usually followed by a regretful, "Someone should have kept a better eye on that child," meaning Emmett, himself, I'm sure.

I don't believe that any of the little deaths was from neglect, only disease and bad fortune. In the Bible record, there are two boys, Zachary Taylor and Horace Greeley. They were infants who died within days of each other, most likely from some local epidemic sweeping the cradles clean. I do remember holding one of them, I think. He had a sweet face, but whether he was Zachary or Horace, I cannot say.

Perhaps, in the end, there were so many small ghosts on the other side, my mother crossed over just to tend to them all.

I don't know why I'm the child who made it this far. Maybe I was better at steering clear of well shafts and keeping my feet dry. I feel bad about it sometimes, like I pulled off a trick I never taught the others, especially the littlest ones. I should have whispered a few tips to them while they suckled on their sugar-rags. Other times, I suspect it was a mistake that I was spared—maybe Death lost count and forgot about me. One of these days, he'll realize he's short a Lightfoot and slip up behind me when I'm not looking.

Later, at Emmett's desk, by lamplight—

Near sunset, I determined to face Seitz, the landlord, and I set out for his butcher shop. When Evie and I were small, we found Seitz's establishment to be a fearsome and a fascinating place. The gutted carcasses of cattle hung from a timber opposite the butcher's door, their only dirge the drone of flies. When Seitz would step out onto the plank walk, cleaver in hand, to hack down one of his beeves, we'd shriek and scatter like pullets in a barnyard.

I gathered my courage and stepped into the darkness of the store. The walls were lined with headless pigs and sheep. Seitz was behind the counter, grinding scraps.

"Mr. Seitz," I called.

He turned to me, his apron stained red. "You have my money, Miss Lightfoot?"

"I'm working on it."

He frowned, black brows almost concealing his pale eyes. I felt a sympathy for the lambs dangling on hooks. I pulled out the Captain's pouch of gold and set it on Seitz's scale.

"Mr. Seitz, I've been blessed by a benefactor. I hope this might buy me a bit more time in my rooms, until I can make plans."

"This should go toward your debt."

"Perhaps. But if you just--"

"My cousin loses money while we wait."

"Please."

Seitz lifted the pouch and weighed it in his hand, then poured the dust into a saucer. It gleamed, even in the shadows of the butcher shop. He poked it about with a bloody finger. "All right, Miss Lightfoot. Until Monday. No more. You're gone by then, or we turn you out."

I was hard put to say, "Thank you." That dust should have bought me two weeks. I merely nodded, then made my way out onto the street and into the realm of the living. At least I shall have shelter through Independence Day.

On the way home, I cut through the alley behind the Greyhound Saloon. The Star Troupe must have arrived--a bright new poster has replaced the old bill, and a couple of locals hefted wicker baskets of costumes from a wagon into the theatre. Dunlap bustled about in his checkered coat. I kept my eyes peeled for Mr. Edwin Booth, but I saw no one who looked like an actor, let alone a "star."

As darkness settled in, I passed one of the new houses to the north of

Main. It was no miner's shanty, but a white frame house with a front porch and roses in the yard. There was a dining room beyond the window, and this evening, in the lamplight, a family was seated around the table. I stood for a moment in the dusk outside and wondered, "Do they feel as loved as they look to be?" Though there was only glass between us, their lives seemed as separate from mine as if we were on other sides of the world.

WEDNESDAY, JULY 2. *Early eve—*

All of Placerville is sprucing up for Independence Day. The board sidewalks have been swept clean, and the muckiest horse troughs drained. The local vermin are grieving for their rubbish piles. Red, white and blue bunting draped along Main Street turns even the sorriest storefronts cheerful.

Today, I determined to find employment. I donned my best clothes and made the rounds through town, to no avail. I was graciously welcomed in the stores I visited, but no one was able to offer me what I needed, a position and a wage. California's boom has desperately gone bust, and some of those shops may be no better off than the *Rattler*.

As I trudged home, I remembered Mrs. Gee's offer of aid, and I detoured to the door of the Lucky Wash House. Mrs. Gee greeted me cheerfully, but when I asked for employment, she stared at me as if I had escaped from the asylum. "Emma Lightfoot, you're a smart girl. You read. You can get work someplace on Main Street."

"No, ma'am," I replied, and I recited the list of employers that had turned me down.

"The wash house is hard work, Miss Emma. Your fingers bleed."

"I'm not afraid of hard work, Mrs. Gee. I kind of need hard work right now."

She gestured to my hands. "Show me."

I held up my palms, ink-stained but soft. I am no stranger to a wash tub--we have met upon occasion--but Emmett sent most of our laundry to Mrs. Gee.

"Lye soap every day, Emma."

"I'll manage."

Mrs. Gee frowned. "I think about it, okay?" She must have seen the disappointment in my face, for she added, "I see what I can do."

I'm not sure if that was a promise, but it put a tiny bit of hope in my heart.

I started back to the *Rattler* office and had just turned onto Main when I heard a cry of "Emma! Emma! Wait!!" It was Evie, hastening after me in Miss Alice's green wagon. She halted long enough to toss the dry goods she'd fetched into the rear and help me up onto the seat beside her. Then she drove us up Cedar Ravine, to a spot where the horse could nibble ferns, and two friends could converse.

Evie was in high spirits. "I was going to sneak away later and come by, but you've saved me the trouble!" She held out a newspaper. "Look, Emma, the *Democrat* is out—I know, it's the competition—but they've listed all the doings for Independence Day! I thought perhaps we might find a way to have at least a little fun!"

"I don't know, Evie. I'm not up to a celebration. And I'm short of funds, to boot."

"Well, me, too, but we deserve to celebrate as much as anyone else. It would be a shame if we couldn't find something to do. Here. Take a look."

Evie spread the *Democrat* across our laps. Its pages bore a long list of festivities. There was the usual parade up Main Street. Colonel B.F. Washington, a cousin of General George, was bringing his illustrious heritage and some inspiring words to the picnic oration, and a grand ball was being held at Mr. Levan's Union Hotel. "All are invited!!" the *Democrat* enthused.

In the midst of the theatrical column was a sizable advertisement for the Star Troupe's *Iron Chest*. "Look here, Emma," Evie said, "there's a play on Independence Day! You know how much you love the theatre. You could go!"

I felt a lump in my throat. "I was supposed to go, Evie, with Emmett. I was going to write the review. It was to be my first byline."

"You could still see the play. Can you afford a ticket?"

"I have a ticket. I just haven't the heart, or *The Rattler* to print the review in."

Evie patted my hand. "That's a damn shame."

"Could you go with me? Could you slip free of the Red House just for the show?"

She sighed. "On a Friday night? On the Fourth? It'd take a miracle, Emma. But you could tell me all about it."

"Well, it doesn't matter."

"Now, you stop that, Emma Lightfoot. It does matter. Your father would want you to go. Even if he can't fill his seat, his spirit will be there, right beside you. You take that ticket and go see that play. Write your review, even if it's only for the two of you. No, the three of us. I'll read it, too!"

"I'll take it into consideration."

"You better." She giggled. "My, I'm getting opinionated, ain't I? Now, let's see what we might just do together!"

We turned to the other festivities on the list. Evie thought her best bet for escaping Miss Alice was the parade at ten, when most of "the girls" were sleeping in. With luck, we'll meet on the Fourth at Coloma and Main streets, nine-fifty on the dot.

THURSDAY, JULY 3. *Early—*

I write this morning on a stool, in the yard behind the office. It is a beautiful day, no heat yet. The sun filters down through the oaks and pines. A woodpecker has been stashing acorns in the bark of a big ponderosa and chattering to its friends. I had been sitting here with my coffee, trying vainly to formulate a plan for my life, when I was greeted with the most AMAZING SIGHT!

In truth, I heard it first––a gentle creaking of ropes, a swish of air. I glanced up, and high above the town floated an immense globe, golden yellow against the blue, blue sky. It swept toward me from the west, steady, graceful, magical. It might have been a huge round angel, but as it neared, I spied a wicker basket suspended from its bottom. A hot air balloon! And then I remembered the poster I'd seen by the Round Tent Store--"PROFESSOR WILSON will ascend in his BALLOON, the GLORY, on July 4! Passengers may embark from the Amphitheatre on Main Street. LADIES FREE!" As the balloon passed over my spot, a head peered above the rim of the basket. "Hello, down there!" Professor Wilson doffed his hat and waved it at me. I waved back as he sailed to the east, and stood, my mouth wide, for the only reply I could muster was a sigh of wonder. Was this a practice ascension? Where would he come to rest? Oh, to be one of those ladies riding for free, sailing up and beyond my trials on the ground.

The beauty of this vision has lent me courage. I must find my own way to fly, to cut the ropes that bind me here and rise.

As I make lists in my mind of reasons to stay or to go, I wrestle with fear of either choice. I am scared as a baby. Although I know more than

I sometimes wish, I am still young and green and ignorant of much in the world. But fear is profitless. And as I ruminate, one memory keeps coming to me--the girl on the prairie.

When I was small and traveling west with Emmett, our company of wagons came upon a girl by the side of the trail, sitting on the tongue of a battered prairie schooner. Just beyond, were mounds of graves, some large and some small. The girl was alone except for a sorry-looking horse, who was at least relishing the green grass and the break in his journey. But the girl was mournfully still, gazing out over the plain. The men stopped to talk with her, to find out what had happened. Her family had sickened and died, she said, mother, father, younger brothers and sisters, and the baby. Their party had been nervous about the sickness. They had waited a couple of days but then moved on. She and her brother next to her, a year older, had buried the family by the road there. While the baby was still alive, her brother had taken the good horse and ridden back toward Fort Laramie for help. He'd left her with the weaker horse and her father's rifle. He'd be back any time now.

Of course, our party hadn't seen anyone on the trail. No matter, she said, he'd be back. Our folks begged her to come with us, but she refused. What would happen if he returned and she was gone?

"He could catch up."

"No!"

Emmett wouldn't let me get too close because of the sickness, but I was near enough to glimpse a look in that girl's eye that wasn't quite right, the look I now know too much grief can give. Maybe the girl didn't truly care if her brother showed or not. She'd keep her promise, and then go lie down by the fresh graves and let her troubles cease. Some of our party tried to lead her away from her wagon, but she carried on and broke loose. She ran and kept her distance then, like a wild creature waiting for the humans to clear out. Our people finally stocked her wagon with some corn meal and salt pork, and a tiny bit of white sugar from someone's special hoard, and left her there on the prairie to wait. We started off west, and when I looked back, she was warily returning to perch on the wagon tongue. I kept my eyes on her until her thin shoulders disappeared in the high grass.

There are some people who become ghosts in our memories, just take up residence there forever. Maybe her brother came back, maybe not. Today, those graves have surely vanished under the wagon tracks, or there's a settlement above them, no sign of that girl's sorrow. But in my mind, she will always be waiting on the prairie, a desolate ghost of dim hope. That ghost is with me now, in the days after my father's death. I can sit in this town and grieve, and wait on the wagon tongue for some kind of salvation, or I can use my savvy to jump out of the grave of this life and into something new. In the end, it don't suppose it takes too much thought.

Friday, July 4, 11 a.m.—

I have a few minutes, so I shall record the happy events of this morning while they are fresh in my mind!

I rose early, to the patter of a quick rain shower, a surprise for this time of year. It was just enough to bring the freshness out of the sand and willows down by the creek. Then the sky cleared to pure blue.

About nine-thirty, I set off in search of Evie, but the crowd for the parade was already dense, packing the plank sidewalks along Main. When the band struck up down in the Plaza, I cut off into back alleys to make better time, and hastened so quickly that my spectacles nearly bounced off my nose! As I neared Coloma Street, I hoped Evie would be there, and I hoped I hadn't missed too much. My heart leapt as I spotted my friend, Sparky at her heels. "Emma!" she shouted, and waved. She'd managed to snag us a good spot, in a patch of shade. I pushed my way to her side, and she handed me a paper cup of shaved ice, drizzled over with red and blue berry syrups. "I was afraid I'd have to put this away all by myself!" she laughed. I tasted it. It was cool and lovely after my dash across town. Then, I glanced out at the parade.

Right before my eyes was a big wagon, drawn by four magnificent bays. "The Star Troupe" was painted in red and gold on the canvas cover. "It's the acting company!" I shouted to Evie. Where was Mr. Booth? I made out a half-dozen "actor types," but none appeared to be the star of the show. "Do you see Mr. Booth, Evie?" I asked.

"Oh, I don't know, Emma, I can't tell one actor from the other. Perhaps he's in that bunch on horseback at the front." Up the street, ahead of the wagon, were more riders. They had passed by just before I arrived. Evie pointed to a man on a pinto. "Maybe that fellow. He was handsome enough."

All I could make out by then was a figure in a black coat and the back end of a horse. As the wagon rolled by, I spied a treasure chest lashed to its rear, a chilling skull and crossbones painted upon it. Lettering above the skull announced, "*The Iron Chest*," this evening's drama. I might have to get myself to the play, after all, to look upon the famed Edwin Booth.

The rest of the parade was splendid. The firemen had polished their wagon until it glinted in the sun. They tossed molasses candy into the crowd, to the delight of scampering children. The Masons and the Sons of Temperance marched in all their regalia, passing in file under the flags strung across the street, and the spirit of Independence Day prevailed over all. I had only one twinge, at the thought of how Emmett loved these processions, and how he could hardly have waited to record the day's delights on the front page of *The Rattler*.

Finally, the last of the parade marched on up the street. Evie breathed a wistful sigh. "I must get on back," she said. "Tell me all about the play and Mr. Booth. I'll lay down money he was on that pinto!"

I waved her goodbye and stood for a moment on the corner, tempted by the pleasures of the afternoon. Should I take in Washington the Younger's oration? Wade in the creek?

Just then, I heard, "Emma! Emma Lightfoot!" It was Mrs. Gee, pulling Lily and May through the stragglers on the street. The little girls clutched American flags, and their cheeks bulged with molasses candy. They hastened over to me. "I got a job for you, Emma!" exclaimed Mrs. Gee. "You still need work?"

"Yes, ma'am, you know I do!" I abandoned any thought of lazing by the creekside.

"This morning, a man from the theatre company come by. He want to hire for the day."

My heart did a little dance of joy. "From the Star Troupe?"

She shrugged. "At Placer Theatre."

"That's them, Mrs. Gee!"

"They have costumes, all wrinkly from the trunks. And it's hot, so the shirts and petticoats get stinky. You wash and iron, maybe sew on a button, not too hard. A dollar for the day. What do you say?"

"Oh, yes!"

Maybe I showed too much enthusiasm, for Mrs. Gee shot me a frown. "You be careful, Emma Lightfoot. I only send you over there because I know you need money."

"I don't believe I'll be in any danger, Mrs. Gee," I said.

"You're a young girl, Emma. You wear plainest clothes, cover up.

Those are *actors*."

Though many people have a low opinion of the theatrical profession, I was surprised to hear such words from Mrs. Gee. Still, I knew she was watching out for me and I held my tongue.

"You get your money up front, too," she added. "Don't let those people owe you—you never see your cash then. After the show, poof, they disappear."

I took that thought under advisement. Mrs. Gee handed me a slip of paper with a name written on it. "You talk to this Mrs. Burnham, nobody else. Be at the theatre three o'clock."

I thanked her again and wished her and the girls a happy Independence Day. Then, I hustled back home. I will have a quick dinner, wash up and change. It won't be hard to follow Mrs. Gee's advice to "wear plainest clothes." The state of my wardrobe these days is exceedingly plain—mostly work clothes and a leftover funeral dress. But I do have a blue blouse that is just a cut above the rest. If I must wear washerwoman clothes to the theatre, they will be my best washerwoman clothes.

Saturday, July 5, about 1 p.m. *The yard behind the* Rattler *office, in the shade—*

Twenty-four hours is a lifetime ago.

I left home yesterday with time to spare. Emmett's watch read two p.m. as I slipped it into my apron pocket—along with a ticket for *The Iron Chest*. Even though I skirted some of downtown, the party had already started for many of Placerville's citizens and was spilling out of the drinking establishments onto the streets. One crowd of ne'er-do-wells at Krahner's Saloon was doing its best to live up to the term "public nuisance." I recognized a few of them—mainly miners and odd-jobbers, with a sprinkling of vaqueros and drifters thrown in. All I could do to avoid their taunts was to keep my head high and my step speedy.

It was a relief to near the west end of Main, and a wonderful surprise to see a huge globe rising over the rooftops. Professor Wilson! I rushed down to where the amphitheatre stood in a field beyond Stevens's livery. I remembered ladies were free, so I did not hesitate to invite myself as close to the "Glory" as I dared. The balloon was surrounded by Professor Wilson and his helpers, who positioned it over the fire from whence it drew hot air. It rose like a gigantic golden loaf of bread, billowing upward toward the sky. Soon, it was airborne. The men strained at the ropes that kept it tethered to the ground. Professor Wilson arranged the bags of sand in its big wicker basket and prepared for his ascension. My heart sank as I took in the long line of ladies and their gentlemen companions hoping to ride the sky. I wanted to shout, "ME! Please take ME!" and rush to the head of the line. I knew I had work waiting for me—work at the *theatre.* But, oh, what a hard hope to relinquish. "Another time," I told myself. "It will happen. You will fly."

The chosen few boarded the basket. Professor Wilson, in his silk hat and frock coat, delivered a short speech on the wonders of aeronautics, gave the signal, and the ropes were loosed to a thunder of cheers. The "Glory" lifted straight up, ascending much higher than when it had passed over the *Rattler*, to two or three thousand feet. There, it caught a bit of wind and floated to the east, passing above the length of the town. From below, at each stage of its journey, rose shouts of wonder and delight, until it was a tiny orb moving over field and forest. Then, it transformed—the globe shifted to the shape of an open umbrella, the bottom half rising upward into the body of the balloon as the air within it cooled. Quickly but gracefully, the Glory descended from heaven and once more touched upon the earth.

I glanced again at Emmett's watch. It was ten minutes to three! I hurried back up Main and made my way to the rear of the Placer Theatre. The lot was almost deserted in the afternoon sun, save for the wagon, a few horses tied in a fringe of shade, and a young man bringing the animals buckets of water. "Mrs. Burnham, please?" I inquired, and he pointed me toward the theatre. I ascended the stairs, took a deep breath, and stepped through the double doors leading to the auditorium.

Even though the shutters on the narrow side windows had been thrown wide in hope of a breeze, the theatre was dim, as a church might be when you enter out of the bright sunshine. My eyes took a second to adjust, but I soon made out a crew bustling about the stage, practicing scene changes. As painted "wings" and backdrops shifted in and out of view, one setting dissolved like magic into another, a garden becoming a manor house, then a forest. I have always loved the surprise of scene changes, and I stood in the shadows for a moment, enchanted by the conjuring onstage.

Shortly, I realized a woman was in charge of this operation. She was tall and slender, with a regal profile, and she guided the stagehands with enthusiasm. "Yes! That's it! That's perfect! Now, try it on a four-count, Buck!" I did not dream of interrupting her, but, at last, she moved toward the back of the auditorium to get a wider view of the stage and she spied me. She stopped in the aisle. "Who are you?"

"I'm Emma Lightfoot," I replied. "Mrs. Gee sent me."

She stared at me. "You're not a Chinese."

"No, ma'am. But I'll work just as hard."

She looked me over. At length, she nodded. "I'm Harriet Burnham. Come down here and talk."

We perched on the edge of the stage. Though her hair was falling loose, and her dress was workaday, she was quite beautiful. Her eyes were deep hazel; her gaze was direct. "We need someone to care for the costumes," she said. "Someone who can wash, iron and make repairs. Can you sew?"

"Oh, yes ma'am. I love to sew. I'm a fine seamstress." (This was a boldfaced lie, of course. I hate to sew, all those gussets and nonsense. But I can stitch on a button, and if I set my mind to it, a hem isn't beyond me.) "I can take on most any repairs."

She smiled. "Good. Pay is one dollar for the day. If you do well, we'll bring you back tomorrow for *Taming of the Shrew*."

This was wonderful news!

"Right now, we need you to steam the velvets and press the other pieces. Then, you'll stay backstage during the show, and afterwards, you'll collect the laundry and take care of repairs. Can you handle that?"

"Yes, ma'am!" Then I hesitated. I feared to even bring it up and spoil my chances, but I had no choice. "Mrs. Burnham," I ventured, "I have a ticket for tonight's show. I've had it ever since the bills went up."

She grinned at me. "A paying customer?"

"Well, more or less, yes," I replied. "Is there any way I can see the play and still do the job?"

Perhaps she was moved by my earnestness. "I expect so. This is our opening show, and the costumes are in good shape. Just for tonight, you keep backstage until right before the curtain. Then go claim your seat but skedaddle on back as soon as the last act rings down. Agreed?"

"Oh, yes," I replied. "Thank you!"

"Then it's a deal." She rose.

I debated once more whether to open my mouth, and then I took the plunge. "Mrs. Burnham? I need to have my dollar up front, please."

She regarded me as if I had just dropped from the moon before she let out a laugh. "You drive a hard bargain, for a skinny girl in spectacles." She pulled a change purse from a pocket near her waistband. "All right, Emma Lightfoot. Here's your dollar." She handed me a coin. "Now, show me you can earn it."

"Oh, yes. I will!"

"Jeriah!" Mrs. Burnham called. A man appeared from the wings, balding, with grey in his drooping mustache. "Mr. Leach, meet Miss Emma Lightfoot, our new laundress and wardrobe supervisor." She turned to me. "Mr. Leach is our stage manager. What he says backstage, goes. If you have any problems, you talk to him. Right now, he'll set you up with the costumes."

Mr. Leach was polite and businesslike. He began with a quick trip through the dressing rooms. In the Placer Theatre, they are squeezed behind the stage, one for men, one for women, and a couple of cubbyholes for the stars. The costumes for the evening's show had already been pulled out of their trunks and champagne baskets and hung from hooks on the walls. As we passed through, Mr. Leach scooped up as many as we could carry, then led the way out of the building and down to the back lot.

A line had been strung between tree limbs, and it was there that I draped the costumes, while Mr. Leach hauled an ironing board and a big straw basket out of the wagon. The basket was cunningly packed with the smaller necessaries--a couple of flatirons, a steam kettle, and a big glass sprinkler bottle. There was also a little brazier. It was way too warm in the theatre to start up a stove, but the brazier meant I could heat the flatirons out of doors. Mr. Leach soon had it fired with bits of pinecone. "My nephew Jimmy will bring you water for steam," he said, and waved over the youth I'd spied tending the stock. Jimmy was barely older than Evie or me, with big brown calf eyes and a shy shuffle. Soon, he delivered a bucket of water up from the creek.

I determined to work diligently and with great care, to prove to Mrs. Burnham that I could "earn my dollar." Still, I could not resist pausing to run a palm over the sleek velvets of the cloaks, or to finger the cool silk of a sleeve. From Mrs. Burnham's cubby came a lavender gown, off-the-shoulder, with yards of fabric in the wide crinoline skirt. Mr. Booth's dressing room yielded an elegant, black, cutaway jacket, and tailored charcoal trousers. I pressed those pieces with extra special care, for I could imagine how splendid they would appear in the glow of the footlights.

As I labored, I kept an eye out for members of the company. Shortly after I heated the flatirons, Mr. Leach hastened downstairs with the same "Buck" that Mrs. Burnham had called to earlier. He resembled Jimmy, but he was bigger and furrier, with a full beard and shaggy hair. If Jimmy was the calf of the company, Buck was the bear, albeit an affable one. As Mr. Leach introduced us—"Miss Emma Lightfoot, my elder nephew, Mr. Buck Bliss"—Buck offered his hand. I took it, and my own hand disappeared within his huge grizzly paw. "Nice to meet you," he growled.

A few minutes later, an older gentleman with a dog turned into the lot, parked himself on a stump in the shade, and perused the day's edition of the *Democrat*. The dog flopped at his feet, only stirring to snap at the occasional fly. The man was tall and lanky, perhaps in his thirties or early forties, and nattily garbed in a grey jacket, waistcoat and bow tie. The dog was a mongrel of indeterminate pedigree, grey and lanky, too. They rested there maybe twenty minutes; then the man neatly folded his newspaper, and they made their exit.

I kept hoping for a glimpse of Mr. Booth. How would I know him? Perhaps he would simply have "star quality." Or be imposing, like his father. Or dignified. But no such personage appeared.

About four-thirty, another pair made an entrance—a little blonde girl, in the company of a thin woman with sharp features. The woman's countenance was plain, yet there was a resemblance about her cheeks and chin to the beautiful child. I reckoned she was the girl's mother. She did not introduce herself, but she marched on over to where the child's costume hung neatly on the line and began inspecting each frill. The girl turned her curiosity to my implements—she squatted in the dust to peer at the flatirons heating on the brazier. I held my breath as the mother pored over my work, even though I knew I'd done my best.

"Passable," the woman finally announced. "No scorches." She turned on her heel with a "Come along, Louise," and was several yards away when she realized Louise hadn't come along at all. "Louise! Don't touch those, they're hot! Now, get on over here. And stay out of the dirt, please." Louise obediently followed, though she stayed directly behind her mother, out of her line of sight, and kicked up little dust clouds with the toes of her boots all the way to the staircase.

By six o'clock, the theatre was nigh empty—most of the actors had cleared out for supper--and I began to deliver the costumes back into the dressing rooms. As I entered the women's room, I passed a piece of looking glass nailed to the wall and saw Emmett gazing back at me. My heart nearly stopped. When I got the courage to look again, I realized I had been spooked by my own reflection, and I studied it. Emmett was indeed in the mirror. We share the same sandy hair and freckles, straight noses, and smallish hands with ink stains. Still, there are differences in my eyes and the corners of my mouth--I think those come from my wispy mother. Emmett always said I had her laugh, too, though I do not believe I have her light heart.

I saved Mr. Booth's costume for last, double-checking to make sure it was perfect. Then, I hurried up the stairs, turned into his dressing room, and almost fell over a stagehand catching a snooze! He was a slight man in a worn pair of trousers. He had planted his posterior in Mr. Booth's chair, tilted it back against the wall, and deposited his muddy boots on the dressing table. Despite the heat, he had thrown an old serape over himself and hidden his face beneath a slouch hat. I could only think that he was a day hire, like me, shirking his responsibilities by hiding out in a quiet corner. I couldn't even slide past the miscreant to hang the costume on its hook. "Hey, there," I demanded, "get those dirty boots off Mr. Booth's table."

A chuckle sounded from beneath the hat. Its wearer slid the brim aside, regarded me out of keen brown eyes, and drawled, "Thank you, ma'am. I'm pleased to see someone is looking out for my interests."

I was mortified. "Oh, Mr. Booth, I am so sorry. I had no right—"

"No," he replied. "I deserve your rebuke. My boots are a disgrace, and the rest of me isn't much better, though I clean up well, Miss…?"

"Lightfoot," I blurted. I felt the heat of a blush sear my face, until the tips of my ears were on fire. "Here," I mumbled, and shoved his costume into his arms. Then I rushed out of the theatre and took refuge behind the wagon.

Why had I opened my mouth? I was brought up to be kind to people. But it had seemed so insolent, Booth's dressing table violated by the muddy heels of a ne'er-do-well. How could I carry on through the evening after shaming myself so?

Steps came my way. "Miss Lightfoot?" Mr. Booth rounded the wagon. I could not meet his eye. "Please," he said, "don't be embarrassed for my sake."

"I was so rude."

"Not at all. I shouldn't have mocked you. Please." He offered his hand. "We can forgive each other." His voice was deep and soothing. I raised my gaze to his face and was rewarded with a smile. He was quite young and very handsome. I clasped his hand, and my spirit lifted. "Besides," he added, "my costume has been excellently pressed. I should regret being at odds with a lady who can work such wonders."

This was pure flattery, but it was meant in kindness, and I dearly welcomed it.

After a delightful minute, Mr. Booth went about his business, and I leaned against the wagon until my heart settled. The next hour was quiet, save for firecrackers popping away across town. I'd packed along a supper, and, as I nibbled, I spied Mr. Booth, a red-haired man, and the older gent relaxing in the shade, smoking and swapping stories. Every once in a while, they'd burst into laughter. Soon Mrs. Burnham arrived, on the arm of the fair-haired man with the chipped tooth. As the couple neared the foot of the stairs, Mr. Booth hastened to them. His jovial demeanor shifted to a somber one. At first, their conversation was hushed. But as the argument built, I picked up every word. It had something to do with the bills posted around town. "Let me stand on my own two feet, for God's sake," demanded Mr. Booth.

"Ted, the Booth name is our draw," said Mrs. Burnham.

"Don't put me in my father's shadow," Mr. Booth pleaded. 'Heir to the mantle—?' I am not the old man, and if I try to pass myself off as him, they'll crucify me."

The fair-haired man stepped between them. "Those bills are already paid for and posted, Ted. They've been up for days."

"I want new ones for tomorrow."

"What the hell—"

Mr. Booth cut him off. "I'll pay for it out of my own pocket, Burnham. Take it from my first week's share of the house. Throw in a couple of dollars for Buck and Jimmy to paste them up around town."

"Ted, it's no secret that you're Junius's son," said Mrs. Burnham. "People will make the connection whether it's on a bill or not."

Mr. Booth sighed. "Please. All I want is the chance to rise or fall on my own merits. I need some room to breathe."

Mrs. Burnham hesitated, then nodded. "All right. Fine. If that's what it takes—"

Mr. Burnham shot her a frown. "Hattie!"

"If it's what he needs to give his best performance, so be it, Ben."

Mr. Burnham shook his head in disgust. "Actors. My God."

"Ben, he has a point."

"Thank you, Hattie," said Mr. Booth.

Mr. Burnham scowled. "All right, all right, new bills. But it's out of your cut!"

Mr. Booth gave a grim nod and disappeared upstairs. I did not see him again until shortly after sunset.

As dusk came on, the company gathered at the theatre, and the sleepy mood of the afternoon shifted to bustle and excitement. This was opening night! Bouquets of flowers arrived for the actresses, and little gifts piled up on the dressing room tables.

I was officially introduced by Mr. Leach as Miss Lightfoot, and stationed backstage with my sewing kit, ready to be of use. The women fluttered and worried as they dressed. I was called on more than once to pull those corset laces "a little tighter," and to assist with crinolines and hair pins. Laughter rippled about the men's dressing room, as razors and paint worked their magic. I was faced with only a solitary repair—I sewed a button back on a jacket belonging to Mr. Brown, a pleasant young man. When I finished, he beamed at me and exclaimed, "Bravo!"

Before long, this afternoon's troupe of workaday actors had become the elegant characters of *The Iron Chest*. Presently Dunlap appeared backstage, grinning ear to ear, with the announcement that, despite the Grand Ball at the Union Hotel, the house was sold out! The buzz of the audience echoed all the way back to the dressing rooms. I was thrilled for the Star Troupe, until I remembered…my ticket! I was in danger of losing my seat for the play! I rushed to Mrs. Burnham, "May I head out front now, ma'am?"

She nodded. "You may! And you'd better hurry!"

I did, dashing for the side door leading to the house. As I wove my way through the wings, I almost collided with a figure pacing in the shadows. It took a moment to recognize the man beneath the makeup and the refined cutaway coat. "Oh, please excuse me, Mr. Booth," I whispered. But when he turned his eyes to me, he was not the same Mr. Booth who had comforted me by the wagon. His countenance was lined, and his eyes held torment and a tinge of madness. I said no more, but gave him a wide berth and hastened out into the auditorium.

The theatre was packed. Miners and merchants mingled with farmers, wives, and an occasional "fancy woman." I scanned the crowd for the chance of a seat. The air was hot and close. I finally spied a sliver of bench beside a gentleman in a clean shirt, and I squeezed myself onto it.

The wall sconces glowed, and the footlights illumined the curtain, painted with advertisements for our local establishments. Above the ads stretched a landscape of the snowcapped Sierras. As the footlights flickered, the pines on the mountainsides gently swayed. Dance melodies from the Grand Ball floated in through the open windows, "Shenandoah" and "Virginia Reel." Mr. Burnham strode to the front of the stage and welcomed us to the "premiere performance of the Star Troupe's classic tragedy, *The Iron Chest*." Then the curtain rang up!

REVIEW.—The Star Troupe opened their new season at the Placer Theatre last night to a full house and a standing ovation. The play was THE IRON CHEST by George Colman, the Younger, and, in keeping with the spirit of Independence Day, it arrived with no less than a "bang."

The evening's tone was set early in the first act, when a wag in the audience tossed a lit string of firecrackers to the base of the stage. At the incendiary "pop-pop-pop," the stage manager, Mr. Jeriah Leach, made the quickest entrance of the night, rifle in hand. However, Mr. Ben Burnham found a more pleasant way to defuse the situation. Leaping down into the auditorium and seizing the miscreant by the collar, he reminded him that the best place for fireworks was on the stage, not under it, and hustled the "gentleman" out of the theatre, to laughter and loud applause. He then returned, took his bow, and the production commenced from precisely the point it had left off.

THE IRON CHEST boasts a cast of melodrama favorites—innocent damsels, rowdy robbers, and an almost-noble hero—as well as a trunk containing a dastardly secret. The story tells of the struggle between good and evil in the heart of Sir Edward Mortimer. Mortimer's young clerk, Wilford, pries into Sir Edward's iron chest, and finds evidence that Mortimer has murdered his beloved Helen's despicable uncle. This opening of "Pandora's box" unleashes all the tragedy of the remaining scenes.

There is plenty in THE IRON CHEST to cheer for and boo against, and the audience put their hearts and their voices into it. We heard only a solitary criticism. When one of the characters had gone on at length spouting noble sentiments, the gentleman behind us muttered, "Open the damned trunk and get to the ro-mance."

What made the evening such a splendid success was the cast, especially Mr. Edwin Booth as Sir Edward. We cannot find enough superlatives—his performance lit up the stage; it crackled in the air. In his scenes with his clerk, Wilford, there was no doubt that "twenty blue devils were dancing jigs and hornpipes" in his head, or that, at the end of the play, when he collapsed to the cry of "I am brain-scorched," he was suffering the torments of hell. During these scenes, the audience, quiet as church mice, perched on the edges of their seats. We have no doubt that, had the fiery Mr. Booth stepped into the auditorium instead of toward the terrified Wilford, several of the theatre's patrons would have fled the building in a panic.

The supporting cast was also outstanding. Mrs. Harriet Burnham played Sir Edward's gentle love, Helen, and brought the audience to tears. Mr. Harry Brown was a winning young Wilford.

Not all was melancholy in this play, as the comic relief proved. Miss Sophie Griffith as Helen's saucy "rosebud" of a maid, Mr. Sumner Moone as a "low comedy" servant, and Mr. Augustus Thayer as the old retainer had the audience in gales of laughter. Mr. Jeriah Leach and the Bliss brothers provided support as servants and lusty robbers, while Mrs. Clarissa La Rue sustained the old peasant mother. Mr. Ben Burnham portrayed Mortimer's half-brother, described in the play as having a "pleasant, harmless mind." While Mr. Burnham does not have the natural style of Mr. Booth, he did provide a merry contrast to the dark soul of his "sibling."

Although there was no doubt that Mr. Booth and Mrs. Burnham were the "stars" of the evening, they were given a run for their money by La Petite Louise La Rue, the company's "fairy star." She is an incandescent performer, even at her tender age, whether she is playing the poor, sweet Barbara in THE IRON CHEST, or singing her entr'acte melodies. This night, she was the miners' delight at her final note, the audience showered the stage with flowers, pokes of dust, and even jewelry, which she dutifully handed to her mother at the pianoforte. Then she dipped into a dainty curtsey, to even more applause.

Other lively entr'actes were provided by the song and dance numbers of Griffith and Moone, and by Mr. Thayer and his dog, Ulysses. Ulysses is a charming cur who does very little and does it very well, provoking roars of laughter from his audience, particularly when he lifted a leg and "baptized" the inconvenient post in the middle of the stage.

The properties and scenery were all well appointed.

The costumes were impeccably pressed.

—Emma Rose Lightfoot

As soon as the curtain was rung down, I hurried backstage. The mood was celebratory, with hugs and compliments of "Good show!" I spied Mr. Booth shaking Mr. Thayer's hand and grinning—Sir Edward Mortimer's spirit had vanished, and the sweet man of this afternoon had returned. A few minutes later, I caught a glimpse of the Burnhams in their cubby with Dunlap, delightedly counting the night's receipts.

With guidance from Mr. Leach, I collected the washables and made sure the silks and velvets were draped on their hooks. As I stashed my sewing kit in the wagon, I observed that admirers had gathered in the lot, most of them young ladies. A few were hoping for a sight of Mr. Brown, who is, indeed, a handsome youth. He greeted them with charm and obliged them with autographs. But most had their hearts set on meeting Mr. Booth, who never appeared—although a slight person in a slouch hat and serape slipped right through their midst, with no notice at all.

As I wrapped up my duties backstage, the theatre became suddenly quiet. It was empty, save for Mr. Leach, closing up windows for the night. I hastened over to him. "Sir? Has Mrs. Burnham gone? I hope I didn't miss her."

"No, Miss Lightfoot," he replied, "you'll find the Burnhams on the staircase."

"Oh, thank you!" I ran through the lobby and out onto the landing. Below me, the Burnhams sat side by side on a step.

Mr. Burnham struck a match, lit Harriet Burnham's thin cigar, and then removed the cigar from her lips to deliver a kiss in its place. I slipped back into the lobby for a moment, and returned with a heavier footstep. "Ma'am?"

She smiled up at me. "Miss Lightfoot! Fine job tonight."

"Thank you. Shall I come back tomorrow?"

"Ten a.m. for laundry."

"Yes, ma'am! Thank you! I'll be there!" Mr. Burnham rose to let me pass, and I made my way down the stairs. But I couldn't resist stopping to exclaim, "The play was wonderful!"

I traversed the back lot, empty save for the horses breathing softly in the dark. It wasn't until I turned onto Main Street that I confronted the dilemma I'd earlier shoved to the back of my mind—how I would manage the considerable distance to home. The Independence Day celebrations were still in full swing at the Union Hotel and in every drinking establishment on the street. I could dodge the revelers by crossing the creek and following the far bank, but it was pitch black over there. Better, I figured, to stay on Main Street, where light spilled out onto the sidewalks, and where there would at least be witnesses if some rowdy gave me trouble. I kept my eyes down and walked swiftly up the street.

Mostly, the drunks were harmless—a couple of them even wished me a "Happy Fourth!" I had almost passed the worst of the saloons when a door swung open, and a barkeep tossed an unruly patron into the dust at my feet. The man's mouth was bloody and one of his eyes was swollen shut. He frightened me. I backed away, but he tottered to his feet and called out, "Puddin'!" Then I ran. The last thing I needed was Clarence McPhee.

I sped back toward the theatre, praying he was too drunk to follow, but his footsteps were close behind me, and shouts of "Emma! Darlin'!" rang down Main. I wove through strangers on the street and darted from one side to the other, but I couldn't shake him. Finally, I ducked into the back lot of the theatre and rushed up the stairs. The theatre door was locked! I squeezed into the shadows of the shallow vestibule. Down below, McPhee lurched into the lot and eyed the staircase. I held my breath. He started up but, after two steps, gave out and collapsed against the rail. He bellowed my name one more time and stumbled off into the darkness.

I did not stir, although my heartbeat shook my ribs. I huddled in the shadows until the music had faded from the Union Hotel and even the saloons were silent. Then I made my way, quiet as a ghost, to the nearest safe haven I could think of. The back door of the Lucky Wash House was open—I let myself in past old Yip snoring on his pallet, made myself a nest of laundry sacks, and fell into a fitful sleep.

I was awakened shortly after dawn. "Miss Lightfoot?" Mr. Yip bent over me, worry in his eyes. He put a warm cup of tea into my hands. I assured him I was well, only mentioning that I had worked late, and that I knew Mrs. Gee would not object to my napping there. Would he please tell her I did well at the theatre, and that I was asked back for today's play?

Then I returned to the *Rattler* rooms to freshen up, and made it to the theatre by ten a.m., in time to do battle with the laundry. Jimmy Bliss helped me heat water in a big metal tub, but my back is aching and my hands stinging from the soap and the washboard. I put too much starch in the men's collars--they stiffened so, I feared they'd crack--and I had to scrub them all again. I almost wept at the effort. Now, thank Heaven, the wash is drying on the line, and the *Taming of the Shrew* costumes are pressed. I am not needed back at the theatre until six p.m., so I have spent the afternoon writing, which helps me to order my thoughts. The office is calm and quiet, although I've kept the little rifle close at hand.

I'll leave here by four o'clock. I've errands to complete before I return to the Star Troupe.

I have a plan.

SUNDAY, JULY 6, 2:00 A.M. *My room, on my coverlet. The light flickers—*

I cannot sleep, so I shall write as long as the candle holds out.

I stopped by Captain Smith's stable before yesterday's show. I know him to be a fair man, unlike some folks in his trade. I found him in the back of the barn, doctoring a hoof. "Miss Emma!" he exclaimed, as he dragged over a hay bale. "Make yourself comfortable. I'll be done right quick." He deftly medicated the hoof, whispered something soothing in the mare's ear, and invited me into the office.

"How are you, Emma?" he asked, as we settled by his big desk.

"Oh, tolerable, Captain."

"Still in your rooms?"

"Yes, sir, but not for long. I've decided to take your advice and find other accommodations--although, for what I have in mind, I need a horse."

"A horse?"

"Yes, sir. As you know, I am rather short on funds just now, but I am prepared to offer some fine books in trade--books by Tennyson, Hawthorne, and other notable authors, and an almost-complete collection of Shakespeare. You're a learned man—perhaps they would cover the cost of a mount."

"Your father's books?"

"Yes, sir." I also had a few dollars and cents tied up in a sock, but I hoped to hang onto that for the next few days.

The Captain studied me. "Emma, dear, I know your predicament has been difficult, but is it worse than usual?"

"No, sir," I replied. "Things are looking up."

"Good. And how does a horse fit into the picture?"

I could have come clean about my plans, but I had to have that horse. I chose to spin a small tale, although it did not sit well with me. "I have found a nice family to stay with, Captain. They have a spread out on the Coloma Road. I'll help with the chores and the children, particularly little Ira, who is a dickens. But I'll still need to get into town to wrap up my father's affairs. A good horse will see that I make it there and back with speed. And safety."

The Captain frowned, in the manner of a man who would like to see me at Miss Ford's School for Young Ladies. "Do I know this family?"

"No, sir. I don't believe so. They're new to the county."

He was silent. I kept my eyes on my reddened hands. At last, he said, "All right. What are you looking for? A smooth gait and a good disposition?"

"Yes, sir!" I said, breathing again. "What about that little chestnut you had for sale a while back?"

"She was skittish and needed work, Emma. Anyway, she's sold. How good of a rider are you?"

"Middling."

"Umm-hmmm. And how far off the road is this family I don't know? How sure-footed does this animal need to be?"

"Sure-footed would be good."

"Well, come with me."

He escorted me out to the farthest corral. There were a couple of fine horses along the way, a roan gelding and a shiny black mare, but we passed them by. "Now, Emma," the Captain said, "give some thought to this fellow."

In the corner of the pen stood the ugliest mule I have ever seen. He was a dirty grey, with black spots. He had a nasty, crescent-shaped scar over one eye, and the rest of his hide was pitted with old wounds. The Captain spied my displeasure. "Don't judge a book by its cover, Emma. I know this old boy. I've traded him in and out of the stable more than once. He's as sure-footed as they come, and he has a pleasing disposition."

"He's not much to look at, Captain. I've never seen a mule with spots like those."

"His mother was a paint, I believe, although I doubt she was a pretty one. But he's a good old mule, saddle broke, and he can pack for you, too. His last owner struck yellow and traded him in for that fancy chestnut. Worked him hard, then left him behind. He could use a little kindness and an easy shift. Trotting you back and forth to town might turn out dandy for the both of you."

The "left behind" part played on my heartstrings some, but I still didn't see myself on this dusty old mule. The captain gestured me into the corral, slipped a halter over the mule's head, and led him over to me. That crescent scar gave him a ferocious aspect, but as I patted his neck, he turned a benign, sad eye to me. "Hey, mule," I said, "has life been rough on you lately?" He straightened up his ears, then moved right in to lean his big forehead against my shoulder.

"I believe you have a mule," said the Captain.

I sighed. "I reckon so."

"He won't disappoint you. He's reliable, and sturdier than most horses. Throw him a few oats when you can, and he'll make a good friend."

"He won't be coveted by thieves, anyway. Does he have a name?"

"As many as he's had owners. Spot, Dusty. Dammit."

He deserved a better appellation than Dammit. Something with a little dignity to it. He had the long, melancholy face of one of those Bible elders wandering the desert. Lemuel! And so it was. "I christen you, Mr. Lem Mule!" I said, and the mule nickered.

The Captain and I headed back to the office to work out the details. "Now, Miss Emma," he said, "do you really want to part with your father's books?"

"No, sir, I don't. But they are cumbersome to truck about just now. I had hoped they would find a home with you."

"Then I shall take them on loan. But when you have finally settled, Emma, you come and fetch them back. Understood?"

"Yes, Captain!"

"As for the mule, I shall give him to you on credit. When you can—and only then—you come to me and square up."

My heart sang at this kindness. "Thank you, Captain! My father would thank you, too, if he could."

"Now, Miss Emma, I usually seal a deal with a whiskey, but I have something more suitable for a young lady right here."

He pulled a tin out of his desk drawer and lifted the lid to reveal some elegant sugarplums, dressed up with squiggles and rosebuds. "Help yourself, Emma."

"From San Francisco?"

"Yes," the Captain nodded. "Can't get that quality around here."

For a moment, my thoughts went places my heart did not wish to follow, but, as Emmett used to say, every good man has his failings. I took one of those sugarplums, the one with the fanciest squiggle on the top. The taste of it was bittersweet.

When I arrived at the theatre on my old mule, I half-expected some humor at my expense, but the back lot was empty. I tied up Lem Mule in the shade and went to work pressing the morning's wash. Shortly, Mr. Booth passed by, a copy of the *Democrat* peeking from his coat pocket. He delivered me a nod, found an out-of-the-way spot under a digger pine, and pulled out the paper. While he checked the theatre notices, I pretended to attend to the laundry, but when at last he smiled, I mustered the nerve to call over, "Good news, Mr. Booth?"

He grinned. "Wonderful, Miss Lightfoot! We are a success!"

As I ironed, a scruffy child made her way up from the creek and squatted with a jar in the long grass at the rear of the lot. Her smock was dirty, and her hair rolled in rag curlers. I was beginning to wonder if this stray had a home when Mrs. La Rue stepped out of the theatre and called down, "Louise, I told you to come in ten minutes ago. Get up here, please." Only when Louise glanced toward her mother, and I spied her beautiful eyes, did I recognize her.

"In a minute." Louise didn't move.

"Now." Mrs. La Rue started brusquely down the steps.

Louise held up the jar. "I have three caterpillars and a grasshopper."

"Set them free."

"No."

Mrs. La Rue seized the jar and emptied it into the grass. "Go on in. I asked you to stay tidy, and look at you. Go."

As Louise trudged up the staircase, a frown creased Mr. Booth's brow. Later, before the performance, Louise came to him with more of her finds. "I have a button in my pocket," she whispered. "And six rocks. There's gold in them!"

"Lovely, Miss Louise," Mr. Booth whispered back. "Wait just a minute, now." He disappeared into his dressing room and returned with a shiny tobacco tin. "Why don't you keep your treasures in here?" Louise's countenance lit up like a candle, and she hugged the tin to her chest.

The cast of *Taming of the Shrew* was in high spirits before the show. Mr. Booth was no longer lurking in the shadows but spreading merriment backstage. The only actor not having a pleasant time was young Jimmy Bliss. He is new to the acting profession. He had "dried up" onstage on opening night—the presence of an audience had sucked his words right out of his brain—and, last night, he was terrified he'd forget again. He kept running to the privy out back, to a chorus of chuckles from the rest of the cast. Then he would take refuge in the wings, repeating his single line over and over.

Finally Mr. Thayer took pity and put a gentle hand on Jimmy's shoulder. "You just stay cool, young man, and give it your best."

And Jimmy did. He made his entrance, pale with fear, and spit his line out to perfection. Never mind that his character had the twang of a farm boy, the words were strung right, a triumph for Jimmy Bliss.

While Mr. Thayer was looking out for Jimmy, the other half of his team had taken an interest in me. Ulysses, the mongrel, kept me company as I went about my tasks, his paws clicking behind me on the boards. Maybe it was because I had slipped him a biscuit from the supper I'd brought, but the dog was fond of me, settling at my feet when I lighted somewhere for a minute, and turning his eyes upon me as if I was his new best friend.

As the actors dressed for the show, I stood by, ready and attentive. At one point, Mrs. Burnham caught the hem of her skirt on a nail, and I managed to stitch it up quickly and cleverly, so that the tear almost disappeared into the folds of fabric. She was pleased, and so was I, for I hoped to make myself indispensable. I was cheered that she shared her good opinion of my repair with Mr. Leach.

Mr. Leach, the stage manager, is a busy man. He keeps things moving backstage so that the performance plays out like magic for the audience. He dashes about, giving orders to the Bliss brothers during the scene shifts, and seeing that the actors don't miss their cues. Then he throws on a hat and a smock shirt, plays his own scenes, and rushes back into the wings to see that the curtain rings down. Though he's stout, he has the quickness of a river otter, and with his droopy mustache and side whiskers, he looks a bit like one, too.

Though I have not seen *The Taming of the Shrew* before, I have read Emmett's copy of it. It is a rollicking piece, about two lovers who meet their matches. Petruchio, a fortune-hunter, has decided to marry Katherine, the shrew. Katherine has other ideas—she's spirited, and not about to be bossed around by any man.

The house was as full last night as it was on the Fourth, and the audience put on as much of a show as the players. Some cheered for Petruchio, some for Katherine. In the wooing scene, when Petruchio invited Katherine to "Come sit on me," there were hoots of approval from his faction; when she called him an "ass" in return, her supporters hollered out, "You tell him, little lady!" When he stole a kiss and she roundly smacked him, you could hear the audience from one end of town to the other—and that was only in the first act! None of this commotion bothered Mr. Booth or Mrs. Burnham—they were having too good a time themselves to be distracted. It was a delight to watch them argue over whether it was the moon or the sun in the sky, and pound at each other behind her long-suffering father's back.

From my stool in the shadows, I also observed a scene not written by Shakespeare. Miss Griffith and the redheaded Mr. Moone, I have discovered, are a couple both on and off the stage. Onstage, they are an affectionate, talented team. But, as they waited for their entrance in the wings, and Mr. Moone wrapped his arms about Miss Griffith's waist, she pushed him away with a toss of her curls befitting Katherine. He scowled and slumped into a chair, not at all the gleeful fellow I had taken him to be, although, when he heard his cue, he jumped up with the merriest expression on his face and made his entrance as if nothing had happened.

As the curtain descended on the final bows, it was time to play my own scene. The Star Troupe was moving on in the morning. The actors quickly stowed their costumes and makeup, and in no time, their champagne baskets were stacked by the theatre door, ready for loading into the wagon on the morrow. I had deliberately not asked for my "dollar up front" earlier in the day, so I might have good reason to speak to Mrs. Burnham after the play. I spied her in her cubby, still in a dressing gown, settling up with Mr. Burnham and Dunlap. They were buoyant, a sign of the evening's success. I waited until the men had left, and then I stepped into the doorway. As soon as she saw me, Mrs. Burnham set her cigar on the lip of the dressing table and hollered out, "Ben! I need that cashbox!" He circled back into the room. She fished out my dollar and smiled. "You decided to take us on faith today, Miss Lightfoot."

"Yes, ma'am. I figured you'd do right by me."

She chuckled. "Well, I hope we deserve your high opinion. Sometimes we do. Thank you for your help." She turned back to her dressing table and began to wipe the powder off her face. As Mr. Burnham headed through the door, she called out, "Ben, let's make it early tomorrow, to beat the heat."

"I'll have the wagon ready by six. Georgetown Road can be a trial for the team." He tipped his hat to me and disappeared down the hall.

I remained by the doorway. Mrs. Burnham sighted me in her mirror. "Miss Lightfoot?"

"Did you approve of my efforts, Mrs. Burnham?"

"Yes, you were fine. My skirt is good as new."

"Then I would like to offer my services for the rest of your tour. I'm a hard worker, I have clean habits, and I'd be no trouble. You wouldn't regret it."

She turned in her chair, took a puff on her cigar, and replied, "That's not possible, Miss Lightfoot. We're a small company. We simply can't take on the expense. When we hire for the day, it costs us for that show, and no more. When you travel with us, you need to eat, have a place to sleep, and make enough cash to cover that."

"I need very little," I came back. And though I hated to say it, I added, "I will work for seventy-five cents a day."

"How old are you, Miss Lightfoot? Fourteen? Fifteen?"

"Sixteen," I replied. She threw me a doubtful glance. "Last May."

"I already have a child to look out for in this company. And Mr. Brown and Miss Griffith are hardly grown up. I can't afford to turn this tour into a children's crusade. It's a rough road out there."

"Ma'am," I said, "I grew up in these camps. I know rough. I've seen it right here."

Her expression was not unkind, and my hope rose that she was well disposed toward me.

"Please, just give me the opportunity. You can always send me back," I said. "I am a very independent person."

"I'm sure you are." She leaned toward me and looked me straight in the eye. "Miss Lightfoot, this is not a life for anyone who has better choices. Be glad you do. Be wise, and go back to your family. Be happy you have a home to go to."

I had no response to that, none that I cared to share. She rose and squeezed my hand. "I'm sorry, but no." Then she passed me by and headed out toward the stage. "Jeriah!" she called, "Let's lock up!"

The weight on my heart nearly crushed my breath. I found my way down the stairs and across the lot to where Lem Mule waited quietly under the trees. I leaned against his warm side, and he allowed it, patiently. At last, I mounted up, and we made our way out to Main Street. I was grateful for the mule's company, as he delicately picked his way through the dark. My plans had turned to ashes. I longed for Emmett, and my memory wandered to the words he had whispered to me. "Don't let the grass grow under your feet. Chase your dreams. Have courage, and believe I'm always with you."

Well, now is the time for courage. I have nothing to lose. The Star Troupe is leaving tomorrow at six a.m. They will need a laundress at their destination, and Lem Mule and I shall be there. Having no other compass, I shall follow in their wake. I shall not despair.

I have picketed Lem Mule behind the *Rattler* office, where there's a patch of green grass, and I have rewarded him for his sweetness with a handful of oats from the bag the Captain tied to his saddle horn. My necessaries are packed in a bundle, and Emmett's books are loaded into sacks to be slung over the back of the saddle. I tucked the family Bible and his scrapbook in there, too, for safekeeping.

I completed one more task before departing. I lit the lantern by the printing press, then set the type and ran off three copies of my review. I cannot yet give Emmett an obit, but I shall give him something to be proud of.

While I worked, his ghost was all about. His desk was as he left it—chewed pencils, smudged foolscap, an opened volume of the Farmer's Almanac. As I inked the press, he was at my side—the smell of printer's ink is the smell of my father. This closeness to him was both comforting and sorrowful to me. We were putting out our last "edition" together, and then there would be no more.

I will leave at first light and make a few stops before I fall in behind the Star Troupe.

WELL PAST 7:00 A.M. *A hill north of Hangtown Creek—*

From our spot on this rise, sheltered by scrub, Lem and I can peer across the creek and catch glimpses of the back lot of the Placer Theatre and the Star Troupe wagon. There has been no early departure—not yet. Mr. Burnham had the team hitched by six, and Mr. Leach, with Buck and Jimmy, saw the wagon loaded. Mrs. Burnham passed through several times, her voice raised in consternation. The dog has been trotting about. But a good portion of the company appears to be missing in action. And so, as I wait, I shall write.

I believe I have everything I shall need, especially my journal and two of Emmett's books, wrapped in oilcloth. (These are small editions of *The Tempest* and *David Copperfield*—I cannot bear to part with everything.) What money I have is tied up in an old sock.

I am garbed in my father's shirt and trousers, relics of his mining days, and have donned his big, wide hat to keep the sun off. Emmett was a smallish man, and his clothes are not that outlandish on me. They make it easier to ride, but it is also my hope to pass unnoticed on the trail. I suppose anyone could tell, at second glance, that I am a girl, but perhaps, if I am nondescript enough, I can escape the first glance. I'll have to trust to my spectacles, a broad hat brim, and an old mule to make myself disappear.

This morning, as I readied to depart, I said goodbye to our *Rattler* rooms and to the ghosts that live there yet; goodbye to my penciled height marks on the doorjamb and to the wild rose bush beyond the window. I stood for a moment by our press, shipped up from San Francisco with so much delight and anticipation, and touched its beautiful eagle farewell. Then I locked up and stepped out into the early light.

My first stop in town was the most difficult. I tied Lem Mule by the blackberry bushes and stepped softly to Evie's door. Sparky was not in his basket, a good sign, so I gently knocked. From inside, I heard, "Just a minute," and presently Evie appeared, pulling her wrapper about her and rubbing the sleep out of her eyes. She stared at the sight of me, in my trousers and shirt. "Emma, did they put you into a play?"

"Oh, no, Evie, this is for real."

"Why?" And then, before I could answer, she knew. Her eyes filled with sorrow. I took her by the hand and we settled on her mother's quilt, where Sparky yawned a greeting.

I revealed to her my plan. She nodded but said little. To soften things, I added, "Perhaps they won't take me on, Evie. I might be back in a day or so."

She shook her head. "I will always remember you, Emma."

"Oh, Evie, I will write to you. I promise. Check the post office. And someday soon, I'll come back, and we shall eat ice cream until we bust. All right?"

I finally got a tiny smile.

"Evie," I went on, handing her a copy of my review, "I did go to the play, and now you can read this. Thank you. It means the world that you believe in me."

"I'll read it. I'll keep it right by my side."

"And here," I said, "I treasure my ring, and I shall always wear it. I do not have a ring for you, but I want you to have this as a remembrance."

I handed her Emmett's pocket watch. Her eyes widened. "Oh, Emma, I know how much this watch means to you—"

"You are my friend," I replied. "I trust you will care for it. And just think, every minute that ticks away is another minute that brings us together again."

She threw her arms about me and held me tight. I felt how fragile her shoulders were, and I knew I had to go, while I still could. We parted at the doorway. "Goodbye, dear Evie," I whispered.

"Goodbye, Emma. Be safe. Be happy. Write to me."

I strode across the yard to Lem Mule, trying not to look back. I did so only once, as I climbed into the saddle. Evie flashed me her loveliest smile. Cradling Sparky close with one hand, she waved me a brave farewell with the other. That is a picture I shall always hold in my heart.

From the Red House, I made my way to Captain Smith's stable. I passed through the warm darkness of the barn to his office and left the little rifle and Emmett's books piled neatly on his desk, along with a short note and two dollars of my debt to him. I did not go into detail about my plans—I saw no need to stir up worry—but I thanked him for his help and promised to keep in touch. I also added a postscript: "Lem is a fine mule. Best regards, Emma Lightfoot."

It was a stone's throw to Sacramento Street and the Lucky Wash House. No one had wakened yet, and I left a note much like the Captain's by old Mr. Yip, who was dreaming away on his pallet. I was sure he'd find a way to put it under Mrs. Gee's eyes without stirring up too much fire. I omitted any talk of "theatre people." I wished, for all her kindness, I could have told Mrs. Gee the truth to her face, but I could not risk an argument on this morning.

My last stop was only a short ride up the hill to the cemetery. As I arrived, the sun was peeking above the horizon, pale gold light making the place seem a little more lovely than it would ever truly be. Emmett's grave now has a wooden marker, with "C. E. Lightfoot, Editor" burned into it. I figure it should last a couple of winters, at least.

He is the only person I know who might have approved of my actions, and I stood by the grave wishing that, in some way, I could make him proud. Then I took his copy of the review from my pocket, unfolded it, and placed it under a rock by the marker. I turned Lem Mule into the sunrise and headed down the hill.

Things are now looking up over by the theatre. Mr. Moone and Mr. Thayer have been present for some time. Mr. Brown arrived right on their heels, mounted on a handsome black horse with white stockings. Miss Griffith strolled into the lot a few minutes ago. She arranged herself in her sidesaddle and trotted right past Mr. Moone, snubbing his greeting, to place herself on the far side of the wagon. Finally, La Petite Louise came dashing around the side of the building, and was hoisted by Mr. Leach into the wagon. Mrs. La Rue hurried after her, scolding all the way.

The only actor still unaccounted for is Mr. Booth. I heard Mrs. Burnham demand, "Where the hell is he?" and someone, maybe Buck Bliss, reply, "He wasn't at the hotel." I know where he was last night after the play. Lem Mule and I were returning to the *Rattler* when out of the darkness I heard, "Goodnight, Miss Lightfoot."

My heart skipped a beat, though I quickly I realized it was not Clarence McPhee. McPhee's voice is high and has a piggish tone to it. This voice was rich and deep, with the hint of a drawl. I made out the rainbow colors of a serape on a bench before one of the German taverns that huddle at that end of Main.

I called back, "Goodnight, Mr. Booth," and kept on going. Sunk as I was in my own troubles, I did not think of it again until this morning.

Closer to 8 a.m.—

Mr. Booth just appeared in the back lot. He looked a bit unsteady—I hope he's not ill. Buck Bliss helped him up onto his pinto. Mrs. Burnham mounted her fine dappled grey and shouted, "We're booked tonight! Let's move out!" Mr. Burnham echoed her sentiments in much more "colorful" language and leapt onto the wagon seat. We're on our way.

Georgetown, the middle of the night—

A long and eventful day.

Lem Mule and I waited on the hill until the Star Troupe had moved on up Coloma Street and almost out of sight. Then we fell in behind them. Within minutes, we were past the saloons and storefronts of town, heading north into open country. I was glad that I had brought Emmett's hat, as the sun was already beating down upon the trail, burning the grass on either hand to gold. I kept my distance from the Troupe, to remain invisible and to spare myself eating their dust.

It being Sunday morning, there was little traffic. Lem and I came upon a buckboard packed with a churchgoing family, and we pulled to the side for a dray, loaded with barrels. The teamster nodded my direction as if I were just another miner on a mule.

Soon, we fell into a pleasant rhythm, hoof beats mingling with birdsong. We turned into a stretch of road fringing a dry creek bed. As we climbed the ridge, the hills to our sides crowded in upon the creek's hollow, casting morning shadow. Tall oaks, not yet hacked for the town's timber, threw a canopy overhead, and the air on the trail cooled palpably.

Lem and I carried on in that shady piece for half a mile. Nigh the crest of the ridge, we journeyed back into daylight. At first, I thought my eyes had failed to shift from the dimness of the hollow to the brightness of the sun. Then, I perceived that the very air had taken on a darker tint, as it had during an eclipse that Emmett and I had witnessed through smoked glass. I pulled Lem about and faced south. Beyond the hills rose a massive cloud, like one of the thunderheads that gather above the high Sierras in the summer—only this was a solitary cloud in a clear sky. Its white billows were tinged with brown, its underbelly with gunmetal grey, and the disc of the sun, trapped behind its veil, glowed orange. I was raised in these foothills, and it took me but an instant to realize the terrible import of that cloud.

Placerville was going up in smoke.

As I gazed, the cloud lifted higher and boiled at the edges. I could only think of what floated skyward with it: the theatre, Miss Ford's white house with the pointy window, the *Rattler* office—save for the iron bones of the printing press—all whirling toward heaven. And what of the Captain, and Emmett's books? Of Mrs. Gee, Lily and May? Of Evie??

I gave Lem Mule a squeeze and set off downhill at a quick trot. The wind shifted, sweeping smoke and ash about us and driving bitter grit against my teeth. Lem squinted and set his ears back, but he did not slacken his pace. After a quarter mile, we happened upon the buckboard of the churchgoing family. The patriarch of the bunch, pouring sweat, raced his steed back the way they'd come. The children, in their Sunday best, held on for dear life, terror in their eyes. "How bad is it?" I shouted.

"Bad!" was the only reply, and they galloped off in a storm of dust.

The mule and I kept on. I pulled my shirt collar up over my nose and tried to determine how I could reach the Red House. If I could only get to Evie, scoop her up behind me on Lem Mule, and hightail it out of there, all might yet be well for my friend.

As we hastened toward town, traffic rushed out of Placerville—at first, a stray rider or two, then wagons loaded with chests, quilts, even a parlor organ. Soon, Lem and I struggled against a current of panicked men and skittish beasts. We dodged off the trail and battled through the scrub until a couple of sooty-faced horsemen came our way, their beards grey with ash. The Cole Brothers! "Bob!" I hollered. "Elton!" They slowed a bit and looked about. I pulled Lem around and fell in beside them. They stared at me. "Bob!" I exclaimed, "It's Emma Lightfoot!"

Bob drew in a breath. "Oh, my Lord, Miss Lightfoot, I thought I'd seen a ghost. All you need is a set of whiskers."

"What are you doin' in your daddy's clothes?" wondered Elton.

"Traveling," I replied. It was no time to fret about fashion. "Listen, you fellows appear to have been in the fire. Is it as dreadful as it looks?"

"Oh, it's terrible," said Bob.

"Real terrible," echoed Elton.

"Main Street's gone," Bob added. "All of it."

"All of it," Elton sighed. "And Coloma Street, and—"

"Smith's stable?" I asked.

"All ashes, Miss Lightfoot," said Bob.

I was afraid to put the next question. "And the Red House? Have you boys been that way lately?" They traded a sheepish glance. This is not something one brings up with a "nice" young girl, even if she is in her father's clothes. "Please tell me."

"Well, we done come from there," said Bob. "I expect we was about the last customers that establishment had."

"Yup, the last." Elton shook his head in disbelief.

"It's gone, too, Miss Lightfoot, I'm sure. And it's a shame." Bob's mouth twisted up as he bit back his grief. "The roof was alight as we mounted up. Miss Alice was having her wagon hitched for the girls."

My heart grabbed at hope. "Did you see Evie about? Or her little dog?"

"No. We spent last night up in the big house, and everybody was in such a stampede to get out this morning, I don't believe we noticed her," said Bob. "Did you, Elton?"

"Nope."

"She's your friend, ain't she?" said Bob.

"Yes, she is."

"Well, don't worry none. Miss Alice wouldn't leave one of her girls behind."

"I hope not," I said, though I was not convinced. "Thank you, gentlemen." I whirled Lem about and hastened once more towards town.

I'd covered but a few yards, when Elton grabbed Lem's reins and pulled him to a halt. The man delivered me a stern look out of his good eye, and this time he was the one who spoke first. "Don't be a fool, Miss Lightfoot. It's too late for rescues. Everybody who could get out already has. All you'll get for your pains is a quick trip into hell."

"Yup, the fires of hell," said Bob.

"Somebody will have to risk their life to rescue *you*. Use your sense, Miss. Why don't you ride with us a piece? I reckon we're "traveling," too."

Elton kept a tight grip on Lem's reins. My head knew the wisdom of his words, though everything in my heart said to go to my friend. For a long while, I hesitated, and, in the end, I could not speak, only nod. Choosing to ride away from Evie is the hardest thing I've done, short of putting Emmett in the ground. "Come along then," said Elton, and we joined the river of refugees flowing along the Coloma Road.

Yesterday, I could not have imagined taking up with the Cole brothers, but tragedy makes for odd companions. We held a steady pace, purposeful, but not rushed. Though I was shaking inside, there was comfort in having a Cole on either hand.

The brothers had suffered in the flames. Elton's fist, which had grasped Lem's bridle so tightly, was badly blistered. Patches of Bob's shirt were singed away, leaving the skin on his arms bright red. And they weren't alone in their troubles. The fugitives swelling the road were blackened with soot; tracks of tears lined the faces of men and women alike. A buggy clattered by us with a couple on board. The woman was still in her nightdress. She clutched an orange cat with singed whiskers, bundled in a baby blanket, and her eyes met mine with shock and puzzlement. I had chosen to leave Placerville. This woman had awakened in her own bed, and, in minutes, had wound up on a dusty trail with no home to go to.

Shortly, despite the smoke and traffic, we arrived at the fork where the Coloma and the Georgetown Roads divide. The Coles spoke of a third cousin out Coloma way who farmed a pear orchard—would I care to come along? The wife had six little boys and would welcome a bit of feminine company at the table.

"You're very kind," I said, "but I have word of employment up Georgetown way. That's where I was traveling to this morning."

Elton frowned. "Oh, Miss Lightfoot, you'd be much better off at the farm."

"Yes, indeed," added Bob. "That's a rough road for a young girl, and our cousin ain't but a few miles from here."

"I thank you from my heart," I said, "but I must go. Don't fret for me." I turned Lem up the Georgetown Road and hastened away. When I glanced over my shoulder, the Coles were still watching from the parting of the roads, like faithful shepherd dogs. They remained there until I was out of sight, but by then, I had surrendered any hope of backtracking toward the fire. My only chance was to find the theatre company.

I set Lem Mule at a lope, urging him toward the ridge top. I kept an eye out for the Star Troupe's wagon, but I almost overlooked it as I hurried by. The company had pulled off the side of the trail, and the wagon was nearly masked by a stand of manzanita. I caught sight of Miss Griffith first, perched on her little sorrel. In her elegant riding costume with the plumed hat, she stood out against the scrub like an exotic bird in a weed patch. Beyond her, by the rim of the hill, stood the slight figure of Mr. Booth, and then, in a sheltered spot, the team of bays. The horses stamped and shifted, spooky from the smoke, as Mr. Burnham held the smaller lead horse's head, soothing him in a soft voice and adjusting the blinders on his harness.

I spied Mrs. Burnham in the shade of an oak, seated on a fallen limb. She fanned herself restlessly with her hat, and I tried to gauge her mood. My plan had been to show up in Georgetown and offer my services at the moment I was needed. I could still head back up the road and tail the company to its destination. Or I could just ride in and present myself now, while I had an extra argument in my pocket—I was a refugee upon the road. "Mrs. Burnham," I called. I gave Lem Mule a nudge, and we made our way into the clearing.

Hattie Burnham glanced up, and for the second time in our acquaintance, demanded, "Who are you?" She squinted against the sun. "Do I know you, young man?"

I doffed my hat and let my braid tumble down. "It's Emma Lightfoot, ma'am."

Mrs. Burnham rose, shaking her head. "You are full of surprises, Miss Lightfoot. You've switched the script on us. Here we were, pondering the burning of Troy, and suddenly we're knee-deep in a comedy, where the girl gads about as a boy. *Twelfth Night*, perhaps."

"Perhaps," I replied. And I could not resist, "Shall I 'make me a willow cabin at your gate?'" (I'd used those words for filler in the *Rattler* more than once.)

Mrs. Burnham knitted her brow. "Miss Lightfoot, why are you here spouting Shakespeare?"

"I'd hoped you might reconsider my request for a position, ma'am."

"I thought I told you to go home."

"I don't have a home, Mrs. Burnham." I nodded southward. "I expect that cloud of smoke is all that's left of it."

"Where's your family? Wouldn't you be safer with them?"

This time around, I was better prepared to put the sad facts of my family life to good use. "I am an orphan ma'am, without friend or family."

"Oh, dear God," said Mrs. Burnham.

"I have nothing to return to," I went on, "and am solitary upon the road."

"I believe you should be on the stage, Miss Lightfoot, rather than behind it."

I slid off Lem and went to her side. "My original offer stands, Mrs. Burnham. I will perform my duties for seventy-five cents a day. I have my own mule and bedroll. I am a hard worker with a cheerful attitude, and I believe you could use me."

Mrs. Burnham almost smiled. "You are nothing if not persistent, Miss Lightfoot."

"Desperate times—"

"Yes, yes, desperate measures. I know. Although why you would choose to go traipsing through the camps with the likes of us is a mystery to me."

"It's not a choice," I said. "It's a necessity."

"I believe you will find it's a hard life. You would be far more comfortable in another line of work."

"I do not seek comfort, Mrs. Burnham. I simply want the chance to do my best for you."

"'O, that I served that lady?'"

"Something like that, ma'am."

She studied me—the specs, the baggy trousers, the boots. She finally gave me a rueful nod. "All right, Miss Lightfoot. You have spirit. I can appreciate that. And, under the circumstances, I can hardly throw you back upon the road. Which I am sure you counted upon. We will try you out, one day at a time. But I cannot make you any offer before I speak to Mr. Burnham. He's in charge of funds."

"Thank you!"

She crossed to her husband, who had been observing us from the wagon. She leaned in toward him and spoke quietly. At first, he threw me a glance and vehemently shook his head, but Mrs. Burnham persisted. I claimed her spot on the oak limb. The La Rues huddled nearby in the patchy shade, the mother clutching a handkerchief to her face to fend off the smoke. She had tied a bandana over La Petite's nose and mouth—it lent the child the look of a small, blue-eyed bandit. Mr. Booth remained on the rim of the hill, somberly observing Placerville's funeral pyre. Even at our distance on the ridge, crimson tongues of flame could be glimpsed rising off of town and shooting toward the heavens. He gazed my way only once and tipped his hat in recognition before returning to the cloud of smoke. His eyes were red with tears.

Ulysses the dog was undaunted by the conflagration. He trotted my way, tail a-wag, and plopped himself at my feet, panting. Shortly after, Mr. Brown ambled over on his black horse, a twinkle in his eye. "Miss Lightfoot," he said, "are you setting a new fashion trend? I thought Hattie Burnham had cornered the market on the latest thing, but you have outdone her." I glanced over Mrs. Burnham's way, where she was still head-to-head with Mr. Burnham. She was garbed in one of those new "bloomer dresses" that had caused such a stir, where the skirt serves as trousers. Mr. Brown went on, "I believe 'early miner' makes a much more daring impression. And can be quite fetching." He leaned down and extended his hand to me. "Pleased to see you again, Miss Lightfoot."

Just then, Mrs. Burnham headed our way. "Harry," she said, "go bedevil someone else. Miss Lightfoot and I have business to take care of."

I must have burst into a smile at the word "business," for Mr. Brown gave me a wink and rode over to chat with Miss Griffith.

"Miss Lightfoot," Mrs. Burnham began, "these are our terms. We will pay you one dollar for each day—you won't make it on seventy-five cents. But you must be responsible for your own meals and for putting yourself up at night. You'll also have to see that that mule is fed and watered. I'm not quite sure how you'll manage, but you appear to be a determined young lady."

"I am."

"Sometimes the Bliss brothers cook up a company meal from our stores, or put on a pot of coffee. You are welcome to partake of that. Buck and Jimmy also have sleeping rights to the wagon, but they seem to prefer to camp out on the ground. I don't expect they'd mind if you slept in there on occasion. There isn't much room, but if you can find a corner, you'll most likely be welcome to it."

"Thank you, Mrs. Burnham!"

"For your dollar, you take care of costumes and anything else that needs to be done. Help us load and unload, run errands, make yourself useful. And you keep that 'cheerful attitude' and exemplary personal habits. Stay out of trouble, Miss Lightfoot."

I don't believe I'm a troublesome person, but I nodded, "Yes, ma'am."

"Good," said Mrs. Burnham. "Welcome to the Star Troupe. Get yourself on that mule and be ready to fall in."

By now, Mr. Burnham had done the best he could to calm the bays. The rest of the troupe mounted up, but for the La Rues, who climbed aboard the wagon, Mrs. La Rue keeping a tight grip on Louise's hand. "To Chili Bar," shouted Mr. Burnham, as he signaled the team, and we were once more upon the road. I took my place at the very rear of the caravan, despite the dust, because I am new to this company, and, though Mrs. Burnham announced my employment as we departed, I am still a stranger to their world.

The descent to Chili Bar is precipitous, snaking down the north-facing slope of the American River canyon, but it is also shady, which blessedly helped to abate the heat. Still, the shifting wind played havoc with the smoke. Sometimes the air was tolerable; then, in a blink, we choked on ash that filtered like snowflakes through the pines.

Slowly, we worked our way down toward the river. The actors proved to be confident riders, and Mr. Burnham handled his team with skill, easing the big wagon downhill like a knife through butter. Once or twice, Louise peered out the rear, grinning at those of us riding behind her, before Mrs. La Rue yanked her in to safety.

Most of the company rode in "costumes" of their own choosing—Mr. Booth in his Spanish gear, and Mr. Thayer in his tidy grey coat. Mr. Moone wore a plaid waistcoat, a cravat with a gold stickpin, and a tall beaver hat that added inches to his small stature, and the women were outfitted in their riding habits. But Mr. Burnham had packed away his hat with the beaded band and his fancy clothes and was garbed in the plain shirt and denim pants of a driver, a role he played with relish.

After a couple of miles, the road spilled us out onto the rocky bank of the American, where the cabins and storefronts of Chili Bar hug the narrow canyon. Some of Placerville's refugees had already pulled off the road, to watch and wait from the safety of the river. A few had even settled in, squeezing between the claims to set up camp until they could return to their homes—or knew for sure they couldn't. Others had chosen to continue on and crowded the entrance to the Chili Bar Bridge. Mr. Burnham slipped the wagon into line.

The current runs swift and deep at Chili Bar, even at midsummer. The stout wooden bridge is a traveler's boon. Despite its heavy traffic, the tollkeeper, with his weathered face and battered hat, kept things moving. So it was a surprise when Mr. Burnham suddenly raised his voice in a heated exchange with the man, then backed his team and drove to the side of the road. Mrs. Burnham and Mr. Leach hurried over to him. The rest of the company kept a respectful distance, but we all had our ears pricked for a clue as to what was up. At first, Mr. Leach and Mrs. Burnham spoke in low tones, much like Mr. Burnham had spoken to the spooked horses a while back. But Mr. Burnham was worked up, and his exclamations sailed our way. "Does he think I'm a fool? I drove a stage on this road every day for three years. I know what the damn tolls are!"

Mrs. Burnham murmured a reply.

"No!" Mr. Burnham shouted. " He's doubled his price. And the old bastard thinks he's got me over a barrel!"

La Petite poked her face out of the wagon. Mrs. La Rue planted her hands over Louise's delicate ears and hauled her back in.

Mr. Leach chimed in then, calm but audible. "It's not about you, Ben. The man sees an opportunity in other people's misfortunes and he's taking it. He's sticking it to everyone. It doesn't speak well for his character, but there it is. We need to get across this river."

"We'll cross downstream."

"Ben, the next bridge is all the way over at Coloma. That's miles. We'd have to backtrack the whole piece up the canyon, and then catch the Coloma Road."

"We can ford the blasted river. I've done it before!"

"In this stretch of canyon?"

Mr. Burnham was silent.

"With a child and all those costumes on board?"

At last, Mrs. Burnham spoke up. "Oh, Ben, just pay the damned toll before the man decides to triple it. We have a show tonight. It'll cost us a hell of a lot more than the toll if we miss our booking."

Mr. Burnham scowled. The company held their breaths. In the end, he gave the lines an angry shake and maneuvered the wagon back onto the road. When he arrived at the booth, he slapped the toll into the keeper's hand, but the man just grinned and coolly dropped the cash into his box. We filed onto the bridge. The sound of hooves on wood was music to the company's ears. For all that we sweltered in the heat, I don't believe anyone relished the thought of swimming the American today.

On the north bank, the road followed the river for a short piece, then headed straight up the slope of the canyon. It was nigh unto midday, and the sun glared down upon us. The horses heaved and sweated foam as they labored up the trail, the bays straining against the weight of the wagon. Lem Mule put one hoof patiently in front of the other. Mr. Booth, up ahead on his pinto, looked unwell and remained very quiet. When we finally attained the canyon rim, both man and beast were grateful. Our spirits lifted as we followed the trail toward Georgetown. Smoke still lingered, but the air tasted less like cinders.

We were up on the "Divide" now, between forks of the river, higher and cooler than before. We traveled to the tune of Mr. Thayer's mouth organ and made good time. Within a mile or two of Georgetown, we arrived at a bend in the road. The wagon and riders before me suddenly halted. Silently, a horseman slid from the trees, a pistol drawn upon me. A rough voice up ahead growled, "Dismount! Every last one of you!"

I hustled off of Lem Mule, and the outlaw with the pistol herded Mr. Brown, Buck Bliss and me up the road. There stood the rest of the company, surrounded by four more armed bandits. "In a line, at the side of the trail!" ordered the rough-voiced man.

Ulysses let out a ferocious growl. Mr. Thayer quickly grabbed his collar. "Ulysses! Down!" The dog obeyed, to Mr. Thayer's relief, although the pistol that had been meant for the canine was put to Mr. Thayer's head. Mr. Moone and Mr. Brown also felt iron at their ears.

I found myself standing just a step behind the Burnhams as we formed our line. My knees trembled no matter how fervently I bid them be still. Mr. Burnham was the only member of our party who was visibly armed, with a Colt revolver at his waist. His hand moved stealthily toward it, but one of the outlaws, a spare, dark-complected man, seized the firearm from Burnham's holster and thrust it into his own belt. The outlaw cracked a smile, and his gold tooth gleamed.

All of the highwaymen were fearsome, but the ringleader clearly enjoyed the role of desperado. He was tall and muscular, with fair hair and a goatee. Bowie knives hung from his belt, and five or six revolvers were slung about his waist and across his chest. Around his torso, he sported a metal breastplate, like a knight of old, except that it was crudely cobbled together from boilerplate and rivets. Hard living had ruined his looks. He might once have been a handsome man, but his steely grey eyes could not redeem his nose, which was smashed in at the bridge and lent him a fierce and frightening appearance. He stood boldly in the road, and boasted, "I'm Tom Bell, highwayman! My gang and I are here to lighten your load, so if you will drop your valuables into the collection plate, no harm will come to you. If you hold back, this gang is a desperate crew, and I cannot vouch for their good manners." He grinned at his own joke.

Tom Bell's name had made headlines in the *Rattler* for months, as his gang prowled the roads about the camps. They had not yet committed murder, a fact with which I tried to comfort myself. Their foul deeds were confined to robbery and borrowing, without permission, other people's horses.

Two of the bandits worked their way down the line, collecting cash and jewelry and tossing their plunder into a pile at Tom Bell's feet. As they drew closer, Miss Griffith did not hesitate to cling to Mr. Moone. The other bandits rummaged the wagon, whooping when they discovered the Star Troupe's cash box under the driver's seat. "Goddamn it!" muttered Mr. Burnham. The gold-toothed outlaw grinned and demanded Burnham's pocket change. As the bandit approached me, I prayed that Emmett's loose trousers would conceal that old sock of dollars pinned in the leg. My friendship ring was nestled amongst them.

A scream ripped from the wagon. "Don't you touch that child! Leave her be! No! No! NO!" The highwaymen glanced toward the cries, and Mrs. Burnham slipped a hand, quickly and subtly, to her waist. She removed something from her pocket—I caught a flash of silver, as one might spy a minnow in the depth of a stream—and concealed it in the folds of her bloomer dress.

An outlaw burst from the rear of the wagon, with a frantic Mrs. La Rue slung over his shoulder. Right on his heels scrambled his partner in crime, cradling La Petite Louise. Louise remained cool as her captor deposited her before the ferocious Tom Bell. The desperado knelt down to the child's level. "Leave her be!" shouted Mrs. La Rue, but Tom Bell simply smiled.

"Now, I wouldn't hurt her," he said, and his voice was almost kind. "What's your name, young lady?"

Louise met his gaze straight on. "Miss Louise," she replied.

"Well, Miss Louise, what is a pretty child like you doin' with this scruffy bunch?" He gestured to the wagon canvas. "The Star Troupe, is that right?"

"Yes, it is. I'm an actress."

"Oh. And what can you act?"

"I can recite."

"Umm-hmmm."

"And I can sing."

"You can? Then sing us a song, sweetheart."

Louise turned to Mrs. La Rue, pinioned by the outlaw. "If you let my mother go."

The head of the gang snorted and nodded to the bandit, who released his grip. Mrs. La Rue shot Bell a furious look, but, daunted not a whit, he took Louise's hand. "This child has sand," he said, and lifted her onto a boulder. "What shall it be, Miss Louise? I'm in the mood for a sad song."

"'Pretty Saro?'"

"Why, yes, that's splendid. Give us 'Pretty Saro,' darlin'."

And Louise did. Perched on the boulder, she filled the trail with sweet sorrow:

Farewell, pretty Saro, I'll bid you adieu,
But I'll dream of pretty Saro wherever I go.

I cannot say that the wolves about us were turned to lambs, but their brutal faces softened, even as they kept hard grips upon their pistols.

As Louise held her final note, Tom Bell applauded, drew a gold piece from a pouch at his belt, and pressed it into the child's palm. "Nymph," he said, "in thy orisons be all my sins remembered."

"That's Shakespeare," Louise replied.

"Yep," nodded Bell. "I had aims to be an actor once. I decided highway robbery was a steadier line of work."

"Did you play the bad men?" Louise wondered.

Tom Bell hooted, a wild, lunatic laugh. "No, darlin', I was a sweet young man back then."

Louise handed him a skeptical look.

"All the ladies loved me."

Mrs. Burnham squinted hard at the highwayman, and her shoulders relaxed the tiniest bit. "Tom," she called out. "Tom Hodge, is that you?"

The outlaw leader stared back at her and snarled, "I'm known as Tom Bell, ma'am."

Mrs. Burnham wasn't fazed. "Tom, it's Harriet. Harriet Carpenter. From the *Sweet Dream*, out of Cincinnati."

A light came into the highwayman's gunmetal eyes. "Hattie? Hattie

Carpenter? That riverboat girl who sang like an angel and swam like a fish?"

"I suppose so." Mrs. Burnham smiled, although her hand remained concealed in the folds of her bloomers.

"Time has been kind to you, Hattie. You've grown into a fine woman."

Ben Burnham frowned but said nothing.

"You're quite someone yourself, Tom," Mrs. Burnham said. "I hardly knew you."

"It's the nose, ain't it?" Bell grinned, which flattened his nose more than ever.

"Or the knives. Or the boilerplate. But, yes, you did have a fine nose once."

"Never argue with a Mexican cavalry horse. That old nag packed quite a kick." The outlaw chuckled, though his gang kept their pistols leveled at us. "This is your outfit then? The Star Troupe? You traded in the river for the camps?"

"Quite a while back, Tom. We're booked into Georgetown tonight, then all up and down the foothills. We put on a good show, if I do say so myself."

"I have no doubt," replied Tom Bell, admiration in his voice. He took a step toward Mrs. Burnham. She stood her ground and looked him right in the eye. He was nigh enough to me that I could smell his tobacco.

At that moment, a strange figure stampeded down the trail. The highwaymen swiftly took aim, but held their fire and stared. Was it a tall, skinny man? Or a deer? No, the critter was a giant bird of some sort—tiny head on a long neck, bobbing hips, and legs as lanky as Tom Bell's. It ran pell-mell into our midst, then wished it hadn't and dashed about frantically, dodging horses and wagon and outlaws. Louise cheered it from her spot on the boulder, while the highwaymen howled, and a bandit in patched pants fired into the air. This only set the bird off more. It almost ran down the Bliss brothers before it found an opening at the far end of the bend and bounded off along the road.

"What the hell was that," wondered the bandit with the gold tooth.

"I believe the circus is on its way," said Mrs. Burnham. "Unfortunately. I know Joe Rowe is traveling about these parts."

Tom Bell hooted again. "Well, I ain't about to take on strange birds and acrobats this late in the day. That's it, boys! We're done here!"

His gang holstered their weapons and made for the pile of booty in the road. But Bell let out a shrill whistle, the kind you'd use to call off a pack of dogs. The highwaymen halted. "Not this time," said Bell. "This one's on us." The gang scowled, but they slunk back.

Tom Bell turned one more time toward Mrs. Burnham and stood close before her. She let loose of the silver object. A tiny pistol slid down the rear of her bloomer dress, coming to rest in the dust of the trail. She took a quick half step back to conceal the gun with her hem, but it had skittered beyond the skirt's reach. It gleamed up at me. My knees turned once more to water.

"Goodbye, Hattie Carpenter," murmured the outlaw. He reached for the same hand that had so recently gripped the little weapon and delivered it a chivalrous kiss, much to Mr. Burnham's chagrin.

As the outlaw bent his head to Mrs. Burnham's hand, I took a deep breath and slid my trembling foot toward the little pistol. The inches seemed a mile, but Emmett's boot at last concealed the bright metal. I pressed it into the earth and swore to hold my ground.

"I expect complimentary tickets to your shows," Tom Bell rasped. "A lifetime's worth."

"You'd take the chance of coming into town, Tom?"

Bell flashed her a bold smile. "You'd be surprised."

"Then gladly," Mrs. Burnham smiled back.

She had come out ahead on that deal. A lifetime of tickets for Tom Bell wasn't likely to add up to much. He tipped his hat to her, the gang mounted their horses, and they vanished into the trees as silently as they'd appeared.

The company rushed to the pile of valuables in the road. Mr. Burnham seized the cash box and stowed it back on the wagon. Mr. Booth lifted Louise down from the boulder and delivered her safely to her mother.

Mrs. Burnham began to shiver. Mr. Thayer hurried to her side and helped her down onto the grass. He crouched beside her. "Hattie?"

"Thank God he's gone. I couldn't have kept that up much longer."

"A nasty piece of work, isn't he?"

"Yes. The devil's own. But, once upon a time, he was truly a sweet young man. He'd leave pink roses on my dressing table."

Mr. Thayer patted her hand. "Life changes people."

Mrs. Burnham shook her head. "No. Sweet or not, he always had a wild streak—and that crazy laugh. My father threw him overboard one night when the till came up empty."

My legs had steadied enough that I could finally lift my boot from the little pistol. I retrieved it from the dirt and handed it to Mrs. Burnham. She looked up at me, surprised. "Thank you, Miss Lightfoot."

Mr. Thayer regarded her in disbelief. "Hattie, did you really think that toy would make a dent in boilerplate?"

She shrugged, "Maybe a little dent. I was worried about the child."

"Well, I'm glad you fell back on your charm. You shot that sinner right through the heart."

"If he even has one," she sighed, and tucked the silver pistol back into her pocket.

"Oh, he does," said Mr. Thayer. "Your aim was true."

Mrs. Burnham rolled her eyes, "Lord, Gus, I don't even want to hear that," and Mr. Thayer grinned.

As they spoke, hoofbeats pounded up the trail. Mrs. Burnham started. But the rider who turned into the bend was no rough outlaw. He was a trim, handsome man, who sat upon his shiny steed with grace.

"Hello, Rowe," said Mr. Burnham. "Looking for a bird?"

Rowe pulled up his horse and nodded. "Our new attraction, Othello. He hails from Africa, and he's determined to get himself back there."

"He was just one hell of an amusement for Tom Bell and his gang."

"You were robbed?"

"No. You might say we were saved by the bird," said Mr. Burnham. "Can the dang thing fly? Or swim?"

"Not a chance," replied Rowe. "He's an ostrich, a land bird."

"Then the river might slow him down some." Mr. Burnham gestured back toward the American. "He was headed thataway."

"Thank you," said Rowe, and added, a little sadly, "I expect the creature misses his own kind."

He lifted his hat to Mr. Burnham, and was about to trot off on Othello's trail, when Mr. Thayer stepped forward and called out, "Howdy, Joe!"

Mr. Rowe brightened. "Gus Thayer! Good God, it's been ages! I didn't know you were traveling with the Burnhams. How's that old dog?"

"Tolerable. Is Eliza with you on this trip?"

"Yes, indeed."

"And you've expanded your bill to include strange fowl?" Mr. Thayer chuckled.

"It seemed like a good idea—we thought he might draw a crowd," replied Mr. Rowe. "But he's the dickens to keep track of."

Mrs. Burnham strolled over. "Where you been, Joe? Georgetown?"

"Oh, no, Greenwood."

"How was the house?"

"Excellent," Rowe replied. "Shame about Placerville, though. We'll lose four performances there. But we have hopes for Spanish Flat tonight."

"Spanish Flat." Mrs. Burnham mustered a smile. "Then I wish you well, Joe."

They exchanged a bit more small talk, and Mr. Thayer filled Rowe in about Tom Bell. Then Rowe disappeared down the trail in search of his wandering "star." The Burnhams gazed after him. "Cheer up, Hattie," said Mr. Burnham. "Spanish Flat is still a ways from Georgetown. Rowe shouldn't hurt us too much."

"I surely hope not," Mrs. Burnham replied. "Damn the circus."

When the Burnhams were out of hearing, I sought out Mr. Brown as he repacked his saddlebag. "Mr. Rowe is a pleasant man," I said. "But the Burnhams weren't happy to see him."

"No," said Mr. Brown. "No one wants to travel behind a circus. It's like following locusts. They swallow up the patrons' cash, their stock eats up the grazing. And some stage people think the circus is beneath them, it isn't 'legit,' you know, not the real 'drama.'"

"I love the circus," I said.

Mr. Brown delivered me a broad smile. "I love the circus, too!"

I loved it even more when Rowe's company passed us by a few minutes later. Except for an empty cage on a wagon bed with "OTHELLO" emblazoned on its side, the circus was made up of acrobats and equestrian acts. I don't know what was more pleasing—the beauty of the horses or the elegance of the riders. Perhaps they were one. Some of the performers rode bareback. All of them were young and agile. They waved to us amiably, and a young man spoke a greeting in a foreign tongue. At the head of their caravan pranced a gleaming stallion, the name "Adonis" worked into his bridle. A slender woman perched on his back, reins held lightly in one gloved hand. The procession glided by to its own music of hooves and breath. When the last rider disappeared down the trail, I felt the same sadness as on the final notes of Louise's song—something beautiful had come and gone.

I must end here for now. I have not even spoken of Georgetown, or of the evening's performance. But my last candle stub is about to sputter out, and I should have slept long ago. Yet, as I write, I sense Emmett by my shoulder, and that is a deep comfort. I shall finish on the morrow. For now, I must catch what sleep I can in this corner of the wagon. Dawn will break in an hour or two. I send up a prayer for Evie.

> MONDAY, JULY 7, ABOUT 3 P.M. *Coloma. The laundry is drying on the line. My hands are almost too tender from lye soap to pick up a pencil, but I expect that will improve with time—*

It was nigh unto five p.m. yesterday when the Star Troupe rode into Georgetown. The place is situated on a ridge, not crammed into a creek bed, and it has some spread to it. Main Street is about a hundred feet wide, lined with arching oaks and Chinese trees of heaven. We had no trouble locating the theatre on the second floor of Mr. Pratt's bank building, or Mr. Leach, who was already on the premises, having ridden on ahead at Chili Bar. He had thrown open windows and doors to disperse the heat, and a smart, fresh bill was posted out front—a bill that made no mention of Mr. Booth, Senior. What was missing, Mr. Leach informed the Burnhams, was our "welcoming committee," comprised of Pratt and a couple of other local merchants. They had long ago wearied of waiting for us. Mr. Burnham launched an expedition to the bar of the Georgetown Hotel and shortly returned with our hosts. They were in good cheer, if a little embarrassed about their recent whereabouts. "Delighted to see you all," exclaimed Mr. Pratt. "We're honored by your presence!"

His acquaintance, a Mr. Graham, added, "We almost gave you up for dead. Leach assured us you hadn't burnt to a crisp in Placerville, but we was worried you might have fallen off the mountain."

A third local, Mr. Clegg, chimed in with, "We figgered the least we could do was to hoist you a memorial toast."

"And so we did," chortled Mr. Pratt. "More than one."

"We didn't tumble down the mountain, but we did come up against trouble," said Mr. Burnham. "An unhappy encounter with Tom Bell."

Mr. Pratt let loose a whistle. "Tom Bell. That rooster's going to wind up at the end of a rope one of these days." The gentleman pushed his spectacles up on his nose. "No one injured, I hope?"

"No."

"Praise be. Then you have arrived safe and sound. We welcome you, Star Troupe!"

This was the cue for a burst of activity, and every company member played their part. The wagon was positioned at the foot of the theatre stairs and quickly unloaded. Mr. Burnham took charge of the team, while Mr. Leach and Mrs. Burnham set up the stage. Mr. Booth emptied his wicker champagne basket, then lashed it to the rear of the wagon and draped the skull and crossbones of *The Iron Chest* about it. The other men rolled up their sleeves and hefted stage properties, whilst the women toted costumes, and I helped wherever I could. In fifteen minutes the business was, to my wonderment, done.

Even more wondrous was the transformation of the actors themselves, from road-weary travelers to bright and beautiful performers. There was no rest until the parade had toured, and within another fifteen minutes, the company was ready for its entrance upon the streets of Georgetown. Horses were brushed until they shined, and the team put in fine harness; Ulysses sported a ruff. While Miss Griffith wove bright ribbons into her hair, Mr. Moone added a jaunty feather to his beaver hat. Mr. Booth, in the costume he would wear that evening, was splendid upon his pinto. With a musical flourish from the Bliss brothers, the Star Troupe set off along Main Street.

The parade route was not a long one—up Main and back down Church—so the troupe made the journey twice. Jimmy Bliss's drum and Buck's bugle drew people out of their doors to cheer the company on, and by the time the procession returned to the theatre, it had collected a small crowd. Mr. Burnham leapt off the wagon and bounded to the top of the building's steps. He spread his arms wide and, in a booming voice that carried nigh unto the city limits, addressed his audience something like this:

"Ladies and gentlemen of the fine city of Georgetown, welcome! Tonight, the illustrious Star Troupe presents Colman's fine play, *The Iron Chest*, fresh from its triumph in Placerville. Indeed, we have fought our way to you through fire and highway robbery! We have survived the violent assault of Tom Bell"—(hisses could be heard from the crowd at Bell's name)—"to present this outstanding production. At the top of the bill are Mrs. Harriet Burnham, Empress of the California Stage, and Mr. Edwin Booth, the Young American Tragedian, making his last tour of the mines before conquering the Atlantic States!"

Mr. Burnham then beckoned onto the plank sidewalk the different company members, each giving a taste of the delights awaiting the crowd at the evening's performance. "Princess of the Fairy Stars, La Petite

Louise!" lifted her voice in a lively version of "Sacramento," followed by a cunning hornpipe. Mrs. Burnham and Mr. Booth, stunning in their *Iron Chest* costumes, played the scene where Lady Helen visits Mortimer. When a tear ran down Helen's cheek, the eyes of half a dozen spectators glistened, too. Not to leave off on a sorrowful note, the scene was followed by Griffith and Moone, "fresh from their triumphant tour of Australia." The couple delivered a smart duet of "Blue-Tailed Fly" and wrapped up with a jig, their feet tapping the boards in perfect unison. If only they could get along as agreeably together as they can dance!

Next, Mr. Burnham introduced Mr. Thayer, "that fine New England artist, master of comedy and tragedy alike," and Ulysses, "the most talented canine in the States."

Offstage, Mr. Thayer has a rich voice with crisp, clear diction, but he can shift his sound in an instant. Now, he became a simple yokel. He sidled over to Mr. Burnham, the dog at his heels, and confided, "Ben! How the heck can this mutt follow those other folks? They put us to shame!" He shot a glance at Ulysses that gave new meaning to the term "hangdog." Ulysses came back with an even sadder look, and the audience giggled. "You'd best come up with something, dog," Mr. Thayer demanded. "Play dead!" He fired off an imaginary shot at the dog. Ulysses wagged his tail. "No, no, Ulysses!" wailed Mr. Thayer, and he fired from all different directions—over his shoulder, under his knee. Ulysses remained cheerfully standing. Finally, Mr. Thayer apologized to the audience for his "temperamental artist" of a dog and slunk away in despair. "Come, Ulysses," he called over his shoulder, and the dog fell upon the sidewalk, paws in the air. Mr. Thayer's long, sad face filled with surprise, and the audience roared as he scooped up his "dead" dog and took a bow.

Mr. Burnham requested a round of applause for all the actors and reminded the crowd that the performance began "right on this spot at eight p.m.—a portion of the proceeds for the benefit of the Placerville fire victims. Come to the show and tell your friends!"

In a blink, the company stowed costumes and instruments and hastened away to supper. Mrs. La Rue pleaded a headache and insisted Louise join her for a rest in their room at the hotel. When Mr. Burnham led the team off to be stabled, only the Bliss brothers and I remained in the theatre lot. It was too late to wash any costumes, but I did need to press a few bits. As I worked, I pondered the news that Mr. Booth was leaving the West. Why did this make me sad?

Buck Bliss was kind enough to offer me some jerked beef, and I nibbled it as I fired up my little brazier and heated the flatirons. I was barely ten minutes into my labor when Louise appeared. She played around the edges of the lot, collecting bits for her tobacco tin. Mrs. Burnham emerged from the theatre and caught sight of the girl. "Louise," she called, "Aren't you supposed to be napping?"

The child glanced up sweetly from where she crouched in the dust. "No."

Mrs. Burnham hesitated, then decided to go on to supper.

Not long after, I felt a pair of eyes upon me. Louise was at my elbow. "My father's dead," she announced.

"Oh," I said. "Well...so is mine."

"He died in Grizzly Flat. He's six feet under."

"How did that happen, Louise?"

She shrugged. "I don't remember. But he's a goner."

"Hmm." I spied the tobacco tin under her arm. "Find anything good today?"

"Yes," she replied. She cracked open the tin and began laying treasures on the end of the ironing board. "Here's a green rock. And this one's quartz, with gold. See it sparkle?"

"I do," I said, and leaned over the tin. "What else?"

"Oh, don't look!" she said. "It's my secret box. Here." She lifted the lid just a tiny bit and, with great mystery, slipped out a handful of stuff. "I found these nails, too. And now, I have three buttons."

"Nice!"

She would have hauled out more, but just then, Mrs. La Rue marched around the side of the theatre. She had a pinched air, and, for the first time, I noticed the dark circles under her eyes. In a weary voice, she said, "Louise, I've been searching for you. We were both supposed to have a 'lie-down.'"

Louise met her mother's gaze. "I did. But I woke up."

Mrs. La Rue knew she was being worked, but she had no energy for anger. "Come on in now. Miss Lightfoot, thank you for minding her."

I hadn't minded her much at all, but I reckoned it was politic to take what credit I could. "You're welcome, ma'am." Mother and daughter headed back to the hotel.

Louise is an odd girl—and a marvelous one, too. She can spout verse that would confound many grown folks, yet she fancies squatting in the dirt to find rocks and bugs, as any other child might. But then, I was an odd child, too, with my nose in books and my feet in a creek, so perhaps I'm not one to judge.

As dusk came on, the actors reappeared about the theatre, and I hastened to finish up. One of the first to arrive was Miss Griffith. She started up the stairs, then turned and rushed over to me. "Miss Lightfoot, isn't it?"

"Yes, ma'am," I replied.

"Oh, please don't call me ma'am," she giggled. "It makes me feel so ancient. I don't expect I'm much older than you are. What's your age?"

"Sixteen, last May."

"Well, there, you see? I'm seventeen. We're just the right ages to be friends."

"Yes, ma'am. I mean, Miss—"

"No, no. You call me Sophie. And I'll call you...?"

"Emma. My name is Emma."

"Welcome, Emma. Do you have family in Placerville?"

"Until recently."

"Did they have to flee the fire?"

"No, ma—Sophie. They're deceased."

"Oh. My." A tiny frown crossed her brow, and then she brightened. "Well, now you're a part of *our* family."

"You're very kind," I said. I handed over her hair ribbons, and a lace collar I'd pressed.

"Oh, this is lovely. May I bring you down a few more small things before the show?"

"Of course."

"Why, thank you, dear Emma!" She leaned in toward me and whispered, "Now, if anyone gives you any trouble, you just let me know." Then she winked and was off.

I'm not quite sure why she adopted me so quickly, but she was kind, and I can't fault her for that.

A few minutes later, I headed into the theatre to make deliveries. Mr. Booth was the only person in the men's dressing room, placing some of his costume pieces back into the champagne basket. He waved me in. I hung a shirt up on a hook by his Mortimer coat. I couldn't help admiring the stitching on that coat, and the velvet lapels. "This is so very fine," I said.

"Much finer than I can afford. It was my father's."

"Your father played Mortimer, too?"

"When I was a boy, I must have seen him play it hundreds of times."

It crossed my mind that Emmett would have loved to have this conversation. "I've heard people speak of his Richard the Third," I ventured. "He was much admired in that role." Mr. Booth stopped packing the basket and gazed up at me. "Have you seen my father act, Miss Lightfoot?"

"Oh, no. But I've heard your father was always well regarded by those who witnessed his performances. He must have been a very great actor."

"He was," replied Mr. Booth.

For a moment, I could almost feel the ghost of the senior Booth in the room with us, about to don Mortimer's coat. I longed for Mr. Booth to speak more of him, but nothing else was forthcoming, and I grew tongue-tied. I could only manage, "Have a good show, Mr. Booth," before I started for the door.

"That's 'break a leg' in theatre lingo, Miss Lightfoot," said Mr. Booth, and he smiled at me. "So as not to tempt the gods with our audacity."

"Well, break a leg, Mr. Booth," I stammered, and then, as I felt my face and ears getting warm, I made a hurried exit.

I consider myself a sensible person. I do not blush in ordinary conversation. I have now blushed before Mr. Booth twice. I don't know what that is about.

When I reached the women's dressing room, it was already lively. At one end of the makeup table were the La Rues, and at the other end Mrs. Burnham, Miss Griffith, and Mr. Brown. The ladies were still in dressing gowns, but Mr. Brown was already in costume, popping peppermint candies into his mouth from a little paper sack. He chattered away, to peals of laughter from Mrs. Burnham and Miss Griffith and the rapt attention of La Petite Louise. His tale concerned the notorious actress, Lola Montez, and a nefarious manager, Crosby, who had skimmed off Lola's share of the take.

"Now, Crosby is a smallish man," said Mr. Brown, "not much taller than our Petite Louise here. When Lola cornered him in his office, the man shook in his boots but still declined to account for Lola's losses. Lola was obliged to resort to fiery curses—which shall not be repeated—and a drubbing from her infamous whip."

"Oh, that man was in dutch!" exclaimed Miss Griffith.

"Yes, indeed," continued Mr. Brown. "Lola chased him about the office like a squirrel in a cage, until his shrieks aroused the alarm of Mrs. Crosby, who is *not* a smallish woman. She has a good hundred pounds on Lola. Mrs. Crosby seized the whip and basted Lola up and down until the weapon shattered into pieces. Then she resorted to tooth and claw and attempted to remove every strand of the lovely Lola's hair."

"Oh, no!" cried Louise, clutching her own rag-wrapped curls.

"Not to worry," said Mr. Brown. "Most of Lola's tresses were imported French ringlets, which fell away in hanks. Lola fled, minus funds, to Frisco, where she nursed herself with milk baths and champagne and awaited a new shipment of French locks."

"Dear, dear Lord, I shouldn't laugh," said Mrs. Burnham. "The woman is my friend. But, oh, my, I can just see it."

"Every word is true," said Mr. Brown. He crossed his heart and tossed another peppermint into his mouth. Then he offered the bag of candies to the others. Louise took two, but Mrs. La Rue uttered a curt, "No, thank you," and turned back to the mirror. Mr. Brown hesitated a moment, then took this as his cue and, with a gentlemanly bow and a "See you on stage, ladies," left the room.

"Is there a problem, Clarissa?" asked Mrs. Burnham.

"He doesn't belong in here," snapped Mrs. La Rue.

"It was only a funny story," said Miss Griffith. "He minded his language."

Mrs. La Rue frowned. "It was tasteless. I don't want Louise exposed to such tales, especially about Lola Montez. She's coarse and morally bankrupt. Besides, he's a man, and this is the women's dressing room."

Miss Griffith slipped her costume bangles onto her wrists and jingled them. "Oh, he's just a boy, Clarissa. And he's lovely company."

"He's harmless," said Mrs. Burnham.

Mrs. La Rue glared at them. "I don't want him in here."

"Well, we'll just keep him down at our end of the room!" declared Miss Griffith.

I decided this was not my business. I handed off the rest of my deliveries and ducked out into the back lot.

Mr. Leach was placing benches and stools under the trees. It was much cooler out of doors than up in the stifling rooms of the theatre, and, as the twilight deepened, that's where the actors gathered, some only half in costume, to wait out the minutes before the show. The men smoked, and the women fanned themselves. Louise perched on a stool to keep her costume clean, her hair now combed into perfect curls. Mr. Booth demonstrated the art of blowing smoke rings to the child, much to her delight. Once he had formed them in the air, she played with putting her fingers through them as if they were truly rings.

When Mr. Booth had finished his pipe, he pulled out a big white pocket handkerchief and deftly knotted it into the shape of a rabbit. "How d'ye do?" the rabbit saluted Louise, in a high, plummy voice. "Maybe you don't know me—I'm Sir Hare-old the Valiant! Yes, I am! You might think it strange a rabbit should speak. Only a rabbit of the highest rank may address a lady!" Sir Hare-old bowed, and his linen ears flopped forward. Louise giggled. Though I should have been headed upstairs just then, I couldn't help but linger as the Young American Tragedian took on the role of a bunny.

"How may I serve ye, dear damsel?" requested Sir Hare-old.

Louise became suddenly regal. She glanced over toward Mr. Brown, still savoring his candy. "Sir Hare-old, I wish for another peppermint!"

Sir Hare-old addressed Mr. Brown. "Varlet! The lady demandeth tribute—a peppermint!"

"Gladly!" replied Mr. Brown, pitching a candy to Mr. Booth. Mr. Booth stuck it between the cloth paws of the rabbit, who delivered it with a flourish to Louise. She placed it in her mouth with great satisfaction.

"What other boon may I grant, m'lady?" asked the royal rabbit. "Command and I obey!"

Louise looked about her kingdom. "Protect me from that dragon!" she demanded.

The dragon was sweet Ulysses, napping under a bench. But Sir Hare-old began to tremble. "Oh, no, dear lady! I dread a dragon! Any other deed, I beg ye, but not a dragon!"

Louise was relentless. "I command you, Sir Hare-old—the dragon!"

Mr. Brown held up a twig. "You need arms, dear fellow. Here," and he tucked the twig between the bunny's paws.

"Alas!" groaned Sir Hare-old. "Is this a dagger I see before me?" The rabbit made his way over to the "dragon," shaking like a leaf. "I challenge thee, monster!" Ulysses opened one eye. The rabbit shrieked and retreated under Louise's stool. "Oh, oh, I do fear these nasty dragons, yes, indeed, I do!"

But by and by, with encouragement from Louise and Mr. Brown, the noble rabbit tiptoed back to the "dragon." "Zounds, I do believe he eats little rabbits, bones and all." He shivered so, his ears flew about. "Oh, dragon, ope not thy ponderous and marble jaws!" On cue, Ulysses offered up a huge, toothy yawn. "Oww, yow, YOW!" Sir Hare-old screamed. "He hath breathed his fiery breath upon me—singed me whiskers, and scalded me little tail! Yow, ow, WOW!"

Louise laughed so, she almost tumbled off the stool. Sir Hare-old took refuge first behind one of her shoulders, then behind the other, and finally shot into the air. Ulysses leapt up, seized the rabbit's remains, and made off with them to the far side of the lot to enjoy a chew.

"Farewell, valiant hare!" said Mr. Booth with a twinkle, and then, "Miss Lightfoot, are there any clean kerchiefs about? I need to wipe away a tear for our fallen comrade."

Just then, Miss Griffith hurried down the stairs toward me. "Emma! Emma, dear, have you seen my brooch?"

"Ma'am? I mean, Sophie?"

"My brooch, for the cloak I wear when I visit the old servant. Shaped like a butterfly, you know?"

"I think so," I replied. "I saw it in Placerville. It has blue stones."

"I can't find it anywhere. Might you have put it somewhere while you tended the cloak?"

"No. I only pressed the small pieces this afternoon."

She turned to the rest of the company. "Has anyone seen it? Anywhere?"

No one had, but we all began a search, in the theatre, in the wagon, and around the lot. Nothing had turned up by the time Mr. Leach announced ten minutes until the performance. "We might come across it during the show," offered Mr. Leach. "I suggest we get *The Iron Chest* on the boards and hunt up that brooch later."

I did not watch much of the play that night. Mr. Pratt wouldn't wish to hear it said, but his theatre was not all that fine. It spared the actors a post in the middle of the stage, but it was hot and cramped. Mrs. Burnham had found the drop paintings shabby, and the space in what the actors call the "wings" at the sides of the stage was so squeezed, I would have been in the way if I had tried to see the show from there. I spent most of the evening out on the back stairs, where there was the tiniest night breeze, and I only went into the wings when I was needed to hand off a costume piece.

As the performance played out, the actors began to exit the stage with an air of discouragement. There were empty seats out front, instead of the full houses of Placerville. (Although, to Mrs. Burnham's relief, no outlaws had demanded tickets.) This was a Sunday night, not the festive Fourth. Those folks who did attend the play struggled to give their full attention in the sweltering auditorium. Messrs. Pratt, Graham and Clegg dozed in their front-row seats, the victims of too many memorial toasts.

Phrases like "second show letdown" and "off night" were whispered backstage. The actors carried on valiantly, even though, as they came from their scenes, sweat trickled down their powdered faces.

The actor who suffered most, it seemed, was Mr. Booth. He had "dried up" several times, leaving out whole sections of dialogue. "I guess we didn't need that scene," joked Mr. Thayer, after one of his entrances had been skipped. "The audience was tired of my old mug anyhow."

Mrs. Burnham was more worried. When I tiptoed backstage for a moment to collect an apron, I caught a glimpse of her in the wings, frowning as she watched Mr. Booth perform out on the stage. When at last she made her entrance, I listened for a moment to their dialogue. Whatever sentiments were voiced in the shadows backstage, Mr. Booth sounded fine before the audience.

When the curtain fell for the last time, the company swiftly packed costumes and properties, ready to load them into the wagon in the morning and move on. Mr. Leach allowed as I could keep the candle stubs left behind in the dressing rooms, as long as I cleaned the tables and mirrors with industry.

Miss Griffith was still upset over her brooch. She had had it "made especially" for the play. She recruited Mr. Moone and the Bliss brothers to scour the theatre, but it did not turn up, even after everything else had been packed. Miss Griffith would have searched for it all night, save that she was turned away from the task by an offer of sympathy (and a little whiskey) from Mr. Moone and Mr. Brown.

I had every intention of climbing into the wagon and closing my eyes as soon as I could, but it was crowded with properties and provisions. I squeezed myself in amongst them. My blanket scarce could soften the rough wagon bed; my knees and elbows ached in the confines of my corner. I have slept in a wagon before, when Emmett and I traveled west, but I was half the size I am now, and my father fashioned me a snug bunk, with a downy tick and a flannel quilt; his cheerful lullabies eased me into my dreams. I so longed to be home in my own bed, my father whistling in the office below me, that I sank into sorrow. But, as I bit back tears, voices drifted through the wagon canvas. Except for Mrs. La Rue and Louise, the actors had not departed for their hotel rooms, which were no doubt as stifling as the theatre. Instead, they had gathered again in the back lot. A small fire was built to shine a little light, and a bottle was passed about. The Blisses hauled out their fiddle and guitar, and Mr. Brown pulled his Jew's harp from his pocket. Mr. Moone produced a concertina, Mr. Booth his banjo. Melodies rose up from the darkness, and everyone sang to lively tunes like "Camptown Races," and sweet, sad songs, like "My Old Kentucky Home," and "The Last of Gowrie." As I listened from the wagon, Mr. Brown called, "Miss Lightfoot? Are you in dreamland?"

"No, Mr. Brown."

The young man offered me a hand. He helped me down and pulled me toward the fire, into the merry company of the actors. My heart lifted, at least a bit.

The Bliss brothers are the best musicians in the bunch—their music is where they shine. Buck has a wondrous deep bass voice, Jimmy a clear baritone, and they work magic with their instruments. Still, Mr. Booth can give them a run for the money—he has a pleasing voice, too, and his fingers dance across his banjo. As the evening wore on, the three of them began to improvise. They would pick up a tune, make it swirl upon the strings, then toss the melody from one to the other, in a sort of competition to see who could have the most fun with it. In the end, though, the contest always came to rest in perfect harmony.

As the night deepened, the company thinned some. Mr. Burnham and Mr. Leach shared cigars and a drink and then departed. Mrs. Burnham stayed on, conversing softly with Mr. Thayer and sometimes casting a glance in Mr. Booth's direction. Finally, she spoke to the musicians—"Not too late, boys, we have an early call"—and she departed, too. I could no longer keep my eyes open, and I crawled into the wagon, curled up in my blanket, and sank into sleep to the rhythm of the banjo.

I was awakened by a scream. I wasn't sure if I had dreamed it, but then I heard another—a child's scream. I peered out of the wagon. Whimpers and a woman's voice led my eyes to an open window on the top floor of the hotel next door. "It's all right now," the woman said. "Hush, hush, shhh. It's only a nightmare." The child began to weep. The voices belonged to the La Rues.

I glanced over toward the embers of the evening's fire, still burning in the darkness. I could make out three figures on the ground. Two of them were the Blisses, neatly tucked into their blankets. But the third figure was sprawled in the dry grass on the border of the lot. Something glowed red in his hand. I climbed out of the wagon, my covers about me, and made my way over to him. It was Mr. Booth, quite asleep. In his hand was his lit pipe, ready to tip into the tinder of the grass. He had the stink of whiskey about him. I took up the pipe and gently shook his shoulder. "Mr. Booth?" It took some doing, but he came to. When he realized how he'd been found, he was abject—"My deepest apology"—and helped me douse the fire. Then he bowed, whispered, "Good evening, Miss Lightfoot. You have my everlasting gratitude," and wandered off unsteadily into the darkness of town.

It pained me to see him so, but I was too tired to fret about it, and, as Louise had quieted, I hoped to slip back into my own dreams. But my brain was now abuzz with the happenings of the day. I rose, dug out candles and my journal, and put my thoughts to paper until sleep at last came upon me.

7:30 P.M. *The American River, under the willows at the water's edge. No performance tonight—*

I awoke this morning a little after daybreak. My mind was busy, but the weight of my worries for Evie kept me from rising. I stayed curled in my blanket long after I sensed other company members stirring about the lot. And I wished for a newspaper.

A few of Placerville's dispossessed had straggled into Georgetown last night. They all had their stories, but the only true picture of the fire that emerged was, as the Coles had put it, "terrible."

As I lay in the wagon, I heard Mr. Burnham's voice, speaking with Mrs. Burnham and Mr. Leach about Placerville and a Wells Fargo wire. I pulled myself together and scrambled out of the wagon. "Please, Mr. Burnham," I said, "do you have any news? Was anyone hurt?"

He gave a grim nod. "The fire took out Main Street, and Coloma Street, too. It's all ash. Quite a few people were injured."

"No one died?"

"One person, so far," he replied. "The body's too burned to know who it is, yet. It was lying in the street by the *American* office."

"Do they know if it was a man or a woman?"

"The wire didn't say. But there was a dead dog by its side."

My heart began to pound in my ears.

"I'm sorry for the bad news, Miss Lightfoot," said Mrs. Burnham. "I'm sure you have acquaintances who may have suffered."

"Yes, ma'am, I do," I replied. "Thank you, Mr. Burnham, for giving me word." Then I scurried back to the wagon and ducked into my corner until I could breathe again. As my heart settled back into my chest, I resolved that I would not despair for my friend until I knew the truth. There is more than one dog in Placerville. When I could see the facts in print, then I could rejoice or grieve. Or both. Until then, I would simply have to hope. And keep myself busy with work.

In a few minutes, there was a knock on one of the tailgate planks. It was Jimmy Bliss, shyly handing me a tin mug of coffee and a fresh biscuit. "You're very kind, Mr. Bliss," I said.

He looked at his toes, and mumbled, "Buck sent 'em over."

"Well, please thank Buck, too." I hadn't expected breakfast in "bed." The biscuit was still warm, and it cheered me just enough that I could finally face the business of the day.

By then, most of the other company members had gathered to load the wagon. I quickly packed my laundry supplies and pitched in where I could. Miss Griffith was still hunting for her brooch. At one point, I saw her in a hushed but fervent conversation with Mr. Leach. They glanced over my way a time or two, and it made me uneasy. Presently, Mr. Leach came my direction. He doffed his hat and spoke quietly, though I felt the whole company could tell what this was about, and it shamed me, even though I had no reason to be ashamed.

"I hate to have to ask you this, Miss Lightfoot," said Mr. Leach, "but Miss Griffith is upset. You were working with the costumes yesterday. Did you see that brooch?"

"No, sir, I haven't seen it since Placerville," I replied.

"Are you sure?"

"Yes, I am. You can search through my bundles, Mr. Leach. You'll find no brooch."

He hesitated. I knew he did not relish his role. And then I spied Louise by the wagon, hugging her tobacco tin, listening to every word. I saw what I had to do and I didn't like it any more than Mr. Leach did. "Excuse me, Mr. Leach," I said, and I made my way to Louise. I went down on one knee so I could look her in the eye and I smiled. "What have you found this morning, Louise?" She bit her lip and clutched the tin tighter. "May I see your treasures?"

"No."

"I know they're special, but you showed me before."

"No!" she shouted, and started to skitter away.

"Louise!" hollered Mrs. La Rue.

Mr. Thayer stepped quickly into the child's path, and said, gently, "Miss Louise, I believe you need to let us take a look."

"They're secret."

"You can share a secret with me," he said, "and Ulysses, and Miss Lightfoot here. We don't mean any harm."

"No!" Louise tried to dodge Mr. Thayer, but he was tall and quick and once more cut her off. He extended his big hand. Perhaps it was his sheer size that compelled her to relinquish the tin. "They're mine," she whispered.

"Yes, Miss Louise." Mr. Thayer nodded. He pried off the lid and spread her treasures on the back stairs, complimenting each rock and nail, until he finally fished the brooch out of the bottom of the tin. He passed it to Mr. Leach, as Louise cried out, "I found it! I found it on the floor. It's mine!"

Mrs. La Rue was on her like a duck on a June bug. "Louise, that was very wrong! You cannot take things—"

"Most likely, she did simply find it, Mrs. La Rue," said Mr. Thayer. "The clasp isn't strong, it could easily have fallen off the costume."

But Mrs. La Rue was worked up and not ready to hand Louise the benefit of the doubt. "She knows better! She worried everyone. I am so sorry, Miss Griffith—"

"Oh, it's fine," said Miss Griffith. "I have my brooch back."

"Yes, it's settled now, Mrs. La Rue," said Mr. Thayer. "Everything's all right."

Louise was in tears. Mr. Leach scooped the rest of her treasures into the tin and handed it to her. Mrs. La Rue, humiliated, offered a last apology to everyone. "We are so sorry for the trouble, aren't we Louise?"

Louise managed a nod and a "Yes." Then Mrs. La Rue dragged her off toward the wagon.

Miss Griffith hastened over to my side. "I am so sorry, too, Emma. I don't know what I was thinking. Can you forgive me?"

I reckoned, in my situation, it was savvy to be owed some. "Thank you, Sophie. I can forgive you just fine."

Sophie beamed. "Emma, dear, a few of us are riding out ahead of the company today. Would you like to come along? We'll have our own little adventure!"

Before I could even consider it, there was a ruckus in the wagon. Though she tried to keep her voice low, Mrs. La Rue was still having at Louise.

"Don't you *ever* do that again."

"I found it."

"Don't tell me fibs."

"But I did!"

"This is our chance to make things better. Do you want to ruin it?"

Louise did not reply.

"Do you want to wind up back in Grizzly Flat?"

"No!!" The child jumped out of the wagon and sped off around the corner of the theatre.

Mr. Brown watched her disappear. "Oh, my dainty Ariel! There she goes!"

Mrs. Burnham threw up her hands. "Damn it. Buck and Jimmy, go fetch the fairy star. I had actually hoped we might get out of here on time."

But Louise was elusive. The Blisses, Mr. Brown, Mr. Moone and Mr. Leach all fanned out and searched the town. It was half an hour before she was spotted in front of the theatre, trudging her way back. She stepped right up onto the wagon seat.

"Where were you?" demanded Mrs. Burnham.

"Up a tree."

Mrs. Burnham shook her head. "Of course. Where else? A tree." She turned to the rest of the company. "I'd suggest we get on the road. We're late. Again."

"Maybe you haven't noticed, Hattie," said Mr. Burnham, "but our other 'star' is missing. Be a damn shame to lose Booth, too."

Mrs. Burnham paled. "Where is he? Have you seen him?"

"Last night," said Mr. Burnham. "In the bar of the Nevada House, as they were closing up. The boy can't hold his liquor, so I told him to get back to the hotel. I haven't seen him since."

"Buck," said Mrs. Burnham, "please run and check Mr. Booth's room."

Buck Bliss hurried over to the hotel and was back in minutes.

"His room was never slept in," Buck said. "The clerk hasn't seen him since yesterday."

"Dear God," sighed Mrs. Burnham. "I'm herding cats. Harry? Buck and Jimmy? Can you take a look around? We need to make this quick."

"Shouldn't take long," said Mr. Burnham. "Check behind the saloons."

On this cue, Mr. Booth appeared around the side of the theatre. His hair was tousled, and his clothes were dusty from last night's nap in the lot.

Mr. Leach delivered him a scolding. "You missed your call, Ted. Where have you been?"

Mr. Booth shrugged. "In my room. The bedbugs were ferocious. Couldn't catch a wink."

Mr. Burnham snorted. Mrs. Burnham looked daggers at Mr. Booth but said nothing, only mounted up. Buck Bliss brought Mr. Booth's pinto over, and Mr. Booth managed to get himself into the saddle.

I had no sooner climbed onto Lem Mule, when Miss Griffith waved me over to where she posed on her pretty sorrel. "Emma! Emma, dear! Ride with us!"

The "us" turned out to be Miss Griffith, Mr. Moone and Mr. Brown, the "young people" of the company. Their plan was to ride ahead of the rest of the party as far as Johntown, then meet up with everyone again before we headed down into the Coloma Valley. To be truthful, I was bashful about the idea. These were talented, fine-looking people (even Mr. Moone, for all that he was short and had red hair), and they were provided with handsome horses. I was back in my "early miner" get-up and mounted on an old mule.

"Miss Lightfoot, please honor us with your company," said Mr. Moone, doffing his beaver hat.

"Oh, yes, Miss Lightfoot," added Mr. Brown. "We shall perish by the roadside if you deny us."

Miss Griffith giggled. "You hear, Emma? You must come along, or they shall suffer dreadfully!"

I threw my worries to the wind. "Then I expect I must!" And Lem and I fell in with their little group. We nodded farewell to the Burnhams and started off through the streets of Georgetown, then southwest onto the Coloma Road.

How lovely the morning was! Nature had given us a respite from the heat, and the breezes shifted the residue of Placerville's smoke back from whence it came. The sky above was clear and deep, and remnants of dew flashed upon the long grass. The road took us through patches of woodland, where the sun sifted in lacy patterns upon the forest floor, and bright woodpeckers flitted about. Then it opened into rolling meadows. Here, the grass grew green and revealed small treasures—wild roses, orange poppies, and bright buttercups—as yellow-breasted meadowlarks sang out the sweetness of the day.

While Mr. Brown and Miss Griffith chattered away, I tried to let the beauty of the morning into my heart, in the hope that it might wash away some of the sorrow for my Placerville friends. But Mr. Moone sensed something was up. He fell back beside Lem.

"My apologies, Miss Lightfoot," he said. "This bunch loves to hear itself talk, and we've hardly let you get a word in edgewise. How are you today?"

"I'm fine, Mr. Moone," I lied.

"I'm glad to hear it."

"Perhaps I'm a little shy around actors. I don't believe I have your wit."

"Oh, don't be, Miss Lightfoot," replied Mr. Moone. "We're just paid fools." He pulled a comical face, and I could not help but grin.

"That's better," he said. "You've seemed a little melancholy this morning."

There was such sweetness in his manner that I could not hold my troubles back. "I am. I am very concerned for my friends in Placerville. For one friend in particular. I don't know if I can rest until I know her fate."

Mr. Moone nodded. "Yes. I know what it is to worry for a friend." He smiled at me. I saw then how young he really was—the only lines in his face were small laugh lines. "We must cheer you up, Miss Lightfoot. We cannot waste this gorgeous morning in despair." He launched into song. Mr. Brown and Miss Griffith turned and laughed, then joined in with as pretty a harmony as I've heard. The meadowlarks should have been impressed:

Begone, dull care!
I prithee, be gone from me.
Be gone, dull care!
You and I shall never agree.

Their voices rang out over meadow and through woods. "Sing, Miss Lightfoot!" urged Mr. Moone. "Let's make it a quartet!" I expect I croaked like a crow next to their beautiful tones, but I gave it my best.

And so we made our way down the road, singing and telling stories (or at least the actors told stories—I tried to be a good audience), and taking in the lovely world about us. My spirits rose. So did Lem's. That old mule has an affinity for music—on a good, rousing chorus, his step is absolutely sprightly. Mr. Brown suggested we bill him as "The Dancing Wonder Mule" and make our fortune.

Shortly before we reached Johntown, the actors began the "Shakespeare Game." Miss Griffith and Mr. Moone would throw out a phrase from a Shakespeare play, and Mr. Brown would have to name the play and the character. The contest was funny and fierce—Mr. Moone and Miss Griffith conspired to come up with the most obscure verse they could, and Mr. Brown pretended he was at a loss and groaned over his answer, when he knew it all along.

At last, Griffith & Moone handed him a passage that genuinely confounded him, "I see a man's life is a tedious one: I have tired myself; and for two nights together have made the ground my bed. I should be sick, but that my resolution helps me." As Mr. Brown puzzled over this one, Miss Griffith giggled.

"Oh, don't dismiss me so quickly," said Mr. Brown. "It's one of those girls in trousers, I know it is. Like our Miss Lightfoot here. 'For one night together, she hath made the wagon her bed.' I know it—"

"No, you don't, you're just stalling!" said Miss Griffith.

"Never!" said Mr. Brown. "It's...uh...it's...oh—

I couldn't stand it any longer. "It's Imogen," I said, "from *Cymbeline*. Act III, scene vi!"

Mr. Brown's jaw dropped. "Is it?"

"It is, indeed," said Mr. Moone.

All eyes were upon me, and in an instant I realized I may have let more of the cat out of the bag than I should have. Did I want to appear to the company as anything but a washerwoman just yet? My heart could not speak to them of Emmett and *The Rattler* without tears.

Mr. Brown was not one to let the moment slip. "Ah-hah!" he said. "Our laundry lass is more than meets the eye! So, who are you, Miss Lightfoot? A famous actress incognito, down on her luck? A princess dodging her enemies behind a laundry tub?"

"Hardly that romantic, Mr. Brown," I replied.

"Oh, tell us, Emma!" pleaded Miss Griffith.

"I'm just the girl who does the wash," I said.

Mr. Moone came to my rescue. "Rosekranz's store is just around the bend, if we want some dinner."

And so I was spared further questions by our arrival at the Johntown General Mercantile. We stopped long enough to pick up a few morsels for a picnic lunch—cheese and bread and dried apples—and continued on for a couple of miles to where the road wound out onto the rim of the ridge, just before its descent. There, we found a shady spot under a stand of pines and gazed out over the Coloma Valley.

The town of Coloma is just another mining camp, gouged out of the banks of the American, but the valley is still a beautiful place. The narrow canyon we struggled through at Chili Bar gives way at Coloma to a broad bowl, encircled by rounded, golden hills, their clefts lined with grey-green oaks. Along the valley floor curves the river—shining, translucent, like the jade necklace I've seen about Mrs. Gee's throat. Far below our spot on the ridge, two red-tailed hawks floated over field and riverbank. I wondered if this was the view Professor Wilson might have in his hot air balloon—the sort of view angels might be allowed.

I knew that somewhere down there on the water's edge was what was left of Colonel Sutter's sawmill, where the gold nugget that began the rush to California had been found. Where would any of us be now if Marshall and his men hadn't pulled it out of the mill race? Where would the actors be? And my family? Would Emmett be happily alive in Vermont? Or buried under the linden tree? It makes my head spin to think of all the thousands of lives whirled about by a little nugget.

We settled under the pines to enjoy our dinner, and the games and songs went on. I was glad to see Mr. Moone and Miss Griffith laughing together again. Perhaps they were past their troubles. Mr. Moone amused us with handstands and stunts with his beaver hat. He would roll the hat along his arm and flip it into the air so that it landed precisely on his head, to applause and ripples of laughter from Miss Griffith. Then he gathered a handful of deep pink vetch blossoms and placed the flowers delicately in Miss Griffith's hair. He invited her to dance, and as he whistled a waltz, they swayed gracefully under the trees, the wide valley at their feet.

Mr. Brown sighed, "I feel positively left out, Miss Lightfoot." He rose and bowed. "May I have this dance?"

"I don't dance, Mr. Brown," I replied. "I don't even know how."

"I shall teach you." He offered his hand.

"I left my ball gown at home."

He chuckled. "Never mind. I just love ladies in miner's boots."

He was way too charming to fend off, so I took his hand, and while he danced, I managed to stomp all over his toes. He had the good grace to laugh off his injuries, and, as we twirled on the canyon rim, I laughed, too, as strange as the sound of my own laughter seemed to me.

Mr. Moone soon abandoned his whistled waltz for a merry song. In a breath, Miss Griffith and Mr. Brown joined in. "Out of the way, for old Dan Tucker, he's too late to get his supper!" Faster and faster we spun under the pines, until Mr. Moone lifted Miss Griffith into his arms and whirled her about. The blossoms, loosened from her hair, floated down onto the grass. Between our songs and merriment, we hardly noticed the riders trotting down the road until they hailed us.

"It's Thayer," panted Mr. Moone. "And Jimmy." He lowered Miss Griffith, her cheeks pink as vetch blossoms. "Time to pack it up, ladies!"

As we gathered together our dinner scraps, Mr. Thayer dismounted and hurried our way. "Hello, Thayer!" said Mr. Brown. "Come to join the ball?"

Mr. Thayer frowned and looked us over, his long face even more melancholy than usual. "You don't know," he said.

"Know what?" said Mr. Moone.

"It's gone," said Mr. Thayer, in the hushed tone of an undertaker. "The whole blessed town, I'm sure."

"Placerville?" asked Mr. Brown.

"Oh, no." Mr. Thayer turned back toward the trail and waved a bony hand at us. "Come on out from under those pines."

We left the shadows of the trees and followed Mr. Thayer to the road. Jimmy Bliss had turned his horse and was staring back the way he'd come, calf-eyes wide.

An ugly cloud rose from the direction of Georgetown. It bubbled up higher than Professor Wilson's Glory could ever hope to lift, dwarfing the landscape below. Then it hit a wind that swept it in a broad, dark plume south over Chili Bar.

"Dear Jesus," whispered Mr. Moone.

And those were the only words spoken as we stood in the rutted road, mouths agape, and the cloud's shadow spread over wood and canyon. Ulysses let loose a little whine and wandered from one to the other of us for reassurance. His wet nose nuzzled against the palm of my hand.

Up the road, a wagon rattled. It rounded the bend in a whirlwind of dust, and Ben Burnham pulled the sweating team to a halt. "Mount up quick," he said. "Let's get off this mountain and across the river." His tone was low and deadly serious, none of yesterday's bluster about it. Mrs. Burnham, on her dappled grey, said nothing, though the pallor of her cheeks made her eyes burn darker. We needed no urging. In seconds, the "young people" were in our saddles, and the Star Troupe moved on down the precipice into the canyon.

The morning's road from Georgetown had been a fair one, following the ridge top, but now, the trail narrowed, clinging to the mountainside like a tattered ribbon. It curved and switched back as it snaked on down, and I no longer admired the view—I told myself not to look, to keep my eyes on the rider before me. Lem picked his way carefully along the rocky roadbed. Mr. Burnham kept the team reined in, though the wagon tilted perilously toward the trail's downhill side. The smell of burning leather drifted back to the riders as brake shoes squealed against the wheel rims. Slowly, we descended.

We had reached the valley floor when we were overtaken by riders fleeing Georgetown. Amongst them was one of our hosts. Mrs. Burnham hailed him, "Clegg! Clegg! What do you know?"

He tipped his hat to her. "It's all gone, ma'am. Just a big wall of flame from one end of Main to the other. It didn't take but minutes. A wind come up and whipped it around something fierce."

"Where did it start?"

"Best anyone can figure, the rear of Murphy's Bank Exchange, by the hotel. But there ain't been no fire in the stove there for weeks."

"Then how?"

"They're saying it's incendiary, ma'am. If they find the fiend, they should hang him high as Haman."

Mrs. Burnham drew in a breath. "Thank you, Mr. Clegg. We're very sorry for your loss."

"I welcome your sympathy. But we'll rebuild, I have no doubt." He nodded to both the Burnhams and hurried on his way. Mr. Burnham urged the team to a trot, despite the steepness of the road, and we were soon in sight of the bridge.

Coloma's population had clearly swelled since yesterday. The meadows edging the town on the east side of the river were packed with sooty tents and wagons. The ashy faces of the campers bespoke Placerville, and I searched each countenance in vain for someone I knew. Many of the refugees simply stood about, strangely still, waiting for God knew what. Some stared in disbelief toward the east, where the smoke cloud loomed and bursts of dust on the mountainside trail marked the flight of Georgetown's victims.

Mr. Booth pulled his pinto out of the line of riders and trotted him over to a campsite. A family abided there—barely. The father lay upon a quilt in the grass, hands bandaged, face blistered. A thin woman bent over him, surrounded by half a dozen children and a wailing baby. Mr. Booth dismounted, fished his penknife from his pocket, and ripped away the seam of his jacket. He pulled out a gold piece and handed it to the astonished woman. Then, with no pause for thanks, he leapt onto his pinto once more and rejoined the troupe.

As we neared the tollbooth, Mr. Burnham took on a ferocious aspect, determined as he was not to be overcharged this time around. He leaned in toward the tollkeeper, an old man who resembled the trolls I've seen in picture books, trolls who were fond of lurking about bridges. They exchanged a few words, and Mr. Burnham burst into a laugh. "I'll be damned!"

"Yes, sir," replied the troll, "Coloma has embraced the unfortunate. Our citizens are fetching the destitute into town in their own wagons. There's no toll for anyone today. Pass, friend!" He waved the Star Troupe onto the bridge.

As we crossed above the lovely, rippling river, its coolness rose through the timbers to welcome us. On the far side, we rode past the ladies of the Episcopal Church, who were handing out bread from a makeshift booth. We turned down Main Street and, shortly, we spied Mr. Leach, awaiting us before the performance hall. He had a grim set to his jaw. Beside him stood a tall, rawboned gentleman with pleasant blue eyes. "I'm Wright, the manager," said the tall gent, introducing himself to the Burnhams. "I'm afraid we have a situation."

The management journeyed over to the vestibule of the hall to confer. The rest of us tried to give them room and act as if we weren't attempting to make out every word.

"These are terrible days for some," Wright began.

"Yes, we know," said Mr. Burnham.

"The city has decided it's a time for charity towards our neighbors of Placerville—and now Georgetown—and that we'll aid them as best we can. They're welcome in our valley—"

"And?" cut in Mr. Burnham.

"And," continued Wright, unfazed, "The long and the short of it is, the hall is filled with women and children who have no other roof over their heads. I doubt there will be a performance there tonight."

"Then what do you propose we do?" said Mrs. Burnham.

Mr. Leach stepped in. "Wright and I have pondered this. He believes we can have these families—"

"And the ones coming down the mountain right now—" added Wright.

"Taken into the homes of Coloma's citizens by tomorrow."

"Perhaps we can even have the hall cleared for you by morning," said Wright.

Mr. Burnham frowned. "Mr. Wright, we have a contract—"

But Mrs. Burnham put her hand on his arm. "Ben, misfortune doesn't give a damn about contracts. Let's just weather this and go find the hotel."

Mr. Leach rubbed his bald head as if it ached. "Hattie, there are no hotels. They're full to the rafters."

"Of course," she sighed.

"Right now, the back lot is full, too, but Mr. Wright thinks he can shift folks a bit."

"I believe so," said Wright. "There's still plenty of room along the river."

"So, it looks like our best bet right now is to make camp and hope for a good show tomorrow night," said Mr. Leach.

"I reckon we have no choice," said Mrs. Burnham. Mr. Burnham grudgingly nodded.

Wright beamed and shook their hands. "Coloma will thank you for your understanding. We'll do our best to bring you a grateful audience."

"I suggest my partners and I announce our performances as benefits for the sufferers," said Mr. Leach. "Ten percent of profits for their relief."

Wright's blue eyes lit up. "Splendid! Then come along, everyone, please!" And he disappeared around the back of the hall with the Burnhams and Mr. Leach.

The rest of us waited in hope that we would have a safe haven for the night, and we were not disappointed. A shady spot in the back lot was made ready for us. We unloaded poles and canvas from the wagon, and, in short order, set up a pleasant camp. The back lot sloped down to the banks of the river, sweet-smelling with sand and willow. Jimmy Bliss and Mr. Leach led the stock back across the bridge to graze the fields on the other side, as the stables were full and the theatre lot claimed by so many humans. I could spy Lem happily watering on the opposite shore. Wright went from one to the other of the company members seeing to their needs, a lanky guardian angel. Mrs. La Rue was the only one to object to the camp—she insisted that she and Louise be allowed to sleep in the wagon, that it was not "safe" out of doors. I shall be quite squeezed into my little corner tonight.

In the late afternoon, I washed and pressed some of the costume shirts and petticoats. As I knelt in the dust by the brazier, Mr. Brown sang out, "Cinder-Emma! Leave your nasty old hearth and come along into town."

I was nearly finished, anyway. "Where to, Mr. Brown? I don't have much cash on me."

"Neither do I. That's why I need to find Wells Fargo. I'm hoping for a letter and a little extra from my father. I can't support my bad habits on an actor's income."

I stared at him over the top of my specs. "Like all those peppermints, Mr. Brown? A wicked habit, indeed."

He grimaced. "Ouch, Cinder-Emma, you've wounded my vanity to the quick. All right, yes, peppermints. And a shave, with a little barbershop cologne. We all have our weaknesses. What are yours?"

"I have a need of a newspaper. I shall be happy to accompany you, Mr. Brown." I quickly stowed the flatirons, and Mr. Brown and I headed off down Main Street. Along the way, we spied a posted bill for Professor Wilson! He will be here, ascending in the "Glory" tomorrow. I can't wait to see the balloon rise above the treetops and float across the river!

Wells Fargo was but a stone's throw down Main. I had no expectations of a letter for myself, so, while Mr. Brown went inside in hope of improving his fortune, I made my way over to Clark's stationery store. They had a newsstand, and, with both prayer and trepidation, I secured myself a copy of the day's *Sacramento Union*. I hastened out onto the bench before the store. The headline on the front page was dire:

Placerville almost entirely Destroyed by Fire—

Several Citizens Burned to Death—Loss about $1,000,000—Printing Offices Totally Destroyed—Great Suffering—Dreadful Scenes, &c., &c.

The fire ravaged the whole of Main from Sacramento Street to Cedar

Ravine, and most of Coloma Street. The *Rattler* office perished, and the *Democrat* and the *American* offices, too. Captain Smith's stable (with Emmett's books, no doubt) was leveled, and the Red House was reduced to ash, along with the establishments of just about everyone I know. *Except*—the fire did not devour all of Sacramento Street, which gives me hope for Mrs. Gee and her family.

The article updated the headline that pronounced "several" deaths. The only human mortality, and the one that had given me such anguish, was that of the body found beside the dog. To my great relief, it was not Evie, but I sorrow nonetheless. A silver dental plate revealed that the victim was old Mr. Benham, who ran the toll road through Big Cut, south of town. Mr. Benham and his hound, Walleye, were inseparable. I could not help but dwell on their last moments. Perhaps they were both brought down by the flames at the same instant. If Walleye alone had foundered, Mr. Benham, aged as he was, would have carried him out. But if only Mr. Benham had gone down, Walleye would have stayed by his master's side to the end.

I will think a good thought for their ghosts. And I will hope for Evie. Newspapers might detail the losses to a town's "finer citizens," but they don't pay much mind to residents of a place like the Red House. Somehow, I must find out more. I know Placerville will rebuild, just as Georgetown will. Perhaps, in time, I can write to the Captain and see what he knows.

Be safe, dear Evangeline.

I found Mr. Brown before the Wells Fargo office. The grin on his face advertised good news for his finances. He suggested we celebrate with a trip to the candy counter. "You've encouraged me to work on my bad habits, Miss Lightfoot," he said. "I suggest we add licorice to the list!" I did not object. We crammed our cheeks with the gooey stuff and were hard put to escape choking. Evie would have enjoyed such an adventure!

It is now nigh unto midnight. My day's scrounged candle stubs are at an end, but I have put off crawling into my blanket in the wagon. I have had no wish to encounter Mrs. La Rue's scolding or to wake with La Petite's screams at my ear. Still, unlike many tonight, I at least have a spot of my own for a "lie-down." I am weary enough that the river's song is a lullaby, so I shall tuck my saddle-sore self into my tiny wagon corner and hope for rest.

Tuesday, July 8, midafternoon. *It's hot. I write in the shade of a big cottonwood—*

In the end, I should not have worried about sharing quarters with Louise. She slept through the night like the baby she is. It was Mrs. Burnham's voice that woke me in the wee hours, speaking in low tones not far from the wagon. "Gus, go into town and see if you can get wind of them."

"Where's Ben? Isn't this something he should handle?" Mr. Thayer whispered.

There was no reply at first, then, "He's probably found a game somewhere. He's not the one I'm worried about."

"They'll come back when they're ready, Hattie."

"Please, Gus. Ted's a spooky boy. He's been on the bottle, and God knows where he'll lead the other two."

"He's twenty-two years old. I'm not his nursemaid, Hattie. Neither are you."

"Gus, if we lose him, we haven't got a season. He's our star. We're banking on him."

"All right, all right. I'll see what I can do. Let me get some shoes on."

He stirred a bit in his tent; then, through a gap in the wagon canvas, I watched him disappear into the darkness, Ulysses at his heels. Mrs. Burnham slipped into her own tent. A match glowed as she lit one of her thin cigars. I curled back up in my blanket and heard no more until morning.

By sunrise, there was already a stir in the camp, and tongues were wagging about the three missing men—Mr. Booth, Mr. Brown, and Buck Bliss. They had sallied forth last night to enjoy Coloma's hospitality. They had ended the evening right where Mr. Thayer found them—in jail, a nasty little stone cage at one end of town. Mr. Burnham had gone, at first light, to reluctantly pay their fines and obtain their freedom. Mr. Brown's arrest, in particular, was a surprise. Perhaps he has more bad habits than his Sunday school looks lead one to believe.

While we awaited the return of the three bad boys, Mr. Moone arrived with the morning's newspapers, and we passed them around. Georgetown's fire was as sad and terrible as Placerville's, and every article pronounced Georgetown's demise the work of an incendiary, "a heartless wretch." It is strange to imagine that someone who walks the same streets as we do wishes us such a fiery fate. Mrs. La Rue muttered, "A rope is too good for that kind of beast!"

Shortly after, Mr. Burnham arrived with our very own criminals. He delivered them to Mrs. Burnham with the news that their fines were to be deducted from their pay. Mr. Leach ordered Buck Bliss across the river to check the stock, and Buck headed for the bridge as quickly as he could. Mr. Brown, his hair in disarray and his good shirt stained, ducked sheepishly into his tent. Mrs. Burnham glared at Mr. Booth. "Ted, I'd like to speak with you," she said, in a manner that gave Mr. Booth no choice in the matter. They went into her tent.

I have discovered that a theatre company lives like a family of twelve in a tiny, one-room cabin. There's no way to stay out of each other's business, even when we want to. Right now, few wanted to, and we conjured ploys to stay within earshot of Mrs. Burnham's tent. I stared at a newspaper, never turning the page; Miss Griffith buffed her lovely nails; Mrs. La Rue, balanced on the tailgate of the wagon, wove rag curlers into Louise's locks, though the evening's performance was many hours away. Mrs. Burnham and Mr. Booth tried to keep their voices down, but they drifted right through the canvas walls.

"I'm sorry, Hattie," Mr. Booth began.

"It was a fool thing to do," Mrs. Burnham said. "We have a show to sell tonight, in the middle of disaster."

"It was only a joke."

"It was not funny. Take some responsibility, Ted."

Mr. Booth said nothing.

"If for no other reason, do it for the rest of the company. We depend on you. We can't afford to lose you."

"This is the first I heard I was lost."

"It's easy to disappear down a bottle. Tench went down one and never came up again."

"I'm not as fragile as Tench, Hattie." There was an edge in Mr. Booth's tone.

"Ted, when you're sober, there's no one I'd rather be on stage with. Please don't betray that. You owe it to yourself, you owe it to June—"

"June thinks very little of me."

"June's your brother. He's put his bankroll on the line for you. Don't let him down."

Mr. Booth was silent.

"Try, Ted."

"I am."

"Try harder. Put your heart into the shows and get ready for New York. If you can't do it for yourself, do it for Ben and me. We've sunk everything into this tour. And you may not have noticed, but I'm not the sweet young thing I used to be—"

Mr. Booth managed a chuckle. "You're always sweet, Hattie—"

"Uh-huh. Very nice. So I'm not the young thing I used to be. Dear God, I'd like some small ship to come in—some bitty rowboat, even—before I make an exit. Please, Ted."

"Yes. Yes. I'll try. I'll do what I can," said Mr. Booth, his voice filled with sincerity. "If only to help out the aged and infirm."

"You're a devil. But I'll hold you to it. I need your word."

Mr. Booth paused, then replied, "You have it, Hattie."

He started for the tent door. The rest of us suddenly turned to our assorted tasks with great industry.

"And do not lead my juvenile player and my best bugler down the road to perdition."

"No, ma'am," promised Mr. Booth. "We shall nip their sins in the bud." He stepped into the open and looked about. Our subterfuges did not fool him. He lifted his hat to us and, with a grim smile, retreated to his own tent.

Wright was true to his word—with help from Mr. Leach and other Coloma citizens, the families sheltered in the performance hall were shifted to happier accommodations by early morning, and the Star Troupe moved in. Mrs. Burnham announced *The Taming of the Shrew* as the evening's entertainment, in the hope that the comedy might be a tonic for the ills about us. My task for the morning was to launder the company's regular clothing, as the costumes were mostly in order. I went from tent to tent gathering piles of hose and chemises. When I arrived at the Burnhams's tent, their laundry lay waiting just inside the tent flap. I stepped in.

The tent was furnished, aside from the bedrolls, with stage properties—a scrap of Oriental carpet, a regal-looking armchair from *The Iron Chest*, and a vanity fashioned from a stool and a table, with a shawl thrown atop it. I could not resist a closer peek at the vanity. Mrs. Burnham had carefully laid out a shiny mirror and comb set and an elegant little box that cradled her thin cigars. Near the rear of the table stood a small daguerrotype in a silver frame. It was a baby, and it gazed back at me with Mrs. Burnham's deep, smart eyes. The Burnhams had never mentioned a child. Where was it? Perhaps it didn't make sense to drag a baby through the camps. Maybe it had been left somewhere safe, where it could take its naps and suck its sugar rag in peace. Yet, the child regarded me as if it had a story to tell.

Suddenly, I didn't belong in the midst of these private things. I hurried out of the tent and collided with Mr. Brown. My armful of laundry spilled into the dust.

Mr. Brown helped me gather it up. "Cinder-Emma, your work is never done," he laughed. "Oops, don't forget this stocking."

"Mr. Brown," I replied, "I don't know if I should speak to you, now you are such a desperado."

He hung his head. "I was led down the primrose path. Can you forgive me, Miss Lightfoot?"

"Of course I can, if you tell me all about it. Sit right here!"

And so, as the laundry water boiled, Mr. Brown and I shared the stairs, and he unfolded the tale of his fall from grace.

"It was all tomfoolery," he sighed. "Ted and I were having supper in the hotel when Buck came in, hoping to buy Ted a round and talk music a bit. This turned into a grand tour of Coloma's saloons, starting with the reputable ones and working our way on down. Do you know how many drinking establishments there are in this town?"

I shook my head.

"Well, good. I don't know why I tried to keep up with them, except my father's money was burning a hole in my pocket, and the company was just so amusing—when Ted's on a roll, he has me in stitches. We finally stumbled into a dive at the far end of Main and took a table in the corner. 'All right, boys,' whispered Ted, 'time for 'Bandito.''' He slumped in his chair, his hat way down over his eyes, and growled out, 'I had aims to be an actor once. I decided highway robbery was a steadier line of work.'

"I laughed so hard I choked on my beer. But Buck picked his cue right up, 'That actor bunch up on the Georgetown Road was sure a passel of fools. How many hundreds did we skin off of them, Tom?'

"'Enough for a few more rounds,' said Ted. 'But they was just actors, not worth nothin' compared to what we'll take off tomorrow's stage. Now listen close.' And he laid out the whole crime, boastful, just like Tom Bell, and loud enough for the whole saloon to hear. I had to fight to keep a straight face. Ted doesn't look a thing like Bell, you know, but he was covered in that serape and the hat, and he had the voice down pat. 'It's the nose, ain't it?' he said, all rumbly. 'Blasted nose. It sours the ladies on me.

All except Hattie Burnham, bless her soul. Now there's a woman! Perhaps she'd like to swap the theatre for an outlaw band!'"

Mr. Brown started to laugh, and I did, too. "Oh, forgive me, Miss Lightfoot. I'm supposed to be repentant, but I can't help myself."

"So how did you wind up in jail," I asked. "Is there a statute against impersonating highwaymen?"

"I expect there is, in this town. Someone took us seriously and skedaddled to the sheriff, who showed up with a deputy and a couple of shotguns pointed our way. That part was not funny. When the sheriff realized we were a bunch of actors, for God's sake, and he wasn't going to collect one cent of the reward for Bell, he booked us for public drunkenness. He'd been dragged out of bed in the middle of the night, and he was not a happy man."

Steam blew from the kettle, and I went to pour the water into the tub. Mr. Brown followed me over and perched on the tailgate.

"Mr. Brown," I said, "where's the Burnhams' baby? I didn't realize they have a family."

Mr. Brown looked surprised. "They don't."

"I saw a picture," I said, "in the tent. A baby."

"Oh," said Mr. Brown. "I imagine that was Henry. Henry was Hattie's baby, not Ben's. Her baby with Tench Fairchild."

This was news. "Oh. Then where are they?"

Mr. Brown took the kettle from my hands and refilled it with water from the bucket. "They're gone, Cinder-Emma. Both of them. They're dead."

I'm a Lightfoot. I should have known.

"I met Tench once," Mr. Brown went on, "when I was a little boy. He and Hattie were playing San Francisco. He was a small fellow, dark hair, good-looking enough for leads, sang like an angel. Not a shade like Ben Burnham. Couldn't keep him off the bottle, though. He even worked Temperance for a time to hold himself on the straight and narrow, but it was no good, and the drink killed him."

He handed me the kettle, but I set it right down. "What about Henry, then?"

"Oh, for a while, Hattie cared for Henry by herself. She quit acting and worked for a milliner over on Market Street. But then the diphtheria took him. I reckon that finally broke her heart."

"It breaks mine." I simply stood there for a moment, weighed down by the sadness of it all.

"So Hattie doesn't touch alcohol. She may smoke like a chimney, but you never see her take a drink. At least, I haven't." Mr. Brown returned to the tailgate. I hopped up by his side.

"Neither have I, Mr. Brown."

"You mustn't call me Mr. Brown any more. Every time you do, I look over my shoulder for my father. Please, it's Harry."

"All right. Harry. What would your father think of your adventure last night?"

"Oh, he'd have a fierce attack of dyspepsia. But he's a dear old gentleman, and he can't hold a grudge against me for more than a minute, even when I drive him crazy. He'd forgive me."

"Are you his only child?"

Mr. Brown laughed. "Oh, no. I'm his baby boy, but I have six sisters who spoil me, and a fine elder brother who I bless every day for being the responsible one. He went into my father's bank at an early age, and he removed any burden from me to follow in the old man's footsteps. You see before you the black sheep, who has cast his lot with the theatre. My father doesn't understand it one bit, but he's always in the front row on opening nights, my mother right beside him."

"I expect I should like him," I said. "Was it hard growing up with all those girls?"

He laughed. "Oh, no. I love sisters."

I returned to the tub and began to scrub long johns against the washboard, trying my best not to scour my knuckles. Harry was silent for a moment, watching me.

"You're very clever, Cinder-Emma. You've gotten me to talk of my life, but I still don't know a blessed thing about you."

"I like to listen," I said, "and you have some fine tales to tell. You are what they call in the newspaper business, a 'great source.'"

"And what do you know of the newspaper business, Emma?" he fished.

"Only a bit."

"Tell me."

As much as I like Mr. Brown, I know that anything I tell him will be news for other ears, as his stories this morning were for me. I wasn't ready for that.

"Sometime I will, Harry. Today, I'm simply the girl who does the wash. Those are stories for another time."

"Promise?" He gave me a look so winning, I found it hard to refuse.

"Perhaps."

Still Tuesday. After the play, on a rock by the river—

Buck Bliss has taken a liking to Lem Mule and slipped me a few oats for the old boy. So, this afternoon, after the laundry was hung out, I crossed the bridge to the far side. Jimmy Bliss was there, keeping an eye on the stock, but he's not one for conversation. I gave Lem the oats, a good scratch between his ears, and some kind words. He pressed his big head against my shoulder, quite content.

Afterwards, I decided to explore upriver a piece. I hoped to find a woodsy spot where I could stick my feet and maybe a little more of me into the river, to shed some of the sweat and trail dust. I headed south under the bridge and picked my way along the shore until I thought I'd left most of the camps behind. I came upon a sandy stretch, thick with willow scrub and sheltered by a stand of cottonwoods. I pulled off my shoes and had just dipped my toes when a man shouted a few feet away, right beyond a tangle of vines. I froze. He sounded plain deranged. I clutched my shoe, ready to toss it in self-defense if the lunatic burst through the bushes. The shout shifted to a rough whisper, "Honour, thou bloodstained god! At whose red altar sit war and homicide, O, to what madness will insult drive thy votaries!"

The speaker was indeed deranged—I had stumbled upon Sir Edward Mortimer ranting at the river's edge. Or rather, Mr. Booth, trying to put his "heart into" the role, as he'd promised Mrs. Burnham.

I stood there, gripping my shoe. Should I back off quietly and leave him to his rehearsal? Sir Edward was pretty worked up. "Desperation cried vengeance! I stabbed him to the heart!"

I didn't care to meet him face to face. On the other hand, I did want to eavesdrop—Mr. Booth would put a line out there one way, then stop, and come up with a whole new way to say it, until, beautifully, the words brought me almost to tears.

I listened there until my toes froze in the cold river water. Finally, I tiptoed up on the sand and peeked around the vines and scrub. Mr. Booth stood in a clear spot, very still. Then he crouched and said, under his breath, "To be, or not to be." We weren't in the land of *The Iron Chest* anymore; this was *Hamlet.* Mr. Booth's voice became younger as he struggled with whether to live or to die. Soon he began to speak to an imaginary person, "'Soft you now! The fair Ophelia!" As he went on, he paced the clearing like a tiger in a cage. At last he came within a foot of my hiding place and stared straight my way, madness in his eye. "Where's your father?" he demanded. I turned to run and caught my sleeve on a nasty twist of berry vine. My shoe tumbled into the brush.

"Oh, Mr. Booth, I am so sorry," I cried. I expected Mr. Booth to reply, but it was Hamlet who took me by the wrist and dragged me into the clearing. "Wise men know well enough what monsters you make of them!"

"But, Mr. B—"

"'God hath given you one face, and you make another," he hissed. And then he pulled me into his arms. Terrified as I was, this was not such a bad place to be. He smelled of soap and tobacco, and something else very nice. But the words were scolding, "Go to, I'll no more on't! It hath made me mad!"

He loosened his grip and stalked away. "I'm sor—" I began.

Like lightning, he turned. "To a nunnery! Go!"

I hesitated, only a second, but the crazy person did not leave his eyes. "Go!"

I grabbed my shoe, and I ran. I'm not quite sure, but I believe I heard laughter behind me.

I owe Mr. Booth an apology for sneaking up on him. But I can't even pass him by without a blush scorching my cheeks. I don't know what I shall do.

This evening's performance was a success. Mr. Wright helped round up a full house, and Mr. Booth appeared to have "put his heart into" Petruchio and remembered his lines, to much laughter and applause. The Burnhams were all smiles. Mr. Booth dodged the adoring ladies waiting at the back stairs, and I believe is now upriver with the others—I can hear his banjo sing through the night. But I cannot bring myself to join in the merriment.

Mr. Burnham did not dodge the ladies after the show. I saw him speaking at length to one of them. She stood a bit too close for propriety, although she disappeared as soon as Mrs. Burnham came downstairs.

Mr. Thayer passed by a few minutes ago. "Professor Lightfoot," he remarked, "are you writing an encyclopedia? You're wearing those pencils to nubs every night."

"It's just a little pastime," I replied. "Taking notes on nature, and such."

He smiled. "Well, you are quite a scholar for one so young. By the end of the tour, you'll need another mule to pack all those pages out. Have a good evening, Miss Lightfoot." And Ulysses and he wandered off toward the music.

I now have an abundance of names. Different company members have cast me in different roles: Cinder-Emma, Emma Dear, Professor. I have cast myself as The Girl Who Does the Wash. I'm not sure who I was to Mr. Booth this afternoon. Fool, perhaps.

The beauty of the evening, however, lifts my soul. The bowl of heaven is splashed with the stars of the Milky Way. I hardly need my candle, though the moon has just set, leaving a glow behind the western hills. The star shine bathes the valley with light; the river sparkles and dances with it.

I must stop here for now.

A little later, still by the river—

As I sat with my journal, I spied a figure making her way along the water's edge. She meandered upstream towards me but did not, at first, see my candle. Once she did, she started. "Mrs. Burnham," I called.

"Yes. Is that you, Miss Lightfoot?"

"Yes, ma'am."

"Why aren't you with the others? The music's picking up over there."

"This suits me for tonight," I replied. "There's a fine sky and a shine on the water."

"Yes, it's lovely," she said. "O blessed, blessed night!" She pulled her shawl about her shoulders. But, instead of moving on, she gazed out at the river. Then, she stepped carefully through the sand and willows toward me.

"Are you studying away, there?"

I set aside my journal and blew out the candle stub. "Just taking some notes."

"Am I interrupting you?"

"Oh, no."

"Good. May I share your boulder, Miss Lightfoot?"

"Of course."

She scrambled nimbly up the rock and smoothed her skirt over the granite. She had washed off Katherine's paint and powder and was the more beautiful for it, although I thought for a moment her eyes might be swollen. But in the half-light of the stars, I couldn't be sure, and it would have been rude to stare. In truth, I felt a little shy being that close to her, the cat looking at the queen. It was as if one of those celestial lights had descended to settle by my side.

"How are you and that old mule surviving? It's been a lively couple of days," she said.

"Lem's a sweet creature, he doesn't ask for much," I replied. "And I'm fine. Saddle-sore, though."

She chuckled. "You are not alone. It'll go away, but for now, we all wish to be in Sacramento with a hot bath and a soft bed."

"That would be heaven. But the river is a comfort, too. To my mind, if not my backside."

"It certainly is." She gestured toward my journal. "You can read and write, Miss Lightfoot, and sling a little Shakespeare. You're a young lady of learning. How did you come by it?"

"School. Professor Bitman loved recitation, and he was generous with his books."

"I should have liked to go to school. I was not ignorant, my parents saw to that, but we didn't stay in one place long enough for a real school."

"Tom Bell called you a 'riverboat girl,'" I said.

She nodded. "I grew up on a showboat. My whole family acted—brothers and parents, and my uncle, too. The *Sweet Dream* played every stop she could navigate along the Ohio and the Mississippi, and even some stretches of the Missouri."

"Do you miss it?" I asked, for I heard longing in her voice.

"Oh, yes. I adored the *Sweet Dream*. My parents handled most of the work and worry, more than we children ever knew. Once we learned our lines, we amused ourselves with catching catfish and swimming off the side of the boat." She laughed, a silvery laugh that rippled like the starlight on the water. "My brother Daniel was a daredevil and drove my mother crazy. I can't tell you how many times she thought she'd lost that boy over the edge. She'd be grieving by the rail, and he'd swim around to the other side, climb back aboard, and sneak up on her from behind. She'd have a fit. Do you have brothers, Miss Lightfoot?"

"I did, ma'am. We had a daredevil, too, but we lost him down a well."

Mrs. Burnham turned to me. Her eyes were indeed swollen. "I'm sorry to hear that, Miss Lightfoot."

"It was before I was born." And, truly, there wasn't much more I could say about Charley. I really wanted to ask her about another lost child, about Henry, or why she might have been weeping, but as quickly as the thoughts came to me, my courage melted away. Instead, I ventured, "Professor Bitman was not my only teacher. My father was a learned man. He loved his books." There. I'd done it. I'd spoken of Emmett before a stranger without shedding tears.

"My father was a learned man, too," smiled Mrs. Burnham. "He had a 'library' on the *Sweet Dream*. It was really just a cubby that he'd crammed with books, but I spent hours there. He had so many volumes, the boat always listed a little bit to that side. He'd read law before he'd taken to the stage. But most of his books were plays or poetry."

"I should like to have seen your father's library," I said.

"Oh, it ended up on the bottom of the Mississippi years ago. The *Sweet Dream* had an unfortunate run-in with a barge one night, just below Memphis. My family took to playing on land after that. But those books are still up here." She tapped her temple. "They are good friends to me. I would give odds that you know that feeling, Miss Lightfoot."

"Yes, I do," I answered, but I could not elaborate. My favorite books are Emmett's gifts to me, and this time, at the thought of him, I had to fight off a sting at the back of my eyes. I shifted the talk. "Is your family still performing back East?"

"No. They're mostly gone," she replied, "to death or to distance. But the water, any river, brings them back to me."

We stared out over the American and for a long while sat silently side by side, mesmerized by the swirl of the water and its flashes of silver—no, quicksilver is the better word. Our thoughts flowed like the current, taking us home, even if our true homes had vanished from this world.

By and by, the musicians upriver strummed out "Wayfaring Stranger." Mrs. Burnham hummed along softly until the second verse. Then, backed up by Buck Bliss's fiddle and the deeper accompaniment of the river, she sang out in her rich alto, "I know dark clouds will gather o'er me, / I know my pathway's rough and steep; / But golden fields lie out before me / Where weary eyes no more shall weep." Louise has a lovely singing voice, but Mrs. Burnham's is even more beautiful, as if she were not merely a fallen "star" but a seraph touching down on the river's edge. "I'm going there to see my mother, / She said she'd meet me when I come. / I am just going over Jordan, / I am just going over home."

As the last note rose and fell, the river played on solo. Mrs. Burnham smiled at me. "You're doing a fine job, Miss Lightfoot. Keep it up. I'm glad we have you on board."

"Thank you, ma'am," I said.

She stood. "And now, good evening to you. Come on in before it's too late. You never know who you'll run into wandering the riverbank."

She was half-joking, of course, but the point was well-taken. "Yes. Goodnight, ma'am." She headed off upstream, in the company of her ghosts. I gathered my candle, but I could not leave just yet. The spell of the glittering river and the luminous canopy above held me there on the water's edge.

Soon, I did encounter a surprise wandering the riverbank—what seemed a shiny stone, round and brown, moving through the shallows. It was a sizable beaver. I was amazed to see him there—between the miners and the market for hats, there's hardly a beaver left in the foothills. He looked much better navigating the rocky shore than he ever would on Mr. Moone's head. I hoped he had a safe haven to go to up some creek bed, where his kin awaited him. With a splash, he dived into the deeper water, and nose above the current, drifted downstream on his solitary journey.

WEDNESDAY, JULY 9. *Still in Coloma. Afternoon—*

Early this morning, I persuaded Harry Brown to slip away with me in search of Professor Wilson's ascension. His bill had proclaimed that the Glory would leave the earth at eight a.m. sharp, and so we hurried through Coloma, hoping to sight a golden orb rising above the rooftops. Near the north end of town, we came upon a banner stretched between two trees—"Professor Wilson presents The Miracle of Flight! Tickets $5, Ladies Free!"—and beyond, in a clearing, the beautiful balloon itself, billowing as the crew tugged at the ropes.

Harry let out a whistle of admiration. "That is something to behold, Cinder-Emma!"

"Isn't it lovely? I should so like to fly in it," I said. But once again, I could already see a line of hopeful passengers, and I realized, too, that I did not witness any single "ladies" anticipating a free lift to the heavens. All the ladies in line were in the company of gentlemen willing to pay for the privilege.

"You have more courage than I do," said Harry. "She's a beauty, but I prefer to keep my feet on the ground."

This surprised me some, but it did not dampen my enthusiasm. "Someday, Harry, I shall float up in that basket and see the world as others can't."

"I don't doubt it. I'd buy you a ticket today if it weren't for the little matter of a jail fine."

"Thank you, Harry," I said, "but the time will come when I shall buy my own ticket to heaven. And for now, watching is as free as the air."

After a fanfare from a bugler in a blue silk shirt, Professor Wilson made his little speech about the wonders of aviation and invited a half dozen customers to board the wicker basket. Amongst them were Wright and a young lady friend, decked out in their Sunday bests for the occasion. Professor Wilson fussed about, making sure all were safely positioned. The crowd on the ground shouted good wishes and a few jests—"Steer clear of them lightnin' rods!" and "Hold on to your breakfast, there!" And then, as the passengers waved, and the well-wishers cheered, the ropes were loosed, and the Glory rose above the clearing.

She lifted more sedately than she had in Placerville, then lolled over our heads for a short piece until she caught a breeze that moved her toward the river. Harry and I, and most of the rest of the crowd, chased along on the ground.

When we arrived at the riverbank, we found it lined on both sides with a multitude of admirers. The Glory floated out gracefully over the American, caught the canyon zephyr, and began a delicate dance downstream.

The crack of a rifle sounded, echoing off the bowl of suntanned hills. No one knew what to make of it, until we saw the Glory's side rip open and the torn silk flutter. The balloon's crown collapsed in, and she spiraled down. Professor Wilson had time to throw out a sandbag or two, to little avail, and then began to pull frantically at the ropes. The young woman's screams rang out across the water. The wicker basket twirled crazily, but somehow, Professor Wilson managed to keep the tattered balloon over the river—not the middle, where the current was strong and swift, and not the bank, hard and rocky, but the shallows near the edge, where the Glory descended with a tremendous splash. Her canopy spread out across the water's surface, and, as it caught the current, tilted the wicker basket on its side and began to pull it downstream.

Professor Wilson was the first to scramble from the basket. Wright had been thrown clear, and between them, they gripped its edge, and dragged out the terrified young woman, a boy, and several men, one of whom was barely conscious. As they clutched at the wicker, a dozen of the spectators along the far side—mostly refugees camped on the bank—dived in and rushed to their aid, guiding the passengers from one savior to another until they were safely on shore. Professor Wilson remained in the water, vainly struggling to keep the balloon from vanishing downstream, until more of the rescuers joined him with strong hands and lengths of rope and towed the fallen Glory to the bank.

It was a sorrowful sight, Wright and his weeping young woman in their soaked Sunday bests, the distraught boy, the wounded passenger lying by the water's edge. The Glory has since been spread in a field to dry. This afternoon I glanced across the river and could spy the Professor limping disconsolately from one of the balloon's wounds to the next.

I do not understand the mind that would commit such an act. Was it done out of mischief? Vengeance? Just plain cruelty? I remarked on it to Harry Brown, and he suggested it was the same sort of mind that would set a town on fire.

I still do not believe in Vigilance Committees, but there should be a consequence for the person who would shoot the Glory out of the sky and threaten the souls she cradled. She caused no more harm than a butterfly, and she brought us more beauty.

I took my sadness for Professor Wilson back to the theatre and tried to assuage it with work. Midmorning, I found myself in need of red thread. Mrs. Burnham doled out fifty cents and sent me to the variety store. I completed my purchase and, as I stepped out onto the sidewalk, almost bumped into Mr. Booth. The familiar burn spread across my cheeks. I knew I should apologize for yesterday, but all I wanted to do was disappear. I tried to duck back into the store, but he called out, "Miss Lightfoot, please don't run from me. Please!"

There was no escape. I faced him, squeezed my eyes shut, and blurted, "Oh Mr. Booth I am so sorry I deeply deeply regret spying upon you—"

"Oh, no, Miss Lightfoot," he began.

"I ruined your rehearsal I know I was where I didn't belong and I apologize from my heart and—"

"Miss Lightfoot," he cut in. "Stop. Please. Once again, the apology is mine. Open your eyes, for heaven's sake."

I did. He was looking right at me, but I saw no trace of the madman in the woods on his countenance, only kindness and concern. He smiled. "We don't have to play this scene on the street. There's a soda fountain two doors up, right beside the saloon. May I offer a refreshment?"

He sounded sane. Nonetheless, I said, "I must get back to work, Mr. Booth. I have sewing to do. Grumio's hose."

"A pox on Grumio's hose. If Hattie Burnham gives you a hard time, Miss Lightfoot, I'll take the blame. Come, what will it be? Cherry phosphate or lemon?"

He offered his hand. I screwed up my courage and took it. This time, his grip was gentle and he led me, not to a nunnery, but to Pike's Fountain. We found a table near the back, and he pulled my chair out in the most gentlemanly fashion. I requested a cherry phosphate. He ordered coffee, black. When we had been served, he said, "Now. My formal apology. I had no right to treat you so despicably. I didn't think you would take it so to heart—I didn't think at all, I'm afraid—but from the way you've been avoiding me, I'm sure I was hurtful."

"You were rehearsing," I began.

"That's no excuse to embarrass you."

"You did frighten me," I confessed. "I thought you might be truly mad."

"I sincerely hope not. Though I sometimes have my doubts." He frowned into his coffee. "Madness runs in the family, you know."

I did know. Though I refrained from quoting Emmett's opinion, that the old Booth was "crazy as a loon."

"I have heard that your father was...eccentric," I said.

Mr. Booth half-laughed. "'Eccentric' is an understatement, Miss Lightfoot. How's your phosphate?"

"Lovely. I like the way the bubbles tickle my nose."

"Can you see it in your heart to forgive me?"

How could I not? He was so earnest and remorseful. "Of course, Mr. Booth."

Giggles erupted from the counter. The two girls running the fountain had their heads together, whispering and sneaking peeks in our direction.

One of them gave the other a little shove, and she sidled to the table, clutching a playbill. "Mr. Booth?" she said. She had an Irish brogue. "Mr. Booth, Minnie and I saw the play last night. It was wonderful, wasn't it, Minnie?" Minnie nodded vigorously. "You were wonderful, Mr. Booth. Would you please to sign our playbill?"

I know by now how determined Mr. Booth is to dodge the crowd at the stage door, but he replied, "I would be happy to. And your name is?"

"Margaret. Oh, Minnie, bring a pencil!" And Minnie did, blushing all the while. Mr. Booth signed over his best wishes to the both of them. They thanked him profusely and only left our table when customers called them back to the counter.

"I'm sorry for that, Miss Lightfoot," whispered Mr. Booth. "A peril of the profession."

"I can't blame them a bit," I whispered in return. "The play *was* wonderful last night."

We sipped our refreshments, though Minnie and Margaret were still sneaking glances our way. I was suddenly self-conscious—perhaps they weren't simply admiring Mr. Booth, perhaps they were wondering what a handsome "star" was doing with a girl in specs and a wash apron.

"Don't mind them," said Mr. Booth. "They'll tire of us soon."

"I wish I was more presentable, Mr. Booth."

"You're lovely." A twinkle came into his eye. "The apron's a step up from your miner's costume, although the trousers were captivating in their own right."

"They served their purpose. I felt safer in disguise, you know."

"Yes, I do. I'm in disguise all the time, Miss Lightfoot." He smiled at me over his cup. His present disguise was charming.

"I don't mean to pry,"' he went on, "but how did you come to be on the road in miner's denim? Was it because of the fire?"

It wasn't in my heart to spin him a story. "No, Mr. Booth, I had determined to leave long before any spark was struck."

"You're young to be out here on your own. What about family? Might someone be grieving for you back in the ashes?"

"No. I have friends, but no family."

He did not reply, but the tenderness in his countenance led me to confess, "My father has passed away."

"A fatherless child," he murmured. "There are a few of us in this company."

"I know your father is gone," I said.

"Yes. Although, lately, he seems as alive as ever. And as contrary. He refuses to behave like a proper apparition and only show up when I need him. He makes his entrance in the middle of performances. I'll be out there thinking the role is all mine, and then I hear his voice pop out of my mouth—now that *will* drive you mad. That was the wasp under my blanket when I was rehearsing by the river. I suppose I was just trying to shake the old man out of those roles with devilment."

"I admit, I listened for quite some time, Mr. Booth. The way you kept speaking the lines in different ways, everything sounded new to me."

"Oh, I imagine it did," he said.

"No, no, I don't mean the 'nunnery' business," I replied. "I mean—oh, well, I hope you know what I mean."

"I think I do, Miss Lightfoot. Thank you."

I couldn't believe I had just tried to critique Edwin Booth's acting. I began to blush again, but he said, gently, "How long have you been alone, then?"

"Just since June. Although I don't know if I'm truly alone, either. Sometimes I feel my father traveling with me, right behind me on that old mule. If he's there, he's having a grand time. He loved the theatre. He wrote a beautiful obit for your father."

"Obit?"

"Yes. He was a newspaperman, Mr. Booth. I was his assistant."

"Did you write for the newspaper, too, Miss Lightfoot?"

"Some. I did a little of everything. And a lot of the practical things, so my father could do what he loved best, turning out those editorials."

Mr. Booth nodded. "Yes. I know that role. I came to California with my father four years ago, the last time I toured the camps. I wasn't much older than you. I played small parts, but my main role was my father's keeper—to make sure he trod the straight and narrow, that he got to the theatre at night. But he left the tour before we finished. He was tired, he couldn't handle the trail, and he longed to go home. I wanted to stay, so I let him go off by himself. We were playing the town of Nevada, in a snowstorm, when I got the word he'd died alone on the Mississippi."

"I remember," I said. "My father wept over that news."

"I should have been with him," Mr. Booth went on. "That was my job. I was supposed to keep him safe. I didn't. And now I feel his ghost more strongly with every camp we play."

"I was with my father at the end, Mr. Booth, and there wasn't a blessed thing I could do to hold off death, though I tried with all my heart. What's worse? Failing when you're near someone you love, or failing when you're far away? I don't know as it makes much difference."

He looked me in the eye, and then he reached across the table for my hand. For a second, I feared we were back in *Hamlet.* But he raised it to his lips and very delicately kissed it. I heard a titter from behind the counter, but I did not care. This was my first kiss! Or does a kiss on the hand count? I think I shall simply decide that it does.

I hardly remember returning to the theatre, except that my feet barely touched the ground. I do recall that when we left the soda fountain, the heat on the street hit us like an oven. A thermometer before the dry goods store read over a hundred degrees. We arrived to find the back lot of the theatre nigh deserted—Miss Griffith and Mrs. Burnham were reading in the shade, and a few others had sought naps in their tents. Mr. Booth gave me a courtly bow and a "Thank you for a fine morning, Miss Lightfoot," before he, too, disappeared in search of a cool spot. I tackled the tear in Grumio's hose.

As I stitched, I ruminated over the morning. I realized that, as I had spoken to Mr. Booth about Emmett, there had been no tears to fight back. Perhaps, with time, it will be easier to smile for my father.

STILL JULY 9. *Night, after the play. By the wagon—*

By midafternoon, the heat was at its worst. I was writing in my journal when I heard, "Emma dear! Emma!" Miss Griffith hurried my way. Her hair was pulled up in a ribbon, and she clasped a towel and a big bar of lavender soap. "Emma, it's so hot and nasty, the girls have decided to bathe down by the river. Will you come along?"

"I can think of nothing better, Sophie. Thank you!" I said. I rummaged in my bedroll for soap and a comb while the other "girls"—Mrs. Burnham and the La Rues—joined Miss Griffith by the wagon. Then we headed for the water.

It is no mean task to find a bathing spot for five females within Coloma city limits. The American's shores are rocky, and miners have stripped much of the timber from the bank. Louise was for diving in as soon as we spied the water, but her mother held her back. We found one passable spot not far below the bridge, but it was in plain view of the tents across the river, and Mrs. La Rue declared she was "in no mood to give the dispossessed a show." Mrs. Burnham urged us further downstream, and, after picking our way through the scrub, we found a lovely spot where the bank curved around quiet water, and a big cottonwood sheltered us from the worst of the sun. We stripped down to our shifts and waded in.

Sophie and Mrs. Burnham floated out into the deeper part of the pool, laughing and gasping at the icy water. The cold made my feet ache, but that soon passed. When it's a hundred degrees in the shade, a chilly river is a balm.

The La Rues kept to the shallows. Mrs. La Rue pulled soap from her canvas bag and set about lathering Louise's hair, then sponging the both of them down. Mrs. Burnham, Sophie and I paddled about a bit, and then followed suit. Soon, the sweet smell of Sophie's lavender bar mingled with the scent of willow and damp earth. Sophie giggled to see Mrs. Burnham and me crowned with suds. We dived under to rinse and came up clean.

I am not a strong swimmer. I like to be able to touch the bottom with my toes, so I bobbed about with Sophie in the quiet water. But Mrs. Burnham struck out for the deeper stretches of the river, near the swift current, and played about like a young otter. When she finally returned, grinning, she pulled herself up on a broad, flat rock to warm in the sun. Her shift revealed her bare arms—it was plain to see that she was not round and gently plump, like Sophie, or thin, like me. She was lean and strong, bringing to mind a Greek girl I'd once seen in a picture, who only lost her footrace because she stopped to gather golden apples.

The La Rues did not swim at all. After the child had been scrubbed, Mrs. La Rue directed her to a safe spot along the bank, where she amused herself by building flutter mills from sticks and bits of gravel. Mrs. La Rue spread a blanket by the river's edge and pulled *Pickwick Papers* from her bag.

"Why don't you come on in with us?" asked Sophie.

"Yes!" shouted Louise.

"Louise doesn't swim!" replied Mrs. La Rue. "And I don't either, not well. That current is dangerous."

Mrs. Burnham, lounging on her boulder, sat up. "Yes, but all we have right here is a little eddy. And you can touch bottom almost everywhere. Didn't you ever play in the water as a child?"

"Of course, but—"

"Then you must remember how sweet that is." Mrs. Burnham rose and waded into the river to her knees. "See? It's fine. It's safe. Here." She offered her hand to Mrs. La Rue.

"Please," said Sophie. "It's lovely. Come on in."

Mrs. Burnham smiled and continued to hold out her hand. To my surprise, Mrs. La Rue clasped it and gingerly followed Mrs. Burnham out into the pool. Louise looked on in wonder. "You see?" said Mrs. Burnham. "You're fine. Feet on the bottom?"

Mrs. La Rue nodded.

"Excellent." Mrs. Burnham let go of Mrs. La Rue's hand. "Now, may I?" She swam over to Louise and lifted the girl onto her back. "We shall show this child how pleasant a river can be. Don't worry, we'll stick to the shallows. Hold on, Louise. Just don't pull my hair." Mrs. La Rue's mouth tightened, but she did not protest. In fact, as we floated and twirled, and our shifts billowed about us like water lilies, she actually laughed. Louise shrieked happily as Mrs. Burnham ducked with her beneath the surface and popped back up again.

By and by, we tired and began to feel the cold. Then we traded the river for warm spots onshore, where we stretched ourselves out like happy lizards in the sun. I had nearly dozed off when I was roused by men's voices calling, "Lay-deez! Oh, lay-deeez!!" A rustle in the scrub announced the appearance of Harry Brown and Mr. Moone.

"Hello, mermaids!" shouted Harry.

"We searched high and low for you beauties!" said Mr. Moone. He had a length of rope wrapped about his shoulder, and a burlap sack. He set them down, and the two men began to tug at their boots.

Mrs. La Rue pulled her blanket about Louise and herself. "This is ladies only! You are not invited!"

"Yes, they are," said Sophie.

"Clarissa, this is the only good spot on this whole stretch of river," said Mr. Moone. "Besides, no one will see anything they don't see backstage every night." He began to undo a shirt button.

"Stop!" shouted Mrs. La Rue, clamping a hand over Louise's eyes.

Mrs. Burnham stepped in. "Why don't you fellows wait a few minutes? We're nearly finished here anyway."

Harry Brown abandoned his cheerful air. "I'm sorry, Clarissa," he said. "We can find another place. Come on, Moone."

"No," replied Mrs. La Rue. "We're going. Pack up, Louise. Hurry."

Louise gave her mother a pained look but reluctantly obeyed. They scooped up their things, and the child trudged off upstream after her mother.

"We didn't mean to spoil the fun," said Harry.

"No, indeed," added Mr. Moone. "We are the bearers of good tidings." He reached into the sack and pulled out two big bottles.

"Ooh, champagne," squealed Sophie.

Mr. Moone grinned. "The manager of the Sierra Nevada House saw the show last night and delivered this with compliments. Here, cool it in the water, sweetheart."

Sophie tripped down to the water's edge, a bottle in each hand, nestled the champagne in the shallows, and dived in. Mr. Moone and Harry pulled off everything but their trousers. Then they threw the rope over a branch of the cottonwood and secured it. With war whoops, they swung out as high as they could over the deepest part of the pool and dropped in, making tremendous splashes. Mrs. Burnham couldn't resist—she took a dive off the rope, too. Then Harry Brown turned to me. "Emma, it may not be the Glory, but this is the only way you'll get to fly today. Are you game?"

Well, I was. It took me a swing or two out over the water to get up the nerve, and I confess it is no mean feat to keep one's shift modestly about one when dropping into a river from a rope, but I did it. I flew, if only for a second. Hallelujah.

In no time the champagne was cold—or cold enough. Mr. Moone fetched a bottle, loosened the cork, and aimed it out over the river. The cork flew into the current with a hearty "pop" and hurried downstream toward the Pacific. Sophie cheered.

"Who's shooting?" came a voice through the willows, and Ulysses bounded out of the scrub. Right on his tail were Mr. Thayer, Mr. Booth, and the Blisses. Mr. Thayer thrust his hands in the air. "We surrender!"

"And we offer generous terms!" said Buck Bliss, lifting another burlap sack.

This one, it turned out, contained green bottles of beer, which were soon cooling by the remaining champagne.

In seconds, Mr. Booth and the Blisses, too, were down to their trousers and swinging out into the water. Mr. Thayer preferred his long johns for a swimming costume. The thought crossed my mind that the more we dipped the company in the river this week, the less laundry I might have to do.

By and by, a contest began between Mr. Moone and Harry Brown to see who could launch himself from the rope in the most spectacular fashion. Harry could spin in the air and kick his feet out in comical ways, but Mr. Moone was an acrobat—he could turn a flip before slicing into the water.

Mr. Moone tried to recruit the Blisses and Mr. Booth to the competition, but they declined, declaring they had no desire to break their necks on such a lovely afternoon. Finally, Harry cast an eye on Mr. Thayer, who'd been bobbing quietly in the shallows. "Come on, Thayer. You're not in a wheelchair, yet," he teased. "Show us what our elders can do."

"Oh, I don't know as I should," said Mr. Thayer. "My arthritis, you know."

"Don't worry," said Harry. "We'll haul you out if need be. Come on."

Mr. Thayer reluctantly dragged himself out of the water and crossed to the bank. "All right. But I expect kind words from you at my funeral." He gripped the rope and swung out once, twice, three times, until he was high over the pool. Then he released, curled into a perfect double somersault, and disappeared beneath the surface.

"My God," exclaimed Harry, as we all applauded. But the seconds went by, and Mr. Thayer did not reappear. Mr. Moone dived under and came up, shaking his head, just as a whoop sounded from far out in the river. Mr. Thayer waved at us. Ulysses yipped and paddled out to join him as he swam back toward the pool.

Harry let loose a laugh. "You bastard."

"Gus did time with a circus, Harry," said Mrs. Burnham. "And he still has a few tricks up his sleeve."

Mr. Thayer just smiled and returned to laze in the shallows.

Shortly, the men broke out the beer and popped the last bottle of champagne. Mrs. Burnham did not drink, nor did Mr. Booth. Jimmy Bliss, it seems, is Temperance and he did not imbibe, either. But we all floated happily about. I threw a stick for Ulysses and he paddled after it. He never seemed to tire, just ferried that stick back a dozen times and dropped it before me, joy in his eyes.

The champagne bottle was passed around—I was surprised when Sophie handed it to me, as I had never tried alcohol. "Here you go, Emma," she said. I could have refused it, but since I had already collected my first kiss today, I leaned toward living dangerously. I gave it a go. I savored the bubbles, although the champagne was more tart than my cherry phosphate had been. I took another sip. And perhaps one more. All went well until my knees grew wiggly and weak. I was glad I had the water to hold me up. The sensation wasn't unpleasant, just strange.

Harry Brown floated my way. "Cinder-Emma, has an evil stepsister gotten you tipsy? Your cheeks are all rosy."

"I don't think I'm drunk," I replied. "I'm just feeling...oh...pleasant."

Harry chuckled. "Stay out of the deep water, young lady."

I suspect the champagne had left Sophie feeling a little "pleasant," too. As the afternoon pressed on, she got herself back up on the rope and sailed out over the water, dropping perilously close to Mr. Booth. She surfaced with a giggle and wrapped her arms around his neck. He swam her gently over to Mr. Moone and, with a smile, announced, "Delivery for you, Sumner." Mr. Moone embraced her, but she broke free. She swam away, lifted herself out onto a rock, and turned her lovely back on the both of them.

A little later, Mr. Booth took to his own rock, to warm in the sun and light his pipe. He caught my gaze and winked, then blew a smoke ring. My knees got even weaker, and I can't put the whole blame on the champagne.

The afternoon shadows lengthened, and the hills on the far side of the river turned deeper shades of gold. Ulysses had abandoned his stick and was lolling on the sand; the empty bottles circled lazily in the eddy. I floated about—it's a fine thing to hang there, water almost up to your nose, and gaze at the green ripples as they dance downstream and at the sun flickering through the cottonwood leaves.

Most of the company was already drying out on the bank, although I didn't see Mr. Moone or Mr. Thayer.

Presently, we heard distant hollering, barely audible over the rushing of the river. Mrs. Burnham swam past me toward the deeper stretches and frowned as she peered upstream. "Oh, dear Lord," she said. "Look at the bridge."

We scrambled for a view. Way upriver, two men were perched on the bridge's rail. They shouted and gestured at us. "I believe that's Moone," said Harry. "And is that Thayer?"

"I'm afraid so," said Mrs. Burnham. "Oh, no."

The troll tollkeeper had spotted the men from his booth and scuttled toward them, yelling and waving his arms. They waved back, laughing, until he was almost upon them, and then they kicked off from the bridge and dropped into the middle of the American. Mrs. Burnham gasped. At last, two heads appeared above the current, drifting downstream as swiftly as champagne corks. When they arrived opposite our swimming hole, they struck out for shore. Relieved as Mrs. Burnham was to see them safe, she couldn't help but scold, "You idiots! Who'll go on for you tonight if you're at the bottom of the river?"

Mr. Thayer swam toward her and wrapped her in his arms. "Oh, Hattie, you know we wouldn't drown on your watch." And he planted a kiss on her cheek.

That was the afternoon's finale. We packed up and headed back to the theatre. The Burnhams and Mr. Leach threw open the performance hall's windows and doors to catch whatever breeze might be about, and most of the company went in search of a quick supper before the play.

This evening, Mr. Booth was in the dressing room ahead of the other actors, putting on his stage makeup for Mortimer. I did not wish to be caught spying again, so I didn't linger by the dressing room door. But I did find plenty of reasons to pass by. He possesses a beautiful wooden makeup case, with drawers of brushes and powder and false hair, and he sits in deep concentration before the scrap of mirror. His fine fingers stroke the brushes deftly across his countenance, as an artist's hands might play across a canvas, and step by step, he becomes someone else.

In between my peeks at Mr. Booth, I came upon another scene. Mrs. Burnham and Sophie were combing out their hair in the women's dressing room. Sophie complained, "He was such a fool today. That was all about wanting attention, you know."

Mrs. Burnham simply shrugged.

"Sometimes he's the best friend you could ever have," Sophie went on, "But then, when I'm pleasant in return, he pushes me for more."

"Sophie, how old were you when you were engaged to Sumner? Fourteen? He's loved you for a long time."

Sophie sighed. "I know. But I just don't love him anymore. I wish he'd stop moaning around about it. It's pathetic."

"Be kind to him Sophie," said Mrs. Burnham. "If not for his sake, then for the company's—just to keep the act together until we get through this tour."

Sophie squinched up her pretty face as if she'd sucked on a lemon. "When I'm kind to him, he takes it all wrong. Oh, Hattie, he's making me crazy."

Mrs. Burnham tugged the comb through her hair. "I hate lovers' quarrels. They're messy and they're bad for business. Why didn't you tell me what the story was before we handed out the contracts?"

Sophie snorted. "And miss the chance to eat trail dust and sleep in cheap hotels?"

Then she saw me behind her, and quickly shifted to the role of best friend. "Emma, dear! Are those my second act stockings? You are so kind!" No more was said of Sumner Moone.

There was a run on face powder in the dressing rooms tonight. Sunburn from our afternoon at the river made the fairer members of the cast pay for their pleasure. Sophie glowed pinker than usual, and Mr. Moone, with his crimson face under his orange hair, resembled a human spark. He had little need to redden his nose for Grumio. Mr. Booth and the Burnhams had browned up in a way that rendered them even more handsome. Not so Jimmy Bliss, or, alas, myself. As I'd been running my errands backstage, I'd felt the heat rise in my face. When I passed Harry Brown in the hall, he laughed, "Miss Lightfoot, have you been boiled or steamed?" He marched me to the mirror, and my countenance was the color of smoked ham.

"Oh, no," I wailed, for I knew what I was in for, the pain and the peeling. Harry was ruddy, too, but, like Mr. Booth, in a way that made him all the more good-looking.

" You'll have to skip the ball tonight, Cinder-Emma. Your cheeks will clash with your gown."

"Don't even try to make me smile, Harry. It hurts."

"I'm sorry. I truly am." He put on a somber face, but it only made me giggle.

My remedy was to dig the bottle of witch hazel out of the wagon stores, splash myself with as much of it as I dared, and then pass it on to the sufferers in the dressing rooms. I comforted myself with the thought that Mr. Booth could no longer see me blush—my cheeks were already as red as could be.

Sunburn or no, the evening's performance was a success. Perhaps because it was a benefit for the fire victims, the theatre sold out, with patrons standing in the rear of the hall. Mr. Booth was at his best, and the rest of the cast shone as well. After the play, the company presented extra entertainments and closed the evening with one of Louise's songs. Mrs. La Rue dedicated it to those who were burned out of their homes or far from the ones they loved. She refrained from accompaniment, only plucked a single guitar note, and Louise's clear voice rang out in a hymn. "There's a land that is fairer by day, and by faith we can see it afar; / For the Father waits over the way, to prepare us a dwelling place there." The child sang simply and soulfully, and the audience of rough fortune seekers listened in hushed silence. "We shall sing on that beautiful shore the melodious songs of the blest, / And our spirits shall sorrow no more, not a sigh for the blessing of rest."

Louise's spell worked its magic backstage, too. In the wings, all eyes were on the girl. "In the sweet by and by, we shall meet on that beautiful shore...." I could not help but long for Emmett, and my mama whom I hardly remembered. "In the sweet by and by-eee, we shall meet on that beautiful shore!" Louise's last note echoed sweetly. Then she curtsied to a wave of applause that belied how small the performance hall really was.

When the curtain fell, the company swiftly "struck" the show and readied for the morning's departure. Then they went their ways—some ambled down to the river for a last night of music and a mite more beer. Mr. Thayer and Ulysses retired to their tent. The La Rues bedded down in the women's dressing room, while the Burnhams and Mr. Leach counted the take in the men's. I was coiling a laundry line by the wagon when I heard a shout from backstage. The theatre door flew open, and Mr. Burnham charged out, cash box under his arm. Mr. Leach and Mrs. Burnham were right behind him. "Ben," pleaded Mrs. Burnham, "we're a week out of Sacramento."

"Another day won't make any difference," Mr. Burnham said.

"We've promised a payday," said Mr. Leach. "The actors are counting on it."

"They can wait."

Mr. Thayer appeared in his long johns, frowning. "Is there a problem with salaries?"

"No!" said Mr. Burnham and stormed into his tent.

Mrs. Burnham rushed in after him. "Where did it go, Ben?" she demanded.

At that moment, Mr. Leach caught sight of me, laundry line in hand. "This isn't for your ears, Miss Lightfoot," he said. His tone was not unkind, but I could have differed with him. My dollar a day is dear to me, and my pay was as much at stake as anyone else's. I obliged him by retreating to the wagon—I don't know where else he expected me to disappear to. But

I could hear every word in there as well as I could outside. The Burnhams went on at each other.

"This won't cover the pay. It's short," said Mrs. Burnham.

"There were expenses, Hattie. New playbills for our illustrious star—there's money down a rathole—and fines for the company jailbirds, theatre rent, stables, feed—"

"Five card stud—"

"And fires!" Mr. Burnham roared.

I heard a whisper at the tailgate. "Cinder-Emma?"

"Here," I whispered back.

"You've got a box seat for this melodrama. May I join you?"

I nodded, and Harry Brown slipped in by my side. We crouched together in the wagon bed while Mr. Burnham ranted on, "Those damned fires have eaten away at our houses—the take has gone up in smoke."

"Ben, we sold out Placerville! And the theatre was packed tonight!"

"We lost a whole show here, Hattie."

There was a silence. Then, even in the wagon, I could hear Mrs. Burnham sigh. "I know where you've been at night. Poker and women come at a price." Mr. Burnham did not reply. "What happened to that 'new day' you promised?"

"Don't start, Hattie—"

"What happened to 'partners?' 'We'll strike our own gold mine.' Weren't those the words, Ben?"

"We will."

"You know, you put me in mind of that Greek story, that Prometheus. He tries all night to survive, to grow his liver back, just so a vulture can rip it away the next day. You're the vulture, Ben, only you pull us apart at night at the card tables. You bleed us out."

"You're the vulture, Hattie. You chew away at a man until he's hollow—"

"We have to pay the company!" Mrs. Burnham shouted.

"Fine. You want the payroll, I'll get the damned payroll."

"At a poker table?"

"Come along, if you like."

"Ben!"

"With you or without you, it makes no difference to me."

Mr. Burnham strode out of the tent. Mr. Leach stepped into his path. "Burnham," he said, "don't be an ass. Let's cut our losses right here. We'll work something out—"

Mr. Burnham brushed him aside with a curt, "Out of the way, Jeriah," and stomped off into the night.

Mrs. Burnham muttered, "Dear God." She threw her shawl over her shoulders and hurried after him.

Mr. Leach was right behind her. "Hattie, I'll take care of this. Stay in your tent."

"No. I can't," she cried, and hastened on. Mr. Leach threw up his hands and followed. Mr. Thayer watched them go. He shook his head and, with a whistle to Ulysses, retreated to his bed.

Harry and I climbed out of the wagon. "I believe I'm in need of a late-night stroll, Emma," he declared. "I shall keep you posted on the sights I encounter." He grinned and disappeared after the Burnhams.

I finished packing up the laundry equipment, lit a candle stub, and pulled my journal from my bedroll.

Tonight, with the La Rues camped in the theatre, I'm once again the wagon's sole lodger. Though I'd trade its tight quarters in a heartbeat for a real bed in a quiet room, the wagon is for now my home. Its planks lift me off the earth; its canvas shelters me from the night. It's a comfort to once more claim it for myself.

I know this claim is fragile. I am the lowliest member of the Star Troupe. The La Rues or any of the others could evict me, and so I am grateful for each evening that the wagon is my cradle. What shall I do if it is lost to me?

As a Lightfoot, I should know that each bright morning presents a hundred roads to ruin. The wagon could tumble off a mountain trail or be swept off a bridge. Worse, the Star Troupe could fail, as Hattie Burnham fears. Payroll could vanish across a card table, or Mr. Booth could wander off in an evening, never to return, a star who leaves us in the dark. Where is home then?

I hope that Emmett's spirit is close by, as he promised, to help me fight off these black thoughts.

THURSDAY, JULY 10. *Auburn, in the heat of the afternoon. Costumes are ready—*

Before dawn, I dreamed of Emmett. I was so happy to see him. He looked well and hearty in his finest coat, his notebook in his pocket. He sat at the head of a table in the dining room of a white house with roses in the yard. He greeted me with love in his eyes and asked me to sit in the chair beside him. I did, and he took my hand. "Say hello to your family," he said. My brothers and sisters ringed the table in their Sunday bests. I could hear their sweet laughter, but I could not make out their faces. My mother's chair was empty. I prayed she was in the kitchen, fetching our meal, but she did not arrive. "This is our newest addition," Emmett said, beaming and pointing to a very small boy in a high chair. His was the only child's face that was clear to me. I looked into his deep, bright eyes. "Welcome, Henry," I said.

Then, I awoke. I still sensed Emmett holding my hand, so I did not stir from my bed until the sun was up. When I finally poked my head out of the wagon, I found our camp to be the picture of peace. The tents were quiet, save for a few snores. Only Louise was up and about, in her nightgown. She had collected the company's cast-off bottles from the riverbank and arranged them by color and size, where they caught the morning sunlight and sparkled.

Soon, the Blisses threw off their blankets, grunted and stretched, and set about starting a fire. The camp filled with smells of coffee and biscuits. Jimmy Bliss threw an oilcloth over a rickety property table, and Louise graced it with a jam jar of wildflowers. Buck fried up plenty of bacon, enough for all, and as the breakfast was spread on the table, and the sleepy actors gathered around, the back lot took on the feel of home.

Mr. Booth did not appear, although Jimmy Bliss called at his tent flap more than once. Finally, Buck went over and growled, "Ted, I only do room service for the ladies. If you want breakfast, get your backside up and come to the table." There was no reply, but as Buck turned away, a boot flew out of the tent and right into his backside. Harry Brown laughed so hard he spilled his coffee on his shirt.

The surprise of the morning came when Mr. Moone appeared from his tent, followed a few minutes later by Sophie. Despite her protests that she was not in love with him, the two had been very friendly down by the river the night before. Mr. Moone grinned as he put away his biscuits and bacon, and Sophie had a certain flush about her that was more than sunburned cheeks. The rest of the company tried not to stare, although I could see a few folks biting back their amusement. We all went on with breakfast as if there was not an elephant in the room, except for Louise, who exclaimed to Sophie, "I didn't know you were married!"

The Burnhams and Mr. Leach put in appearances, but they had dark circles under their eyes and barely nibbled at breakfast. Mr. Burnham took only a sip of coffee before he mounted the backstairs and announced that pay was ready in the men's dressing room. At the news, the lines on Mr. Thayer's brow relaxed, and Harry Brown shot me a smile. "Later," he whispered. One by one, the company members ascended to the hall for our pay. I was positively joyful to have my dollars in hand—I gave one to the Blisses for their kindnesses toward Lem Mule and stowed the others in my old sock.

The last of the company to rise was Mr. Booth. He wandered over to the breakfast table to find naught but crumbs and an empty coffee pot. He stood there, his hair mussed and his countenance mournful. "Mr. Booth," I called out. "Here." I held up the extra biscuit I'd wrapped in my bandana. "It's yours, if you like."

He smiled. "Are you sure? I don't want to take your last bite."

"Absolutely."

He set the biscuit on a tin plate and drained the last few drops of cold coffee into a cup. "Thank you, Chicken," he said. "When we're out on the trail, my stomach shall thank you, too," and he slipped back into his tent.

"Chicken?" I don't regard myself as poultry. I suspect it was meant as an endearment, and that I am not sprouting pinfeathers. Still, even "Emma dear" and "Professor" have a sweeter ring to them. Perhaps, in time, he'll come up with something better—I shall simply have to live in hope.

Right after pay was disbursed, Mr. Burnham and Mr. Leach journeyed to the far side of the river for the horses. They returned to camp in short order, Mr. Burnham in a dudgeon. Passage over the bridge, he reported, was no longer free. The troll's benevolence had expired the day before, and he wasn't about to make exceptions for a passel of actors who'd abused his bridge for diving practice. He'd already made Mr. Burnham and Mr. Leach pay twice—for going over the river and back—and he'd piled on more charges for the horses.

Our management huddled in a far corner of the lot. "We'll ford the river," announced Mr. Burnham. "It's summer, the water's low—"

Mr. Leach shook his head. "I haven't seen a passable stretch of this river yet."

Mrs. Burnham touched Mr. Burnham's arm. "Ben, we've got the child. She doesn't swim. And costumes—everything we own."

"Hattie, you're the one who's so worried about cash. Why throw away money on the bridge?"

"Is there a safe place?"

"To the north, around the bend. I drove that crossing for years when the bridge was out. If I can get a stage across, I can handle a blamed wagon."

"I don't know, Ben," grumbled Mr. Leach.

"You and the boys already caulked the hell out of that wagon bed. She's tight as a ship."

Mr. Leach gave it up. "All right. But play it careful. Save the drama for the stage."

Lengths of oilcloth were passed out to the actors and lashed tightly about costume baskets and trunks. I'd bound my journal and Emmett's two books in oilcloth when I left home, but I figured another layer wouldn't hurt. The company dressed in old clothes—Sophie's feathered hat and Mr. Thayer's grey coat were packed away for a drier day. I was grateful I still had Emmett's trousers and boots. And I was thankful for Lem Mule, too—the old boy was so pleased to be on the trail again that he let out a tremendous bray to inform Coloma of his feelings on the matter.

Wright stopped by to bid us farewell. One arm was in a sling and his forehead was bruised from his crash landing in the Glory, but nothing could dampen his cheer as he waved us down the road. "Come again soon!" he cried after us. "All the world's a stage!" We headed north along the main street, which soon became an open road, following the curve of the river.

I kept to the rear of the caravan. Harry Brown dropped back and fell in by my side. "Dumb luck," he said. "Dumb luck and nerve."

"The payroll?" I asked.

"Umm-hmm."

"So you found the Burnhams last night."

"I certainly did," he replied, and promptly delivered me his report. "I trailed The Management until they came upon an all-night game at the Virginia Saloon, where the stakes were worth the while. By the time I slipped in, Burnham had managed to claim himself a seat at the table. Hattie and Leach were stationed within spitting distance. I settled for a beer at the bar. Leach had a full bottle of whiskey in front of him, and Hattie had lit up one of her skinny cigars.

"The players were a tough-looking bunch. One of them had the leathery face of a rancher, but his boots and jacket said money. Another

I'd peg for a drummer—flashy waistcoat, and he laughed too much for someone with no front teeth. The last gent would have given Tom Bell a run for the money. He was a big man, short an eye, and he let that empty socket hang out for all the world to see. His good eye was sharp as a snake's, though.

"For a while, Burnham played it close to the chest. He'd win a few hands, then lose a few, and he barely let out more than a grunt. Meantime, Hattie would burn through one cigar and light up another from the stub. Leach nursed his whiskey.

"Along about two in the morning, the drummer started drawing the cards, and soon he was up hundreds of dollars. The rancher looked none too cheerful; the big man kept his snake eye on the drummer's fingers. There was grumbling about a shaved deck, and then shouting, except from Burnham, who said not a word. At last, the rancher exploded, and the drummer's hand went for his pistol. Old One-Eye grabbed the drummer by the collar, and all three headed out toward the street, where there was bellowing and fists laid on. But Burnham just relaxed at the table, his eyes on the pot, and let the others do the dirty work. Only One-Eye returned, bleeding from his mouth. Burnham and One-Eye tossed the drummer's winnings into the pot, Burnham dealt two hands from a fresh deck, and they played it out. One-Eye grinned with his bloody mouth, as if he'd eat you for breakfast, and kept raising Burnham. Burnham didn't break a sweat, even when all the company's cash was on the table. One-Eye finally called, and, closing in for the kill, spread his hand, pairs of kings and tens. Burnham took a long gander at his own hand, then laid it on the table—a full house, fours and nines. One-Eye flashed him a snake stare. Burnham held fast, and then One-Eye growled, shoved the pot across the table, and stalked out. Leach tossed back the last of his bottle, Hattie breathed again, and that is how you and I were paid our pittance this morning. Dumb luck, and a hothead who kept cool for once. It was historic."

How Emmett would have delighted in this young man's nose for news!

In a short while, the company arrived at Mr. Burnham's "safe place," where the river was indeed wide and shallow. Mr. Burnham and Mr. Leach scouted the water on horseback for rocks and holes. They journeyed to the far side more than once before announcing our path.

The ladies, except for the La Rues, ventured across first, each of us with an escort. Mr. Leach and Mrs. Burnham led the way, and shy Jimmy Bliss kept me company. I was grateful once again for Lem—Mrs. Burnham's grey needed urging into the water, but dear Lem calmly set one hoof in front of the other, as if he forded rivers every day.

The crossing was mostly smooth, the water barely above the animals' bellies, but midstream, we hit a deep patch. Lem plunged in up to his neck and swam. I floated up out of the saddle—I laughed in surprise—then quickly gripped the horn and pushed my legs back down into the stirrups. Lem simply snorted, pleased at the coolness of the current, and safely delivered me to the bank on the far side, where he brought us up, dripping, onto dry land. Mrs. Burnham and Sophie were already ashore. They were laughing, too, from the exhilaration of our dip.

By now, the wagon was almost midriver. Mr. Burnham took his time with the team, gently coaxing them along. Buck Bliss rode near Burnham, on the upstream side, while Harry, Mr. Thayer and Mr. Booth brought up the rear. When the wagon arrived at the deep water, the team lifted their heads and swam toward us. The wagon bobbed in the current, seaworthy as a schooner. Louise peeked out, delighted, from behind Mr. Burnham's shoulder.

The team arrived at the spot where they should have touched bottom. The larger lead horse easily found his footing on the rocky riverbed, but his partner in harness stumbled. As the animal struggled to find his balance, he slipped again and went down, head and all, below the water. In an instant, he resurfaced, frightened and floundering, dragging the rest of the team off balance. The current gripped the wagon, swung its tail downstream, and threatened to snatch it away, team and all. Mrs. La Rue's screams rang from the wagon bed, "We're going to die! To die!"

Mr. Burnham had no intention of dying—he gripped the lines and shouted commands to the team, while Mr. Thayer swam his mount to the tailgate of the tilting wagon and scooped Louise from her mother's arms into the safety of his saddle. Buck Bliss was at the bigger lead horse's head within seconds, clutching the harness and guiding the animal toward shore, while Mr. Booth hastened to reach the panicked horse on the downstream side. As he grabbed for its line, the horse careened into his pinto and sent Mr. Booth flying from the saddle. The spooked pinto jerked away and began to swim downriver, Mr. Booth's ankle still twisted in his stirrup.

I was the first to spy Mr. Booth flailing to keep his head above water. I urged Lem into the current, but Mr. Moone's horse was quicker than my steady old Lem, and Moone dashed ahead of me, crying, "Ted, hold on!" By the time he reached the pinto, its rider had disappeared. Mr. Moone thrust down into the water and hauled Mr. Booth up by his shirt, keeping him afloat until Mr. Booth was able to fight his way up into his saddle. Then Mr. Moone seized the pinto's bridle and turned his head toward shore. All I could do was to guide Lem toward the pinto's side and stay close. Buck Bliss and Mr. Burnham calmed the frightened team and drove the wagon up onto the bank.

Mrs. Burnham had watched in horror as Mr. Booth had nearly floated away. Now, she rushed out into the water to grasp the reins of the pinto from Mr. Moone and lead her star to safety. "Are you hurt?" she cried. Mr. Booth slid free of his horse and winced—his trapped ankle had taken a battering. This was Sophie's cue to cast herself as Florence Nightingale. She helped him to a dry spot, then fluttered about him as Mrs. Burnham tried to determine how badly injured he might be.

"We could have lost you," Mrs. Burnham said.

Mr. Booth gave her a grim smile. "The Booths don't do well on water, do we? But I guess it's not my time, yet."

"Oh, Ted, don't even think such things," Sophie moaned.

The two women removed his boot. The ankle had an angry look about it, although Mr. Booth assured everyone that, no, it was not broken, and, yes, he could handle the trip to Auburn and perform *The Iron Chest* on top of it. The women were unconvinced and hovered about him until he protested, "Ladies, you have my thanks, but I'm more likely to drown in sympathy than in the American."

Mr. Moone stood alone, dripping, as he took in this scene. Later, Mr. Booth thanked him, and Mrs. Burnham gave him a quick, "Well done, Sumner," but to Sophie he was invisible. And, though he had salvaged the crossing, Mr. Burnham was granted little credit from Mrs. Burnham. He scowled at the fuss over Mr. Booth and turned to check the wagon for damage.

Mr. Thayer, however, received his due and more. As he lowered Louise from his saddle, she delivered him a hug, and when he lifted the weeping Mrs. La Rue from the wagon, he was deluged with gratitude. "Oh, Mr. Thayer, thank God for a gentleman, thank God for your courage," she cried, and on and on.

The company took a short spell to catch our breaths, then moved north toward Pilot Hill, and beyond that, to Auburn. As we journeyed up out of the canyon, Mrs. Burnham glanced back down at the Coloma Valley and smiled. "What do you think she sees?" I wondered to Harry Brown.

"Nothing, Cinder-Emma. Nothing but blue sky. That's why she's so pleased." And indeed, not even a wisp of smoke clouded our wake.

The road from Coloma to Pilot Hill was smoother than the trails we had so far encountered. It rolled through gentle hills, dotted with oak and pine, and put most of the company in good humor, despite our tangle with the river. Lem Mule had a cheerful spring in his trot and a desire to nibble the long grass by the roadside. I confess, I was an indulgent mistress and gave him his head when I could.

We made good time and rode into Pilot Hill a little before noon. There's enough there to call it a town, I suppose—a couple of stores, a post office, and a hotel. We found a shady spot off the road for the wagon and the stock. Some of the company dispersed to find a quick dinner. I watered Lem at a small brook and let him softly nose a few oats out of my palm.

Over by the wagon, a private talk between Miss Griffith and Mr. Moone was becoming a public argument. Sophie abruptly turned her back on her lover. "Leave me be!"

"No. I won't let you humiliate yourself," said Mr. Moone. "Why do you throw yourself at Booth? He's not interested in you. Have a little dignity."

Sophie wheeled on him. "How can you talk about dignity? Moping around after someone who doesn't give a plug nickel for you?"

"Is that what last night was worth?"

"Damn right!"

"You had me fooled. I guess I'm just a sucker for a second-rate performance, as long as there's enough sentiment and sound effects."

"Stay away from me," Sophie shouted. "Don't speak to me again, Mr. Moone!"

"*Mr.* Moone? Look, Sophie—"

"Miss Griffith to you!" she shrieked, and started away.

"Sophie, please—" Mr. Moone placed a conciliatory hand on her shoulder. She whirled about, and epithets flew from her rosebud mouth that I could never have imagined.

The ruckus gathered onlookers, until Mr. Thayer stepped in with a, "Why don't we save the drama for a paying audience? You two can figure this out when you're calmer, yes, Sophie?" He took her by the elbow and tried to lead her gently into the wagon. She pushed him away, but he persisted, speaking in a low voice, until she was finally tucked out of sight in the wagon's quietude.

Harry Brown went over to Mr. Moone's side. "Sumner?" But Mr. Moone could only stumble away, his shoulders sagging.

Thank heaven Mr. Booth was nowhere in sight.

Later, on the road, Harry Brown and I brought up the rear of our caravan, out of earshot of the others. "Emma," he said to me, "if I am ever in love, just hit me over the head with a big stick and knock some sense into me, will you?"

"Happily," I replied, and then, "Mr. Moone is a smart man, Harry. Why would he want to stay with her if she doesn't care for him?"

"I haven't a clue, except that he's known her for a long time. They were engaged."

"I heard since she was fourteen."

"Yes. I suppose he's been waiting for her to grow up, but I don't know how soon that's going to happen. I do know it gets complicated when you have an act together."

"Do you think she'll stay with him?"

"Probably. They do this all the time—one minute, Sophie's happy as a lark with his company, and in the next minute, it's the Punch and Judy show." Harry smiled my way. "Now, what's your story, Miss Lightfoot? Spill—how did you come to know about *Cymbeline*, Act III, Scene vi?"

Mr. Brown is an affable person, and I no longer wished to remain a mystery with him. Perhaps I could not yet trust him with deep secrets, but I could trust him to listen generously to what I chose to share. Right there on the trail, I confessed to him my tales of Emmett and *The Placerville Rattler*, of Evie, and even of my almost-remembered family. He was delighted. "So that's why you scribble away in that journal day and night. You're a member of the press!" He raised his eyebrows. "Uh-oh. Does this mean I must be wary of what I say to you?"

"Oh, no. I shall never misquote you. And you shall always be a 'confidential source.'"

He laughed. "I wish I had known Mr. Lightfoot. My father is a pleasant sort, but he's a banker, you know, and stodgy as starch. You would never catch him on a street corner with a notebook in his hand and a turkey feather in his hat."

"Emmett would have enjoyed your acquaintance, too, Harry," I said. It crossed my mind that Charley might have turned out much like Harry—lively and funny and inquisitive—if he hadn't plummeted into that well.

Harry grinned. "I should have picked up the clues about you days ago. I'm a good detective, but you eluded me. Where are your inky fingers? Put out a hand."

I did. It bore blisters, and the knuckles were raw from lye soap, but the printer's ink had vanished. "I've been on my own for some weeks now, Harry. My former life has washed away."

"Hmm. Mr. Dickens should write a book about you, Cinder-Emma. An orphan girl, secretly a writer, who dons her father's clothes and stows away with ragtag actors. Oops, wait, maybe Shakespeare's already been there."

"Does the story turn out happily?"

"Absolutely!"

And so we rode on, amusing ourselves. Up front, I could I could see Mr. Booth on his pinto, his wounded ankle hanging free of the stirrup. He was handling the ride well enough but keeping to himself. I wished I could speak with him as comfortably as I spoke to Harry, without blushes or hesitation. Our talk in the soda fountain had been easy enough, even intimate, but it had not been repeated. I confess I felt a small envy of Sophie this morning, as she had thrown herself before him without an ounce of shyness and wrapped his injured foot.

"Harry," I said, "has Mr. Booth ever mentioned his family to you?"

"God, no, though I know about his father. But Ted never talks about anything personal or grim. He just crams it in between the lines. If you want to know about Ted's father, watch Mortimer lose his mind. It scares me to death to play that scene with him." Harry caught my eye and smiled. "You're the reporter, Emma Lightfoot. Have you got a scoop? Something I don't know about?"

"Oh, no," I replied. "I just wondered."

"Thayer once mentioned that Ted has some private place he goes to in his mind, where no one can follow. What you see on the outside is only Ted playing Ted."

I took that into consideration. I realized that the door that Mr. Booth had opened to me at the soda fountain was perhaps more than was given to most, and it cheered me.

I must stop here for now. The afternoon has flown. I have just had an invitation to take a quick walk to Wells Fargo before the play begins. More later.

After the play, in the wagon. It's late but too hot and noisy to sleep—

A few minutes after Harry and I spoke of Mr. Booth this afternoon, Mr. Leach grabbed a roll of theatre bills and hastened on ahead of the company. As he trotted by the wagon, he called out, "The bridge this time, Ben!" Mr. Burnham glowered but remained silent.

I had never traveled the road to Auburn, and so I was surprised when the gentle hills and fields dropped off into the chasm of another river canyon, vaster than any we had yet encountered. There is more than one fork of the American, it seems, and the north and middle forks find their confluence at the bottom of the abyss that lay before us.

"There's our road," said Harry, pointing out the fine line snaking up the canyon wall on the far side. "It's a shame we can't sprout wings and fly over."

As we paused, Mrs. La Rue peered out from under the wagon canvas, caught a glimpse of what awaited, and disappeared back inside. Mr. Thayer dismounted, whispered into the wagon, and returned to Louise with a length of rope. He made sure the child was securely seated in his saddle, looped the line a couple of times about her waist, and made it fast to the saddle horn. "Just like the circus," he said with a wink. Then he gripped the reins, ready to lead the horse along the treacherous descent.

We knew by then what the road demanded of us and gently urged our mounts downward toward the river. I gave Lem his head and kept my own low, eyes on the trail. After miles of wicked switchbacks, we arrived at the bridge, slung across the river below a jumble of huge, dark rocks. It was a contraption of wire and rope, with a sway to it, and it did not inspire confidence. Still, the American's deep middle fork ran swiftly here, and fording was not even to be imagined. Mr. Burnham silently surrendered our tolls to the keeper, and we moved cautiously out over the river. It made me dizzy to look down through the plank floor to the current racing below. I forced my gaze upward and fixed it on Lem's long ears, monuments to mulish calm. Then I sighed, deeply, as he descended once more onto the earth of the trail.

The passage up to the north rim of the canyon was grueling, It finally leveled out onto the divide, and we found ourselves on the fringes of Auburn. We began to spy posted bills—those of our own Star Troupe, which Mr. Leach had just hung, scattered in with bills for Rowe & Co.'s Pioneer Circus. The latter bore the image of a beautiful rider dancing on the back of a spirited steed. We also spotted a "wanted poster" tacked to the trunk of an oak, but the illustrated visage of the fugitive was not Tom Bell's. Big eyes glared out at us from a tiny head—Othello the ostrich was once more on the lam. "Six feet tall," the description read, "and of passionate disposition. One hundred dollars REWARD!"

Mr. Burnham hooted. "Hell, we could've made a bundle off that bird, and we let him slip right by us."

Mrs. Burnham handed him a glum look. "Maybe we should send out a search party."

"Maybe we should," laughed Mr. Burnham. "We could pay the actors for nigh unto a week off that critter."

Soon, we rolled into Auburn's main "plaza." Every town the Star Troupe has played has had its own look about it. Georgetown is perched on a ridge. Coloma is in a wide, beautiful river valley, open to the sky. But Auburn is in a hollow, as if a giant had laid out the town on two flat hands and then cupped them together, crumpling the place into the creases of his big palms. All streets pour into the plaza, marked by the sign of a huge watch hanging from a jewelry store. Breezes do not stir much down there. The alleys are narrow and the buildings close.

Mr. Leach awaited us down Main Street before a handsome, two-story building. He introduced the Burnhams to the proprietor, Mr. Holmes, who beamed with pride over his new theatre and its appointments and immediately gave the company a tour. The theatre sits on the building's top floor, above a bowling alley and a billiard saloon. An elegant chandelier graces the lobby, which holds another, smaller drinking establishment. The auditorium has fine new seats with backs—no rough benches here—and the mirrors in the dressing rooms are not cracked! All is polished and tasteful and, as Holmes said, "Built of brick, too!"

What the theatre lacks is a good back lot, squeezed as it is down in the center of town. There is barely room to unhitch the wagon, little grass and no trees or water. All the horses must be boarded, and Lem, too, which shall cost me dearly from the stash in my sock. Not that the old boy isn't worth it.

As soon as the company had checked out the hall, Mr. Leach gave the signal, and we rushed into action, loading in *The Iron Chest* and staging a quick parade around town. Then almost everyone disappeared into hotel rooms to catch quick siestas. The thermometer before the Star Bakery read one hundred and three degrees. Perhaps the best medicine for such misery is to snooze through it, but I found my comfort in this journal.

The sun was low when Harry Brown stopped by the wagon for our jaunt to Wells Fargo. We had ambled a short piece down Main when we spied a crowd gathering in the plaza. We hurried over and looked up. A thick rope had been strung from the dry goods store all the way to the roof of the new American Hotel, a three-story brick building. Halfway up the rope, in crimson silk and dainty slippers, balanced a young woman. "Madame Barry," an onlooker whispered to us. "One of Rowe's folks." The crowd stared in silence as Madame Barry placed one small foot before the other, inching her way up the rope. She carried no acrobat's pole, and naught separated her from the plaza but thin air. For a moment, she teetered on one leg, struggling to keep her equilibrium. The crowd broke their silence to gasp, then exhaled as she found her footing. Had she tumbled, she would have lain in the dust like a broken bird. But she did not fall, although, as she rose, she appeared ever more lonely against the sky. When she finally gave a little hop and lighted upon the brick ledge of the hotel, she did so with a confidence that made me wonder if her earlier peril was simply a part of her performance. She turned to her audience, cheering in the plaza below, and curtsied, a delicate queen.

"I wish I was like her," I said to Harry Brown. "Sure and brave."

"Maybe you are, Cinder-Emma. Just don't look down or back. Come along now, or we shall be late for the show."

On our way to Wells Fargo, we passed the *Placer Herald* office. I caught a quick glimpse of Mr. Burnham picking up freshly printed handbills from a woman behind the counter. I felt a twinge of envy toward her, a longing to be back in the world of presses and paper and ink. I lingered just a moment at the door. Mr. Burnham leaned across the counter and whispered the punch line to some joke into the woman's ear. The woman giggled, Mr. Burnham roared, and I realized I had best be moving on. I hurried after Harry.

When we arrived at the express office, Harry's hope for another draft from his father was dashed. But a quick stop at the post office produced a letter full of family news from his sister Georgianna, and he once more brightened. I wished for a letter, too, although I had no hope of one. Evie has no idea where I am, and post is not delivered from beyond the grave, no matter how much a missive from Emmett would have comforted me.

Perhaps I'll write a letter to myself sometime soon and sign his name to it. I could mail it ahead to one of our destinations—or I could save myself the postage and simply deliver it to myself when I am most in need.

Harry and I passed a grocery as we neared the theatre. Neither one of us had eaten supper, and neither of us had much change to spare. I found four bits' worth in my apron pocket, and Harry pulled out thirty-five cents. Between us, we managed a little bread and cheese and a handful of dried peaches, not a bad meal all told. We settled on the edge of the sidewalk and nibbled it down as the sun sank at the far end of Main. "A feast," declared Harry. "A poor man's feast, but a feast nonetheless."

"We could do worse," I said.

"We certainly could," said Harry, as he relished the last dried peach.

When we arrived back at the theatre, we heard the news—the act of Griffith & Moone had been dropped from the bill. They were announced instead as Miss Sophie Griffith, Songbird of the West, and Mr. Sumner Moone, King of the Comic Stage. Sophie sailed through her evening's solos. Mr. Moone didn't have the heart to launch his own act quite yet. He played a duet on his concertina with Mr. Thayer, got himself through *Iron Chest*, and called it a night

Otherwise, the performance was a fine one. As Mrs. Burnham had feared, the house was disappointingly small because of the circus, but the patrons who did show were enthusiastic. The actors gave them their best, even though the elegant little theatre could not shut out the thunder of bowling balls sounding up through the floor during the tenderest moments of *The Iron Chest.*

"I'd have each hour, each minute of thy life a golden holiday," crooned Lady Helen, followed by a rumble from below.

"Sweet, sweet Helen!" murmured Mortimer, underscored by a boom and the crash of pins.

Mr. Thayer was laughing in the wings as Mr. Booth exited. "I didn't know you were doing Lear in the storm, Ted. 'Blow, winds, and crack your cheeks!'"

"Very funny, Gus," replied Mr. Booth, although, offstage, he was on the edge of laughter, too.

Mr. Thayer had to suffer his own share of ribbing between scenes. "I believe the widow La Rue has taken a shine to you, Thayer," said Mr. Burnham. "Must be your good looks."

"Oh, no, it's his money," said Buck Bliss. "And his fine manners. Ready for a family, Gus?"

Mr. Thayer simply rolled his eyes and escaped into his entrance.

After the play, I passed by the women's dressing room. Mrs. La Rue was gently brushing out Louise's hair. They were unusually serene—Louise with her eyes closed, relaxing into the rhythm of the brush strokes, and her mother calmly, tenderly working through the child's gleaming locks.

I thought of my own mother. She was nothing like Mrs. La Rue, with her fears and frown lines. My mother was lighthearted, floating through her life like a dandelion wisp until she missed a beat and perished. But I am sure she must have brushed my hair, too. I can almost remember it—or perhaps I only remember the wish.

I long to sleep. The bowling alley still rumbles, and Buck Bliss snores right under the wagon. There is no breeze off the river to cool the night air, and no matter which way I turn, my sunburned shoulders sting. Strangers wander through this small patch of a lot, headed from one saloon to another. Mr. Burnham just passed through, too, from the direction of the American Hotel to heaven knows where.

Shall I write more of my mother? Perhaps I could finish a Lightfoot Family Obituary if I only knew where to start. I remember my mother wore a silver comb with her Sunday best. But were her eyes blue or green? And her laughter would ring from the kitchen as she worked, but why was the kitchen in my dream silent? She frightened me so by her absence. Had she lost herself as well as her children?

The only one who can really help me remember is Emmett, and Emmett is now a memory.

Well. I shall lie down and try to get some rest, despite Buck's trumpeting below me. Sometimes memories come best between waking and sleeping.

FRIDAY, JULY 11. *We remain in Auburn. It must be about 3:30—*

Auburn roused itself early, trading the din of saloon traffic for the hum of business—doors slammed, shopkeepers called to their neighbors, and a stagecoach pulled from the front of the American Hotel and rattled down Washington Street. I rummaged through my bundle for a clean blouse and combed my hair before I ventured out in search of a newspaper.

The morning *Placer Herald* was just coming off the press. I longed to buy a copy outright, but I knew my change was best spent on breakfast. I bought a roll at the Star Bakery and bided my time. A newspaper passes through many hands in a mining camp, and sometimes it gets lost in the shuffle. I took a few minutes to savor my roll and then went fishing along the plank sidewalks before the hotels and restaurants. I hit pay dirt on a bench by the barbershop. I reeled in an abandoned *Herald*, neatly creased, not a page missing. A little beyond, by the Orleans Hotel, lay another treasure, the *Sacramento Union*. I hurried back to the wagon with my finds.

The *Herald* updated the fires, mostly with news of rebuilding. It cheered me to see Captain Smith listed amongst the optimists, though there was, sadly, no mention of the Red House girls. I sifted on through opinions on the Whig and Temperance parties, and the discovery of mastodon bones down Sonora way, until I found a paragraph headlined "Theatrical," buried on a back page. The critic had attended *The Iron Chest* last night. He complimented Mr. Booth ("a superior actor") and the Star Troupe and wished us well, although his review was but a few lines long and easy to overlook. Emmett would have given the company the front page.

The other paper, the day's *Union*, offered a plentitude of homicides and corruption cases, but page two held an article that stopped my heart. Here it is:

REMARKABLE COINCIDENCE

Edwin Booth played in Placerville immediately before the fire. As he was ascending the hill on the way to Georgetown, fire broke out. In Georgetown, he played one night, and shortly after he left, that town was burnt down. While childish "fairy stars" are the rage in the Mother Lode, we sincerely hope that a "Fiery Star" has not also graced her stages.

Mr. Booth & the Star Troupe are now performing in Auburn. We bid them a safe and successful engagement in that fair city, and pray that Auburn escapes the flames of destruction upon Mr. Booth's departure.

I went in search of the Burnhams. Mr. Burnham was nowhere about, but I did spy Mrs. Burnham in the restaurant of the American Hotel, finishing up her coffee. She was perusing a copy of the *Herald*, opened to our little review, and she looked pleased enough. I hated to break into her moment, but I wove through the tables to her side and set the *Union* down by her plate. "Have you seen this yet, Mrs. Burnham?"

She had not. She read the article and murmured, "This is vile." She glanced up. "Thank you, Miss Lightfoot. I'll take care of it. May I borrow your copy?" She quickly paid her bill. Then, newspapers under her arm and purposeful as Joan of Arc marching on Orleans, she left for the theatre. I stayed close behind.

The theatre lot was deserted except for Mr. Leach. Mrs. Burnham spoke to him in an urgent whisper, and he rushed off into town. She sank onto the theatre steps, her head in her hands and the *Union* at her side, until he returned at last with Mr. Burnham. Then all three of them hurried upstairs into the theatre and shut the door tightly behind them. This time, there were no angry voices filtering down into the lot. I had last night's laundry to do, but I dared not go up into the dressing rooms for it. A few company members appeared—Buck and Jimmy Bliss, then Mr. Thayer and Mr. Moone—only to find the theatre door locked. Mr. Thayer had a copy of the *Union* in his hand. It was over an hour before the door was once more opened. Mr. Burnham descended and stalked off toward the street. Mr. Leach called Buck and Jimmy Bliss up to ready the set for *Taming of the Shrew*, with a tone of business as usual. As I went about gathering the laundry, I caught a glimpse of Mr. Thayer, Mr. Moone and Mrs. Burnham huddled in the shadows at the rear of the auditorium. I could guess the drift of their conversation.

Mr. Booth was the last to arrive at Holmes Hall, a sleepy look on his face. Mr. Leach spied him from the upstairs landing and quickly waved him into the theatre. He emerged five minutes later and, without a word to any of us, disappeared around the corner and down the street.

For the rest of the day, what was *not* said out loud hung over the company, as the sky weighs down heavily before a storm. The *Union* article had stopped short of calling Mr. Booth a firebug but had left the notion dangling boldly in the air. In these days of "incendiarism" and Vigilance Committees, it is a dangerous and a frightening thought. I cannot believe Mr. Booth capable of such horror, but there is a power in the printed word to make the innocent appear guilty and to allow insinuation the ring of truth.

As news of the article spread through the Star Troupe, the actors were stunned. Now and then, a handful engaged in hushed talk that abruptly ceased when anyone else passed by. Mr. Burnham did not hold back. As he and Mr. Leach hung a banner out front announcing the evening as another benefit for fire sufferers, he grumbled, "More damn trouble than he's worth." Then he caught sight of me and dried up. Mr. Moone and Buck Bliss worried in whispers as they shared a smoke, and Sophie confided to me her opinion of the *Union* writer: "Emma dear, it's that hack who should burn, burn in the flames of hell! Poor Ted!" The only one who seemed not a whit rattled was Mr. Thayer, who passed the morning reading a novel in the dressing room. Mr. Booth did not reappear.

By early afternoon, the laundry was done and the costumes for *Shrew* were hanging neatly on their hooks in the dressing rooms. As I tidied up, Louise appeared, right on schedule. Her mother was nursing a headache with her afternoon "lie-down," and the child had slipped her leash. Her treasure tin was tucked under one arm, but she mostly crouched under the stairs, watching the comings and goings of the citizens of an ant hill. She did not acknowledge me. Finally, I called, "Louise?" but she gave me the cold shoulder.

I walked over to her. "Louise, I'm sorry I had to get you in trouble. I was in trouble, too." She ignored me. "Look what I found in the street, over by the bakery," I said. I pulled a tiny bottle from my pocket. "I believe it held perfume. It's kind of fancy. What do you think?"

She finally looked up. I held the bottle to her nose, and she sniffed. "It's sweet," she said, with the glimmer of a smile. "The glass is pretty."

"That color is called 'midnight blue.' It's yours if we can be friends again."

She studied me with those eyes that can look right through you. "All right." The bottle was swiftly squirreled away in the safety of the tin. Then she wandered over to where the Blisses were working on a damaged wheel rim, to sift the dirt for their cast-off nails and bits of metal.

A ruckus sounded in the street before the theatre, and Harry Brown came dashing into the lot. "The rebel has been captured!" he announced with a grin. "Come see!"

We all rushed out to Main Street. Othello had been rounded up by a pair of vaqueros, who were parading him down the dusty boulevard to hoots and cheers. He had two nooses about his long neck, secured to his captors' saddle horns, but he hadn't completely surrendered. He stood tall, in the proud manner of a vanquished warrior king. As the cowboys led him around a bend, one of them was foolish enough to let his nag drift too close to the bird and was rewarded with a ferocious hiss.

By the time we ambled back to the rear of the theatre, the heat was settling in. Harry perched on the stair landing, swinging his long legs over the edge. "I'm sure you saw the *Union*," he said.

"Oh, yes," I replied. "I had a high opinion of that publication until this morning."

He gazed about the lot. "Cinder-Emma, this is a gloomy old place today. There is a curse upon the kingdom. What do you say we journey to the rival realm and see what's up?"

"You wouldn't mean the circus?"

"Of course I do! We'd have to sneak on over there, given the opinions of the management—fraternizing with the enemy and all—but it might just cheer us up."

"I'd love to see the horses," I said.

Buck Bliss rendered the wheel rim a final tap and exclaimed, "So would I!"

"Me, too!" added Jimmy, his voice louder than I'd ever heard it before. "We'll be through here in a blink."

"I've finished with the costumes," I said. "Let's go!"

As the Blisses cleared up, Louise returned to the staircase and huddled underneath, a sorrowful look in her eyes.

"What's the matter, Louise?" asked Harry. "You want to go to the circus, too?"

"Yes, but my mama wouldn't like it."

"She's resting, isn't she?"

"Yes. But she says not to talk to circus people."

"She says not to talk to most people," said Harry.

"She says not to talk to us," added Buck. "Now, how can you be unfriendly to folks who have such beautiful horses?"

"Come on, Louise," said Harry. "We'll only be gone for a little while. We'll get you back here in no time."

Louise smiled, a big, wide smile. "All right!"

The Blisses quickly stowed their tools and wiped their hands. Louise stashed her tin in the wagon, and I pulled off my apron. I confess we took a glance about, to make sure there were no witnesses, as we hastened away from the theatre. We set our course for the "enemy encampment," the circus lot out at the end of Sacramento Street.

We had no trouble spotting the big canvas tent that rose up behind the jumbled buildings of Chinatown. The circus lot was so much finer than the tiny bit of space at the theatre—it held ample room for Rowe's amphitheatre, plus all the circus stock.

No one was about, although we soon came across the circus wagons, parked in a row. Oh, they were lovely! The Star Troupe's wagon is fine enough—it lets people know we're in town—but these wagons were a wonder, just singing out with gilt and bright colors.

Othello's wagon stood at the end of the row. Sure enough, there was the big bird, back behind bars. He looked mournful. "I know how he feels," said Harry. "I was a jailbird, too, you know."

"I wonder what he likes to eat," I said. "A treat might cheer him up."

Harry fished in his pocket and pulled out a peppermint, but Othello would have none of it. He studied us out of a wily eye, decided we weren't worth much, and stalked away.

"What are you doing?" demanded a gruff voice behind us. My heart flip-flopped. We whirled about. A big man in a dark blue coat glared at us. He carried a pistol at his waist. "We don't allow trespassers here," he growled. "If you don't have a pass—and from the looks of you, you don't—you can just skedaddle."

I eyed our little group. Harry was presentable enough, he's generally spruce, but I was decked in my specs and wash clothes. The Bear and the Calf were smeared with axle grease, and Louise, for all her beauty, wore a dusty smock and rag curlers. We were hardly the sorts to possess a pass, but Harry was undaunted.

"We're emissaries from the Star Troupe, sir. Fellow artistes, who have paid you a visit out of admiration for your circus."

The big man scowled. "I don't care if you're President Pierce and his cabinet, you need a pass. Show it or leave!"

"But Mr. Rowe is my cousin," said Harry, all smiles. I stared at him—I couldn't believe what had just come out of his mouth. "On my mother's side," he added. "She was Maybelle Rowe before she married—"

"Leave!" the man shouted.

"But we want to see the horses!" cried La Petite, and she burst into tears. Perhaps they were genuine, perhaps not—she's a good little actress—but they were effective. The big man was suddenly flustered.

"Oh, now, miss, we can't let just anyone wander about—"

Louise wailed louder. Othello hissed. A woman came out of the big tent. "Mr. Gersch, is there a problem?" I recognized her as the slender woman who had ridden Adonis when the circus passed us near Georgetown.

"Just trespassers, Mrs. Rowe. I'll handle it."

Harry jumped right in. "No, ma'am. We're actors. From the Star Troupe."

"Hattie Burnham's company?"

"Yes, ma'am. We merely hoped to look. You see, we love the circus. Right?"

And the rest of us nodded, except for Louise, who sniffed as one exquisite tear rolled down her cheek.

"And who is this?' asked Mrs. Rowe. She stooped to Louise's level, wiped away the tear, and studied the child's face. "Why, I know you. You are a lovely singer. I saw you once in Sacramento. What's your name again, dear?"

"Louise," the child replied, giving new meaning to the word pathetic. "Please, may we see the horses?"

"Absolutely. I'll show you around myself." Mrs. Rowe offered her hand, and Louise grasped it. "Mr. Gersch, we'll be fine. Thank you."

Gersch grunted. "Do you have a cousin named Maybelle?"

"Perhaps," said Mrs. Rowe, in a silvery voice. "I'll have to check with my husband."

The big man slunk away, a chastised mastiff.

"I'm sorry about our policeman," said Mrs. Rowe. "He's new and a little taken with himself. Have you met Othello?"

"We certainly have," said Harry. "We were wondering what might whet his appetite."

"I'll show you! Jake!" she called, and a boy of about ten appeared from the tent. "This is Othello's special friend, Jake Barry. Jake, do you have a treat about you?"

Jake smiled and reached into his pocket. He held out what looked like dried corn. The bird hurried over and ate right out of the boy's hand.

"Can I feed him, too?" wondered Louise, and in a trice, with Jake's guidance, she had the ferocious Othello eating out of her palm. The bird looked almost happy. The child beamed.

We all introduced ourselves to Mrs. Rowe, not as her shirttail cousins but as our own selves. When Mrs. Rowe heard that I was a "wardrobe mistress," she led us back to the wagon before Othello's. "Take a look in here," she said, and opened the wagon door as one might lift the lid of a treasure chest. I cannot tell you what shone more brightly, the sunlight pouring down outside the wagon, or the costumes hanging within. The silks and velvets and woolen band jackets blazed with a rainbow of colors, and their spangles and jewels sparkled and shimmered. Feathered hats lined the shelves, and shiny boots and delicate slippers stood in their places along the wagon floor.

"May I touch?" I said, hardly daring to ask.

"Of course," said Mrs. Rowe. And I reached out for a moment to the rich fabric of a skirt decked with "diamonds."

"Thank you," I smiled, keeping Louise in sight out of the corner of my eye. The vision of all those sparkles had the child's mouth hanging open, but, for once, she seemed happy to keep her small hands empty.

"Shall we move on to the horses, then?" asked Mrs. Rowe.

"Oh, yes, ma'am!" said Jimmy Bliss.

"Adonis and a couple of the others are rehearsing in the ring, but most of them are out in back." Mrs. Rowe walked us around the tent to a big field, where the horses were picketed in the shade of a few oaks. She led us from one to the other of her favorites, all beautiful with their glossy coats. Jimmy Bliss said more in those few minutes than I'd heard from him on the whole tour.

"This is an Arab, isn't it ma'am? Isn't that color grey special to the breed? Look at that neck, Buck! I hear these horses are strong and smooth, but I don't know if they can match our fox trotters. Back in Missouri, that's what we raise, ma'am, fox trotters, and they are fine horseflesh!" and so on. I glanced over at Harry, and he was as amused as I was to see Jimmy so delighted. We might have stayed with those horses all afternoon if Jimmy'd had his way, but Mrs. Rowe finally invited us into the tent.

"Colonel Rowe is just finishing up the Indian Chieftain routine. I don't suppose he'd mind if you watch."

We slipped into the tent. The ring was surrounded by hundreds of seats. Red and white hangings lent an air of elegance. As we watched, the band kept up a tom-tom beat. Mr. Rowe jumped on and off his steed, Adonis, as he loped about the ring, man and animal in perfect rhythm. Then he stood on the horse's back, leapt into the air in a backwards flip, and landed gracefully right where he'd begun. He circled about and dismounted. Adonis gave us a graceful bow, his front leg extended. Mr. Rowe lay on the ground before the horse, took a piece of bread from his pocket, and placed it between his teeth. Adonis bent down, delicately lifted the bread into his own mouth, and whinnied his thanks. Rowe sprang to his feet.

"Joe," called Mrs. Rowe, "we have guests. From the Star Troupe!" Mr. Rowe hastened over, smiling. He is a handsome man, with his blue eyes and trim beard, not big in stature but strong and agile. "Delightful!" he exclaimed. "Welcome!"

Mr. Rowe led Adonis to meet us. The horse had a bright, almost human intelligence, his ears pricking up at our every word. Mr. Rowe smiled down at Louise. "How old are you, child?"

"Seven."

Rowe turned to the horse. "I'm afraid I didn't quite catch that, Adonis. How old is that little girl?"

Adonis proceeded to tap out Louise's age with his hoof. She stared in delight—she was the happiest I have ever seen her.

I expect Jimmy Bliss wanted Adonis to tell his age, too—but he was too shy to ask, and he knew he'd take a ribbing later.

We thanked the Rowes with all our hearts and hurried on back toward the theatre. We'd been gone much more than a "little while." As we passed by the circus wagons, I spied a woman doing laundry, her hair falling loose across her face. It took me a second to realize that the washerwoman, in her faded calico, was Madame Barry, who could defy gravity like a beautiful silken bird.

I fell in beside Jimmy Bliss. "So, Jimmy, you're from Missouri?" I said.

But Jimmy's shyness had returned, and all I got back was "Yep."

"Do you miss it?"

He met my gaze. "Every day. I wish I was home."

I nodded. "I long for home sometimes, too. Is your family still there, then?"

"Except for my uncle and Buck. My brothers are on the farm, and my pa and ma—oh, I can't even say how much I miss my mother."

"He's a mama's boy, Miss Lightfoot," joked Buck, and he gave Jimmy a little shove.

"So what?" said Jimmy, shoving him back.

"We came out last year to help our uncle get his herd started down Stockton way. Then he caught this 'theatre bug.'" Buck pronounced it "thee-*ay*-ter."

"Mr. Leach has a ranch, then?"

"Yup. A big one," declared Buck. "And some fine horses. The team is his. The wagon, too, and the company's mounts. He's only renting them to the Star Troupe." This was news.

"Jimmy," I said, "You must be having some fun in California. You liked the circus."

Jimmy tried to smile. "I guess so. But I sure as hell wish I was in Missouri."

We'd made it back as far as the Empire Stable, a few doors down from the theatre, when we heard, "Louise! Looo-eeeze!!" Mrs. La Rue was up and about, and we were in trouble.

"I'll scout a bit," said Harry. "Wait right here. Don't you worry, Louise." He sneaked on ahead to see what was what.

Louise gripped my hand. Harry was back in minutes. "Your mama's out in the back lot, Louise. So we'll just surprise her. You come with Miss Lightfoot and me. Mr. Bliss the elder and Mr. Bliss the younger will slip in behind the theatre, if they don't mind, and distract your mama with a little quick conversation."

Buck grinned. "I believe we can oblige."

So, the Blisses returned to the theatre by the same route we'd left it, cutting through the back lots. Harry, Louise and I hustled over to the front of the theatre and up the main staircase. We ducked in, dusted most of the dirt off Louise's pinafore, and made our appearance through the stage door at the top of the rear stairs. Mrs. La Rue was below us, by the wagon, grilling the Blisses. "You're sure you haven't seen her?"

Buck shook his fuzzy head. "Oh, no, ma'am, not lately, have we Jimmy?"

"Here she is, Mrs. La Rue," called Harry, cheerful as a cricket. "Right here."

Mrs. La Rue peered up at us. "Louise, I've been calling and calling. You were supposed to stay in the hotel."

"Oh, she was with us," Harry said. "Playing in the lobby, keeping cool. She stayed nice and clean, too." He smiled sweetly. So did Louise.

Mrs. La Rue's lips tightened, then she uttered a terse, "Thank you. Louise, come on down. We need supper."

Louise skipped down the stairs.

I turned to Harry. "You are such a liar, Harry," I whispered. "And who the heck is *Maybelle* Rowe?" His laughter rang through the back lot.

Friday night, after the show—

As the afternoon shifted to dusk, the company readied for the play. Word was that the evening's performance was selling well enough, but the mood backstage was edgy. By seven-thirty, all the company was accounted for except Mr. Booth. I was in the women's dressing room, plaiting ribbons into Sophie's hair, when Mrs. La Rue started in on Mr. Booth's character. "He's moody and unreliable. How do we know what he might do?"

"Ted Booth is one of the kindest people on earth," said Sophie.

"He's full of secrets," Mrs. La Rue went on. "His father was insane, and half the time, he is, too. He's put us all in danger—"

Her talk riled me so, I almost jumped in, but Sophie saved me the trouble. "Oh, shut up, Clarissa! You are ignorant and tiresome, and I don't want to hear another word!"

Mrs. La Rue's jaw dropped. We were spared her retort by Mrs. Burnham's arrival—Mrs. La Rue and Sophie glared at each other but put a lid on it for the time being. Mrs. Burnham sank into her chair and stared at her mirror, until Mr. Leach popped in about ten minutes before the curtain. "Is he here?" she asked.

"No," replied Mr. Leach. "I can go on for him, if you like. I'd have to carry the script, though."

"Of course. Thank you, Jeriah. Can you fit into his costume?"

Mr. Leach took a quick look down at his round belly. "I'll try."

"Tell Ben to make the announcement."

Mr. Leach nodded grimly, and headed down the hall. Mrs. Burnham leaned forward, eyes closed, and rubbed her brow.

"Hattie?" The voice was low, seasoned with a drawl. Mrs. Burnham spun around in her chair. Mr. Booth stood in the doorway. "I can't be the star of a sideshow."

"Ladies, would you leave us, please?" said Mrs. Burnham.

"No, they should hear this. It's the whole troupe's business. I'd rather they stay."

Mrs. La Rue rose, aimed a disapproving look at Mr. Booth, and walked out anyway. From her footsteps, I'd lay money that she stopped just around the corner, well within earshot.

Sophie played with her powder puff, and I kept right on straightening costumes.

"Are you going on tonight?" Mrs. Burnham asked.

Mr. Booth shrugged. "I can't believe it'd do the company any good to have a firebug front and center. It's a little risky, wouldn't you say?"

"No. What's risky is to give in to that kind of trash. It's lies, and we should not dignify it by letting it scare us."

"It scares me."

"Well, me, too. But we should do what we always do, put on a damn good show. This town likes us, and tonight is almost sold out—"

"Maybe they're just out there to see another crazy Booth."

"Ted." Mrs. Burnham reached for his hand. He sank into the chair next to hers. "I admit that article had me in knots this morning and ready to run. And I admit I've been out around town all day, trying to get a feel for which way the wind blows. But all I've heard on the street is good news—not a word about the *Union* piece. Maybe the people in this town have too much to do to waste their time on garbage like that. Maybe the stink of it will stay down in Sacramento."

"Jeriah says the mayor is out front, Ted," said Sophie. "And Mr. Holmes has his whole family in the front row. He wouldn't bring all those little Holmeses if he was worried, would he?"

"Ted, Jeriah is ready to go on for you," said Mrs. Burnham. "God knows how he'll squeeze into that costume, but he'll play Petruchio if you can't. I can't force you—"

Mr. Booth stared at the floor. His hands began to shake the tiniest bit, and he gripped the edge of the chair to steady them.

"Still, I doubt that that audience is out there to see another crazy Booth."

Mr. Booth looked Mrs. Burnham straight in the eye. "What about you, Hattie? Do you doubt me? Suspect I might have a taste for smoke and flame?"

Mrs. Burnham met his gaze. "No. No, I do not. You are a pain in the ass, and you drink too damn much. But I do not doubt you."

"Thank you," said Mr. Booth, and then, "I do not doubt you, either."

For a moment, they sat in silence. Then Mr. Booth sighed. "All right. I shall relieve Leach from duty, while my costume still has seams."

Mrs. Burnham put her arms around him. "We'll get past this, Ted. Do a good show tonight. Stay dry. Tomorrow we'll move on to Nevada. We have plenty of friends there, and we'll make up for all this trouble."

Mr. Booth nodded. Then he whispered into Mrs. Burnham's ear, "Got a match?"

She pushed him away. "What the hell—"

"I need a quick smoke before the show," he grinned.

For a second, I thought she was going to knock him upside the head.

Instead, she kissed him on the brow. "Crazy Booth," she whispered right back.

In a blink, word was out that Mr. Booth was hurrying into costume. Just before the curtain rose, Mrs. Burnham gathered us all backstage for a little stump speech. "Whatever we have encountered offstage," she said, "onstage you have proven yourselves to be true ladies and gentlemen of the theatrical profession. Let's give our audience the best blessed show we can. Break legs, all of you!" Her words, stirring as they were, could not put Griffith and Moone back on the same bill, or sweeten Mrs. La Rue's bitterness, but in some small way, they did give most of us heart, and the cast launched into *Taming of the Shrew* with gusto.

The house was full, and the thunder of bowling balls was drowned out by laughter at the antics of Katherine and her suitor. However troubled they may have been before the curtain rose, Mr. Booth and Mrs. Burnham were never more humorous (or more passionate!) than on this night. They delighted in tickling the funny bones of the audience—even the little Holmeses giggled away in the front row—and they delighted in each other.

Petruchio brought his bride home to his ramshackle house filled with bumbling servants, and he proceeded to tan their hides and deny the starving Kate her dinner. He hollered for "The cook! The cook!" Mr. Burnham, in a greasy apron, edged onstage, knowing he was about to catch holy hell from his master. But before he could open his mouth, a shot exploded in the auditorium, whizzed across the stage, and tore into one of Mr. Holmes's lovely new backdrops. All eyes went to Mr. Booth, who froze in the footlights for only an instant before he pushed Mrs. Burnham to the floor and threw himself over her as a shield. A second shot whistled above their heads. Mr. Burnham staggered to his knees, blood pouring from his scalp, as the shooter hollered, "That's for my wife, you son-of-a-bitch!"

Screams erupted from the audience. Mr. Leach dashed out on the stage, rifle in hand, but the citizens of Auburn beat him to the punch. Three men threw the miscreant to the floor, pounded him, and seized his gun. Then they hustled him out of the building and up Court Street to the jail.

Sophie and Mr. Moone helped Mr. Burnham to his feet, the front of Sophie's costume dyed bright red from Burnham's wound. Mrs. Burnham and Mr. Booth lay for a moment, dazed, in the center of the stage, until Buck Bliss rushed out and hurried them off into the wings. Mrs. Burnham was shaking; Mr. Booth put a gentle arm about her shoulders. Mr. Burnham sank onto Mr. Leach's stool in the corner, as Sophie folded his cook's apron and held it to his head. "Hattie?" he called, but Mrs. Burnham turned her back to him and leaned against Mr. Booth's chest. Mr. Burnham delivered Mr. Booth an evil glance, then winced as Sophie shifted the blood-soaked apron.

As the shooter was dragged out of the theatre, Mr. Leach had tried to calm the audience—"Please, please, it's all over!"—to little avail. The small Holmeses went on shrieking, and some of the women were crying. Mr. Thayer came to the rescue. He strode calmly onto the stage. He has a voice that can wake the dead when he chooses to "project" it. "Ladies and gents," he boomed, "the brave citizens of Auburn have prevailed! What we need to conclude this evening on a happy note is a good guard dog!" He whistled, long and loud. "Ulysses!"

Ulysses ambled out from the wings, his tongue lolling and a big dog grin on his face.

"Ulysses, this is serious business. Sit!"

Ulysses did.

"Salute!"

The dog raised a paw to his nose.

Mr. Thayer seized a property sausage from Petruchio's table and set it down on the stage. "Witness that sausage, Ulysses, and point!"

Ulysses eyed the sausage and did indeed point, absolutely still and unblinking. The Holmes brood stopped their cries, and a few of the other patrons sank back into their seats.

"Now, Ulysses," said Mr. Thayer, "Show these folks just how ruthless you can be. One, two, three—ATTACK!"

Ulysses flopped over "dead," his favorite trick, all four feet in the air. Laughter bubbled through the audience as Mr. Thayer tried desperately to revive the "guard dog," lifting first his front end, then his haunches, only to have Ulysses sink to the floor in the most comical tangles. Almost everyone in the audience smiled, then laughed outright, and chose to stay for the rest of show.

Backstage, no one was smiling. Mr. Burnham's head wound kept bleeding. He lay down on the men's dressing room floor, and Buck Bliss ran for a doctor. Sophie noticed her stained costume, squealed, and rushed to change. Mr. Booth led Mrs. Burnham to the women's dressing room to compose herself, but he looked as shaken as she did. "I thought that bullet had my name on it," he said to her. "I truly did." The rest of us stood in disbelief, except for Mr. Leach, who leaned his rifle against the wall and gazed from the wings as Mr. Thayer and Ulysses persisted out in the footlights. Then he went in search of Mrs. Burnham.

"Ben's through for the evening, Hattie. But Gus is covering out front. What do you want to do?"

Just then, peals of laughter could be heard backstage.

"Are most of them still out there?" Mrs. Burnham asked.

"I believe so."

"Can you finish the show, Ted?"

Mr. Booth looked plain terrified, but he nodded. "We could pick it up right after Ben's exit."

"Then that's what we'll do," said Mrs. Burnham. "Is everyone else all right, Jeriah?"

"More or less."

"Then make the announcement. Give us five minutes to get our hearts back into our chests, and we'll go." She squeezed Mr. Booth's hand. She never did look in on Mr. Burnham.

There's an old adage, "The show must go on," and this night, I witnessed the phrase in its true meaning. Mr. Leach made the announcement just as some of the evening's heroes returned from the jail. He brought them up onto the stage—Walsh the shoemaker, Howard the gunsmith, and the burly Sullivan, proprietor of the Miner's Emporium. They took their bows to thunderous applause, and assured everyone that the lunatic, Bristow—until this evening the *Herald*'s printer—was safely cooling his heels behind bars. Then the curtain dropped and quickly rose again on the actors, framed where they had stood when the shots blew through the theatre—minus Mr. Burnham, of course, and Louise. The child was excused from her small role as Pedro, the page, and whisked off to the safety of their hotel by her distraught mother. I half-expected the rest of the performance to be somber, but the actors carried on in as merry a fashion as they had before, and the audience—perhaps because both the actors and the patrons had all been brave together—applauded them for it.

I confess my heart is still beating in my ears. From the wings, as the first shot boomed, and Mr. Booth fell with Mrs. Burnham to the floor, I thought they had been stricken. I remember hearing my scream rise from my throat, as if I were standing outside myself. I wanted to rush to their aid, but my legs were shaking. By the time I forced my feet to move, Buck Bliss was already at their sides. It is one thing to have courage in one's heart, and another to act upon it. When it comes to action, I suspect I have failed.

SATURDAY, JULY 12, *the city of Nevada, evening. A travel day. No play until Monday—*

It was nigh unto midnight last night when I finished writing, but once again, I could not sleep for the rumble of bowling balls and the noise of the traffic still on the streets.

The company had packed up after the play and swiftly slipped away. Mr. Booth was so uneasy that he did not even stow his champagne basket before leaving—Mr. Leach saw to it for him. As he hurried away, I called, "Goodnight, Mr. Booth. I'm glad you're all right. Take care."

He slowed just enough to reply, "Thank you, Miss Lightfoot. You be careful, too, now." Then he was gone.

The doctor and Mr. Thayer helped Mr. Burnham to his hotel—it seemed he would live, at least. Sophie and Mr. Moone took off in opposite directions. Even the Bliss brothers disappeared, and for the first time, I was left in the wagon with no one at hand. It had always been comforting to know that Buck and Jimmy were curled up in their blankets nearby. Now, with all the late-night traffic through the theatre lot, I did not feel much more safe than Mr. Booth did. I managed to doze for a little piece, only to be startled awake by a rough voice shouting, "Eli? Eli! Where the hell are you? Get out here before I kill you!" A drunken face poked into the wagon. "Eli, you dog! Dammit!" I froze under my blanket, hoping that the man was too inebriated to climb on in. He was, for he shortly wandered off, cursing and staggering.

I could not sleep in the wagon. But where to go? Even if there was a vacant hotel room somewhere, I hadn't the cash for it. And I had no friends with homes I could flee to, as I might have found in Placerville. I threw on my skirt and blouse and grabbed my blanket. There was still enough moon to see my way across the lot and over to the American Hotel.

I had spied the hotel's back stairs earlier in the day on our jaunt to the circus. I made my way up to the second floor entrance but found it locked. The third floor was no better. I tucked my blanket into a corner of the landing, descended, and made my way around to the front and into the lobby. The night clerk leaned across the desk, drowsy face resting on his hand. "Good evening, sir," I said. "I am the chief wardrobe mistress for the Star Troupe, in residence at Holmes Hall. I have an important message for Miss Sophie Griffith from her mother—a family emergency, I believe. Do you have a room number for the lady, please?"

I smiled. I must have looked harmless, for he replied, "Room 306. There's a bunch of them actors up that way," and pointed a weary thumb toward the staircase.

"Thank you," I said, and hurried on up before he could change his mind. Harry Brown would have been proud of me. When I reached the third floor, I made my way through the long hall to the back door and unlatched it. I fished the outside landing for my blanket and hauled it in. Then I looked quickly about.

The hotel was a new establishment, with flowered carpet on the floor and oil lamps in brass sconces. The hallway ran from front to back, lined on each side by half a dozen rooms. At the front end was the stairway to the lobby. In the rear, near the back door, stood a tall chifforobe. Between one side of the chifforobe and the wall was a space just big enough for me. The lamp by the lobby stairs would cast little light at this end of the hall. The lamp by the back door was already sputtering low—I lifted the shade and blew out the flame. Wrapped in my blanket, I scrunched down into the dark corner and disappeared into my dreams.

I was wakened by the click of a key turning in a lock. In the dimness, I made out the figure of a woman in a purple dress, and I smelled gardenia perfume. She dropped the key into her reticule and headed for the lobby. As she passed the remaining lamp and descended the stairs, I could see that it was Sophie, dressed to the nines, the evening's paint and powder still daubed upon her cheeks. She disappeared, and I refrained from speculating on her destination in favor of getting back to sleep.

This was no mean task. The more weary I got, the more awake I became, and the more I heard the noises of the building and voices floating through the dark hallway like the echoes of ghosts. However sturdy the brick shell of the hotel might be, the walls within were thin planks. And the fancy transoms over the doors, because of the heat, were wide open, broadcasting the occupants' secrets to the world.

With my eyes closed, I tried to sort out who was whom. At the far end of the hall, I thought I could hear the Burnhams—her alto and his rough edge—but I could not make out any of their words. Mr. Booth's deep notes resonated from the room just past Sophie's. I caught bits and pieces—"resolve itself into a dew" and "hawk from a handsaw." Was he rehearsing Hamlet again? I jumped when the "madman's" voice suddenly broke through, wailing "O horrible! O, horrible! Most horrible!" in tortured tones.

A man's footsteps echoed on the stairs, and Mr. Booth abruptly ceased. Mr. Moone appeared at the end of the hall. Perhaps he had been drinking, for he wavered as he passed Mr. Booth's door and paused by Room 306, the room Sophie had just departed. I squinched up in the darkness, blanket to my nose. Mr. Moone held a fistful of flowers. Where he'd come up with flowers this time of night I couldn't imagine, except that a few of Auburn's residents might find their gardens bare in the morning.

He knocked gently on the door. "Sophie? Darlin'? Are you awake?" He knocked again. "Sophie? Please open up. If there's something I can do to make this better, tell me, I'll do it. Sophie? Sophie??" He looked up toward the transom and pleaded, more loudly, "Sophie, speak to me." Then right before the door, on the fancy carpet, he tapped out a little comic dance and crooned, as he might when clowning with his concertina, "Heigh! Nellie, Ho! Nellie, listen, love to me!" The only reply was the echo of his own sweet tenor hanging in the hall. He leaned against Sophie's door and dropped his head. I thought he might sink right to the floor, but then, softly, almost to himself, he declared, "'Let me not to the marriage of true minds admit impediments. Love is not love which alters when it alteration finds—'" and he went on to recite the whole, lovely poem. I am used to seeing Mr. Moone play the fool, but now he played the lover, and a fine, handsome one, too, even if he is short. I yearned to shout, "Save yourself the trouble! She's long gone!" but I couldn't bear to embarrass him so. He whispered once more, "Sophie?" There was no response, save a snore rumbling from somewhere down the hall. Mr. Moone propped the flowers at the foot of Sophie's door and slowly made his way down the stairs.

I heard Mr. Burnham mutter, "Idiot."

A few minutes later, Mr. Booth resumed his rehearsal, but he soon departed from anything that resembled text. He spoke in hushed tones in his own voice, broken and melancholy, as if he conversed with a shadow. I wished I could somehow touch his hand, soothe whatever vexed his spirit. I began to write my own speech in my head, "Mr. Booth, I believe in you. You have a tender heart. A person who creates such beauty on the stage could do no harm," and so on. But, of course, I wouldn't have dared to knock on his door wrapped in a blanket and recite to him in the middle of the night.

I didn't get the chance to anyway, for the Burnhams' door flew open, and Mr. Burnham shouted, "Shut the hell up!"

Mrs. Burnham tried to pull him back into the room. "Get in here, Ben. You'll wake everyone up!"

"And he won't?"

"He's working. Or trying to."

"He's babbling. He's a freaking lunatic."

"Get in here!"

The door slammed, but Mr. Burnham stomped about the room.

"Lie down, Ben. The doctor said to stay off your feet."

"I need a whiskey."

"Get in bed. Here."

The mattress ropes groaned as Burnham lowered himself. He groaned, too. "Oh, Jesus. I've got hot coals in my skull."

"I hope it was worth it."

"I didn't think you cared, Hattie."

"You could have been killed. Or gotten me killed. Or Ted. If he hadn't pushed me—"

"Shut up! Shut up!"

Mrs. Burnham sighed. "I don't know why I even bother."

"Then cut me loose and take up with Romeo over there. He's such a goddamn hero! You're all over him most of the time anyway."

"I shouldn't even dignify that. We act together. It's work, and I have never—"

"You were mighty cozy tonight—"

"You should talk. How many women have there been since Sacramento?"

Mr. Burnham started for the door. "The hell with this. I'm going out."

"Fine. Kill yourself. And make sure tonight's tramp is cheaper and easier than the last one. We can't pay a company and fancy whores at the same time!"

I heard a fierce blow, and Mrs. Burnham gasped. Then, low and steady, she declared, "I should have shot you myself."

There was the sound of a second blow, and Mr. Burnham stalked out of the room. His head was bandaged, and, as he passed by the oil lamp, a red stain glowed against the muslin. He staggered down the stairs like a wounded grizzly, growling curses.

For a moment, the hallway was silent, then perhaps—I could not be sure—a soft weeping floated from the Burnhams' room. Mr. Booth paced a few steps, then cracked his door. "Hattie?" There was no answer, not even a whisper of tears. He closed the door, and all was quiet.

Presently, the Burnhams' door eased open, and Mrs. Burnham slipped into the hall. She was barefoot, her hair loose, in her nightgown. She padded soundlessly across the carpet to Mr. Booth's door and listened. Then she raised her hand as if to knock.

She never touched the door. She simply stood there, fist in the air, for an eternity. At last, she turned, and, a ghost in her white gown, disappeared back into her room. The lock clicked behind her.

I huddled in my corner, debating which was worse—losing sleep here, or taking my chances in the wagon. I was too worn to even make the choice. I leaned my head back against the wall, shifted to ease my sunburn, and closed my eyes.

Humming wafted up the stairwell. Harry Brown turned into the hall and headed my way. He stopped at the room closest to my hiding place. As he dug into his pocket for his key, his toes were within inches of mine. I froze and tried not to breathe, but I was no match for Harry's eagle eye. He turned the key in the lock, then stopped and stared my way. "Who's there?" he whispered. He smelled faintly of beer. "Hey."

The jig was up. "Oh, Harry, it's me. It's Emma Lightfoot."

"What are you doing stuffed in a corner?"

"Trying to sleep."

"Here. Come on." He held out his hand and helped me up. "Wouldn't it be easier to get a room?"

"You know I can't afford it, Harry. It was either a room for me or a stall for Lem."

"And you favored the mule."

"I hardly had a choice. I can't hide Lem in a hallway."

"No." He grinned and pushed my hair up out of my eyes. "I tell you what. Share my room."

"Harry—"

"It's a perfectly chaste invitation. I'll sleep in the chair."

"I can't ask you to do that."

"I can't leave you tossed in the corner like a pile of laundry. The bed's soft. There's a feather pillow—"

I so wanted to say, "Yes!" but I hesitated. He glanced over at Room 306.

"Eureka! I have it!" He tried the knob.

"It's locked, Harry."

"What a shame. A good room going to waste." He gazed up. "You're a mere slip of a girl, Cinder-Emma. You should fit through that transom like a minnow through a sieve." He laced his fingers. "Put your foot right here."

"Harry, that's Sophie's room."

"Exactly."

"Suppose she comes back?"

"I doubt it. I saw her ten minutes ago, giggling on the arm of one of the local heroes. Her night is just beginning. And even if she did show, you'd figure out something. Come on, I can't play footstool forever."

"Oh, all right." I planted one foot on his palms and the other on the knob, and I hauled myself up until I was hanging halfway over the frame of the transom. Then the fullness of my skirt jammed in the opening like a cork in a bottle, and there I stuck, my front end in and my back end out. "I'm caught!" I gasped. I wiggled and tried to get some traction on the door, to no avail. I heard Harry snort, and then I began to laugh.

"Shall I call the authorities?" he said.

"Don't you dare!"

"Charming view, Miss Lightfoot."

"Then don't look!"

"Then don't kick me! Here, use my shoulder." He backed up against the door, grasped my foot, and placed it where I could get a little leverage. It was enough to help me squeeze one leg up and through the transom opening, then plant my foot on the inside knob. I eased the rest of myself on over.

"Are you all right?" asked Harry.

"I'm hanging here like a bat, but I'm in." I tried to reach my toe to the chest of drawers, in vain. "I fear I shall have to jump." I let loose the transom frame and dropped to the floor. It couldn't have been more than a couple of feet, but, in the night, the thud carried like thunder.

Mr. Booth's drowsy voice called out, "Are you in trouble out there?"

Harry chuckled. "Oh, no, Ted. Everything's absolutely fine. Go back to sleep." Then he whispered at 306's door, "Open up, Emma."

I undid the latch. He handed me my blanket, and then, with a flourish, Sophie's flowers. "Special delivery! Now don't worry, I'll wake you early. Sweet dreams, Miss Lightfoot. I could say goodnight until it be morrow."

"If it's all the same to you, Mr. Brown, I'd rather get some shuteye." He laughed. "But I do thank you. Goodnight!"

I closed the door and looked about. Even in the dark, the room was heaven, especially the BED! How long had it been since I'd slept in a real bed? I don't even remember my head hitting the lovely feather pillow.

Evie and I were laughing on her mother's quilt as we passed the cat's cradle string from her hands to mine—only we were in her loft room on her parents' farm, not in any Red House crib. Sparky lay beside us, happily panting, as if he was laughing, too. Suddenly Evie stopped, her brown eyes dead serious. "Don't worry, Emma," she said. "I'm all right." Before I could weep, there was a knock at the door. "Don't answer it," I said. "It's only some old miner."

But the knocking went on, louder and louder. "Calling Miss Lightfoot!"

I opened my eyes and frowned. Evie had evaporated, and morning was upon me. I was loathe to move a muscle. The comfort of those American Hotel sheets held me like quicksand. "Harry Brown, is that you?"

"Open up, Sleeping Beauty!"

I dragged myself from the bed. Since I was still in yesterday's clothes, I had no need for modesty. I unlocked the door. "Come on in."

He took one look and laughed.

"Oh, I know, I'm a sight," I grumbled.

"You look like you slept in that outfit, young lady."

True. I was wrinkled from collar to hem. "I should take a flatiron to myself. But I won't. I don't care. The bed was blissful."

"I take it there was no sign of our soubrette."

"Sophie? No. It makes me sad for Mr. Moone."

"We're all wincing for Sumner Moone this morning," Harry said. "Here." He pulled a hotel napkin from his pocket. "Room Service."

The napkin was wrapped about warm bread and butter.

"Oh, Harry, you are a hero."

He almost blushed. "I try. We need to hurry, though. The management is urging a speedy departure." He winked and headed for his own room. "See you down below!"

I devoured the bread and butter, tucked my blanket under my arm, and hustled out the back door of the hotel and over to the livery stable. Lem snorted to see me and pushed his big head against my shoulder. He seemed as happy with his comfy quarters as I'd been with mine. I paid the stablehand and splurged on a small bag of oats for the road. Then I mounted up and trotted Lem over to the theatre.

For once, almost everyone was on time. The team was hitched to the wagon, and the Blisses and Mr. Leach were loading the last of the champagne baskets. Mr. Booth squinted into the morning sun like a critter hauled out of his den, but at least he was present, mounted on his pinto. Mrs. Burnham hurried about, saying her goodbyes to Mr. Holmes and making sure naught was left behind. By the light of day, I made out an ugly bruise on her cheek that powder could diminish but not disguise. Mr. Thayer spotted it, too. He said nothing, but his eyes, usually so kind, filled with fury.

Mr. Burnham appeared after settling with the hotel. His bandage was mostly hidden under his hat, and his demeanor was downright pleasant. But when he put an arm around Mrs. Burnham's shoulder, she tossed it off as if his touch had been a brand and shot him the scowl Medea aimed at Jason before she incinerated his new bride.

We took our leave and wound through Auburn's streets toward the main road. We made only one stop, at the Miner's Emporium, where Sophie stood waiting on the wooden walk. Her purple silk was crumpled, and her powder smeared. No one believed she'd risen early to purchase a pickaxe. I tried not to glance at Mr. Moone, but I couldn't help myself. He bore the countenance of a doomed man. Without a word, Sophie unfastened the reins of her little sorrel from the rear of the wagon, balanced herself on her sidesaddle, and took her place in our caravan.

These small scenes put a damper on my heart and conjured thoughts of a tiny soul called Wing. When I was seven, I found a baby jaybird wiggling in the dirt under a tree. I scooped him up before a coyote could and rushed him home. Emmett looked him over. "He's a scrawny little thing, Emma. His eyes aren't even open, and he's hardly got pinfeathers. Did you see a nest? We could put him back."

"No."

"How about a mama or a papa jay? They might miss their baby."

"Nope. He was all by himself. Nobody cared about him. Can I keep him? Please? His name is Wing."

Emmett hesitated. He liked to see wild creatures wild. But he said, "All right." Then, he went to the shed and fashioned a little box lined with shavings and a soft rag. "You have to keep him warm, Emma, until those feathers sprout." He showed me how to moisten bread, put a dab on the end of a butter knife, and tap Wing's beak until he gaped wide and swallowed.

I tended that baby day and night. When his eyes opened, they lit on me. When he heard me coming, he'd chirp and flap. He grew and started to look like a real bird. But one morning I went to him with his softened bread, and he didn't stir. He had died, curled up as if asleep in his rag nest. Emmett made a lid for his box, and we buried him under the tree where I'd found him.

And then I wept until my eyelids swelled and my throat ached. Emmett gathered me on his lap and put his arms around me. His voice was gentle. "I am so sorry, Emma. Sometimes life doesn't have happy endings."

The theatre delivers happy endings—or at least, some kind of finish to things. Katherine and Petruchio live gleefully ever after. Mortimer is revealed as a murderer, but his wrongs are finally put to right. Next to the world of the theatre, life is plain old messy. Its plots go aimlessly awry. Baby birds die. Emmett cheerfully pens an editorial one day and perishes from a septic splinter the next.

Last night, after Kate and Petruchio found wedded bliss in Holmes Hall, I witnessed a real life play, set in the long hallway of the American Hotel. But my heroes—the actors—pulled off no happy endings.

I would expect the stories that unfolded to belong to mere mortals in the gold camps, where shabbiness and sorrow are all about. But for the actors, who create such beauty and courage on the stage, I wish lives that match their art. I can't help wanting to believe that they can do better than the rest of us. Mr. Booth deserves joy; Mrs. Burnham love and her Henry; Mr. Moone to have Sophie throw open the door to Room 306 and fly into his arms.

In my head, I know the truth of Emmett's words to me as I wept for Wing. But my heart is still a holdout, hoping for happy endings.

Later. Perhaps 10 p.m. or so—

After we gathered up Sophie at the Miner's Emporium, we started once more for the Nevada Road. A coolness lingered in the air. The sky was pale and pure of smoke, and morning light gilded the leaves of the oaks bordering the trail. The Nevada Road is a more gentle, pleasant one than what we have seen—the hills are rounded and golden, and there are no treacherous canyons to struggle through. The only river we came upon was the Bear, a placid stream compared to the American.

From a distance, the Star Troupe may have seemed as peaceable as the landscape, but up close, the waters were troubled. In Auburn, Mr. Burnham had turned the wagon over to Buck Bliss and mounted Buck's horse. He tried more than once to fall in with Mrs. Burnham and converse, but she denied him even a glance and turned her attention to Mr. Thayer. He glared at the pair, then whirled Buck's horse about and rode a fair piece up the road.

Mr. Moone hung to the rear of our caravan in a cloud of his own discouragement, while Sophie Griffith kept her sorrel far to the front. Sophie is not a girl to sink into sorrow, but, as she rode in her wrinkled silk, a sadness settled in at the corners of her mouth.

Soon, she could not bear the burden of her own company and dropped back to find Mr. Booth. He was slouched on his pinto, eyelids drooping, no doubt wishing he were back in his bed. She was suddenly infused with morning cheer. "Up and at 'em, Ted!" He squinted at her, but it was too late. She regaled him with a good half hour of the Sophie show—laughter, jokes and gossip, especially about Lola Montez.

"She's back in town! We're stopping there! Hattie says she'll roll out the red carpet! And Lola's in mourning. Well, practically. Did you know?"

Mr. Booth shook his head.

"That young manager of hers, that Folland, he went right over the side of their ship, halfway between Australia and home. They quarreled. He stuffed his pockets with their profits and sank himself to the bottom of the Pacific. She was left without a cent. She's only here to sell up!"

I sniffed a story there and hoped to hear more, but Sophie broke her monologue with a breath, and Mr. Booth found his moment to make a polite exit. He tipped his hat and rode up to consult Buck Bliss about having his horse shod. Sophie frowned, but then, with a tiny glance at Mr. Moone, she squared her shoulders, put on her best smile, and sought out the company of Harry Brown.

As time went on, Mr. Booth slipped again to the rear of the company, even farther back than Mr. Moone. In the midst of the beautiful morning, he bore the chill of loneliness. I wrestled with the thought of heading his way. I didn't want to be a second Sophie, but I finally nudged Lem Mule in his direction. "Good morning, Mr. Booth."

To my surprise, he smiled back at me. "Good morning, Chicken! You survived the adventures of the night!"

"I did indeed. I stole Miss Griffith's bed, and I don't feel a bit sorry."

"Nor should you. Although it's a shame you were reduced to crawling over transoms to find a place to sleep. Harry Brown told me he found you squeezed between a wall and a chifforobe. Do the Burnhams pay you so little?"

"They don't give me much, but I'm usually all right in the wagon. I was just handed a little scare last night."

"How little, Miss Lightfoot?"

"A visitation from a liquored wanderer. But he passed on by."

"Suppose he hadn't? What would you have done?"

"Beat him off with a flatiron, I reckon."

"I know you're a resourceful person, but you need a safe place at night. Here." He pulled out his penknife and, as he had in Coloma, slit the seam of his coat lining. A twenty-dollar gold piece, a double eagle, slid into his hand. "Please take this."

The gold piece gleamed at me. "Mr. Booth, this is too generous. I could never pay you back."

"No need."

His eyes were so kind, I almost threw my arms about him. But I could not take the coin.

"All right," he said. "If you cannot accept it as a gift, perhaps you'll take it for safekeeping. If you find yourself in another tight spot, put it to good use. If not, give it back to me at the end of the tour. Please."

He pressed the coin into my palm, closed my fingers about it, and squeezed my hand. "Thank you, Mr. Booth," I said. "I can live with that."

"Excellent, Miss Lightfoot. And give up wiggling through transoms. God knows who you might drop in on."

"That's a sobering thought," I said, but I had to laugh, and Mr. Booth laughed, too.

"I hear we're putting new plays on the bill this week," I said.

"You've heard right," he replied. "*Hamlet* and *Richelieu*. Two little pieces of fluff to keep us from getting tiresome."

"I've read *Hamlet*," I said, "but, I confess, I do not know *Richelieu*."

"Have you heard of the novel *The Three Musketeers*, by Dumas?"

"Yes, I have."

"Richelieu is that same foxy old Cardinal in the book, except the story's not the same. You'll get to see yours truly try to add thirty years' age and six inches' height to his person. Should be amusing."

"I'm sure you'll be wonderful, Mr. Booth."

"That remains to be seen. But at least I'll have the chance to work out the rough spots before the New York season."

So, he was, indeed, leaving the West. A twinge hit my heart, though I tried not to show it.

"We'll be playing in a topnotch space in Nevada, too," he went on. "Frisbie's outfitted the theatre again—eight hundred seats and a fancy saloon. And Nevada has good hotels, with decent beds and clean sheets. Which perhaps you, too, Miss Lightfoot, will be able to enjoy!"

"Perhaps." I said. "The town sounds splendid. You must be looking forward to it."

A sudden cloud crossed his countenance. "Yes. Yes, I suppose so."

Had I trod where I did not belong? "Mr. Booth, did I say something wrong?"

"Absolutely not. Your conversation is delightful," he replied.

Yet he said no more. I waited in silence for a moment, then tried to strike things up again, to little avail. His responses were polite, yet the door to his soul had quietly clicked shut. It was time to leave him be.

"Thank you, Mr. Booth, for the double eagle. I shall keep it safe and return it soon."

"You're very welcome," he said. I clucked to Lem and started away. "And Miss Lightfoot—"

"Yes?"

"I do thank you for your company." He managed an apologetic smile. I nodded and took Lem forward of the wagon.

It was not until we had reached the Bear River that I remembered our talk in the soda fountain. Nevada was where Mr. Booth, shivering in a snowdrift on a winter afternoon, had heard of his father's death—the father he felt was more and more at his side with every camp we played. Had the old man's ghost pulled him down into a dark place? I could do no more than speculate. And be thankful that Emmett's shade is such a cheerful one.

After crossing the Bear, we stopped in a grove to stretch our legs and water the horses. As Mr. Leach prepared to ride ahead to post bills, Mr. Burnham muttered, "Frisbie and I have business," and mounted up, too. Mr. Moone, who hadn't spoken a word all morning, saw the chance to escape along with them. Soon, only a swirl of dust on the trail marked their departure.

As the rest of us readied to follow, Mrs. Burnham grinned up at Buck Bliss. "Buck, dear, come down off that wagon."

Buck grinned back. "Do I get that nice grey?"

"You do indeed."

In seconds, Buck was in Mrs. Burnham's saddle. She sprang up onto the wagon seat and neatly clasped the lines. "Head on out!" she shouted, and drove the prancing team smartly up onto the road. Soon her beautiful alto rose above the clatter of wheels and the squeal of harness. "I'm bound for the promised land, I'm bound for the promised land! Oh, who will come and go with me? I am bound for the promised land!" It was a call we could not resist. Mr. Thayer joined in with his booming bass. Harry and Sophie lifted their voices in harmony, and the Bliss brothers followed. Out from under the wagon canvas soared Mrs. La Rue's soprano and Louise's silver tones. I gave it my best try, and even Mr. Booth, still in the rear, picked up a few notes. "Promised Land" spilled into "Roll, Jordan, Roll," and then "Pop Goes the Weasel." A small herd of deer on a distant hillside picked up their antlers and stared at our merry band, as if we were the strangest species that had ever invaded their peace.

Not far up the trail, in the midst of "Oh, Susanna," we crossed another wagon road, deeply rutted, running east and west. I cannot say exactly why—perhaps the way the light fell, or the pattern of the trees arched over the road—but I knew the spot, knew it in my heart before my brain could give it a name. It was a piece of the Overland Trail that Emmett and I had made our journey west on, and we must have stopped, many years ago, in that place, filled with the joy of having arrived together in our own promised land.

Now we are parted, Emmett to sleep on the rugged hill above Placerville's canyon, and me, sundered from our home, on the road to heaven knows where. This is how grief works, I suppose—it lays low, and then it ambushes you when a stretch of scarred earth stirs your memory.

I could no longer sing. But, as my heart whirled about, I took refuge in Lem's sturdy gait, and in the voices raised in harmony on all sides. I forced my throat to make the sounds and my lips to form the words.

"O, Susannah, don't you cry for me!" As we drew out the last note of the chorus, Harry Brown flashed me a smile.

I would have given anything to be back in the *Rattler* office, late at night, setting type by Emmett's side. That was home. But I confess there is a part of me that takes solace in the road and in the company about me. I am a rolling stone amongst other rolling stones, and we are stepping out where the world is wider than a familiar room. There is risk, but there is adventure, too, and the kinship of fellow travelers. Emmett was happy as a lark when we made our way across the country on that worn trail—I suppose he, too, felt the beauty of being in motion. He would understand. He would be thrilled to be on this journey. Perhaps he is.

The Star Troupe was halfway into the chorus of "My Old Kentucky Home" when Buck Bliss trotted the grey up to Mrs. Burnham.

"We have company," he called to her. "Three riders coming up behind us!"

Mrs. Burnham gripped the lines. "Anyone in boilerplate?"

"Nope, but they're gaining fast."

Mrs. Burnham pulled a rifle out from under the driver's seat and offered it to Mr. Thayer, who'd been riding beside the wagon. He squinted back over his shoulder and then he grinned. "No need, Hattie. They're not foes, they're fans. Listen to the fools."

And, indeed, all three riders were shouting at us, "Star Troupe! Ho! Wait up! Woooo! Star Troupe!"

"What the hell?" exclaimed Mrs. Burnham.

In an instant, the young men had overtaken us and reined in their horses, laughing. "We could hear you for miles!" roared a pleasant man with a sandy beard. "We followed the music! Hello, Hattie!"

"James Hamlin! You're a welcome sight! You remember Gus Thayer, don't you?"

"I do, indeed. Pleased to see you again, Gus!"

"Likewise, Hamlin."

"Here," said Mrs. Burnham, "let's get this outfit off the road." She hustled the wagon over to a shady patch, hopped down, and proceeded to make introductions all around.

The sandy-haired gentleman, Mr. Hamlin, was an old friend of Mrs. Burnham and the Star Troupe. "A pillar of support for the Thespian art," was how she put it. He was also the proprietor of a bookstore in Nevada. (I must pay it a visit!). He was accompanied by his "good and true friend," Mr. Sherman W. Fletcher, another of Nevada's leading citizens and its District Attorney. Mr. Fletcher was shorter and stockier than Mr. Hamlin, with bright brown eyes behind his gold spectacles. He was so amiable, I could not imagine him prosecuting the law.

The third man was Mr. Eben Card, one of Mr. Fletcher's cousins by marriage. Mr. Card was a tall young man, newly arrived from Tennessee—indeed, Hamlin and Fletcher had only yesterday met him at the steamboat in Sacramento. He declared he had come to California to mine for gold, but it appeared that he had spent his stake on his wardrobe. He was quite the "dandy," in a bottle-green jacket, checked trousers, and a crazy quilt of a waistcoat. About his middle, he'd draped a gold sash, and about his collar, a bright blue tie, looped in a bow that reached almost to his sideburns. He would have given Petruchio, on his wedding day, a run for the money.

The young men resolved to be our traveling companions for the rest of the afternoon. Mr. Hamlin tied his horse to the back of the wagon and joined Mrs. Burnham on the driver's seat. Mr. Fletcher rode near the rear, by Mr. Booth, Harry Brown and myself, and he and Mr. Booth were soon in lively conversation. Fletcher's profession may have been the law, but his passion was the heavens. Securely tied to the rear of his saddle, swathed in batting and oilcloth, was his new treasure, a telescope he had picked up in Sacramento after its journey around Cape Horn. "You must come up to the roof above my office one night after the play, Mr. Booth!" he exclaimed. "Have you witnessed Saturn's rings or the moons of Jupiter?"

"I have not, Mr. Fletcher. I cannot imagine—"

"Jupiter is golden, Mr. Booth, and majestic, and Saturn's rings divine as halos. And the moon will be full this week—you can pick out the mountains and the craters on her face!" Mr. Fletcher's enthusiasm almost lifted him from the saddle.

"Splendid! How late are you up there on the roof, Fletcher? *Hamlet* runs long."

"Sometimes all night, I'm afraid. I find myself mesmerized by the stars, and, next thing you know, I'm startled by the dawn. By noon, I'm napping on my law books!" He laughed. "This earth is a magnificent place, Booth, but I confess, I wish I were free of gravity. I'd float up and lose myself in the constellations. Imagine looking back down on this Eden as you blaze by on the tail of a comet!" Mr. Fletcher drew an arm across the sky with such vigor that the reins nearly flew from his hand.

"Any comets out there now?" inquired Mr. Booth.

"No. And it's a shame you'll have moved on by August. The meteor showers are magnificent then. Shooting stars dropping down like diamonds."

"I was born under a meteor shower."

"A perfect entrance for a 'star,' Mr. Booth."

"Or an augury for disaster. 'These signs forerun the death or fall of kings.'"

"Shakespeare?"

Mr. Booth nodded.

"Gloomy fellow."

A frown clouded Mr. Booth's beautiful brow. "He specialized in madness and death."

"Well, we're all born to die, Mr. Booth, so death's not worth worrying about. And you're hardly mad."

Mr. Booth shrugged.

"I've seen you *play* madmen, Mr. Booth. But madmen cannot sustain four hours of Shakespeare night after night."

"That very task can drive a man insane."

"Well, I cannot debate you on that point, not having stood in your shoes. I surrender my case for lack of evidence!"

By and by, Harry and I left Mr. Booth and Mr. Fletcher to their budding friendship, and rode to the front of the wagon. We arrived as Mr. Hamlin exclaimed, "I have it, Hattie—Tennyson! His poems would make good plays. I can just see you as the Lady of Shalott."

"The curse is now upon me?" Mrs. Burnham laughed. "Floating downriver to my doom? No thank you, James."

"Poe's the true dramatist," said Mr. Thayer. "Look at 'The Raven.' Now, there's a role for me, ranting to a bird about his lost love. If I could only persuade Ulysses to deck himself in black feathers and bark out 'Nevermore,' we'd be a hit."

"I'd buy a ticket for that," grinned Harry.

Mr. Hamlin smiled my way. "Are you a fan of poetry, Miss Lightfoot?"

"Indeed I am."

"I have some fine new volumes in the shop. You must come give them a look."

"Thank you, I will!" Mr. Booth's gold coin weighed heavy in my pocket, begging to be spent, but I resolved to find book money elsewhere.

"Hattie," Mr. Hamlin went on, "you should drop into the store, too. I have the grandest new editions of Shakespeare. Red Moroccan bindings, gilt spines—"

"They're too elegant for me, James. My copies of Shakespeare are dog-eared and scribbled upon. They see hard use." Mrs. Burnham peered over her shoulder. The La Rues were out of sight in the wagon. "How about newspapers, James? Did you bring anything up from Sacramento?"

"A few copies of the *Union*, and a *San Francisco Call*."

"Any mention of the Star Troupe? For good or for bad?"

"If you mean that little dig about Booth in the *Union*, I did see that, but nothing else."

"No gossip, no speculation?"

"Not in the last few days. Not in Sacramento. But Nevada is a-buzz with your arrival, has been for the last couple of weeks. Everyone wants to see Booth."

He glanced at her, quickly, his gaze just brushing over her bruised cheek. "Where's Ben, Hattie? Is he along on this trip?"

Mr. Thayer's jaw tightened, but he was silent.

"Oh, yes, Ben's with the company," breezed Mrs. Burnham. "He's playing advance man today." She did not meet Mr. Hamlin's eye but kept her attention on the road ahead. "There's Wolf Creek. I suggest we stretch our legs a bit. Whoa!" And she halted the team at a pleasant spot by the water.

I led Lem Mule a short piece off the trail to a spot where the trees curved over the stream, making a cool hideaway. Lem drank and nibbled greenery as I knelt and splashed water on my face. "Miss Lightfoot!" The voice startled me so, I almost fell in. It was the Cousin from Tennessee, Mr. Card.

I'd managed to dodge the boy on the trail, but now he blocked my way back up the creek bank. He was pleasant enough, but he was an endless talker. He'd already tired Sophie's ear and had tried several times to engage Mrs. Burnham, but she'd had the company of Mr. Thayer and Mr. Hamlin to protect her. He'd even tried to chat with Louise as she hung out the rear of the wagon, although her mother had promptly hauled the girl back in. I suspect Mr. Card is lonely—he has probably come west, not to mine for gold, but to mine for ladies' hearts. Now, I was the only claim in the company that he had not yet tried to stake. And what an odd pair we would have made—Mr. Card, a jabbering parrot in his rainbow of colors, and me in my specs and miner's boots. I laughed at the thought.

Mr. Card planted himself right down on the bank beside me, and words tumbled out of his mouth. I confess, I was amused for a short while by his style, more than his substance. His speech was peppered with profanity. He dubbed his horse a "lop-jawed, long-eared lady of the night," and affectionately termed Mr. Fletcher "that damned old polecat, bless him." For a while, he rhapsodized on the virtues of assorted pieces of farm machinery. At last, he leaned in to me, and asked, "Miss Lightfoot, do you have a taste for possum?"

I couldn't say as I did.

"Then you have never feasted on a possum like Old Satan," he said. "That scoundrel haunted the woods about our place in Tennessee. He was the size a sow and the terror of the hen house. He'd run off the hounds with his hiss. If you spied him in the dark, his eyes shining like Beelzebub and his snaggle teeth bared, heaven help you. He was cagier than any possum had a right to be. We'd bait traps, and the danged cuss would dance away free. We'd hunt him with dogs in the night and never catch scent of him, but let some poor soul try to make it to the privy in the blackness before dawn, and Old Satan would be lying in wait. Finally, my Pappy brought home a new hound, a big fella called Leonatus. Leonatus knew no fear, and one summer night we heard him baying like sin. We rushed into the yard, and from the top of the tallest gum tree, flashed two red eyes. Old Satan.

"He was too high in the leaves to shoot. We had to wait him out. Leonatus never left his post, but after days, the vigil grew tiresome. We figured that old possum must have an appetite on him by then. Pappy mixed up some greens and grits with a pint of corn mash, and we stuck it high in the tree. Old Satan feasted—and then he wobbled, did a little dance on his branch, and tumbled into Pappy's arms. In minutes, the beast was in the pot, and *we* feasted. Pappy swears it was that mix of corn liquor and meanness that made Old Satan such a treat. Sometime, you must share a possum with me, Miss Lightfoot!"

I was at a loss for words. I also suspected the veracity of his tale. I have found possums to be shy, slow creatures, who, when threatened, are less likely to hiss than to flop over "dead" and surrender themselves to circumstance. I cannot imagine I would take pleasure in devouring one.

Mr. Card was of that breed of young man who ends up in the West because his family back East has no idea what to do with him. I had no idea either, and I was searching for a way to dodge a dish of possum, when Mr. Thayer appeared through the willow brush.

"Miss Lightfoot, Mr. Card," he said, with a twinkle in his eye, "the company awaits your appearance. And Miss Lightfoot," he added, shepherding me aside, "I must have a word with you about the starch in my shirts."

We mounted up. With Mr. Thayer safely by my side, Mr. Card sought out a new audience. He'd exhausted the ladies, so he settled on Jimmy Bliss, the perfect choice. Jimmy never says a word to interrupt, and he must have been thrilled to hear of farm machinery.

By the middle of the afternoon, we spied the scattered cabins and stores that marked the outskirts of Grass Valley, the "sister city" of Nevada. The road curved and spilled us onto Mill Street. Just ahead, lounging on a boulder in the shade of a pine, was a young man in a straw hat. At the sight of the troupe, he sprang up, gave a wild wave, and leapt down into the dust of the road. "Hattie! Gus!" He ran to the wagon and hopped up onto the seat beside Mrs. Burnham. He threw his arms around her and gave her a big hug.

"I thought we'd catch up with you in Nevada, Frank," gasped Mrs. Burnham.

Frank beamed at her. "No, Lola's putting me up."

"Brave lad," chuckled Mr. Thayer.

"She's been an angel," declared Frank. "She's busting her buttons waiting for the company to show. She sent me out to scout. And now I can return the hero, with my captives in tow. Where's Ted?"

"In the rear."

"Splendid!" And the young man was off again, bounding down the trail to Mr. Booth, who greeted him with a wide smile.

"Frank, my man!" exclaimed Mr. Booth, and he pulled Mr. Mayo up behind him on the pinto. Mr. Booth turned to Mr. Fletcher. "Fletcher, meet Mr. Frank Mayo, the Lord of Misrule!"

Mr. Mayo laughed. "You exaggerate, Booth!"

"Mr. Mayo is joining our company this week," added Mr. Booth. "The ladies love him. He's a blessing to ticket sales."

Mr. Mayo can't be much older than Harry Brown. He has a shock of dark, wavy hair, blue eyes, and a winning smile. He hasn't Mr. Booth's fine features, or even Harry's handsome profile, but he is good-looking in a broad-chested sort of a way, and his laughter lifts you like a wave.

In minutes, we arrived before a pleasant cottage shaded by a wide oak. The front porch looked out over Wolf Creek, and the yard was graced with roses. Just beyond the picket fence stood a sign—"For Sale/All Offers Considered." Frank Mayo grimaced at the sight. "It's a shame, that's all I can say. What's New York got that California doesn't? The only good to come of it is that Lola's breaking all the champagne out of the cellar. Says she can't take it with her, and she might as well spread the good cheer!"

Mr. Booth smiled. "You look a little cheery already, Frank."

"Could be, Ted. Could be," Mr. Mayo grinned back. He slid off the pinto and hurried through the gate. "Countess!" he called. "Your embassy has arrived!"

The cottage door flew open, and Lola Montez appeared on the porch, a white cockatoo on her shoulder. She threw her arms wide and sang out, "Willkommen! Welcome, my dears!" Then she floated down the steps and across the yard to deliver a flurry of embraces and endearments to the members of the Star Troupe.

Sophie's earlier comments aside, Miss Montez did not appear to be in mourning. She was a study in light and dark—the jet of her hair and lashes against the white lawn of her summer dress, the pale lace at her snowy throat, and of course, the cockatoo. Her only hints of color glowed in rosy lips and cheeks, and the brilliant blue of her eyes, which flashed with delight.

This was the celebrated Lola Montez, whose adventures had filled so many columns of *The Rattler* in the last few years. Emmett always pounced on Lola stories, for they sold out many an issue. Miss Montez has been loved by the rich and famous, not to mention the infamous—writers and artists, and even a King of Bavaria—sometimes with fatal consequences for the gentlemen. She has been gifted with a title, Countess of Landsfeldt, and incited a revolution that cost her king his kingdom. And she is notorious not only for her horsewhip, but for her risque Spider Dance, which she has performed all over the world with passion and bravado, and which drew Captain Avery Smith so many nights to her stage door.

We think of "stars" like Lola Montez as larger than life, as being as big as their reputations. Yet here she was, in Grass Valley, so lovely and petite, throwing her arms around Mrs. Burnham and the others and giggling like a schoolgirl. She held Mr. Booth in an extra-long embrace. "Ted Booth," she scolded, as she gave him a mock frown, "I should be angry with you, for the sake of your family connections. That rascally brother of yours, June, has satirized me on the stage."

"June has a golden touch at the box office, Lola," replied Mr. Booth, "and I regret that he was seduced by profit. But you know that no burlesque could ever tarnish the genuine article."

She smiled, her teeth white and very even. "And you know that I could never hold a dark thought against you. I am so happy to see you again, dear Ted!" And she brushed his cheek with her lips.

Those of us who were not old friends were introduced to the lady. When it was my turn, she gently pressed my hand. "I am so happy to welcome you, Miss Lightfoot!" she murmured, and I believe she truly was, even if I am only the washerwoman.

"You must come in for respite and refreshments," Miss Montez called out, already ushering the company through the gate. A table stood in the shade of the oak, piled with plates of cake and other dainties, and big frosted pitchers of lemonade. I longed to step into Lola's little Eden with the others, but the Bliss brothers were leading the stock down to the edge of the creek, and I could not abandon Lem just yet.

My ancient mule has proven himself to be the calmest of beasts, rattled not a whit by misadventure. However, on the far side of Miss Montez's yard, tethered by a chain, stood a bear, regarding all the guests with great curiosity. He was a young bear but sizable, and Lem took a deep dislike to the critter, flaring his nostrils and showing the whites of his eyes. He stamped about and let out a long bray that echoed through most of Grass Valley. I led the old boy right down to the creek, posthaste, tied his reins tightly to a willow, and placated him with a handful of tender leaves.

Once I was down in the creek hollow, I lingered. Laughter and voices rang out up the hill, the hubbub of a fellowship of actors who knew each other as comrades in a way that I did not, and I grew bashful about making my way back up to the party.

Still, it wasn't long before I heard, "Cinder-Emma! There are raspberries with that cake, and you shall have none if you don't get yourself to the table!" Harry Brown appeared, a glass of lemonade in his hand and a smear of red—raspberries, no doubt—at the corner of his mouth. "Don't sit down here by your lonesome, with only a mule for company. Here!" He pulled a bit of cake from his pocket. "Try it!" he said. I could not resist, and good thing, too, for it tasted of vanilla and cinnamon, and it melted in my mouth. I patted Lem farewell and hastened up the hill with Harry.

He guided me to the table. We loaded up with "firsts" for me and "seconds" for him, and then we wandered about Lola's place. The inside of the cottage was cozy and graced with beautiful pieces of furniture, dozens of books, and musical instruments. But it was the yard that Miss Montez had tried to make into her little paradise. You could see that the flower beds had suffered in her absence, but loveliness prevailed in the roses, the fruit trees, and a shady grape arbor. In the rear of her house, we discovered her menagerie. Besides the bear and the cockatoo, she had surrounded herself with goats, chickens, and a ewe and its lamb with ribbons about their throats. We also stumbled across a family of cats that purred against our legs and a half-dozen dogs, including a brace of doe-eyed greyhounds and a sweet little spaniel with "Gip" embroidered on its collar.

Harry and I shared our cake crumbs with the greyhounds and the friendliest of the goats and ambled back to the front of the house. I partook of more lemonade and found myself a shady spot on soft pine needles. Harry gathered handfuls of cherries from under the fruit trees and headed over toward the bear. The animal was pleased to have attention—he'd sit up on his haunches, and, as Harry tossed him a cherry, catch it in his mouth with a happy grunt. He seemed to have been brought up by people, and I wondered what would become of him when Lola Montez sailed for New York. I doubted a bear would be booked passage.

I understand why Emmett liked wild things to stay wild. If the bear is turned loose, he might wander into some miner's camp hoping for a cherry and wind up in a pot. Perhaps his best chance is to find another yard like Lola's, but that might take some luck, even though he's a sweet enough creature, for a bear.

I leaned back on the pine needles and sipped the fine, tart lemonade. A whisper of a breeze was coming up off the creek. I closed my eyes for a moment and heard laughter from all about the yard—Frank Mayo's hoots and Lola Montez's enchanting ripples. Mr. Mayo was up in the branches of the oak, in animated conversation with Mr. Booth, who lounged on a limb, puffing at his pipe. Sometimes Mr. Mayo laughed with such abandon, it seemed he would tumble from the tree into the berry bushes below. Mr. Fletcher and his Cousin had departed for Nevada—

their family was holding its own welcome fete for Mr. Card—but Mr. Hamlin remained. Mr. Thayer and he occupied the big wicker chairs on the porch and carried on a spirited discussion of Mr. Franklin Pierce, while Ulysses stared at the greyhounds sprawled before the door as if they were the strangest pieces of dog flesh he had ever sniffed.

It was Lola Montez who drew my attention most as she danced from one cluster of guests to the next, charming and graceful as a butterfly on the breeze. Her magnetism is partly due to her fame—she is a countess, notorious all over the world—but there is more to it. It is Lola that all eyes go to, if only to see what she'll do next. As I watched, she strolled over to Harry Brown, who tossed the last cherry to the bear. She whispered something to Harry that made him blush with pleasure, and then she spoke gently to the animal while she scratched its head. "Bernard, je t'aime. What a handsome, noble creature!" She offered him a handful of cake, which he devoured in an instant. Then the bear spread his paws and Lola Montez stepped into the animal's embrace, sharing a tender bear hug.

I had almost polished off the last of my lemonade and was thinking of checking on the mule, when I heard "Emma, dear!" and Sophie plopped down beside me. She had scrubbed the paint off her face and changed into a simple blouse and skirt. She looked seventeen again. "Oh, Lola is so lovely, Emma! She let me use her basin, and she has the most wonderful soaps. And lotions! She knows everything about beauty. I suppose she'd have to, with all those lovers and husbands to please. Here, smell!" Sophie held a wrist up to my nose. I sniffed and picked up a faint, sweet scent of roses, oranges, and maybe cloves. "Doesn't it smell just like Spain? Like faraway places?" Sophie gushed. "She mixes her potions from her own recipes, like a beautiful witch. Oh, Emma, I'm sure she'd share some with you, if you'd just ask. Is that lemonade in your glass, dear?"

"It is."

"Are you going to finish it?"

"Probably not. Would you like it, Sophie?"

"Oh, yes, thank you. The trail has made me so dry."

I handed her the glass. She drained the last drop and scooped the leftover sugar out of the bottom with her finger. Then she lay back on the pine needles, gazing up through the branches. In seconds, her eyelids closed, her rosebud mouth fell open, and she was daintily snoring away, a fallen blossom.

She looked so comfy, I followed suit. The pine needles were a fine mattress, the tree above a lacy canopy. I shut my lids but, just before sinking into sleep, was pulled back into this world by voices. I squinted one eye open and spied Miss Montez and Mrs. Burnham spreading a blanket a few feet away.

"This will do, Hattie," whispered Miss Montez. "Our sleeping beauties are off in dreamland. And the breeze is best right here. Sit, please." They settled on the blanket, spreading their skirts. "Now, lay this against your cheek, and keep it there as long as it feels cool."

"What is it?"

"Chamomile, jasmine water, a little alum."

"What's the whiff of barroom?"

"Oh. A hint of white brandy. Purely medicinal."

Mrs. Burnham touched the compress to her cheek and sighed. I decided to stay where I was, eyes almost shut, and feign my trip into slumber.

"Ben stopped by a couple of hours ago," Miss Montez said, "to let me know you were on your way. I should have figured something was up. He was as surly as I've ever seen him—he downed my whiskey and never cracked a smile. And he had that nasty bandage sticking out from under his hat. Was that your doing?"

"Oh, no. A cuckolded husband. He avenged his honor with a pistol in the middle of the second act."

"Lousy shot. If it had been me, I'd have pulled out my horsewhip."

"That would have been a sight," Mrs. Burnham laughed, and then she winced. "Oh, don't make me smile, it hurts." But she giggled again, anyway.

Miss Montez leaned in toward her. "Forgive me, Hattie, but how did you wind up with an ass like Ben? I thought you were a smart girl?"

"You should talk."

"Touche. I've had more than my share of disasters. But I'd hoped you would have better sense than I did."

Mrs. Burnham shrugged. "I don't know, Lola. Why does anyone marry? Because I loved him?"

"Oh, yes, love. The excuse for sanctioned insanity."

"Well, I must have loved him. Or convinced myself I did. Now, I don't even know him. I look at him next to me at night—when he even bothers to come back—and I wonder who the hell he really is."

"You loved Tench."

"I did. Tench would never have struck me. He was incapable of cruelty. Except to himself."

"He was a lovely man, Hattie."

"When he was sober."

"Well," said Miss Montez, pulling a flask from her garter and freshening her lemonade, "we all have our faults, Hattie. Cheers!"

Mrs. Burnham put a hand over her own lemonade, and Miss Montez returned the flask to its hiding place. Hoofbeats pounded before the house. Mr. Booth and Frank Mayo had abandoned the tree and were racing their ponies the length of Mill Street and back, Harry and Buck Bliss cheering them on, and the bear tossing off a roar.

"Speaking of faults," Mrs. Burnham said, "we know, you and I, that we are still in our womanly primes, but doesn't fooling around with Frank amount to robbing the cradle?"

"What makes you think I am having 'un amour' with Frank?"

Mrs. Burnham rolled her eyes.

"Oh, Hattie," replied Miss Montez, "Frank is a big boy. He's full of life, and full of himself, and having a grand old time. He's so young, his heart isn't even formed yet—how could anyone break it?"

"Please, be careful. He's my De Mauprat in *Richelieu*."

"I know. Don't worry. If Frank falls, he'll bounce right back again." She glanced out at Mr. Booth as he galloped by on the pinto, a blur of black and white. "Ted's the one to watch out for, my dear. He's made of glass."

Mrs. Burnham gave a little groan. "Oh, good God, I know, I'm working on it. And he's trying. I believe he's kept to the lemonade—unless you've visited him with your wee flask when I wasn't looking."

"Absolutely not."

"Well, I thank you for that."

"I can't wait to see his Hamlet."

"I'm keeping my fingers crossed for all the shows. Ted's exactly what we need to pull off this tour. So, say a little prayer for the Star Troupe, my dear Countess."

"I will. Do you really need to get over to Nevada tonight? You're all welcome to stay here. There's the guest house, and room in the parlor for a cot or two. Someone may have to share a bed with kittens or a greyhound, but I would love your company, Hattie. And Ben might just appreciate you more if he has to wonder where you are for a night."

"I'm mightily tempted, Lola, but it's not only me. I've got to get this company over the hill and into the theatre. Frisbie is waiting for us there. "

"All right. But then, you must come to my soiree. Friday night, after the show, to celebrate your run. The Frisbies will be there, Southwick from the mine—all the sorts that can do the Star Troupe some good. We shall have a lovely fete. Bring as many of the company as you can."

Mrs. Burnham threw her arms around Miss Montez. "You are a darling, thank you."

"And tell that beastly Burnham to open his eyes to what he has and treat you with some respect. The Countess demands it."

"We shall see. Help me round up my actors and get them on the road before it's too late to get them anywhere. These two already look drunken with Montez hospitality."

Mrs. Burnham gently shook my shoulder, and I opened my eyes. Sophie sputtered to under Miss Montez's touch, and soon, the company was gathered up like a bouquet before the gate. We had sung out a chorus of farewells, the cockatoo had screeched her goodbyes, and the wagon was pulling out into Mill Street before anyone noticed that the pinto and Frank Mayo's roan were missing. Mr. Booth and Mr. Mayo were nowhere to be found.

SUNDAY, JULY 13, *Nevada. Just before 10 a.m. A Rehearsal Day—*

I have been up and about since dawn. The Blisses and I shared biscuits and bacon by the wagon. The Burnhams and Mr. Leach turned up shortly after, with Frisbie and a handful of Nevada's citizens in tow. The latter shall round out the stage crew.

Today is simply a "rehearsal day" for the new plays we shall present. Nonetheless, Mrs. Burnham and Mr. Leach have bustled about with enthusiasm, choosing backdrops from Frisbie's fine store of scenery and admiring the shiny brass footlights lining the rim of the stage. It's only within the last half hour, as the ten a.m. call for actors has neared, that the management's cheer has worn thin. Hattie Burnham's smile has faded. Mr. Leach nervously spits tobacco juice from under his otter mustache. Only Ben Burnham wears a grin. He has abandoned the pursuit of Mrs. Burnham's forgiveness for the prospect of gloating at Mr. Booth missing his own rehearsal. Neither Mr. Booth nor Mr. Mayo has been sighted since yesterday afternoon. The company scoured Lola Montez's house, from chicken coop to champagne cellar, and found nary a trace of them. Finally, Mrs. Burnham gave it up and ordered us on our way.

"Don't fret, Hattie," Mr. Thayer assured her. "They're big boys. They know their way to Nevada." Mrs. Burnham nodded, but every time a rider overtook us on the road, she started about in the hope that it was one of her leading men.

The sun was setting in an orange sky by the time we made it "over the hill" to our destination. We rattled across a wooden bridge, Deer Creek tumbling below, and passed into the city of Nevada, the "Queen of the Northern Mines." We turned down Broad Street, rounded a corner toward Coyote, and came within view of the theatre. A shout arose from the welcoming committee clustered on the wooden walk. The Star Troupe had arrived amongst friends.

At the head of the gathering stood a lively couple. He was perhaps thirty-five, handsome in a blue velvet coat and a wine-colored ascot. She had a lovely, heart-shaped face, framed by a beribboned bonnet. These were the Frisbies, the theatre owners, and they hurried from one member of the company to another, bestowing embraces upon us all, even the girl who does the wash.

The company was escorted into the theatre, where a broad table had been placed upon the stage, laden with a cold supper for the troupe and its hosts—smoked ham and cheese, fragrant peaches and plums, bread fresh from a bakery oven. We fell upon it as if we had died and gone to theatre heaven.

The sole damper upon the festivities was the absence of the company's "star."

"Where's Mr. Booth?" was the oft-heard plaint. The actors put on their best performances. "Oh, he'll be along presently!" or "Personal business, you know, but he has so looked forward to playing Nevada!"

By seven p.m., the company had been fed and had loaded most of the wagon contents into the theatre. The actors disappeared into town—some to hotels, some to the homes of friends. I worried for Lem Mule and myself, as the back lot of the theatre is cramped and dusty. The theatre takes up most of the land; but for an alley behind it and a narrow passage along the theatre's side to Coyote Street, it is hemmed in by other buildings. I was vainly searching for a nibble's worth of grass for Lem when Buck Bliss came to our rescue. "Don't despair, Miss Lightfoot," Buck said. "Burnham's stabled the fancy stock, but Frisbie has a vacant lot up Coyote that will serve for the other horses. And maybe for a sorry old mule, too. Follow me." And so, Buck and I saw Lem up the street a piece to a patch of green and a pail of water. I slipped the mule a few oats, scratched between his ears, and left the old boy quite content.

When we returned to the theatre, we found that Mr. Burnham had squeezed the wagon into a spot by the theatre's back wall. It was a pleasure to retire into it early and to write in this journal until sleep came upon me. As I snuggled into my nest of blankets, Buck and Jimmy Bliss snored long and loud beneath the wagon bed, a most comforting lullaby.

I have just asked Harry Brown to check his watch—time has hastened by. We are now within minutes of the ten a.m. rehearsal call, and there is still no sign of our star. I, too, am beginning to worry that Mr. Booth has lost his way or abandoned the company, but then I scold myself for doubting him. He gave Mrs. Burnham his word that he would do his best, didn't he?

Wait. There has been a shout from the front of the theatre, and Mr. Thayer has hurried into the auditorium. "Hattie, they're here. On the dot of ten. The Prodigal Sons have returned, my dear!"

Seconds later, Mr. Booth and Mr. Mayo have entered the theatre. They look like Hades warmed over, unshaven, in the same clothes they wore at Lola Montez's house, only rumpled, as if they've slept in them—which they no doubt have. Frank Mayo's thick hair stands on end, as though he's been struck by lightning, but they are both at the theatre, on time. Mrs. Burnham has relaxed back into her smile. "Gentlemen," she's announced, "let's rehearse."

Sunday evening, after rehearsal—

This morning, the Star Troupe rehearsed *Hamlet*. I had plenty to do readying our wardrobe, but I still managed to catch glimpses of the proceedings and to listen from the wings. Excitement bubbled through the theatre. The company was opening a new play, with new actors—a passel of locals were on hand to play the smaller roles. The Frisbies dashed about, providing this and that to Mr. Leach. And Mrs. Burnham was in her element, conducting the whole affair. She was swift and efficient, smoothing over Mr. Burnham's scowls, Mrs. La Rue's demands, and Frank Mayo's laughter in moments of high tragedy.

The only soul not visibly fired up was Mr. Booth. Mrs. Burnham ran the new actors through their entire scenes, word for word. And some of the company members wished to speak their lines—Mr. Burnham recited his whole soliloquy as King Claudius, and Miss Griffith wept her way through poor Ophelia's "mad" scene. But Mr. Booth did little except to choose his entrances and exits, although I know how hard he's been working on Hamlet. I finally whispered to Mr. Thayer, "Why doesn't Mr. Booth act his scenes?"

Mr. Thayer chuckled. "Miss Lightfoot, Ted hates to rehearse. Especially this early, and especially with the headache he has this morning."

"Don't you need to know what he's going to do?"

"Oh, we have a pretty good idea. Most of us have played these roles plenty of times, in other companies. A few have even played them with Ted. We know to give Hamlet center and to beware of upstaging the star. And what we don't know will keep us on our toes!"

And so, Mr. Booth hastened from one scene to another—except when it was little Louise's turn to rehearse her role as the Player Queen.

She is only seven, and, unlike Mr. Thayer, she has not played her part plenty of times. When the cast arrived at her cue, Mrs. Burnham paused. "Louise, are you back there?"

Louise and her mother popped from the wings. "Louise needs to run through this business," said Mrs. La Rue.

"Yes, I know that, Clarissa," said Mrs. Burnham. "Gus, can you come onstage? And Ted, do you mind?"

"Of course not," said Mr. Booth.

"Now, you enter with Mr. Thayer, Louise," said Mrs. Burnham. "He acts the part of the King in this little play by Hamlet, called *The Mousetrap*. And Mr. Booth will walk just ahead of you and show you your business as the Queen. What he does, you do, yes?"

Louise nodded.

"You must come into the garden with the King, smiling into his face," said Mr. Booth. "Take Mr. Thayer's hand." Louise slipped her little fingers into Mr. Thayer's broad palm.

Mr. Booth smiled. "Gus, do you think you could shrink about a foot before opening night? And Miss Louise, could you stretch about two feet?"

Mr. Thayer laughed. "We are a mighty unlikely couple, Miss Louise!"

Louise giggled.

Mr. Booth went on, "Louise, what you lack in stature, you must make up for in stateliness. Walk like this, like a queen."

I confess, I have never seen the point of "fairy stars," the child actors who are so popular these days. The prospect of a seven-year-old lisping through the role of Richard the Third or Macbeth gives me pause, although I know the little ones sell tickets. Still, if any child could pull off "stately," it was Louise, as she gravely imitated Mr. Booth.

Within a few minutes, Mr. Booth had patiently acted out the Player Queen's entire role, Louise an intent little shadow at his heels. At the scene's end, Louise bestowed a gorgeous smile upon Mr. Booth, and he gave her an enthusiastic, "Well done, La Petite!"

The rehearsal proceeded apace. Mr. Booth slowed up for a moment in the scene where he runs old Polonius—Mr. Leach—through with a sword. He was careful that no one should truly be hurt, and he acted out the bit of violence several times until it was right—even dragging the dead Mr. Leach by the feet into the wings. "Sorry, Jeriah," Mr. Booth grinned, as he hauled Mr. Leach across the floor. "That stage needed sweeping, anyway."

Then he moved right along until the end of the play, when everything stopped once more for the staging of the duel between Mr. Booth and Mr. Mayo's Laertes. Mr. Leach brought a pair of shiny rapiers from the wings, Mr. Booth and Mr. Mayo rolled up their shirtsleeves, and the two men began to "mark" their swordplay, moving through each bit of the duel as through a dance. "Now Frank, you step forward three paces, I step back, you lunge, yes! I parry, and I drive you downstage, one, two, three, four—mind the pit!" coached Mr. Booth.

When he announced, "Let's pick it up," they went at it more quickly. Mr. Booth handled his sword with grace and precision, but Mr. Mayo is careless. At the height of the duel, his rapier whipped perilously close to Mr. Booth's head. Mr. Booth shouted, "Stop, Frank! If I lose an ear, I'll never play Romeo again!" Mr. Moone, who had been watching with a scowl from the house, stalked up the aisle and out of the auditorium.

"I am so sorry, Ted!" said Mr. Mayo.

Mr. Booth kept his patience. "I know Frank. Let's just work it out." Eventually, both Mr. Booth and Mr. Mayo were satisfied. "Hattie," called Mr. Booth, "shall we give it a go?"

"I guess so," said Mrs. Burnham. "But Frank, remember, my looks are my fortune, too. Keep your distance!"

Poor Mr. Mayo. His cheeks blazed pink. "I'll do my best, Hattie. You know I will."

Mr. Booth and Mr. Mayo were joined onstage by the Burnhams, as King Claudius and Queen Gertrude, and the duel commenced in earnest.

Mr. Mayo, to his credit, finally took Mr. Booth's coaching to heart. The rapiers gleamed, and the theatre echoed with the ring of steel on steel. As the last blow was struck, Mr. Frisbie leapt up from his seat in the front row, shouting "Bravo! Bravo!" The rest of the company followed his cue, and cheers rang through the theatre.

After such excitement, the only thing to do was to announce a dinner break, which Mrs. Burnham promptly declared.

The actors spilled out of the theatre. Mr. Booth and Mr. Mayo, no longer in mortal combat, headed off together, laughing. Miss Griffith watched them leave and sighed. "There go the two best-looking men in the company. With each other."

As I started for the wagon, I spied Mr. Leach across the lot whispering emphatically to Jimmy Bliss. Jimmy shook his head, but Mr. Leach kept at him until he finally nodded and hurried away into town. Mr. Leach gazed my direction. "Can I help you, Miss Lightfoot?"

"No, sir," I replied. I hustled into the wagon and pulled my dinner out of a scrap of oilcloth. Whatever was up, it wasn't my business.

After our break, the company set about staging *Richelieu*. From what I can figure, it is a romantic tale set in old-time France. There are two young lovers, who are helped along by the wily Cardinal Richelieu. There is also a snakes' nest of conspirators trying to undo both Richelieu and the French nation.

It's odd that Mr. Booth, who is himself quite young and handsome, is not playing the youthful hero, Chevalier De Mauprat. That role has gone to Frank Mayo, while Mr. Booth is to portray the old Cardinal. Perhaps Mr. Booth is keen on the Cardinal because he likes to disappear. Frank Mayo, on the other hand, seems never to be in disguise and can hardly make it down the sidewalk without stirring feminine admiration. He will entice the ladies to the box office as honey draws bees.

He'll have to do better with his lines, though—even the washerwoman could tell that his knowledge of the words was fuzzy. Mr. Leach frequently had to prompt him, although it was impossible to be sharp with Frank.

He was humble—"Oh, I am such a dunce, Leach. I shall work all night on this, you have my word. Now what was that again?" Then he would laugh at himself and throw his hands into the air in such a charming way that one just had to hope for the best.

We'll begin our Nevada run with *The Iron Chest* tomorrow, then *The Taming of the Shrew*, and will not see *Hamlet* and *Richelieu* before an audience until midweek. Sigh.

When I climbed into the wagon this eve, I discovered a small gift—four pieces of salt water taffy wrapped in paper and left on my bedroll. They were wonderful. As I turn in, I hear only Buck's snores rumbling beneath the wagon, but if I close my eyes and truly listen, I can also make out the music of Deer Creek, rushing by somewhere down the hill.

MONDAY, JULY 14. *Late afternoon. We open with* Iron Chest *tonight!—*

I woke into the cool of the morning. Buck Bliss was still rolled in his blanket. I combed my hair, donned a blouse and a work skirt, and headed up Coyote Street to Frisbie's extra lot. Lem saw me coming and loosed a bray. I hugged his neck and murmured, "Hey, old boy," before I handed him his oats.

The mule's bucket had been kicked over in the night, and I looked about for a way to fill it. At the back of the lot, the hill sloped to a ravine, but the bottom held only a trickle, and it was muddied, to boot. I loosed Lem from the picket line, and we followed the ravine's course on down, in the hope that it might spill into Deer Creek.

Nevada was quiet, not much bustle yet. We threaded our way through cabins, sheds and boulders, until we descended into the deep creek bed. There we came upon a green spot, softened with grasses and ferns. I knelt down to splash the sweet, cold water on my face. A sizable stick bounced off the back of my head.

"What the—?"

As I looked up, I heard a giggle, and there, in the branches of an oak, perched Louise, grinning like a wicked elf. As we were now "friends" again, I don't reckon the stick was meant to injure, but I didn't favor being whacked in the skull as I went about my toilette.

"Louise, that is not a proper greeting. Why aren't you at the hotel?"

She didn't reply, simply turned her back toward me. I glanced upstream and saw that the child had already staked a claim to the place. At the water's edge, she'd made one of her "flutter mills" of sticks and leaves, and beyond that, she'd set up housekeeping. A broad rock was laid as a table, with flat stones for plates, and acorn cups, and nearby was a bed of boughs, a perfect nest for a small girl.

I let Lem drink as I washed up and thought of what to do. I was tempted to leave the child in her tree—she was happy enough there—but she had also, no doubt, slipped Mrs. La Rue's harness and was headed into trouble.

"Louise," I called. She deigned to cast an eye upon me. "Lem sure needs to be ridden this morning, but you'll miss your chance if you sit up in that tree. Why don't you come down and make this mule happy?"

The girl skittered out of that tree as quick as a kitten.

"I'm a good rider," she declared. "Mr. Thayer says so."

"I expect he does. Here. Let me boost you up. You'll have to ride bareback—can you handle that?"

"Yes."

"All right. Here you go. Now give him a pat, so he knows you like him."

"I need reins."

"Well, we only have the lead, and I have to hold that. But you grab onto his mane, gently now, like an Indian princess."

She did, and the sure-footed mule, the Indian princess and I worked our way back up to Frisbie's lot, and finally to the theatre. Louise was reluctant to bid Lem adieu, but I set her up in a dressing room with a tin full of buttons to sort—if she pinched a few, it was no big loss—and left her happily counting them out in rows.

By now, some of the other company were up and about. Buck Bliss scrambled eggs over the flatiron brazier. Mr. Leach and Mrs. Burnham puttered about the theatre and Mr. Burnham fetched the wagon team over from the stable, to spruce them up for the afternoon's parade.

I was hanging out costumes in the women's dressing room when footsteps clattered in the hall. Mr. Booth hurried by the door, and I called out a cheery "Good morning!" but when I spied the fire in his eyes, I choked back the rest. He was the madman I had encountered on the riverbank. He stalked out onto the stage, and, after a second, I followed. Mrs. Burnham knelt by the footlights, attaching a line to one of the painted drops. Mr. Booth stormed over to her and blasted her with, "I thought you trusted me!"

Mrs. Burnham looked him straight in the eye. "I do, Ted. I said I did, and I do."

"Don't lie to me. I'm not an idiot!"

Mrs. Burnham attempted to rise but caught her foot in the line. Mr. Booth let her struggle. "What in God's name is this about?"

"It's about your spy, Hattie. It's such an ugly thing to do."

Mrs. Burnham made it to her feet. "Who's my spy?"

"Jimmy. Although why you'd recruit a simpleton is a mystery to me."

"I didn't 'recruit' anyone! No one spied on you!"

"Hattie, I know what being followed is. I hid in the shadows outside hundreds of barrooms waiting for my father to stumble out the door. So don't insult me!"

Mrs. Burnham got right up into his face. "Now, you listen to me, Ted Booth! I did not 'recruit' Jimmy Bliss or anyone else to tail you. And if you don't believe me, and trust *me*, you can just go to hell!"

Mr. Booth glared at her, and they hung there, nose-to-nose.

By now, Mr. Burnham had heard the ruckus and rushed out onto the stage. "Hattie, do you need help?"

Mr. Booth turned on him. "Did you have me followed, Burnham?"

"If I cared where you were on your own time, Booth, I could find out for myself."

"Someone sent him," said Mr. Booth. "He wouldn't own up to who, but Jimmy Bliss did not follow me around town last night for the hell of it. Somebody set him on—"

Mr. Leach appeared from the shadows of the wings. "It was me, Ted."

Mr. Booth shot him a look of fury, as if he might run Leach through and drag him off by the heels. "You worry where I go at night?"

"I'm concerned. Yes."

"You think I'm a firebug?"

"I know you disappear, Ted. I know you drink, and I know we've had to bail you out of jail. I don't know about the fires, but I do have a sizable stake in this company. You're an investment, and I intend to protect it. I'm sorry it came down to sending Jimmy—"

"You're sorry he's a fool."

"He's a good boy, but I expect he was up against more than we reckoned with. Where is he? He didn't come back last night."

"Last I saw, he was behind the Polka Saloon, puking his guts out," said

Mr. Booth.

"Jimmy's Temperance, Ted."

"Not anymore."

Mr. Leach squeezed his fists and fought to keep his voice steady. "Stay dry, stay out of trouble, and do your job, Ted."

"I have been doing my job."

"Yes. Well. You just keep it up," said Mr. Leach, and, with a fury of his own, he hurried off to find Buck and throw together a search party for Jimmy.

Mr. Booth said nothing. He lingered on the stage for a moment, then disappeared out of the theatre and off towards his hotel. Mr. Burnham smiled at Mrs. Burnham, but she ignored him and turned her attention back to the canvas drop.

Presently, Jimmy Bliss was wrangled into the theatre. He had been discovered where Mr. Booth had left him, behind the Polka, face down in the dirt. His eyes were swollen, and he was none too steady on his feet. Buck Bliss and Mr. Moone helped him up the stairs and into the theatre. Buck fetched him a pail of water so he could wash up; then Mr. Leach and Mrs. Burnham settled him into a dressing room for a private conversation. When he stumbled out a few minutes later, he ran onto the back steps to dry heave. Then he rummaged for his blanket and attempted to retreat into the shade beneath the wagon, but Harry Brown was too quick for him. Harry knelt down and, with great compassion, said, "I'm sorry you feel so poorly, Jimmy."

Jimmy opened one eye and squinted at Harry.

"You won't feel any better lying there on the hard ground."

"I always sleep on the ground," Jimmy wailed. "Go away."

"I know, but, just for this afternoon, how about a sweet, soft bed in a hotel room?"

Jimmy allowed Harry a bloodshot glance.

Harry smiled, a Sunday school smile. "My bed has clean sheets and a down pillow. There's a cool breeze coming through the window. You can borrow the whole room for a few hours, if you like. Miss Lightfoot enjoyed a real bed the other night, and it did wonders for her health. Didn't it, Miss Lightfoot?"

"It was heavenly," I said.

Jimmy groaned. "Mr. Brown, I can't take another step. My legs are jelly, and my head is about to explode."

"Jimmy, my room's in the New York Hotel, just up the street. And there's a big pitcher of cold water right beside the bed."

Harry offered his hand. Jimmy eyed it with suspicion. "Why are you being so nice to me?"

"Because I'm a nice fellow. Miss Lightfoot will help me get you there. Won't you, Miss Lightfoot? She's pretty nice herself, you know."

"I suppose." With one more moan, Jimmy Bliss capitulated to comfort. He gripped Harry's hand, and Harry hauled him to his feet.

Harry's room was on the hotel's second floor, and a sweet breeze did, indeed, waft in from the street. Harry plumped the pillow and helped Jimmy pull off his boots. Jimmy settled back onto the bed, but before he could doze, Harry slid a chair over to his side. He pulled a brown paper bag from his coat pocket. "Peppermint, Jimmy?"

"Good Lord, no, Mr. Brown--"

"They're an aid to the digestion, you know."

"Truly?"

"Here. You let it melt in your mouth. Peppermint calms the stomach."

Jimmy gingerly set the sweet on his tongue.

"That's it," said Harry. "It's a shame you've had to suffer so. Why did Mr. Leach send you? Why not Buck or somebody older? Did you volunteer?"

Jimmy scowled. "I didn't want to go at all. I told my uncle so. But he couldn't count on Buck. Buck is Booth's friend, and he likes his beer, too. Booth already got him locked up once."

"So Leach thought you'd do a better job of minding Ted?"

Jimmy fought back tears. "Oh, I don't know. I reckon. But I'm as poor a spy as I am an actor."

He had a point. I could have done the deed better, even as a girl. Being a fly on the wall is one of my specialties—poor Jimmy is guileless.

"That Ted Booth is a mean bastard," he hissed. "I hate him."

I crossed to the foot of the bed. "Jimmy," I said, "I've seen Mr. Booth be very kind—"

"I know for a fact, he's mean. And he's crazy."

"What did you see?" Harry said.

"Nothing much—at first. Booth took himself around town at supper time, picked up his mail, bought tobacco and candy."

"Candy?" I wondered to myself. Salt water taffy? But I didn't ask.

Harry kept at him. "So, what happened last night?"

"He walked about a bit with Mr. Mayo. Then they split up, and Booth just wandered around by his lonesome. He kept going in circles, up

Broad, down Main, and back again. He'd stop, light his pipe—I'd have to duck around a corner—and then he'd slip away. I almost lost him a couple of times."

Harry grinned in spite of himself. "I'd say you'd been found out by then, Jimmy."

"You think so?" Jimmy threw his head back onto the pillow in despair. "I told you I was a terrible spy."

"And then, what did he do?"

"Then he stopped in a couple of saloons, just long enough that I'd have to hide somewhere in the shadows and wait. When he went into the Polka, I tried to keep sight of him through the window, but he disappeared into the crowd. Next thing I know, there's a voice at my shoulder. 'Jimmy Bliss!' it whispers, like some sneaky spook. I couldn't breathe. I spun around, and there was Booth, grinning at me, the bowl of his pipe glowing red as hell.

"'Jimmy,' he says, sweet as can be, 'what a pleasure to run into a friend in this part of town. I hate drinking alone.'

"'Oh, Mr. Booth,' I says, 'I don't drink. I'm Temperance, you know.'

"'No, I don't know, Jimmy,' he comes back at me. 'For the life of me, I can't figure out why a Temperance man is making the rounds of saloons this time of night, unless he wants a drink. Can you think of a better reason?'

"He had me. I didn't know what to say. Then he went on, just so pleasant, 'Now, I know why *I'm* at a saloon—for a whiskey. Or at least that's what certain parties expect of me, isn't it? And it wouldn't be mannerly if I didn't buy one for my friend. Would it?'

"He puffed on that blasted pipe, and it glowed even redder. I could hardly come up with a 'No, thank you,' before he had me by the shoulder and pushed me into the barroom. He steered me to a table in the back and called for whiskey for us both. 'To friends,' he says, with an evil look in his eye."

"And you drank," I said.

The tears finally came and rolled down Jimmy's cheeks. "I did. He had me, like a rat in a trap. If I denied the drink, I'd have to spill why I was truly there. So, I downed it, and it burned like brimstone. Then he bought a couple more rounds. I can't remember much, except he kept drilling me as to who'd sent me after him. I tried so hard not to blab, but my face was hot as coals, and I couldn't feel my fingers. I don't know what happened after that, except the dirt behind the saloon was cool, and that was where I wanted to be."

"I'm sorry, Jimmy," I said.

"I'm even sorrier," Jimmy cried. His nose was running, and Harry offered him his handkerchief. Jimmy honked into it. "Maybe I was wrong to spy on him, but Ted Booth is a devil. And a crazy one, too—it wouldn't surprise me at all if that pipe had sparked a few fires."

Harry turned a glance on me, shocked. There had been plenty of gossip around the company, but not even Clarissa La Rue had come out and uttered "Booth" and "fire" in the same breath. "Jimmy, you don't mean that—"

"I do. He could do anything. He scares me."

Jimmy was scaring me. "Harry," I said, "We should let Mr. Bliss have his nap. You promised him the bed, let him enjoy it."

Harry nodded. "Sweet dreams, Jimmy."

"May I have one more peppermint, Mr. Brown?" Jimmy asked, in a small-boy-sort-of-a-voice.

"Here, you take two," said Harry, and he set them on the night table. Jimmy popped one in his mouth, lay back, and closed his calf eyes. Harry and I slipped out the door.

"You're a wicked one, Harry," I said, as we walked back to the theatre. "I knew what you were up to with all that sympathy, and I should have stopped you."

"But you didn't."

"No, I suspect I'm as nosy as you are."

"Once that boy started talking, he didn't pull his punches."

"Nope. I confess, Harry, I feel a little knot in my belly right now."

"Something is rotten in the city of Nevada?"

"Perhaps."

"It doesn't bode well for the Star Troupe, all that nastiness. We have a long way to go yet." Harry pulled out another brown paper bag, this time from his pants pocket. "Well, Cinder-Emma, at least we know what's up. Knowledge is power. What do you say we forget our troubles at the soda fountain? On me?"

"I accept," I replied.

"Excellent!" smiled Harry, and he held out the bag. "Salt water taffy?"

Monday evening, after the play—

Tonight, the company commenced our Nevada run with *The Iron Chest*. The theatre was sold out, all eight hundred seats, and the hopeful waited about for standing room. Just before the doors opened, the street before the theatre bustled with patrons decked in their best. The music of their voices wafted genially into the auditorium. The dressing rooms were gardens, abloom with flowers from well-wishers. In the midst of the women's makeup table stood an elegant display, all white roses; and on fine pale stationery bordered with green was a handwritten note: "Shine on, brave souls! Break all your wonderful legs! Love and felicitations, Lola."

Whatever crises may have consumed the day, umbrage was put aside in the face of such good will. Mr. Booth and Mrs. Burnham played splendidly together, and Jimmy Bliss even remembered his lines. I managed to appear at the right places with the right costume pieces, and, even though I'm not an actor, to share in the excitement of the cast as they played for a rapt audience. At the final curtain, the company was gifted with a standing ovation. Many are still celebrating at the reception in the ballroom of Frisbie's Hotel. The knot in my stomach has loosened with such a grand opening—and I shall celebrate with a good night's sleep in the wagon. Jimmy Bliss turned in early, curled up in his blanket on the ground like an old dog after a rough day.

Tuesday, July 15. *After the play, about 11 p.m. I've collected a wealth of candle stubs!—*

Because we opened *Taming of the Shrew* this night, I spent much of the morning hanging out doublets and hose and pressing the ladies' bright skirts. But shortly before noon, I managed to visit Mr. Hamlin's bookstore. There is a payday tomorrow, and I had just enough cash in my sock that I might allow myself a purchase. Emmett's books are precious to me—I could no more part with the two that I have than with my arm—but I dearly love the fancy of a small book of my very own, with my name penciled inside the cover. I stowed the flatirons and started down Main Street.

I hadn't gone half a block when I spied Lola Montez heading my way, wearing a frock of apple green and pink that set off the roses in her cheeks. She sported an elegant bonnet, a wide crinoline, and dainty gloves. One might think that such a rare creature did not belong on the dusty streets of Nevada, but she picked her way through the potholes with bravado. Her brace of greyhounds imitated their mistress, delicate paws dancing down the street. She waved to me and sang out, "You! Young lady! I know you!"

She rushed to my side. "You're with the Star Troupe! You and Sophie Griffith decorated my front yard the other afternoon—two slumbering angels! You are--Miss Lightfoot! But you've changed your costume, no breeches today!"

"No, Miss Montez," I replied. "Not when I'm in town."

"Pity. I adore trousers. I once had a cunning little ensemble, trousers and a tailcoat. I wore it all about Paris in my younger days. 'Ou sont les neiges d'antan?'" She dabbed at her temple with her lace handkerchief. "The Star Troupe's opening last night was a grand success! My fingers are still tender from all that applause!"

"It did go splendidly," I said.

"I didn't see you at the fete afterwards. You should have come and enjoyed your moment."

"Oh, I can't take credit, Miss Montez. I do the laundry and darn the hose. I'm no actor."

"Miss Lightfoot," she insisted with a smile, "do not denigrate your contribution. Where would the company be without you? On stage in their shifts, with their toes sticking through their stockings!"

She giggled at the thought, and I did, too.

"You are an artiste as well, my dear," she went on, "as much as Mrs. Burnham or Mr. Booth. Now, you must come to my soiree on Friday evening to celebrate your troupe. After the play, chez moi. We shall dance under the moon!"

"Thank you, Miss Montez," I said. "But I'm not—"

"I shall accept no excuses, Miss Lightfoot."

"But I have nothing to wear, ma'am, not to a 'soiree.' I doubt denim trousers will suffice for such an occasion."

She stood back and eyed me. "I have just the gown for you! It will fit beautifully, and if it doesn't, well, you're the wardrobe mistress, you can give it a tuck. I'll bring it to the theatre!"

"Miss Montez," I said, "I'm very grateful, but I can't accept—"

"Of course you can. My dear, I am leaving the West. I am lightening my load. I can't possibly drag dozens of dresses east with me. You will be doing me a favor. Please."

"All right," I capitulated, though not without pleasure. "Thank you so much, Miss Montez!"

Her dogs were sniffing about the entrance to the Pacific Restaurant. One of them lifted his leg. "Dante!" she scolded. "We do not wee-wee on 'la porte.'" As she stepped toward the dog, she peered inside. "Oh, my, there's Ted Booth, having breakfast at noon. I must congratulate him one more time. Miss Lightfoot, I shall see you Friday eve. Dante! Michelangelo! Come!" And she and the dogs swooped in on Mr. Booth.

I turned onto Broad Street and shortly came upon a handsome, new, "fireproof" building, built of brick, not wood, and hung with green iron shutters. Across the front, on the story above the pharmacy, hung a neatly painted sign, "J.E. HAMLIN, BOOKSELLER." I mounted the stairs and stepped into Hamlin's store.

The smells of paper, ink, and leather bindings greeted me like old friends. I closed my eyes. If I stood still and sniffed a bit, I could almost believe I was back in the *Rattler* office, with Emmett at my side.

When, at last, I looked about, I was clearly in a different world. Emmett lived by his own rules of organization, and the *Rattler* office often resembled the wake of a tornado, especially right before a deadline. Mr. Hamlin's bookstore, on the other hand, is a haven of order—not the forbidding kind, but harmonious, like beautiful music. Gilt bindings shine from neatly stacked shelves, inviting you to pick a volume and begin its journey. The store's corners are shadowy and mysterious, but the center glows from a skylight in the ceiling. I could linger long in such a place, had I the choice.

Mr. Hamlin was on a ladder, tending a top shelf, but when he spied me, he smiled. "Miss Lightfoot! You've come for your visit!" he said, and he quickly descended. "I so enjoyed your troupe's performance last night. Hattie Burnham is a marvel!" he declared. "Oh, and Mr. Booth is very good, too. How can I help you?"

"I should like a small book, Mr. Hamlin," I replied. "I have a dollar. I don't suppose that will buy me a fancy binding, but it's what's between the covers that I seek."

"Well, let's see. Have you read Poe?"

"Yes, sir."

"Longfellow? Browning?"

"Yes, and yes."

"Hmm." He scanned the shelves. "Then what about John Keats? He's not a new poet, but I do have a new edition of his poems and letters. It can be yours for the extravagant price of seventy-five cents."

"May I see the book, please?"

"Of course," said Mr. Hamlin, and he placed the little volume in my hand. Its cover was deep blue, simple but pleasing. "You're welcome to sit right here, Miss Lightfoot, and have a look." Mr. Hamlin offered me a stool and, for a moment, pulled up one of his own beside me. "Keats was a young poet, and people your age enjoy him, although old folks like myself also find much to admire. He only lived to be twenty-five—the consumption took him—but he blazed through the world of poetry like one of Fletcher's comets. Are you a romantic, Miss Lightfoot?"

I almost blushed at the question, although Mr. Hamlin meant no harm by it. "I suppose I am," I replied, "though I try to keep my head in tricky situations."

"Then you shall like Keats. He was in love near the end of his life with a young lady named Fanny Brawne. But when he became ill, they had to part. He left England and went to Italy to regain his health, but he died and never saw his dear Fanny again."

"That's dreadful, Mr. Hamlin."

"I'm certain that it was, for Keats. But out of that love came some fine poetry. See what you think."

He returned to the ladder. I perched on my stool under the skylight, while the sun splashed a pattern on the floor about me, and Hamlin's tabby cat purred on a nearby shelf. I opened the little book, flipped through the pages, and found a title, "Bright Star, Would I Were Stedfast as Thou Art." As I read, I realized that Keats spoke to the steadily burning north star, and he wished that his love for Fanny Brawne might be as true. "Still stedfast," Keats wrote, "still unchangeable, / Pillowed upon my fair love's ripening breast, / To feel forever its soft swell and fall, / Awake forever in a sweet unrest, / Still, still to hear her tender-taken breath, / And so live ever—or else, swoon to death."

I was glad that Mr. Hamlin was no longer at my side when I took in those words—I felt a blush come on, as if I'd been spying into Keats's heart. I read "Bright Star" three more times before I turned the page.

I knew I should get back to the theatre, but I could not resist one more title, "When I Have Fears That I May Cease to Be." In this poem, Keats fretted about being robbed by death. Perhaps he knew, even as he was writing, that he would die young. It is a terrible thing to fear that none of life's promises will come true; that you will be cut off and sent into oblivion. The poet's desolation moved me to sniff back a tear. The tabby cat blinked, as if to say, "You silly human."

As I sat in the sunshine and grieved for Keats, I heard a familiar voice. "You're my finest accomplishment. Think well of me in time to come."

My father's ghost was in the room. I could feel him beside me, on the stool Hamlin had just vacated. I did not look that way, for fear his shade might dissolve.

"You suffered like Keats, Emmett, I know you did," I murmured. "I would have done anything to give you one more day."

The ghost sighed. "Dying was indeed a trial. The bitterest pill I ever swallowed."

"Could I have done more?"

"Not a thing, sweet girl. My time was up, plain and simple. And it's not so bad on the other side, although they could use a damn good newspaper."

"Did you find Calla there, Emmett? And the Elysian Fields?"

"I surely did. That dear steed whinnied with delight at the sight of me, and the Fields are pure paradise."

"What about Shakespeare?"

"Oh, a lively fellow, words pop from his mouth like sparks. Hard to get a whiskey with him, though—folks are lined up all the way to Mars hoping for a conversation. Better to shoot the breeze with a Jonson or a Racine—those old boys have plenty of time on their hands."

"Any sign of Booth Senior, Emmett? Any celestial performances?"

"No," Emmett replied. "Word is, the man's been indefinitely delayed."

"Oh." The sorrow in my father's tone led me to take a more cheerful turn. "Then might you have seen a poet named Keats?"

"Young man? Given to praising birds and urns?"

"Could be."

"I ran across the lad not long ago, lolling in the shade of a chestnut with a lovely young lady."

"Was he happy, Emmett?"

Emmett chuckled. "The boy was jubilant. Said he never writes his poems down these days, just thinks them to his dear Fanny, and she wishes her thoughts right back to him, like a heavenly telegraph. Still, I'd rather see a poem in print, myself, on the rear page of *The Rattler*."

I took a breath before my next question. "What about our family, Emmett? Have you found Charley? Or Bessie?"

"Yes," he said, with great tenderness. "It was a joyful reunion, dear girl."

"And my mother?"

I turned toward the stool. It was empty. I squeezed my eyes shut, praying I hadn't lost my father entirely. "Please, Emmett, tell me she's all right. Tell me she remembers me."

Emmett spoke softly in my ear, "She glows at the very thought of you, Emma. Why, look at you! A young lady with gumption. In the theatrical profession! And finding your way to such congenial spots as this. Books and tabby cats, two of life's necessities."

"I tried to have courage, Emmett," I said. "To 'chase my dreams,' like you hoped I would. I guess we'll just have to wait to see how it all turns out."

"I put my money on you, sweetheart," Emmett said. "My time is past. It's your turn, now."

"Please, Emmett, if my mama is nearby, can you ask her to come to me? I haven't seen her for so long."

"She's not far—she's always tending to one babe or another. I'll see what I can do—"

Just then, the store's door creaked open. "I'll always be with you," Emmett whispered.

"Emmett, stay!" I cried, under my breath—but he had vanished.

In bustled Mr. Fletcher. "Miss Lightfoot," he tipped his hat. "Delighted to see you! Has Hamlin been trying to woo you from the theatre and turn you into a scholar?"

"She already is a scholar, Fletcher," Mr. Hamlin came back. "I wish I could turn you into one. Law and astronomy, Miss Lightfoot, that's all Fletcher cares about. Doesn't know his Tennyson from his Pope!"

"My who?" laughed Mr. Fletcher. "Say, Hamlin, have you another copy of *Geography of the Heavens*? I've promised it to Booth. We shall be stargazing tonight!" And Mr. Fletcher launched into a rhapsody of the constellations they hoped to see.

I handed the book of poetry and my dollar to Mr. Hamlin, and while he wrapped the volume neatly in paper, I perused the stacks of stationery set out on a long table. Each pile was marked by a handwritten label: Letter, Foolscap, Gilt, Embossed and Plain. I could not resist running a finger across a sheet or two where the gilt shone and the embossed borders rose in leafy patterns. But the most pleasant pieces were plain, a delicate cream in color, and smooth to the touch, just waiting to be filled in with a pen. At a penny each, I added six of them to my bill. My last indulgence was a most practical one—a sturdy new journal. My first journal, a gift from Emmett, is nigh unto full.

Mr. Hamlin slipped the stationery into a little folder. "Excellent choice, Miss Lightfoot. We received that paper only last week." He held out my purchase.

"Thank you, Mr. Hamlin."

"You are very welcome. Perhaps I'll see you at the play tonight. And let me know how you get on with Mr. Keats!"

I hurried back to the theatre and busied myself with odds and ends. By late afternoon, I had time on my hands. I climbed into the wagon and unwrapped my stationery. I had letters to pen. I pulled a sheet of paper from the little folder and set to work.

My first letter was to Evie, and I copy it here, so I remember what was in my heart:

Dearest Evangeline,

When one begins a new life, one needs an old friend. Someone who knows who you were, and who will listen to your stories of whom you might become. When I feel your friendship ring on my finger, I trust that you hold the old me close in your affection; and remember, as you hear the seconds tick on Emmett's watch, that I cherish and protect the thought of you. So, we shall not be lost.

A person cannot go through fire without change, as iron is beaten into something new on the forge. But I pray that you are safe after the conflagration, and little Sparky, too, as he is such a comfort to you.

I have had adventures, Evie, and I could tell you of the actors, of Mr. Booth and Mrs. Burnham, and of all the folks who have welcomed us along the road. Also of a boastful outlaw, a lovely circus, and a fugitive, man-sized bird, and—oh, but what shall I have to talk about, when we meet, if I spill it all now?

When Placerville burned, I tried to hurry back to you, but I was prevented. Still, sometime soon, I shall return of my own free will. Then, we shall stroll arm-in-arm to the ice cream store, eat every bit we want, and chatter away about our journeys. I believe this. I must believe it.

If you receive this letter, please write to me. We shall be in Downieville shortly, and I shall call at the Post Office. If I found a letter from you in your own hand, what a joy that would be!

Until we meet once more, your dear friend,
Emma Lightfoot

I will post this tomorrow. Perhaps if I mail it to the Placerville post office, care of the Captain, he will know of Evie's whereabouts—if she is about. He is far too aged for her company, even if he is a kindly gent with a good taste in sugarplums, but he is the sole remedy at hand.

Next, I wrote a letter to myself. I had longed for words to cheer me on, but Emmett's visit has cheered me more than any letter I could write. After much pondering, my missive was short and sweet:

Dearest Emma,

Hold a steady course. Do not fear. Keep your stockings dry!

Fondest regards,
Yourself

The delivery of this bit of "wisdom" was instantaneous. I shall keep it close, in my oil cloth bundle, in case I feel myself swept away and need a little anchor.

Later this evening, as I helped the actors into costume, I came upon Lola Montez in the women's dressing room, lounging in a chair and gossiping with Mrs. Burnham. "Is he merely working himself into the Dane," she demanded, "or is he always so glum?"

"Was it early in the day?" asked Mrs. Burnham.

"Noon. A respectable hour for visiting with actors. But he was picking at his eggs and ham as if he were headed to the guillotine."

Clearly, they were talking of Mr. Booth. I took my time laying out Katherine's hats.

Mrs. Burnham tugged at a hairpin. "Did you say something less than tactful, Lola?"

"Of course not. I put an arm around him, and said, 'Brilliant show.' C'est tout. But all I received in return was a grunt."

"I don't know. The boy has his moods. Some if it could be *Hamlet*," said Mrs. Burnham. "He has a lot to live up to."

"Booth Senior?"

"Umm-hmm. Although Ted's already a better Hamlet than his father ever was. He simply needs to believe it."

"He needs to get out from under papa's shadow," Miss Montez went on. "Put a curse on that old specter and send him packing."

"Agreed. But it's not easy for him, Lola."

"Fiddle-faddle," said Miss Montez. She stood and paced the dressing room. "If I let all my ghosts get to me, if I dwelt on all my shortcomings and misadventures, I might as well have jumped overboard with Folland. Ted should have a long talk with the old man's apparition and boot that spook right out the theatre door!"

At that moment, I was called into the men's dressing room to stitch on a button for Mr. Moone. Whatever might have been dragging Mr. Booth into melancholy at breakfast, he was now playing the fool as he readied for Petruchio, dancing jig steps at the dressing room door. His mood spilled over to the rest of the cast and onward into the evening, as *Taming of the Shrew* played to a storm of laughter and applause. At the final curtain, Lola Montez's cheerful "Bravo!!" rang from the center of the balcony.

THURSDAY, JULY 17. *Morning.* Richelieu *tonight—*

Life can shift in a blink.

Yesterday, Wednesday, I stirred in my bed in the wagon shortly before dawn. I was perspiring beneath my blanket. As I struggled to peel it back, a dark figure appeared, framed by the round opening in the rear of the wagon canvas. "Sleeping well, Miss Emma?" drawled Mr. Booth. He scraped a match against the tailgate. As he lifted it to his pipe, it illumined his fine features. As he touched its flame to the canvas, I struggled to utter, "No!" but the word died in my throat. The wagon canopy erupted in fire, casting a blazing halo about Mr. Booth. I twisted to free myself from the blanket, and then I screamed. And screamed again.

"Miss Emma! Miss Emma!" Buck and Jimmy Bliss peered into the wagon. Mr. Booth and his unholy flames had vanished, but the Blisses, roused from their own dreams by my terror, looked as if they had seen a ghost. "Miss Emma, are you all right?" I found enough of my voice to assure them that I was well enough.

But my dream has haunted me since. My heart has told me to be steadfast in my belief in Mr. Booth, but my nightmare betrayed my resolve, creeping up behind me when my waking guard was down. I can only try to push it to the very back of my brain.

Wednesday's workday began as usual, except that a little extra excitement ran through the company—we were opening *Hamlet* in the evening. Mrs. Burnham called the actors to the theatre around eleven a.m. to work a few changes in the entr'acte numbers. I was out back, polishing boots, when I heard, "Excuse me, miss!"

A short fellow in a frock coat strode my way. He was pale, with a round face and blue eyes. He had a familiar look about him. "Is the Star Troupe playing here?" he asked.

"Yes, sir."

He lifted his hat. "My name is John Peele," he said. "And you are?"

"Emma Lightfoot."

"Well, Miss Lightfoot, it is a pleasure to make your acquaintance." He smiled. His teeth were tobacco-stained, but he was friendly enough. "I'm seeking a Mrs. La Rue. Is she about?"

"She's inside."

"Would you mind asking her to come out for a little chat? I'd be most grateful."

The La Rues weren't in the habit of collecting strange gentlemen. I hesitated.

"You can tell her it's her husband," said Mr. Peele.

"Oh," was all I could muster. I remembered where I'd seen those blue eyes before, but Mr. Peele was nowhere near "six feet under." Perhaps the story of his demise was one of Louise's whoppers.

"Miss Lightfoot?"

"Yes," I said. "Uh—of course. I'll be right back." I skittered up the stairs to deliver the good news.

I found the La Rues in the dressing room, where Mrs. La Rue was pinning the hem of Louise's new skirt. "Mrs. La Rue," I announced, "your husband is out in the lot. He's come to see you!"

Both La Rues stared at me. The pins in Mrs. La Rue's mouth rattled to the floor. "That's not possible," she declared.

"Oh, yes, ma'am, he's out there. He says his name is Peele."

"My father?" said Louise. There was terror in her eyes.

"No. It's no one," her mother snapped. "Louise, you stay right here, do you hear me? Miss Lightfoot, keep an eye on her, please," and Mrs. La Rue hastened out to the back stairs.

Of course, Louise made a beeline after her mother. I caught up with the child as she reached the doorway. I wrapped my arms about her and kept her there in the shadows. Mrs. La Rue flew down the steps like a Fury and rushed toward Mr. Peele.

"How dare you show yourself here!" she hissed.

Mr. Peele simply smiled his dingy smile and said, "I've missed you, Clarissa. I've come to take you home."

"Home? And where might that be?"

"I have a new claim, over in Drytown. A cabin and a garden plot. A cow, so there'll be milk for the baby."

"For the baby? You think you can buy us back with a shack in Drytown and a cow?"

"You're my family, Clarissa. I love you."

"You left us," said Mrs. La Rue, in a voice that should have turned Peele to stone. "You left us in a damp, godforsaken creek bottom where the sun never shines. A woman and two sick children, without a penny to keep the wolf from the door. We waited for you, and worried for you, and nigh unto starved before desperation drove us down the mountain. And that baby you're so concerned about—your son—never even made it out. He's buried in his blanket under a scrub pine, no thanks to his father."

"I'm grieved to hear it," said Peele. He hung his head and shuffled in the dust. "I am so sorry, sweetheart. I had an opportunity, you see, and I had to take it fast."

"Really? And what was that?"

"A land deal. Down in Chile. Didn't you get my letter?"

"Damn you, John!" The words exploded from Mrs. La Rue's proper lips. "Don't you try to flimflam me! The sheriff in Murphys told me everything. You were on the run, and then you were in jail. Next time you sell shares in a mine, make sure it exists!"

"I was in Chile!" barked Mr. Peele.

"Chile, hell. You were in San Quentin. How stupid do you think I am?"

"I don't, Clarissa," said Mr. Peele. He spoke softly now—butter wouldn't melt in his mouth. "I'm sorry. I'm sorry I left you in such straits. But I did my time, and I'm starting fresh. This claim looks good—"

"You have to work a claim, John."

Peele stopped and chewed his lip. "I want my family. Where's my daughter?"

Mrs. La Rue paled. "With friends."

"Now you're trying to flimflam me, Clarissa. I read the papers. I know she's here. She's quite the little star."

"Don't you come near her!"

"She's my daughter. I have a right."

"You have nothing. You abandoned us!"

"Unfortunate circumstances, Clarissa. But I'm her legal father. No judge in the state would deny me."

"You wouldn't dare—"

"I can find a judge this afternoon."

"No judge in his right mind—"

"She's mine, Clarissa. And everything she's earned, too. As far as the law is concerned, I'm entitled to my share. You've been stealing from me!"

They were letting it rip by now, playing to the back rows. Louise slipped from my grasp and ran to the edge of the landing. Peele spied her.

"Louise!" he called. "Come on down here! I'm your father. Come on, now!"

He headed up the stairs, but Mrs. La Rue was quick. She dashed up behind him, grasped his coat, and dragged at him until they both tumbled off the steps. They spun in the dirt like cats, screeching and hissing and laying on blows.

Louise stared at them, her jaw dropped nigh unto her pantaloons. "My father is alive," she whispered.

"It appears so, Louise," I whispered back. "In the full glory of his resurrection."

She looked up at me, horrified. "Who do I belong to now?"

She was shaking. I knelt and put my arms around her.

By this time, the caterwauling had drawn the Burnhams and Mr. Leach to the door. They peered out into the lot. "Oh, my God!" exclaimed Mrs. Burnham. "Ben, help!"

They rushed down to the two combatants, still scrabbling and screaming in the dust. Mr. Burnham's bellows of "Stop!" went unheeded;

the management had to lay hands on the couple, taking blows to themselves, to drag them apart. The invectives went on at length, and the threats flew, even as the pair was hauled to separate corners of the lot.

"If you touch that child, I'll kill you!" screamed Mrs. La Rue.

"I don't scare off so easy!" shouted Peele, as Ben Burnham and Mr. Leach gave him the heave-ho down the alley. "I'll be back! I swear I'll be back, and the law with me!!!!"

In the midst of this, Mr. Booth appeared at my side. I followed his gaze, not to the fight below, but to Louise, who still trembled, her mouth open for breath. "Excuse me, Emma," he said. I let go of the child's shoulder, and he scooped her up into his arms, then quickly disappeared with her into the safety of the theatre.

Mrs. La Rue was finally shepherded up the stairs and into a chair backstage. She was weeping, her lip cut and swollen. Mrs. Burnham struggled to get the details of Peele's threats from her. "Do you think he means it? Will he really be back?"

Mrs. La Rue spat blood into a handkerchief. "If John can be counted on for one thing, it's ruining other people's lives."

"I take it you've known all along he wasn't dead," said Mrs. Burnham.

Mrs. La Rue glared at her. "He was dead to me from the day I buried my baby."

Mrs. Burnham took her hand. "Clarissa, I think you and Louise should lay low for a few days. Just until we find out how far Peele will go."

Mrs. La Rue's eyes widened. "Oh, no, no. We have performances to do."

"We'll find someone to fill in, it'll be all right."

"Louise will be devastated. She's happy onstage, if you take that away—"

"She's upset, Clarissa, she's crying on Ted's shoulder right now. Imagine how she'll feel if Peele arrives with a sheriff in the middle of the show. He certainly knows where to find you."

Mrs. La Rue sobbed. "We can't afford to miss performances."

"We'll work out the cash problem later. The company can't afford to have this craziness happen again. We should move you from the hotel, too. Gus Thayer is staying with friends on Nevada Street—maybe they can find some room for you and Louise. I'll talk to him."

Mrs. La Rue calmed a bit at the mention of Mr. Thayer, but she only grudgingly surrendered to the thought that Louise and she disappear for a piece. While Mrs. Burnham went to make arrangements, she huddled in the chair, sniffling. Mr. Leach and Buck Bliss kept an eye out for Peele at the stage door. I was assigned to come up with a cold compress for Mrs. La Rue's lip.

When I brought her a rag soaked in cool water, she seized it from my hand with nary a "thank you," and lit into me.

"Why did you tell him we were here? This never would have happened if you'd kept your mouth shut. Don't you ever, EVER let that man put one over on you like that!"

I wanted to protest that I had no way of knowing Peele was "that man," but it would only have added fuel to the fire. Still, she kept at me, until it seemed she might split out of her skin. At that moment, a majestic voice cut in from behind me. "Mrs. La Rue, it was an honest mistake."

It was Mr. Booth. He went on, with all the authority that his deep tones could deliver, "It is not Miss Lightfoot's responsibility to sort out your private affairs. Your best course would be to put on a calm demeanor for your daughter's sake and go comfort her."

Mrs. La Rue was suddenly still, her mouth agape.

"Louise is in the dressing room. Please go," said Mr. Booth.

Mrs. La Rue rose. She muttered a parting shot, "I'm only trying to protect my daughter," pressed the compress to her mouth, and limped down the hall.

I turned to Mr. Booth. I desperately longed to hug him. Instead, I offered him my hand. "Thank you, Mr. Booth!"

He clasped it, and in his usual soft drawl, said, "It's Ted, Miss Lightfoot."

My ears felt a familiar burn. Ted!

Quickly, accommodations were arranged for the La Rues, and mother and daughter were spirited off to Nevada Street. As soon as they left the theatre, the Burnhams and Mr. Leach gathered the company in the auditorium. "Our first difficulty," said Mrs. Burnham, "is to figure out tonight's *Hamlet*. Clarissa is my lady-in-waiting, and I can live without a lady. But we do need a Player Queen. Ideas, anyone?"

"I vote for Sumner!" exclaimed Harry. "The man of the hour! How well do you handle a skirt, Moone?"

Mr. Moone hopped into the aisle and minced his way down toward the stage. After the nastiness of the last hour, we were all ready for a laugh, even Sophie, and we hooted at his antics. Mrs. Burnham applauded with the rest, but once Mr. Moone had returned to his seat, she confessed, "Truly, Sumner, if you weren't already the poisoner, I'd be greatly tempted."

Her gaze lit on me. "Emma Lightfoot, you can read."

"Yes, ma'am."

"Remind me, what were those lines from *Twelfth Night*? Something about a cabin?"

I knew what she was up to, but I obliged. "I should 'make me a willow cabin at your gate, / And call upon my soul within the house; / Write loyal cantons of contemned love, / And sing them loud, even in the dead of night!'"

"Lovely, Miss Lightfoot. I believe you've been auditioning one way or another since the day we met. Lose those spectacles for the evening, and you shall be our Player Queen!"

My stomach flip-flopped. "Mrs. Burnham, I'm no actor! I've never done more than to recite in class!" Sweat was breaking out on my forehead, and my knees were wiggly, too.

"Miss Lightfoot," Mrs. Burnham went on, "You underrate yourself. It's a tiny role, you'll be fine. Plus—I shall double your salary for today, and for any other day you might take the stage. Is that fair?"

It was the "double your salary" part that gave me pause and settled my stomach just the tiniest bit. I could feel the eyes of the company on me, all of them so skilled at what they did, but I also remembered Emmett's words, "Have courage. Chase your dreams."

"We'll help you, Emma, dear," whispered Sophie from the seat behind mine.

My glance fell on Mr. Booth. He smiled at me.

I took a deep breath. My throat was so dry, I could barely utter the words, "All right, ma'am, I'll give it my best. But—my salary is quite puny. I shouldn't even notice the difference until you triple it."

Mrs. Burnham stared at me, and then she burst into laughter. "You have me over a barrel, Miss Lightfoot! I am forced to agree to your terms. Triple salary—for today, at least. You are now an actress!" And the company delivered me my first round of applause.

Mrs. Burnham and Sophie whisked me off to the dressing room and rummaged in their trunks for pieces suitable for a costume, as there was no way to squeeze me into Louise's get-up, even if her mother had allowed it. By and by, they came up with a skirt and a bodice, which they dressed up with a sash and a paste tiara. Then, they dug through Mrs.

Burnham's box of stage jewelry until they found a ring that fit my finger. Mrs. Burnham slipped it on me, and the "emerald" flashed. Sophie and she stood back, gave me a nod, and hurried me out onto the stage.

We commenced to rehearse my first scene, where the company of traveling players arrive at the Court of Denmark. I was told to go stand in the wings with Mr. Thayer and Mr. Moone. I was to enter with them and go "downstage right." You would think that this would be simple, but it is a different world upon the stage—the minute I stepped out onto "the boards," I felt the place to be rarefied, and it discombobulated me. I headed across the stage until I saw that I was alone. "Miss Lightfoot, other direction," called Mrs. Burnham, not unkindly. "Stage right isn't the same as the right side of the stage from the audience's view. It's your right."

"Thank you," I managed to murmur, though I'm sure I turned bright red.

"Stay with the other actors and you'll be fine. Try that again."

As we moved to the wings, Mr. Moone took my hand. "Here, stick by me, Miss Lightfoot. All will be well." He gave my fingers a squeeze, and I almost believed him.

In the end, the scene went fine, because, except for Mr. Booth and Mr. Thayer, the rest of us had very little to do but watch and look like actors hopeful of employment. At our exit, I even made it into the proper set of wings, "stage left," right on the heels of Mr. Moone. Harry Brown stood there, watching. "Bravo, Cinder-Emma!" he grinned, and he clapped for me.

I was so happy to rehearse this scene first, where I did not have to speak. In the next scene, I was not let off so easily. This was the scene where the "actors" perform Hamlet's play, *The Mousetrap*, in which the Player King is poisoned by an evil nephew. As he had done with Louise, Mr. Booth showed me the Player Queen's moves and Mrs. Burnham coached me from the auditorium. I tried my best to be attentive, although I was distracted by the thought that I was acting with Mr. Booth—there he was, right by my elbow! "Do you have that, now, Miss Lightfoot?" he would ask, so amiably that I had no choice but to nod and hope to goodness I did.

Mrs. Burnham gave the actors their dinner break, but as they drifted from the theatre, she beckoned me over to where she sat in the shadows of the auditorium. "Miss Lightfoot, you did very well. Would you like me to help you learn some of those lines?"

"Yes, ma'am. Thank you! I made a stew out of most of them."

"It's a lot to throw your way at the last minute, but I know you're clever. If you forget your words, if you 'go up' as we say, you'll find Mr. Leach or Buck in the wings on the right—that's 'stage right.'" She grinned. "They're 'on book,' and they'll read the line to you, and then you can repeat it to Mr. Thayer." She glanced at the script in my hand. "The Player Queen was the first Shakespearean role I ever played."

"On the riverboat?" I wondered.

"Yes, indeed. I did love being the Player Queen."

"Then we shall have that in common, Mrs. Burnham."

She smiled at me. "Yes, we shall. Now—let's get to business. Read me your first line."

I did, and then the next line, until we had read through the whole part, and I knew the meaning of everything I was saying. Mrs. Burnham beamed at me, "Miss Lightfoot, I believe you are an actress!" I left the theatre with my head swimming but hope in my heart.

That hope lifted my spirits until I was halfway down the rear stairs. Then my knees began to shake again. Oh, dear Lord! In a few hours I would be standing onstage in front of hundreds of people, pretending I knew what I was doing. Was I insane? I clutched the stair rail to steady myself and kept a grip on it all the way down, until I touched solid earth. Then I took refuge in the wagon and huddled there, making every argument I could about why I should perform that night. "Lem can be stabled. Emmett would be thrilled. And in a hundred years, no one will know if I made an ass of myself or not." But I quickly realized that sitting in a corner wouldn't make me feel more serene about the situation. I was still the washerwoman, and work was the best remedy for nerves. So work is what I did, and I ran my lines through my brain as my hands kept busy darning and pressing.

Through the midafternoon, the theatre was quiet. Sophie was about for a bit, out on the stage, practicing her "mad" scene as Ophelia. She did so by herself, which made her appear even madder, tossing imaginary blossoms to empty air.

Shortly after she departed, Mr. Booth arrived. "Hello, Mr. Booth!" I called across the lot, and he nodded politely, but I could tell that he was not in a mood for conversation. He wandered the theatre for some time. He did not recite aloud as Sophie had done, but I could see that his mind was churning, and that he was not necessarily in the city of Nevada—perhaps he was in Denmark? Or in some other world where only he could go. Eventually, he slipped away, without a goodbye.

About six-thirty, Harry Brown showed up. "Emma!" he waved to me, as he hurried toward the wagon. "I came to wish you two broken legs!" He sat himself on the tailgate. I set down the flatiron and hopped up beside him. "Are you excited?" he asked.

"More like scared witless."

"Don't worry. You'll be wonderful. Remember when I guessed that you were a princess hiding behind a laundry tub? I was close! Except that you're a Queen! And I pay you tribute."

He brought out a rose he'd been concealing behind his back and laid it in my hand. It was deep red and smelled lovely. He is the nicest boy.

"Oh, thank you, Harry!"

"Don't be scared."

"I'm so worried I'll mess things up for everyone."

"It won't happen. If you lose a line, look to the prompter in the wings. Or most likely, the rest of us will just cover for you. Get yourself onstage and offstage on cue, and you'll be fine. Oh, and watch out for the footlights. Keep your skirt away. There was an actress down in Sonora who torched her costume last year—that's the sort of mishap no one can miss. She lit up—"

"Oh, Harry, I don't want the details. They don't cheer me."

He stopped. "I'm so sorry, Emma. Me and my big mouth. You're not the sort of girl to go prancing through the footlights anyway. I know that. Will a butterscotch make things better?"

Of course he had a bag in his pocket, and, of course, I said, "Yes." Candy always makes things better.

"I do have one little piece of wisdom for you, Emma," Harry said, through a mouthful of sweet stuff. "When I go onstage, part of me wants to be perfect, but that's a terrible burden, you know—and acting isn't about being flawless, it's about having the pluck to go out there in the first place. We all applaud you for that." And he kissed me on the cheek.

This was my second kiss in a couple of weeks! I wasn't quite sure what to make of it. I was even less sure when Harry said, "Oh, excuse me, Emma," pulled out his handkerchief, and wiped the stickiness off my face.

Just then, Mr. Thayer and Ulysses arrived. I blushed at the thought of what they might have seen, but Harry simply smiled at me as he tucked his handkerchief in his pocket. "You'll be the belle of the evening, Emma!" he whispered, and, with a wink, accompanied Mr. Thayer into the theatre.

I stowed the last of the costume equipment in the wagon. It was time—I could not deny the inevitable. I put my shoulders back and, with a stab at bravado, marched up the stairs to take on the role of actress.

Earlier, Mrs. Burnham had helped me to find my spot at the dressing room table. Louise's brush and rag curlers had been stowed on a shelf, and I'd set my comb carefully in their place. The comb had looked a little lonely. But when I entered the room this time, I could not even see it for the pile of gifts awaiting me. "Congratulations, Emma!" Mrs. Burnham and Sophie sang out. "It's your debut!"

I sat before my mound of treasure, feeling like a queen. From Sophie, there was a pale blue ribbon; from Mrs. Burnham, a lovely embroidered handkerchief. Mr. Thayer had left a half dozen fresh pencils tied with a string, and Mr. Moone a little bag of dried cherries. And from Mr. Booth, there was a package wrapped in paper from Hamlin's store. I peeled it away to discover a small, red-bound volume with *Hamlet* embossed on the cover in delicate gilt letters. Inside, on the first page, in his own hand, was an inscription:

My dear Miss Lightfoot,

"Speak the speech, I pray you, trippingly on the tongue!"
With all good wishes for your first appearance,
Best regards, and break a leg!

Ted Booth
July 16, 1856

I could not hope for a better gift! Or for as much generosity as the other actors had shown to me. After I thanked everyone, I simply had to sit for a moment before the mirror, *Hamlet* to my chest, and smile.

"Emma, dear, do you have any makeup of your own?" Sophie asked.

"I've promised her some of mine," said Mrs. Burnham.

"Oh, lovely!" exclaimed Sophie. "I'll share mine, too! Have you ever made up before, Emma?"

"No. I've never put anything on my face, let alone painted myself up for the stage."

"Why don't you give it a try? Just remember, you're an actress playing an actress who's playing a queen—a 'play-within-a-play,' you know—so you must be theatrical."

In no time, Sophie had gathered me brushes, powder and rouge, and some black stuff for my eyelashes. I did my best to paint the Player Queen's face over my freckles, but when I finally studied my reflection in the mirror, my heart sank. It was no one I knew. Truth be told, it scared me a bit. My face was almost white, and my eyes ringed with black. My lips were so red, I might have recently tasted blood. Mr. Thayer's King would be hard put to find affectionate words for a Queen who resembled a specter. But what was I to do?

Just then, Lola Montez breezed into the dressing room. "Hattie? Hattie, cherie!"

I dropped my face in the hope she wouldn't spy me. She didn't, at first.

"Hattie, I am so excited for you!" she exclaimed. "I'll be in the box on house left! Break every bone in your body, my dear!" and so on. They gossiped and laughed for a few minutes, and then, with an "Ah bien-toe!" Miss Montez headed for the door. But she caught me out of the corner of her eye, stopped, and stared. "Miss Lightfoot? Oh, dear. What happened to you?"

"I'm the Player Queen."

"Yes, so I've heard. But what is this makeup?"

"I'm supposed to be 'theatrical,' Miss Montez."

"Well, you are that. No one could deny it. Did you do it yourself?"

"Yes, ma'am."

"Ah-hah." She turned to Mrs. Burnham. "Hattie, would you mind—?"

"Not at all, Lola. I would have done something if you hadn't. Please. Go to it."

"May I, Miss Lightfoot?" asked Miss Montez.

"I suppose."

Miss Montez grabbed a towel and wiped the powder from my cheeks. "Now," she said, "let's see what kind of magic we can work. You have a lovely face when you're not behind those spectacles. Here, hold these." She pulled some of her own little paint pots and powders from her reticule. "I make them myself. Beauty is an art, you know. Sometimes a pure fabrication. Please, close your eyes."

She went to work, swiftly and surely, and hummed a little tune as she painted and drew upon me. "Are you thrilled about your debut?" she said.

"Yes, ma'am. And terrified, too."

"Some of us prefer to do the things that terrify us. We long to see life's dragons turned into handsome princes, if we only have the courage to look them in the eye. Perhaps you're one of those souls, Miss Lightfoot."

I sighed. "I can't tell yet, Miss Montez."

"Don't despair, my dear. Don't allow yourself to. Remember, you are a young woman to be reckoned with."

I liked the sound of that. "All right, Miss Montez. I'll try my best."

"Excellent. Now, take a look."

I peered into the dressing room mirror. I'd never seen the woman who stared back at me, but I'd always known her. She was painted, yes, her cheeks rouged, and her lashes darkened—but she had intelligence in her eyes, and in the set of her chin. She was, indeed, someone to be reckoned with. Maybe even a Queen. I met her gaze, and I knew I was only beginning to find out who she really was. "Thank you, Miss Montez," I said.

"It is my debut gift to you, Miss Lightfoot. Now, I suspect the house is about to open, so I must bid you adieu!"

Mrs. Burnham and Sophie were already getting into costume. Sophie cheerfully offered to help me dress. I have never been put into a real corset before, and she tightened the laces with enthusiasm. By the time Mr. Leach called, "Five minutes!" we ladies were ready to go.

I hurried over to the men's dressing room to make sure they had everything they needed. As I passed the open stage door, I spied Mr. Booth out on the landing, in his Hamlet costume. He was gripping the railing and breathing deeply. He turned my way for a second, and, star or not, he looked as pale and terrified as I was feeling. "Places," called Mr. Leach.

Though I was an actress this night, I was the wardrobe mistress, too, and there was no question of being able to watch the whole play. Still, I was able to linger in the wings through the scene where Hamlet encountered his father's Ghost. His friend Horatio had warned him that the Ghost might be an evil spirit, seeking to make Hamlet mad, but Hamlet ran recklessly onto the "ramparts," as a moth darts toward the flame, and rushed down to the front edge of the stage. Silently, the Ghost appeared behind him, floating up from the trap door in the floor as a wraith might rise from the grave. Mr. Thayer was a fearsome Ghost. His gaunt face, lit by the footlights from below, was skull-like beneath his helmet, and his eyes were sunken pits. He groaned, "Mark me!"

Hamlet whirled about. I had a clear view of Mr. Booth's face—it was a mask of terror. He stared so long upon his father's spirit, I thought perhaps he had forgotten his lines, though he never dropped his gaze. At last, with great determination, he seized upon the pledge, "I will."

The Ghost then poured out all the wrongs that he had endured. Though Mr. Thayer spoke most of the words and played them very well, my eyes were riveted upon Mr. Booth. The Ghost challenged Hamlet, "If thou didst ever thy dear father love…."

"O God!" Mr. Booth assured him, from the depths of his heart.

"Revenge his foul and most unnatural murder!"

I began to believe that this was the evil spirit Horatio had warned of. He wasn't like Emmett's ghost, who came to me in love. He was ferocious, and hideous, and demanded that Hamlet commit murder, too, and lose his own soul. What kind of father would ask such a thing of a son? He might as well have led him to his death in the swirling sea.

But Mr. Booth's Hamlet held nothing back.

"Remember me," hissed the Ghost, as he vanished back into the earth.

"Aye, thou poor ghost," said Mr. Booth. "I have sworn it." He was trembling with grief, haunted and nearly mad, but there was no doubt that he would keep his word to the old man, even though he would give his life for it ere the evening was over.

I've seen good actors play Shakespeare's plays. But, often, they have spoken the verse as if they were reciting a poem at the front of the class—you always knew that they were "acting" the words. Mr. Booth spoke as if he was living them, as his audience listened, hushed, in the shadows. I suspect it cost him. I wondered, where did Mr. Booth leave off, and Hamlet begin?

At the end of Act II, we neared the first entrance of the players, and the butterflies in my stomach rioted. I couldn't catch my breath, and the tight corset wasn't the only reason. Black spots began to appear before my eyes. I dashed for the stage door, as Mr. Booth had done, and tried to take in fresh air. Presently, I heard Hamlet speak the players' cue! I would have to either swoon or step onto the stage. I imagined Emmett at my side, "Get out there, girl!" I ran to my place just as Buck Bliss trilled the trumpet flourish for our entrance.

The players were gathered in a little stairwell offstage. We were to mount up three steps into the wings and enter, Mr. Thayer first, then Mr. Moone, and then me. I took two steps and my foot landed on the front of my petticoat, pulling me forward. I tried to save myself with my other foot, but it, too, tangled in the petticoat, and I went down, a fish trapped in the net of my own costume. I landed hard on my knees and palms. The more I tried to fight my way free, the more hopelessly I was caught.

In an instant, a pair of hands was at each of my elbows, lifting me up to the level of the stage. "Are you all right, Miss Lightfoot?" whispered Mr. Moone.

I nodded, "Yes."

"Bravo!" whispered Mr. Thayer. "Here we go!" And the players made our entrance upon the stage.

I put on a smile and did my best to play an actress, cheerful about arriving at the court of Denmark. My knees were stinging, but I felt strangely calm out on the stage. I could hardly have come up with a worse mishap than falling out of the wings on my debut, but I had been rescued by my fellow actors.

In my second scene, the "play," where I was to speak the Player Queen's lines, I tried to remember to pronounce them naturally, yet loudly. But, in the main, I kept my eyes on Mr. Thayer and listened as he spoke to me, knowing that if I faltered, he would reach out. Almost before I could blink, I was gripping the comforting hands of Buck Bliss and Harry Brown, as the company took a jubilant bow before the footlights.

As the actors headed for the dressing rooms, Mrs. Burnham found me in the wings. She wrapped her arms about me and kissed me on the forehead. "Good job, little one!" Emmett used to offer such encouragements, but, since he'd been lost, no one else had rewarded me so. I prayed that Mrs. Burnham would hold her embrace a tiny bit longer, but Mr. Thayer soon swept her away into the back hall.

By the time I finished clearing up costumes, the theatre was nearly deserted, except for the management sorting out the take for the evening—and except for Mr. Booth. As I passed his dressing room, he was hunched in his chair, elbows on the makeup table and head in his hands. I wanted to rush in, thank him for his gift and his kindness in rehearsal, and spill out, "Your performance was wonderful!" but he was clearly spent, even sad, and so I tiptoed away. He must have known he had a gaggle of admirers, mostly women, waiting at the rear of the theatre to congratulate the "star," but he didn't move. A half hour later, he was still in the dressing room, and, though many of his fans had departed, a few still held vigil, living on hope.

What is it about sad, beautiful men that draws women? I know I am not immune. When Mr. Booth is so forlorn, I long to wrap my arms about him. Sophie would happily sacrifice herself on his altar to save him from his sorrows, and so would dozens of the women who come to our plays. This is a mystery to ponder.

While Mr. Booth sat alone and melancholy, the Burnhams counted the evening's receipts, and their laughter and jokes spilled out into the hallway. Mr. Leach locked up the lobby and joined them, his laughter filling out the chorus. Suddenly, there was silence. Then Mr. Leach said, "That's all I want to know, Ben. Tomorrow's payday. Is there enough cash in the till to cover salaries?"

"Of course," said Mrs. Burnham. "We've had packed houses the whole week."

"We have. And so I ask, Ben, can we pay our actors tomorrow?"

"Absolutely."

"Good. And what about the rent on the wagon and the stock?" Mr. Leach went on, calm but persistent. "You're already two weeks behind on that. And on what you owe the boys and me for tending them—"

Mr. Burnham cut him off. "I know that, Jeriah. All too well."

"Then set things right. Maybe you have enough cash to make a dent in the debt."

"Maybe," Mr. Burnham said. "Listen, I'll make you a deal, Jeriah."

"A deal?"

"We've got one more *Hamlet* this week, and two performances of *Richelieu*. We know *Hamlet* will sell, and *Richelieu's* a crowd-pleaser. Let them all run, and I can promise you, the ticket sales will cover your debt and more. Only give me until Sunday."

Mr. Leach said nothing, merely shifted in his chair.

"Jeriah, we're almost past the losses in Georgetown and Coloma. And this town is good to us. Please, we can work this out. I'll make sure of it," said Mrs. Burnham.

Mr. Leach cleared his throat and grudgingly conceded, "All right. Actor salaries tomorrow, the rest on Sunday. The boys and I have kept our end of the bargain, so, for God's sake, keep yours." He rose and came down the hall toward me. His step was tired. I tried to make myself look busy.

But my mind was already on what I would do with my triple salary. I could afford to empty my money sock that night, on the promise of filling it again in the morning. I was now an actress, and I was going to sleep in one of the downy beds in the New York Hotel!

FRIDAY, JULY 18. *Morning. Our second* Hamlet *tonight—*

I was in the wagon Wednesday night, rummaging my money sock for dollars, when I heard, "Emma?" I stashed the sock in the folds of my bedroll and peered out. Harry Brown delivered me an exaggerated bow and declared, "Good evening, miss! Aren't you Nevada's newest actress?"

"For a few hours, I suppose. But fame is fleeting, Harry, and I need to take advantage of every minute." He offered me a hand, and I climbed down off the tailgate. "I'm celebrating by buying myself a real room tonight!"

"Truly? No transoms to be conquered? Where's the fun in that?"

"It's in closing my eyes in a comfortable bed. I was so jealous of Jimmy Bliss the other afternoon, I nearly spit."

"I'd like to have seen that," Harry laughed. "Shall I walk you to the hotel, then? You still have paint on your face--we don't want that weak-chinned night clerk to get any wrong ideas."

He offered his arm, and I welcomed it. It was late, and there were strangers on the street. When we arrived at the hotel desk, the night clerk did, indeed, have an unreliable chin and a scowl of disapproval to go with it. Harry looked him right in the eye and introduced me as, "That fine Shakespearean actress, Miss Emma Lightfoot, who has just appeared opposite Edwin Booth. She requires a quiet, respectable room befitting an interpreter of the Bard."

The night clerk cast a skeptical glance Harry's way but came up with a key, nonetheless. Harry delivered me to my door. "Don't snore too loud, now," he whispered. "I'm just down the hall, and I need my beauty rest." I shut the door upon his cheekiness and made for the washstand to scrub the powder from my face. Then, I shed everything but my shift and crawled in between cool sheets. In seconds, I fell into a deep and dreamless sleep.

Thursday morning, I found myself once more cast as the company's washerwoman. Louise's role in *Richelieu* is as a page, Francois. It appears that it's one thing to garb a small girl in a tunic and tight-fitting hose and call her a boy, but another to try to disguise a sixteen-year-old female. As salaries were handed out, it was announced that the Frisbies' son, Lyman Austin, would step in as Francois that night. I caught sight of his rehearsal later, and he looked promising. He has a strong, clear voice, that, at nine years old, hasn't even begun to crack.

Later, Mrs. Burnham took me aside to apprise me of what was up with *Hamlet*. After twenty-four hours, Mr. Peele had still not put in his threatened appearance, although the company was keeping a vigilant eye out for the man. If it looked as if he had abandoned his claims, Louise would step into our second *Hamlet* on Friday night. If he showed, the La Rues would stay in hiding until we departed Nevada on Sunday. Mrs. Burnham asked me to be ready either way the cards fell. I wished Louise and her mother well, but, I confess, I also welcomed the thought of visiting Denmark once more.

At the end of our talk, Mrs. Burnham added, "Oh, before I forget, Miss Lightfoot, the Frisbies have invited some of us to dine at their home this afternoon, and they've asked me to invite you, too. Will you join us?"

"Oh, yes, ma'am!" I replied. "Thank you!"

"Good! Mr. Booth also hoped you'd be included. He was quite pleased with your performance last night and your grit, too. Why don't you meet us in the lobby at three o'clock, and we'll walk over together?"

She went on with the details, but I hardly heard them, I was so tickled at being invited and, especially, at discovering that Mr. Booth had had kind words about my efforts on the stage. As I readied the *Richelieu* costumes, my feet barely touched the ground. About two-thirty, I turned my attention to pressing my best skirt and blouse and running a comb through my hair. Then, I hurried out to the lobby.

Mr. Booth waited there, with the Burnhams and Mr. Moone. Mr. Moone offered me his arm, and we embarked.

It turns out that the Frisbies live only a stone's throw from the theatre. I had imagined them in one of the elegant frame houses gracing the hillsides above town. Instead, they reside in rooms on the top floor of one of the new brick buildings, the kind that are built to defy flames. I also discovered, as we crossed Main Street and found their entryway, that they are perched next to the office of the *Nevada Journal*. As we mounted the stairs, I smelled ink and heard the sweet, familiar sound of a printing press.

Lyman Austin stood lookout on the landing. "They're here!" he hollered. "They're here!" He bounced so, I feared he might launch himself down the steps and into our arms.

Mrs. Frisbie appeared. She wore an apron over her stylish day dress. "Welcome! We're delighted to have you! And Miss Lightfoot, you made it too, lovely! Please, come on in."

She led us into the parlor, where we were greeted by Mr. Frisbie and Mr. Fletcher, who were sipping lemonade. "Sarah and I are just finishing laying the table," said Mrs. Frisbie. "Please, help yourselves to something cool. Mr. Frisbie?"

Mr. Frisbie smiled. "Of course! What shall it be? Lemonade? Ice water?" He lifted a pitcher from a silver tray, and the music of ice chips tinkled as he poured refreshment into delicate glasses. I savored my lemonade and looked about.

The heavy iron shutters on the windows had been thrown wide, and lace curtains fluttered in the faint breeze from the street. The carved armchairs and settee bespoke elegance, but mostly, the room was comfortable. Shelves were laden with books, and a carpet woven with roses softened the floor. In one corner stood a pianoforte, and by it, on the top of a cabinet, a fiddle, a small drum, and a tin whistle. Posters from the theatre's productions lined one wall, including one for our very own Star Troupe, announcing the week's plays and Mr. Edwin Booth.

"The town has loved *Iron Chest*!" Mr. Frisbie exclaimed. "And *Hamlet*, too! No, everything, by God! I can't walk down the street without some patron heaping praises on the Star Troupe!" Soon, the Burnhams and Mr. Frisbie were in a lively discussion of the theatrical business.

Mrs. Frisbie appeared, having shed her apron, and announced, "Everyone, please, come into the dining room!" Tempting smells had already wafted out to us, and no one lingered. We discovered a table draped with a fine white cloth and laid with china. At each place, silver gleamed. A crystal cruet set sparkled in its stand, and flowers floated in a painted bowl at the table's center. The marble-topped sideboard was laden with platters and serving dishes.

Because we were a bit of a crowd, the gentlemen hauled a couple of extra chairs from the parlor, and Lyman Austin settled himself on a tall milk can. Sarah, the hired Cornish girl, earned her keep and more, delivering one course after another to the table. We began with a soup of oysters and cream; then a platter of pink salmon. Roast beef followed, with tender peas still tasting of the garden, and small, savory boiled potatoes served with tiny onions. Our glasses were filled with red wine or more ice water. Near the end of the feast came poached pears and shelled walnuts; then a mince pie and strawberry ice cream! I barely had room for the fruit, but I reminded myself that ice cream can always be squeezed into one's belly!

Somewhere between the roast beef and the nuts, Mr. Frisbie turned to Mr. Fletcher. "What news of the heavens, Mr. Fletcher?" he asked. "Any comets flashing by?"

"Comets, no, but shooting stars abound, Mr. Frisbie, more than usual for July. Booth and I posted ourselves on the rooftop a few nights ago and counted dozens of them crisscrossing the Milky Way. You must join us one evening."

"He has a new telescope, Frisbie," said Mr. Booth. "I have now gazed upon the face of the moon!"

"Did she wink at you?" said Mr. Frisbie.

Mr. Booth chuckled. "I don't believe she dared. From the distance of earth, you know, she's a radiant maiden, but turn Fletcher's glass upon her and her secrets are out. Her complexion is lined with cracks and pits. Still—like any beautiful woman—her age adds to her mystery."

"My God, Booth," laughed Mr. Moone, "you're a poet!"

Mr. Booth shrugged. "All I can say, Moone, is that my window on the stars has made me very humble. Every night, Jupiter shines above us, holding court in the midst of all his moons, yet we can barely glimpse them with our feeble eyes. The Milky Way shimmers, millions of stars in her current, and yet we shut ourselves away, in dark caverns of theatres, playing out tales that signify nothing."

Mr. Fletcher threw his napkin down upon the table like a gauntlet. "No, no! I challenge your case, Ted. This week, my eyes have been riveted most strongly upon the stars on Frisbie's stage! Each evening, you have eclipsed the night before. *Iron Chest* and *Shrew* blazed at us, and then *Hamlet* burst upon your audience like a galaxy!"

"Here, here!" applauded Mr. Frisbie. "I rule in your favor, Fletcher!"

"And I sit upon the fence," said Mr. Moone. "I am in awe whether I gaze upon the majesty of the heavens or witness the beauty of Lear, weeping for his Cordelia."

"I agree, Sumner," nodded Mrs. Burnham.

Mr. Moone sipped his wine and went on, "Wonder is all about us—in the heavens, on the stage, in the smell of that mince pie. It's a miracle that we're here, alive to witness it. I suppose that's the final wonder."

The table was quiet for a moment, then Mr. Frisbie raised the wine bottle. "We should drink to that. More, anyone?"

He quickly filled the glasses, and we toasted, "To life and to wonder!"

clinking the crystal rims for accompaniment.

Mr. Burnham raised his glass once again. "Wonder is all very good," he said, "but here's to the beauty of this week's box office!" It was hardly an elevated sentiment, but no one could deny its veracity, so we lifted our glasses one more time in a toast to the virtues of profit.

The Burnhams were on their best behavior all afternoon. Mr. Burnham had shed his bandage days before, and his hair covered most of the wound on his scalp. Mrs. Burnham had been carefully hiding her bruised cheek with powder, and, as time passed, its purple hue had faded considerably. You would never know the Burnhams had been wrangling in the worst way less than a week ago. Perhaps they had worked out their differences. Or, perhaps, they were simply good actors.

Mr. Moone was smiling. I had noticed Sophie was not amongst the guests, and I hoped his heart had been able to put his grief for their broken love aside for a short while. He relished scooping the last of his ice cream out of its dainty dish, trying to gather all the bits of strawberry and tiny chips of ice. "My compliments on your cuisine, Mrs. Frisbie," he said. "You are a most excellent cook."

Mrs. Frisbie laughed, and then, seeing the surprise upon Mr. Moone's face, said, "Oh, please don't think me ungracious. I can take credit for planning the menu—but then I merely delivered the order to my restaurant. I have the most remarkable chef over there. He's the one who sweated over the stove, and our feast was dropped at the door right before you arrived!"

Mr. Frisbie smiled at her. "Caroline, I believe you mean *our* restaurant. Frisbies' Restaurant."

Mrs. Frisbie smiled sweetly right back at him. "You're right. Our restaurant." She folded her napkin and set it by her plate. "Of course, it's my name that's on the deed."

Lyman Austin rolled his eyes and slumped in his seat.

"Caroline—" said Mr. Frisbie.

"I don't see what the problem is, dear," Mrs. Frisbie went on. She turned to the rest of us. "You see, we practice a division of labor in this household. I tend to the mundanities, to the restaurant and the saloon. Mr. Frisbie is the patron of the arts, although, heaven knows, I love the theatre as well. But someone has to provide the bread and butter. Then Mr. Frisbie is free to follow his muse. We may toast the box office all we want, but the theatre can be a feast, or it can be a famine."

Mr. Frisbie scowled. "It's done damned well this week."

"It has, indeed," said Mrs. Frisbie. "And our guests are certainly to thank for it. All I'm saying is that a good saloon and a restaurant with hot meals will never go bust in a mining town."

Mrs. Burnham sighed. "Then perhaps it's time for me to pack it in and open that boarding house."

"Oh, absolutely not," said Mrs. Frisbie. "You're a wonderful actress. Never abandon the stage. Leave it to people like me to run the saloons, and you do what you do best!"

"Mother," Lyman Austin said, with a little whine, "Can we please stop talking about business and have some more ice cream?"

"Of course." Mrs. Frisbie turned to Mr. Moone, and with a twinkle, said, "Not everything came from the restaurant. Sarah and I have been cranking that ice cream churn since noon, and it would be a shame to waste a spoonful of it. Can I have her bring you another helping?"

Mr. Moone enthusiastically accepted the offer, as did I, and Mr. Booth, too.

When the last drops of ice cream had been devoured, the gentlemen retired to the parlor for cigars and Madeira. Sarah cleared the table and set out coffee for the ladies. Mrs. Frisbie poured a cup for Mrs. Burnham, but she fetched a second bottle of Madeira from the sideboard for herself. "Miss Lightfoot," she said, "Hattie is a teetotaler, but would you care to join me in a tiny sip of Madeira to celebrate your success on the stage?"

"Yes, ma'am," I replied. "I should like that."

She handed me an elegant little glass, flowers etched in the sides and a small bit of deep golden liquid in the bottom. I sipped it. It was sweet, and smooth, and it made me smile.

"So, Caroline," Mrs. Burnham began, blowing delicately on her coffee, "how did Frisbie consent to your name on a deed?"

"It was that law California passed back in fifty-two. The one that says women can own property in our own rights. My mother had just left me a nest egg, and, despite my affection for Mr. Frisbie, I was determined that it should go into some practical investment. I marched right out and opened up the saloon. Once Frisbie saw the cash coming in, he was much less indignant about the idea. Within a few months, I had enough in the bank to start the restaurant."

"And do you take charge of those accounts, then?"

"Yes, I do. They're in my name."

A frown creased Mrs. Burnham's brow. She set down her cup.

"Lyman manages the theatre accounts," added Mrs. Frisbie. "He adores that theatre, spares no expense. It's burned down five times already, but he always brings it back, bigger and better. He could pour money into it until doomsday. But, at least, with my funds, we'll always have something in our back pockets."

"Ben manages our accounts," said Mrs. Burnham.

"Is that a happy arrangement?"

Mrs. Burnham simply shrugged and took a sober sip of her coffee.

Shortly, Mr. Frisbie popped his head into the dining room. "I am an emissary from the gentlemen's camp. The cigars are now stubbed out, and the air has cleared. Would the ladies care to join us?"

We stepped into the parlor to find Mr. Booth, Mr. Moone, and Lyman Austin crouching on the carpet, laughing and shouting. Books and newspapers had been strewn about, and chairs rearranged. As I picked my way into the room, a small machine scooted across my path. I nearly tripped upon it.

"Beware, Miss Lightfoot," shouted Lyman Austin, "or you shall derail the New York Limited!"

"The what?" I wondered, as it whizzed under the settee and out the other side.

Mr. Booth laughed. "The locomotive, Miss Lightfoot, Have you ever seen such a thing?"

"I've never seen a real locomotive, Mr. Booth," I replied, "so I doubt if I should recognize a puny one."

"Come on down here and join us," said Mr. Moone. "Lyman Austin, please show this wonder to Miss Lightfoot!"

I squatted on the carpet, and Lyman Austin chased the little locomotive down. He flipped a switch on its underbelly, and, with a tiny growl, the wheels ceased their turning. It was a cunning piece of work, made of tin and brightly painted, with a car attached to its rear. "You see, this is the engine," said Lyman Austin. "And here, the bell." He snapped a finger against the bell, and it tinkled merrily. "You wind it on this side, with the key, and it runs and runs. It was sent all the way from New York for my birthday!"

"This is its route," announced Mr. Booth, "a perilous one, indeed," and I suddenly understood that the books on the floor had become tunnels and bridges, and the chairs had transformed into great caverns for the locomotive to conquer. "Give her another turn of the key, Lyman Austin, and let Miss Lightfoot launch her!"

I did, and with a clink of the shiny bell, the locomotive commenced her journey. Lyman Austin played the "engineer," shouting orders, and Mr. Moone dubbed himself the "switchman," dashing about to shift the tunnels and bridges and save the machine from plunging over "cliffs." Mr. Booth was the "stoker," supposed to "put on steam" when the locomotive climbed hillsides of tilted books. In truth, this meant his duty was to give the machine a little push to power her upward, but he was a troublesome hand. "Full steam ahead," Lyman Austin called, and the sleepy stoker replied, "Huh? What? You done ruined my nap!" and snored with all his might.

Then the frantic engineer shouted in his ear, "Stoke her up, you lazy dog!"

"Smoke her up?" Mr. Booth said. "She looks danged smoky to me!"

While they wrangled, the locomotive clicked away, stoked or no. Under Mr. Moone's watchful eye, she managed to wind her way up onto a chair, rattle over a bridge fashioned of a ledger, and finally careen across the refreshment table, past the pitchers on the silver tray and off the table's edge. There, she catapulted into the arms of Lyman Austin, to much applause.

As the boy laid his treasure back into its box, Mr. Frisbie asked, "Caroline, would you play for us?"

"I'd be delighted," replied Mrs. Frisbie, seating herself at the pianoforte, "if Lyman Austin will accompany me."

She searched for sheet music, Lyman Austin tuned the fiddle, and mother and son commenced to spin a web of enchantment through the little parlor, a filigree of melodies woven from bittersweet ballads and toe-tapping reels. We might have lingered under its spell for hours, but all too quickly the light beyond the windows dimmed with dusk, and it was time to head back to the theatre. Mrs. Frisbie wrapped a piece of mince pie in a napkin and tucked it in my hand. I determined to share it with Harry Brown, along with every detail of my adventure.

When I arrived in the back lot, Buck Bliss announced, with a grin, "There's a package for you in the wagon, Miss Lightfoot."

I rushed over to find a cardboard box with a ribbon about it. I tore the box open, and there was the dress that Lola Montez had promised me. It was a beautiful pale blue, with ivory trim. When I had a minute to try it on in the dressing room, I found to my delight that it fit almost perfectly, except for the bosom. Sophie took charge. "Emma, dear, this is nothing that a few stockings can't fix."

Before I could protest, she had stuffed three or four of them into the bodice, and she was right! I checked myself in the mirror, and although I appeared a bit more buxom than usual, I was passable. Sophie had saved me hours of stitching away, trying to fit that gown to my own lack of pulchritude!

I must send Miss Montez a "thank you" note without delay.

This was our fourth opening night in Nevada. By evening, the dressing rooms were again a-buzz with good wishes, and the dressing tables were laden with flowers and gifts. I had bought a little penknife at Hamlin's, and I added it to the pile of small treasures at Lyman Austin's place.

Mrs. Burnham arrived to discover a bouquet of delicate, pink roses, tied with a ribbon and laid neatly before her mirror. She lifted them up and searched for a card. "Does anyone know who sent these?" she wondered. "Did you see anyone bring them in?"

Sophie shook her head. "They're lovely, though."

Mr. Leach popped in at the doorway. "Half-hour."

"Jeriah," said Mrs. Burnham, "do you know who might have delivered these roses?"

"No. They were here when we got back from the dinner break."

"Would you ask in the men's dressing room if they saw anyone come in?"

Mr. Leach nodded, but he returned in a minute with, "No one has a clue, Hattie."

"Maybe you have a secret admirer!" gushed Sophie.

Mrs. Burnham frowned.

"It could be anyone, Hattie," Mr. Leach offered. "Nevada loves you this week."

Mrs. Burnham said no more, simply set the roses aside and started in on her makeup.

By the time "Places!" was called, the house was once again full, with standing room only. The audience settled, and the curtain rose on *Richelieu*. It is a handsome show, set as it is in old-time Paris, and a passionate one. The heroes were rooted for, and the evil Baradas booed. Lyman Austin remembered every one of his lines. It will always be a thing of wonder to me that Mr. Booth and the other actors pull characters out of themselves like rabbits out of a hat. The same young man who played a sleepy stoker in the afternoon can suddenly transform into Hamlet, or the crazy bridegroom, Petruchio, or one of France's most powerful men. I had seen snatches of Mr. Booth's Richelieu at rehearsal and had caught glimpses of him making up—carefully painting the age lines about his eyes and gluing on his grey beard—but, suddenly, there he was upon the stage, convincing hundreds that he was, indeed, thirty years older and six inches taller, and the nemesis of France's enemies.

Frank Mayo's performance as the handsome De Mauprat showed little of Mr. Booth's craft, but I had to admire his bravado. During a duel with the villains, his rapier flew out of his hand and into the front row of the audience. It was sheer luck that it didn't harpoon someone. It landed with a clatter at the feet of an astonished patron, who gingerly lifted it up. Mr. Mayo hopped off the stage and seized the sword with a flourish. Then, exclaiming, "Mercee, Monsoo-er!" he leapt back up into the scene and carried on with the skirmish. The audience cheered at his audacity. Imperfection does not daunt Frank Mayo.

In the last minutes of the play, after Richelieu had saved France from the conspirators and the lovers from their enemies, Mrs. Burnham as Julie rushed into the arms of her beloved De Mauprat, and a solitary hoot of crazy laughter exploded from the balcony. Mrs. Burnham peered quickly out into the darkness, then turned her gaze back upon her lover. When the company took their bows in the footlights, she stared desperately up into the far reaches of the theatre. Mr. Thayer met her in the wings as the actors poured off the stage.

"Did you hear him, Gus?"

"I did. There's either a coyote in the balcony, or—"

"An outlaw."

Mr. Leach spied the pair in the shadows. "I believe Tom Bell took you up on your invitation, Hattie."

"I'd hoped he wouldn't have the sand to show his face. Do you know if anyone saw him come in? Buy a ticket?"

"I doubt he's in the habit of patronizing the box office," Mr. Leach replied. "And if anyone in the company had seen him, they'd have spoken up. He sneaked in somehow."

“He might still be out there,” said Mrs. Burnham.

“He might. Ben and I will lock the doors and look around.”

“Hattie,” said Mr. Thayer, “do you need an escort back to the hotel?”

“No. Ben can get me there. We'll slip out as soon as we can.” She put her hand on his. “But thank you, Gus.”

Mrs. Burnham hastened back to the dressing room. Mr. Thayer stationed himself in the hall until Ben Burnham and Mr. Leach returned with word that Tom Bell had vanished as quietly as dew on a summer morning.

The Burnhams started for their hotel. I sought my bed in the wagon, curled up, and pulled my blanket to my chin. This night, the boards beneath my bones were not so merciless, for I quickly found a happy memory to comfort myself to sleep. At the Frisbies' dinner party, as Mrs. Frisbie and Lyman Austin sought their sheet music, I'd been startled by the rasp of a match, struck against Mr. Booth's shoe. “Forgive me, ladies,” he murmured, “I cannot deny myself one last indulgence in Frisbie's fine stogies.” As he brought the match to his cigar, its flame threw a hint of firelight upon his face, and my heart shuddered at the sight. I quickly chided myself for my dark thought, and in a moment, Mr. Booth banished all my fear. He offered me his hand. His touch was graceful, his palm smooth, his gesture that of a kind friend. He helped me rise up from my spot on the parlor carpet and settle into an armchair, a princess escorted to her throne. I took another sip of Madeira. Mrs. Frisbie and her son began to play the sweet Scottish song, “Ye Banks and Braes,” whilst I relaxed back against the velvet of the chair, and the Madeira warmed a spot in my middle. The lace curtains cast delicate shadows on the floor. Mr. Moone and Mr. Fletcher leaned against the mantle, swaying ever so slightly to the music. Mr. Booth sat on the carpet, Lyman Austin's little engine at his feet, and the pleasure in his eyes as innocent as a boy's. I glanced over at Mrs. Burnham, on the settee, and she smiled at me. I was already smiling, like a child on Christmas morning.

We were not the family around the table in the white house in Placerville, the one I could only witness from the street. Nor were we the faceless family of little ghosts in my dream. But we were a family, few of us related by blood, but all of us tied by something almost as strong. For the first time, in the days since Emmett's death, I was not an orphan. I had found my way home.

I cannot fit another line into this journal, and so, for now, I must declare,

INTERMISSION.

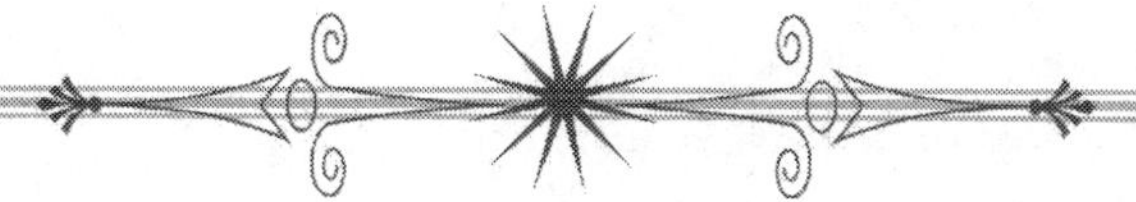

JOURNAL 2

Phoenix Wings

JULY 19 TO SEPTEMBER 2, 1856

"But when I am consumed in the fire,
Give me new Phoenix wings to fly at my desire."

—John Keats

SATURDAY, JULY 19, 1856. *The city of Nevada, State of California. The wee hours. My bed in the wagon behind the theatre—*

It is either very late or very early. I cannot sleep. I know I shall pay for it tomorrow, but the more I try to squeeze my eyes shut, the more my brain races. If I spill my thoughts out of my head and onto paper, perhaps I can rest before dawn breaks over me. The candlelight flickers across my new journal, purchased, with my little volume of Keats, from Hamlin's bookstore. The journal's surfaces, smooth and blank, offer up a mystery. What adventures will fill its pages in days to come? What events that only heaven can yet imagine?

Yesterday, Friday, began calmly enough. I had time in the morning to sort out the *Hamlet* costumes for the evening's performance and to wash hose and shirts. As I labored at my laundry tub, I conjured up a game. In this theatre company, the Star Troupe, I am the washerwoman and, as of this week, an actress in a very small part. But, in my heart, I am still my lost father's daughter, his right hand on our newspaper, *The Placerville Rattler*. I cannot scrub a shirt without seeking its story, and so, as I worked, I spun out "The Language of the Laundry." Even a lowly stocking told a tale of the actors about me and offered the chance of a special secret.

At the top of the heap of laundry was a fine linen blouse, lace at the sleeves and collar. It belonged to Hattie Burnham, our actress-manager, and it smelled of rosewater, a simple scent for a woman of such beauty and determination. Her husband Ben Burnham's clothes bore an overlay of saloon stink and cheap perfume--not, sad to say, Mrs. Burnham's rosewater. Edwin Booth's shirt delivered hints of pleasant, rich tobacco and shaving soap--not a whiff of liquor, at least not on this day. I was tempted to set it aside for a short spell, as if a bit of our star, "Ted," still inhabited it, but then I scolded myself for silliness and tossed it into the soapy water. Right behind it went Sophie Griffith's chemise. The girl's garment reeked of strong gardenia perfume, as if she were trying to pass as more worldly than her seventeen years, and the Bliss brothers' long johns nigh unto whinnied of horses and hay. Mr. Thayer's laundry smelled of bay rum, almost never of sweat, as one might expect of our gentlemanly character actor. And my new friend Harry Brown's stocking had a sizable hole in the toe, in the same spot where my father, C. E. Lightfoot ("Emmett" to me), used to wear his socks out. I liked young Harry all the better for it, and I darned the stocking for him. At last, I turned to Mrs. Burnham's "bloomer" skirt, a thing of fascination with its kinship to trousers and its pocket meant to hide small weapons. I still travel on my old mule Lem in my father's worn shirt and trousers, but perhaps, someday, I shall attain Mrs. Burnham's elegance on the trail!

At the bottom of my wash pile was La Petite Louise La Rue's pinafore, left behind when she and her mother Clarissa fled the theatre on Wednesday. It had pockets, too, still filled with our sweet-voiced "fairy star's" found treasures--pretty stones and a bit of green glass. Louise has had a rough time of it. I know the child thought me a villain for betraying her when she took Miss Griffith's butterfly brooch, but I have done what I can in the days since to regain her friendship. I decided to save the finds in her pockets for the next time I saw her. When life is full of jolts, and one is only seven, small, lovely things can be a comfort.

In the midafternoon, Hattie Burnham met with some of the actors to rehearse bits of *Hamlet*. She began with her leading men, Edwin Booth and Frank Mayo. After Mr. Mayo sent his sword flying into the audience during last night's performance of *Richelieu*, she reckoned practice was in order. The stage door at the top of the stairs was open, and the music of striking rapiers wafted into the back lot.

Mr. Thayer, in his neat grey coat, brought down a dressing room chair and waited in a scrap of shade, his mutt Ulysses at his feet and a newspaper in his hands. Presently, Sumner Moone, the company's song and dance man, came hurrying down the stairs, toting his own chair. He set it beside Mr. Thayer and flopped into it in disgust.

Mr. Thayer raised an eyebrow. "How's it going in there?"

Mr. Moone scowled. "Ted would have ripped into Mayo a half-hour ago if he wasn't his friend. Frank's going to cost someone an eye—or worse—if he can't get control in those fights. I'm lucky I don't make my last entrance in *Hamlet* until after he's dead."

Mr. Thayer shook his head. "I know. The boy is sloppy and undisciplined. But with time, he might even prove passable."

"If we live that long," said Mr. Moone. "He doesn't have a clue about De Mauprat."

I was by the wagon just then, writing in my journal, but I set it down and tuned my ears. De Mauprat is Frank Mayo's role in *Richelieu*. It isn't like Mr. Moone to criticize another actor, or anyone, for that matter, but he kept at it. "No one will think he's a hero just because he has a pretty face. He has to have a soul."

"He does." Mr. Thayer grinned. "A rambunctious one, but he's got some feeling there."

Mr. Moone snorted. "Oh, please, Gus. He shouts the whole damn scene with Richelieu." Mr. Moone jumped up and gave an uncanny imitation of Frank Mayo, hollering and sawing the air with his arms. "'THY ACTS ARE THEY ACCUSERS!!!!!' " The actor threw himself back into his chair. "Mayo's just blamed shallow. And it's a shame!"

As Mr. Moone spoke, I realized he had a point. Frank Mayo *was* loud, and sometimes I couldn't sort out what in heaven he had just said. And then I remembered Mr. Moone's recitation to empty Room 306 in the American Hotel, when he had hoped that the unfaithful Sophie Griffith was on the other side of the door. "Love is not love that alters when it alteration finds," he had murmured. That came from his heart, and every word rang true.

Later in the afternoon, Harry Brown dropped by the wagon. He fished out two shiny apples, one from each pocket, and gave me my choice. We lounged on the wagon tailgate to savor them, and, between mouthfuls, I shared Mr. Moone's criticisms. "You're a good actor, Harry. Do you think Mr. Mayo is 'shallow' as De Mauprat?"

Harry laughed. "Shallow as a dry creek bed. Moone has a point, Cinder-Emma, but then, consider the source."

"Meaning?"

"Meaning Sumner Moone had hopes for that role, himself."

I stopped, mid-bite. "Really? The hero? But he plays the funny parts."

"Usually. But I think, before Frank was hired for sure, that Moone had his sights set on playing De Mauprat."

"But he doesn't look a bit like a De Mauprat," I said.

"No, that's Moone's misfortune, isn't it? He can do anything--sing, dance, turn handsprings across the stage. And he could certainly act the deuce out of that role."

"I believe he could."

"At least, he wouldn't fling his sword into the audience. That was a narrow escape the other night, Emma. For a minute, I could just see the headlines, 'Homicide in the Front Row.'" Harry chuckled and tossed his apple core to the far side of the lot.

Just then, Mrs. La Rue and Louise hurried around the corner of the theatre and up through the open stage door. No one had seen them since they'd gone into hiding after the unfortunate appearance of Mr. Peele, Louise's father, who, contrary to rumor, was not the least bit dead. Harry threw me a look. I tucked what was left of my apple into the wagon--it would be a treat for Lem Mule. Then we both hustled into the theatre after the La Rues. We found them and most of the company on the stage.

Mrs. Burnham took Louise's hand. "How are you doing, Louise?"

"She's fine," said Mrs. La Rue. "She wants to perform tonight."

"We've seen hide nor hair of Peele," said Mrs. Burnham. "Has he been sniffing after you two?"

"No!" declared Mrs. La Rue.

"You know his habits better than we do, Clarissa."

Mrs. La Rue's eyes gleamed with tears. "I never know what he'll do. He may be in Sacramento by now, shuffling from the bottom of the deck in some deal of his. Or he may be so desperate to leech from us that he's still hanging around Nevada. But we'll never get away from him without Louise's salary."

Mrs. Burnham frowned. "Ben?"

"Payday was yesterday," said Mr. Burnham. "She wasn't present."

"You could have sent it by way of Mr. Thayer," Mrs. La Rue snapped.

"Ben, why don't you go fetch the La Rues' pay while we sort the rest of this out?" said Mrs. Burnham.

"Whatever." He stomped up the aisle and through the theatre lobby to the street.

Mrs. Burnham turned again to Mrs. La Rue. "We'd like you and Louise back in your roles, too, Clarissa. But it's a risk."

"Please. We are desperate for funds."

At this moment, young Jimmy Bliss, who had been on sentinel duty by the wagon, ran onto the stage, his calf-eyes wide. "He's coming!" he blurted to the La Rues. "Peele! He must have followed you here! One of the fellows with him is wearing a star!"

Mrs. La Rue paled and gripped Louise's hand. "Oh, no! We have to go!" She dragged Louise toward the front rim of the stage.

"Clarissa, over here! It'll be all right," said Mr. Thayer. He lifted the trap door in the middle of the stage floor from whence he had made his entrance as the Ghost in *Hamlet*. "If anyone knows the bowels of this stage, it's me." He stepped onto the ladder that descended into the hole and held out a hand. "Pass Louise on down. Quickly!"

It was Mr. Booth who scooped up Louise and delivered her to Mr. Thayer. Then he gave the child a wink. "Hide and seek, Louise. Be very quiet!"

Mr. Thayer disappeared with the girl down into the darkness. Mr. Moone took Mrs. La Rue by the arm and steadied her as she descended, too. But boots clattered in the wings before Mr. Moone could close the trap. Mr. Peele appeared, trailed by what looked to be a sheriff and another burly fellow. "They're in here," he declared, with the triumph of a hunter treeing a pesky raccoon.

Mr. Moone leapt into the open trap, only his shoulders and head above the plank floor, and began to sing his droll Gravedigger's song. Then, he ducked under the stage and popped up again with the property skull for *Hamlet*. He tossed it to Mr. Booth, who came in right on cue for the scene at the edge of Ophelia's grave.

"That skull had a tongue in it, and could sing, once!" said Mr. Booth's Hamlet.

Harry quickly stepped to Mr. Booth's side.

Mr. Booth lifted the skull, tilting it to catch the light. "Alas, poor Yorick! I knew him, Horatio." Harry gave a mournful nod. "He hath borne me on his back a thousand times."

By now, Buck Bliss, as the Second Gravedigger, had stooped beside Mr. Moone, and Mrs. Burnham stood back, regarding the "rehearsal" with intense concentration. The interlopers were left to stand at the side of the stage, until Peele protested, "Do something, dammit!"

The sheriff took off his hat and tiptoed over to Mrs. Burnham. "Excuse me, ma'am," he whispered.

"Yes?" Mrs. Burnham replied, her eyes still upon the actors.

"I am so sorry to interrupt," said the sheriff, but then, he lit up. "I saw *Hamlet* the other night. You were wonderful! You were all wonderful!"

Mrs. Burnham was suddenly at her most charming. "Why, thank you so much!" She offered the sheriff her hand and then greeted the big fellow, too, and made introductions all around—although Mr. Moone remained in the trap, and the authorities had to lean down to congratulate him on his success.

Peele was, by now, about to rupture a vein. "Sheriff, for God's sake, it's not election-season! Quit the glad-handing and do your duty!"

"In good time," the sheriff replied. He returned to Mrs. Burnham, fingering his hat brim. "I regret to inconvenience you, Mrs. Burnham, but Mr. Peele is seeking his family. He has an order from the judge for the child's custody."

Mrs. Burnham smiled. "We haven't seen them since Wednesday. Miss Emma Lightfoot, here, has taken on his daughter's role." I delivered the sheriff a small curtsey, hoping to pass as a practiced member of the acting profession.

Peele would have none of it. "They came into the building, and you know it!" he snarled. His stained teeth were more dingy than ever.

The sheriff regarded him with a pained glance, the sort you might turn on a nasty blister. "Do you mind if we look around the theatre?"

"Why, of course not," Mrs. Burnham replied. "As long as you don't mind if we continue our rehearsal. We're brushing up a few spots."

"I don't know how you could improve upon your performance," said the sheriff, with a blush, "but I do thank you for your courtesy!" He bobbed her a little bow, then turned to the irate father. "All right, Peele, now to our 'duty.'"

They began by scouring the auditorium and the lobby. The actors picked up the graveside scene again, and carried on with it until the search party had disappeared into the dressing rooms. We could hear them rummaging about and Peele's increasingly angry protests. Mrs. Burnham suggested, pleasantly, "Why don't we take another look at that final scene in the throne room? Run the duel one last time?"

In a second, Mr. Moone was out of the trap. Mr. Booth helped him close the door as he delivered a furtive wave down to Louise and held a finger to his lips. We hurried the piece of "royal carpet" out onto the stage, unrolled it over the trap door, and set the thrones atop it. Mr. Booth and Mr. Mayo seized upon their swords and went at it.

A few minutes later, Peele and the officers were back, pausing in the wings as Laertes and Hamlet delivered their death blows. The sheriff applauded with enthusiasm, then stepped over to Mrs. Burnham. The carpeted trap door lay just beneath his feet.

"You were right on the money, Mrs. Burnham," he said. "They're not here."

"She knows more than she's saying," muttered Peele.

Mrs. Burnham shrugged. "Perhaps they've returned to Sacramento."

"Well, I'm deeply sorry to have bothered you," said the sheriff. "If you see them, will you let me know?"

Mrs. Burnham looked him straight in the eye. "Absolutely. And I'm so glad you enjoyed the performance. If you wish to come again, we'd be happy to provide complimentary tickets. We always set a few aside for important guests."

The sheriff was tickled at that one. "Thank you, ma'am!"

The search party headed for the rear stairs. The sheriff looked back once, over his shoulder, and Mrs. Burnham fluttered him a little wave before they vanished into the wings.

The company froze right where we stood and listened as their boot steps echoed more and more faintly. The stage door closed with the click of a latch, and Buck Bliss began to lift one of the thrones off the carpet. "Buck, wait!" Mrs. Burnham whispered. "Jimmy, go take a look."

Jimmy made for the door. A few seconds later, he hurried back. "I didn't see anyone."

Mrs. Burnham nodded. Mr. Moone and Buck Bliss shifted the thrones while Mr. Booth stooped for the carpet.

The stage door squeaked open. Mr. Booth swiftly rose, then stepped to the center of the rug. Mr. Peele shot onto the stage like a bullet. He stomped over to Mrs. Burnham.

"I know what's going on," he hissed. "I saw them come in here. I'll find them, one way or another. And when I do, I'll have you up for obstruction of justice."

"I'm not afraid of you, Mr. Peele."

"You should be. You may have buttered up that sheriff today—don't think I didn't see what you were up to—but I'll be back."

"Mr. Peele, don't you think your wife and daughter would be with you, if they wanted to be? Threats can't hold a family together. If you came to them with genuine affection—"

"Affection, my ass. They're mine."

Mr. Booth spoke up, a quiet fury in his voice. "One day you might want to be remembered in more than your daughter's nightmares, Peele."

"What do you know about it? A namby-pamby *actor*?" Peele pushed in toward Mrs. Burnham, his face right up in hers. "If they don't show themselves today, I'll dog you through the camps until they do—"

A rough voice cut through the dark auditorium, "That's no way to speak to a lady!"

A stranger appeared from the shadows, stalked down the aisle to the edge of the stage, and hoisted himself up. He was decked in an ordinary shirt and coat, frayed about the sleeves—an unremarkable figure, until he pushed up his broad-brimmed hat, revealing gunmetal eyes and a ferociously flattened nose. It was the highwayman Tom Bell--Hattie Burnham's "admirer" from her riverboat days, who had haunted the theatre the night before. Even without the boilerplate armor he had sported on the road to Georgetown, his countenance bespoke a man who lived outside the rules. He grinned at the company, then delivered Mrs. Burnham a wink. "Is there a problem here, ma'am?"

"You're damn right there's a problem!" said Peele.

Tom Bell placed a congenial hand on the man's shoulder. "You need a sympathetic ear, my friend. Why don't we find ourselves a whiskey and sort this out?"

"Who the hell are you?" Peele sneered.

Tom Bell's grin grew even wider. "A patron of the arts."

Peele pushed Bell's hand off his shoulder. "This is none of your business. Stay out of it."

"I disagree. I have a deep interest in the theatre. It offends me when piss-ants like you mess with my favorite company. I expect Mrs. Burnham would like to hear your apology."

"When hell freezes over!"

Tom Bell's hand shot out once more and clenched Peele's shoulder so tightly the outlaw's knuckles blanched white. "Owww!" Peele yelped and tried to twist free, to no avail.

"My, you really do need that drink," said Tom Bell. "Now, move!" He propelled Peele toward the stage door. Before they disappeared into the wings, the outlaw turned, yanking Peele almost off his feet, and lifted his hat to Mrs. Burnham. "That was as fine a *Richelieu* as I ever did see, Hattie. You've come a long way from the riverboat."

Peele squirmed. "Let me go, you son-of-a—"

Bell shifted his grasp from Peele's shoulder to the neck of his shirt, squeezing the smaller man's voice to a gurgle. "It's time to leave the lady in peace, hombre. Adios, all!" He shoved Peele out the stage door and dragged him down the stairs.

For a second, no one moved; then a handful of us raced out to the landing. Down below, Tom Bell hustled Peele toward the alley. His gravelly tones drifted up our way, "Now friend, what shall it be? A whiskey or a beer?" and he laughed that crazy hoot of his. They disappeared behind the rear of Frisbie's Restaurant. We headed back into the theatre to find Mrs. Burnham slumped on her throne, a hand to her forehead.

"How long was he out in the house?" asked Mr. Moone.

Mrs. Burnham rubbed her temples. "Who knows?"

"The sheriff never even saw him," said Mr. Booth.

"No," replied Mrs. Burnham. "That doesn't mean anything. He could have been up in the rafters, for all we know."

There was a knock on the bottom of the trap door, and a muffled voice. "Is the coast clear?"

"Oh, dear God, Gus!" exclaimed Mrs. Burnham.

Mr. Booth and Harry pulled the carpet away, and Mr. Moone threw open the trap. Mr. Thayer ascended the ladder to the stage, Louise in his arms. She had cobwebs in her hair, and tears stained her cheeks. Mr. Thayer handed the child to Mr. Booth and helped Mrs. La Rue up out of the hole. She was shaken and tearful, too. "He's gone, then?" she said.

"Oh, yes," said Mrs. Burnham. "Could you hear down there? Tom Bell has taken charge of him. He's 'buying him a drink.'"

"What do we do about that?" wondered Harry.

"Do?" said Mr. Moone.

"Bell's an outlaw. Aren't we supposed to do something about it?"

"An outlaw?" said Frank Mayo, his eyes wide. "That was an outlaw?"

Mr. Booth dabbed at Louise's tears with his handkerchief. The girl whimpered.

"I suggest we let him buy Peele that 'drink,'" said Mr. Thayer.

"They'll never see the saloon, Gus," said Mrs. Burnham.

"Sure they will."

Mrs. Burnham looked to Mrs. La Rue. "Clarissa?"

"I'd say John deserves a 'drink' about now," she said, a steely edge to her voice. "He always liked his whiskey."

At that moment, Mr. Burnham came down the aisle with the La Rues' pay, and Mr. Peele's fate was left to Tom Bell and God.

Mr. Burnham handed Mrs. La Rue a fistful of coins, and she counted them.

"This is short," she declared.

"You missed performances," said Mr. Burnham. "We paid your replacements. We're not responsible for your personal situation, especially since you signed on under false pretenses. You're no widow."

Mrs. La Rue stared down at her pay. Her hand trembled. "We can't get by on this."

"Ben," said Mrs. Burnham, "give them the rest. It can be a loan for now."

"No."

"Fine." Mrs. Burnham lifted her reticule from the side of the stage and pulled out several small gold pieces. Mr. Burnham glared at her, but she handed them to Mrs. La Rue. "This is not a loan, it's pay, and a little extra for the next couple of days. Take Louise back to your lodging, and take tonight and tomorrow off. Louise needs some kindness right now."

"Thank you," said Mrs. La Rue, quietly.

"And you need to stay out of sight. That sheriff might take a notion to claim a house seat."

Mrs. La Rue nodded. "Of course, yes, we'll keep to our room. But we have to perform again soon. We can't afford not to."

"You can join us on Sunday, Clarissa, when we leave town." Mrs. Burnham knelt by Louise, still clinging to Mr. Booth, and brushed a bit of web off her forehead. "Don't worry, Louise, you'll be in the play again in a couple of days. All right?"

"All right," Louise replied, in a very small voice.

Buck Bliss saw the La Rues back to their room, and the Burnhams retreated to the lobby to rail at each other over finances. I rushed to the wagon to touch up my costume, since I would be filling in for Louise and acting the Player Queen this night!

While I heated the flatirons, Mr. Thayer reclaimed his chair in the shade. He patted Ulysses, who had dozed through the whole commotion. Then he pulled his hat down over his eyes and was about to drop off, too, when Mr. Booth appeared. "Ted," he called, "are you going to supper?"

Mr. Booth shook his head. "I've lost my appetite, Gus."

"Louise?"

"Umm-hmm. Children deserve better than to be wrung out by lunatic parents. I reckon I'll remain an old bachelor all my days and spare some poor infant the grief."

Mr. Thayer handed him the newspaper. "Today's *Nevada Journal.* Your notices should cheer you up. They are enthusiastic, in the extreme. Page two." Mr. Thayer rose and straightened his waistcoat. "I am now on my way to partake of that fine mince pie at Frisbie's Restaurant. Ulysses!" The dog yawned and stretched, and they ambled off.

Mr. Booth settled into the empty chair. He picked up the newspaper, and soon, in spite of himself, was smiling at the contents of page two. Then he began to skim through the rest of the news. I thought that I might go speak to him about how kind he'd been to Louise, but he suddenly stood up, scowling, threw the paper in the dust, and rushed from the lot.

I hastened over and retrieved it. The paper was folded open to the page headed "Out-of-Town News," where the editors had reprinted the latest articles from the *Sacramento Union*. Nearly buried at the bottom was the insidious item we had seen before, headed "Remarkable Coincidence." It cast aspersions on Mr. Booth, hinting he had set fires in the towns we had played, and it trumpeted the words, "While childish 'fairy stars' are the rage in the Mother Lode, we sincerely hope that a 'Fiery Star' has not also graced her stages."

Because the offending article was so short and reprinted in tiny type, it was almost invisible in the midst of the other Sacramento reports. Mr. Thayer had no doubt missed it. But Mr. Booth's eyes had been keen and had settled right on the sentences that could wound him.

As we readied for *Hamlet* in the dressing room, Mrs. Burnham helped me with my makeup and gave my hand a squeeze before she went onstage. The butterflies in my stomach, ferocious on *Hamlet*'s opening night, had calmed down considerably for this second performance. When I stepped out of the wings and arrived at the Court of Denmark, I almost felt at home. I could sense the good will of the audience embracing us, even from the balcony, where the candles flickered cheerfully in their sconces. I played my role, small as it was, with all my heart.

The actor struggling through *Hamlet* this night was Edwin Booth. His performance wasn't poor—even when he is "off," he is still very good. But, on Wednesday's opening, he had been inspired. Now, he hit rough patches. Perspiration gleamed on his brow, and several times he was so distracted that he had to look to the prompter at the side of the stage. Between his scenes, he spoke to no one.

I watched his efforts from the wings, and I thought of our talk at the soda fountain in Coloma. Mr. Booth had revealed to me that he often fought onstage to drown out the intonations of his famous actor father, Junius Brutus Booth. He had to push the old man's performances out of his brain before he could find his own voice. Perhaps, tonight, Booth Senior was whispering too loudly in his ear. Or perhaps, as Hamlet flailed about trying to avenge his father's ghost, Ted Booth was reminded of his failure to save his own father from a solitary death on a riverboat. Most likely, though, the *Union* article had simply shaken him into turmoil.

After the play, Sophie and I hurried back to the dressing room to don our gowns for Lola Montez's soiree. The celebrated Countess of Landsfeldt was throwing her doors wide for the Star Troupe! Sophie wound my blue ribbon through my hair and lent me one of her costume necklaces. I was tempted to forsake my spectacles for the evening, but then how should I see the sights? I still felt elegant, even with specs upon my nose. Sophie and I primped in the mirror and giggled like belles. I could only imagine what my dear friend Evie would think, to see me adorned in such girlish splendor!

Most of the rest of the company spruced for the soiree, too. Mrs. Burnham slipped into a stunning burgundy silk. She was almost ready to depart the theatre, when she discovered that Mr. Burnham hadn't even changed. He was enjoying a smoke on the rear landing.

Mrs. Burnham peered through the doorway. "Ben, hurry. We'll be late."

"I'm not going," he announced. "I have business to attend to around town."

"In the middle of the night?"

He didn't reply.

"Ben, Lola's gone to a lot of trouble. She's sold some of her jewelry to cover the expense of this evening. She's our friend."

Mr. Burnham took a draw on his cigar. "She's a witch, and I have no intention of paying court to her."

"Fine!" Mrs. Burnham turned her back on Mr. Burnham and strode off to gather her shawl and reticule.

Mr. Thayer had planned on going back to his hotel, but, once he heard that Mrs. Burnham was unescorted, he decided to ride along to keep her company. And, of course, Buck Bliss and Mr. Moone needed no persuading.

Mr. Booth, however, was in a black mood and had barely managed to towel off his powder. Mr. Mayo observed him for a moment from the hall and then settled into the chair beside him. "Ted, you are a damned slow son of a gun. At this rate, all the whiskey shall be drunk before we darken Lola's door. Move it along, man!"

"I'm not going."

"The hell you aren't! You're the star, for God's sake."

"That's debatable."

"Oh, Ted, don't do this. Come on. Some nights are better, some are worse. I had a good night tonight—I did not skewer a single soul. I'd like to celebrate that, and I'd like you to be with me when I do. You might actually have a good time."

"You're an optimist."

"And proud of it. Ted, come along. As my friend. I shall be desolate if you don't."

"Oh, all right," Mr. Booth groaned. "I can't abandon you to despair."

Frank Mayo gave a whoop and did a victory dance up and down the hall.

A few moments later, Mr. Booth passed by the women's dressing room and spied Sophie Griffith and me playing in the mirror. The frown on his countenance yielded to a smile. "You look beautiful, ladies," he said. "Miss Griffith, charming! And Miss Lightfoot, you never cease to amaze me with your transformations! From mining girl on muleback to a lovely young woman!"

I was so tickled, I could hardly mumble, "Thank you, Mr. Booth!" before he gave us a little bow and went on down the hall.

By and by, Harry Brown appeared at the dressing room door. "Cinder-Emma," he said, presenting me an arm, "May I escort you to the ball?" He offered his other elbow to Sophie, and the three of us marched out of the theatre and into the silver of the full moon.

Still Saturday, July 19. *Very late morning. The wagon—*

I woke, not long ago, to find I'd fallen asleep sometime near dawn with my pencil in my hand. My open journal had been my pillow—my cheeks are still lined with creases from the outline of the pages. Buck Bliss, God bless him, let me sleep in as he rustled up a company breakfast over the fire. He left a tin plate of cornbread and a boiled egg on the blanket beside me.

It is a quiet morning. The day is pleasant, except for a hot breeze from the west, lifting off the baked flatland of the Sacramento Valley. I would guess that most of the actors are still dozing in their rooms. There is no rehearsal for anyone until later this afternoon, when Mrs. Burnham will gather the company to talk over the entr'acte numbers for the benefit tonight. I have washed my face and hung up my party gown, and I shall try to finish the tale of last night's revels.

As Harry, Sophie and I paraded out of the theatre in our finery, we discovered a big wagon waiting by the front steps. Lola Montez had hired it to transport any of us who preferred the comfort of blankets and fresh straw to the rigors of a saddle. Harry lifted Sophie and me up, then leapt in after, and we squeezed ourselves into a comfy spot along the rail.

When the wagon was full, the guests packed in like eggs in straw, the driver shook the lines, and the team gave a brisk start. Quickly, we rolled up Broad Street and turned across the bridge, hooves and wagon rims clattering on the planks. Beyond Deer Creek, we moved into soft darkness, the road pale before us and the pines on the hilltops grey sentinels in the moonlight.

Though nature slumbered, we lunatics in the wagon kept up a sprightly chatter. The journey from Nevada to Grass Valley is only a few miles through the hills, and, with all the gaiety, it seemed mere minutes before we were passing up Grass Valley's Main Street. The inhabitants of the shacks on the outskirts of town had long ago blown out their candles, but the saloons, on a Friday night, were abuzz. Still, as we turned the corner onto Mill Street and headed south, music and laughter advertised Lola Montez's house as the liveliest spot in the camp.

The party was well underway, the premises overflowing with Nevada County's finest and not-so-fine. Miss Montez's automatic piano had been loaded with its roll of music and tinkled through the trees to greet us. Lanterns flickered from branches above the yard, their glow spilling onto dancers swirling below. The hostess had not skimped on the "spread"—tables were laden with ham, and beef, and fat loaves of bread, not to mention fruit and cakes. And she must have emptied her entire cellar of its champagne. As we rolled up to the front gate, Miss Montez reigned from her porch steps, where she lifted her glass to the crowd and exclaimed, "Drink up, ladies and gents, the Countess commands you!"

When she spied the Star Troupe, she rushed down to embrace us all and welcome us into the yard. And when she spotted me in the dress she'd given me, she winked and whispered, "Glorious, Miss Lightfoot!" I felt a blush tint my cheeks, but I can't say that I minded it! Then she put an arm across Hattie Burnham's shoulders and spirited her off toward the house.

Starving actors that we were, Harry, Sophie and I made a beeline for one of the food tables and piled our plates high with every sort of indulgence, then found a corner where we could delight in our haul like greedy children. But the music was, in the end, even more tempting than the food, and, shortly, Harry asked Sophie for a dance. They disappeared into the crowd, whilst I lounged back on Lola's lawn, licking icing off my fingers. The dancers whirled by, all of them lively and most of them graceful, sweeping through the moonlight in their finery. Soon,

Harry and Sophie danced their way back into view, Sophie giggling at something he'd said. Nearby, Mr. Thayer and Mrs. Burnham spun about the yard, and Lola Montez smiled in the arms of Frank Mayo. Later, she smiled in the arms of Mr. Moone, and half a dozen others. Once, when the music was especially merry, she swished her skirts and stamped out bits of what looked to be a Spanish dance, to the delight of the couples about her. Even Miss Montez's pet bear danced, swaying on his back legs at the fringe of the yard, a bright ribbon gracing his collar.

When Sophie finally ran out of breath, Harry dashed over to me and held out his hand. "Honor me with this dance, Miss Lightfoot?"

"Oh, Harry, we've already proven that I'm treacherous to your toes."

"You were in boots then, my dear. And the pleasure far outweighed the pain. Come on!"

"My hands are sticky from that cake."

"Lovely! It'll make you even sweeter than you are. Get up, Lightfoot!"

And so, I did, and we danced until the both of us were silly. We danced the polka, and the Virginia reel, and, soon, I almost had the hang of it!

Harry Brown is a fine, handsome dancer, and a patient teacher. I should not have hoped for more. But I did have a foolish thought that I could not banish--the wish that Mr. Booth would ask me for a turn under the trees. Perhaps his compliment on my dress had stirred my hopes. In fact, he danced with no one. In a moment of stillness, while a hired boy reloaded the piano roll, I caught a glimpse of him through the parlor window, solitary, reading a book by the light of a table lamp. His privacy was short-lived, though. Minutes later, he had been discovered and was encircled by enthusiastic fans—mostly women.

Presently, Lola Montez stepped to the center of the porch and rang a cowbell to catch everyone's attention. She smiled at us—beautifully—and thanked us for being her guests before she led us in an enthusiastic round of applause for the Star Troupe and the Frisbies. Then she lost her smile. "As you know, I am departing for the East Coast. I do so with a heavy heart, but I can see, like any good miner, when the vein is tapped out. I shall seek my fortune in faraway New York, but a part of my soul shall always remain in Grass Valley. This dear cottage is the only home that has ever truly been mine. I shall grieve for my roses, and my pets, and my dear Bernard." The bear let out a tiny roar at the sound of his name—some folks laughed, and some were near weeping. "Most of all, I shall miss you, my California friends, who have welcomed and embraced me. Merci, mes amis, and adieu!" She blew us a kiss and hurried into the house. I believe I saw tears in her eyes, and I believe that they were true.

As Miss Montez made her exit, an imposing gentleman bounded up the steps. He was clad in a finely tailored coat, and a diamond sparkled from his gold watch fob. "Southwick," Harry murmured.

"The mine owner?"

Harry nodded. "He runs the Empire Mine. We're standing right above it, you know. Lola might own enough of this ground to plant her garden, but everything below that is Southwick's."

Southwick beamed at us and announced, "We shall miss our Lola, but she does not desire to leave us in tears. It is my pleasure to introduce her dear friend, the musical artiste, Mr. Ole Bull, who has consented to play us a few numbers on his incomparable violin!"

Mr. Bull stepped out onto the porch, gave a little bow, and placed his instrument under his chin. In truth, he didn't resemble an "artiste," although he was neatly dressed. His blond hair was shaggy, and he had a rawboned build, the sort you might find behind a plow. But his hands drew enchantment from the strings—elegant, pure melodies, that wrapped about his audience like fine gold wire. As he held his last note, we were all silent—all save an owl somewhere up the hill, who joined in with a spirited, "Hoo-hoo!" Mr. Bull laughed and then declared, "A music lover!"

He reached out his hand. Lola Montez emerged once more from the house and stood by his side. "This last piece is a waltz. So, all of you, please, celebrate this evening and our hostess, and dance!" Harry Brown took me in his arms, Ole Bull touched his bow to the strings, and a sweeter waltz Grass Valley never witnessed.

After Mr. Bull drew out the final flourish, Harry and I determined that our throats were seriously dry, and he went to fetch us champagne. I wandered around the outside of the house to the back, to visit with Miss Montez's beloved pets, but the little stables and pens stood dark and empty. No kittens rushed out to rub my ankles, no goats pushed their heads through the rails for a scratch. The chicken house was abandoned. Except for the dogs, the cockatoo and Bernard, Lola's dear ones had vanished.

A cigarette glowed beyond the pens. I made out Frank Mayo, sitting on a stump with a whiskey bottle in one hand. "Mr. Mayo," I called. "Where has everyone gone?"

"To new homes, Miss Lightfoot. The livestock to ranches, the cats to whoever would take them."

"That's sad," I said, "to go from being a Countess's darling to Sunday's roast chicken."

Mr. Mayo nodded. "A serious reversal of fortune. I suggest you don't think about it too much."

"What about Bernard?"

"He's a problem. Not many folks want a bear in their yard. Lola's working on it. I hope she finds him a situation soon, because she leaves next week."

I knew that Miss Montez had been loved by many--the rich and the famous, as well as the infamous--and that Frank Mayo had been her latest conquest. "Will you go with her?" I said.

"No."

"Don't you want to?"

Mr. Mayo took a pull on his cigarette and said, "Miss Lightfoot, I haven't been asked."

So, there it was. Frank Mayo was being left behind, too. He was not the sort to "bounce" back from a broken heart, as Lola Montez had predicted so breezily. He was desolate.

"I am so sorry, Mr. Mayo," I said. "It's none of my business. I should have kept my big mouth shut."

He shrugged. "Don't worry about it, Miss Lightfoot. I was a moth to the beautiful flame. It's not like I didn't know it."

Just then, Harry wandered into the back yard, champagne in hand. "There you are!" he said. "I was afraid I'd have to down this all by myself!"

Mr. Mayo took a long sip of his whiskey. Harry looked from Frank to me. "Did I interrupt something?"

Before I could reply, a small crowd came stumbling around the side of the house, laughing and carrying on, and well-armed with alcoholic beverages. The only person I knew was Mr. Booth. He nodded to Harry and me before he spied Mr. Mayo hunched in the darkness.

"Frank!" he declared. "It's bad business to drink alone. Come on, man, we're bound for the Forest of Arden!"

"Why not?" Mr. Mayo rose and tossed his whiskey bottle into the scrub. "This one's dead anyway. The Forest of who?"

Mr. Booth snorted. "Into the wild, Frank, where nothing is what it seems. 'Once more unto the breach, dear friend!'"

Mr. Booth slipped an arm around the waist of a young woman. From what I could see of her in the moonlight, she was one of the admirers who had pressed in on him in the parlor. She gazed up at him, adoration in her eyes. Then the whole bunch crashed through the brush and ascended into the woods behind the house. Laughter and voices were already ringing out from the very top of the hill.

"What's going on up there, Harry?" I wondered.

"You don't want to know, Cinder-Emma."

I smelled something sweet and smoky on the faint night breeze. "I might. We could follow them."

"Don't you dare."

"Harry, you can't tell me what to do."

"No. But I wouldn't let my sisters go up there, so make of it what you will."

I am not accustomed to taking orders from a young man barely older than myself. I whirled about and stomped away from him, albeit toward the front of the house.

"Emma!" he called out. "I'm just looking out for—oh, for the love of God, be sensible!"

I reached down, picked up a stone, and chucked it at him. I believe, in the darkness, I missed his person, but I did hear a champagne glass shatter on the ground.

"Emma!!"

I ran into the front yard. All I wanted was a quiet spot where I could hold onto my heart until the fury stopped pounding through my veins. Pockets of revelers still crowded the lawn. I glanced up at the porch. One end was empty, and quite dark. I skittered up the steps, settled into a rocking chair, and leaned back.

Yes, I'm the sensible one. I'm not supposed to flare up. I'm supposed to use my head. But, in that moment, I felt anything but sensible, and I'm still not sure why. Was I angry for the pets' sake, creatures who've been forsaken and will never understand the reason? Angry because Frank Mayo truly does have the soul of a lover, and no one gives it mind? Or because Harry Brown bossed me around? He had no right to, but then he hardly deserved a rock aimed at his head, even if I did miss. Or was I set off by the ease with which Mr. Booth embraced that girl? What business was that of mine? He's handsome and he's a star, and only an idiot would expect him to be chaste. Was I an idiot?

I don't know how long I huddled there in the rocker, tossed about by arguments with myself. I finally stopped chewing on them long enough to notice that I had company down at the other end of the porch. Lola Montez and Mrs. Burnham lounged in the wicker chairs, the tips of their thin cigars burning crimson. Miss Montez's cockatoo, up late for a bird, strutted along the rail in time to the piano music, bobbing her head in her own little dance. Her pale feathers glowed in the night like a tiny ghost.

"When I finish this smoke, I have to go," said Mrs. Burnham.

"So soon?" said Miss Montez. "Don't. Stay in the guest house. We'll have a wonderful breakfast tomorrow afternoon. Or, at least, wait for the wagon and ride along with the others."

"Gus will keep me company. He's bringing the horses around. I'll be all right."

"Is this about Ben?"

Mrs. Burnham nodded. "I don't know what he's up to. I probably can't do anything about it anyway, but I'm uneasy being over on this side of the hill."

"Then you'd better go." Lola Montez clasped Mrs. Burnham's hand. "But I'll miss you, Hattie. I don't know when I shall see you next."

"I'll miss you, too. God knows California has its characters, but what will the gossips do without you? We could always count on Lola Montez to stir things up."

Miss Montez laughed. "It's been quite a fete, hasn't it? But it's time. And it's more than the Gold Rush going bust. It's in my bones." She touched a fingertip to her side. "I broke this rib once, in Ludwig's court, dancing an over-enthusiastic tarantella. It gives me a twinge whenever the weather shifts. And, these days, it aches from morn to night."

"Your farewell speech was lovely."

Miss Montez pulled her shawl about her shoulders. "If I think about it too much, Hattie, I shall weep again. Do you know that rose bush by the front gate? With the gorgeous red blooms?"

"I think so."

"It was woefully neglected in my absence. I resurrected it, with love and endless pitchers of water, and, now, I shall have to leave it again, to die at the hands of a stranger."

"Then perhaps you should stay."

"I can't. I haven't the means to keep even a cottage. 'We are Fortune's fools.' One day, a palace, the next, barely a penny."

"Doesn't King Ludwig send you a bit? I thought he adored you."

"I thought so once, too, but who's to say? Perhaps he only collected me. He had portraits painted of all of his women, you know, and there our heads hung on the palace walls, like hunting trophies. Mine just happened to be decked in a flashier frame than the rest. Come, Gip!"

The spaniel, who had been lying at her feet, hopped into her lap and lifted adoring eyes to his mistress. "Now, there's love, Hattie dear," Miss Montez chuckled. "True love."

Mrs. Burnham gave the dog a pat and said, "I'd better get my things."

"Hattie, at least stay for the seance. The Pembertons are very good, they've come all the way from San Francisco. Calling up loved ones is their specialty. I saw them in Oakland, and they were magnificent."

"I don't think so, Lola. I'm in show business myself, I know smoke and mirrors." Mrs. Burnham stubbed out her cigar.

"But, if there was a chance you could speak to Tench, or to Henry--"

Mrs. Burnham was silent for a moment. Harry Brown had told me of her love for Tench Fairchild, her first husband, and their baby Henry, both of them lost--Fairchild to the bottle, and Henry to diphtheria.

"Imagine, Hattie, to hear Henry's voice again--" Miss Montez went on.

Mrs. Burnham cut her off. "No, thank you." But then she leaned over and put an arm about Miss Montez. "I know you mean well. But I prefer to commune with my ghosts in private."

"It might make you feel better. About Ben and all."

"I don't know if anything can do that right now."

"You won't know until you try."

"Do you ever summon your ghosts, Lola?"

"Occasionally. Just to see how much bile is being saved up for me on the other side."

"And do they make you feel better?"

"I don't know. I might feel less guilty if I could talk to Folland. He had a wife and children, for heaven's sake. Not to mention my cash in his pockets when he sank to the bottom of the sea, but we won't dwell on that. It would be sweet to hear that it was a wave that took him over the rail and not something I said."

Mr. Thayer appeared at the gate with the horses. "Hattie?"

"Give me a hug, dear friend," said Mrs. Burnham. "I have to go."

She stood. Lola Montez lowered Gip to the porch and put her arms about Mrs. Burnham.

"I believe your rose bush might make it until the rains," Mrs. Burnham murmured. "And maybe your daffodils, too. They'll lay low until next spring and then pop their little heads right up."

"Peut-etre," Miss Montez whispered back. "They shall be my memorial."

"Lola."

Miss Montez sighed, "I know, I know, I'm going to New York, not to perdition."

"Of course not. And we shall meet again. We always do," said Mrs. Burnham.

"'Auf wiedersehen,' then," said Miss Montez.

They held each other for a moment longer before Mrs. Burnham gathered her shawl and reticule and slipped out the gate. Mr. Thayer lifted her up onto the sidesaddle and mounted up himself; then they trotted off down the road into the darkness.

Lola Montez reached out a hand and ran it tenderly along the porch rail. It was a wistful gesture, and one that I knew—I had touched Emmett's printing press in the same way when I'd bid my own home farewell. Then Lola offered her wrist to the bird, and they disappeared into the house.

I gazed out over the front yard. Guests were still sprinkled about in the moonlight, but Harry Brown was not among them. I was debating seeking him out and apologizing, when my thoughts were cut short by, "Emma! Emma, dear!"

Sophie rushed out of the house. She had a stocky young man by the hand. "There you are! Come along! The seance is about to begin! If you don't hurry, you won't get a place!"

"Sophie, have you seen Harry Brown?"

"Yes, he's gone."

"But he came in the wagon. He didn't have a horse."

"Oh, Sumner gave him a lift on the back of his. Buck went with them, too. A bunch of wet blankets, if you ask me. But don't worry, Mr. Harvey, here, will see us home. Oh, I forgot my manners! Miss Emma Lightfoot, meet Mr. Samson Harvey. Mr. Harvey is a blacksmith!"

Mr. Harvey offered me a hand. "Delighted," he said. He sported a magnificent mustache.

"He's a very nice man," Sophie cooed, and gave him a kiss. Mr. Harvey blushed, even in the moonlight, but he did not resist. At last, Sophie broke off, and giggled, "Let's go ask those spirits if they can do that on the other side!" She grabbed my hand and dragged Mr. Harvey and me into Lola Montez's dining room.

The room was crowded and almost black, lit by a single candle on the sideboard. It smelled of sweat, perfume and champagne. We squeezed ourselves into a corner. Ladies' hoop skirts pressed against gentlemen's knees; elbows and shoulders jostled in the dark. The choice spots about the table were already taken. Lola Montez sat there, and the Frisbies, the theatre owners, and Southwick. The cockatoo dozed on her perch by the china cabinet. I made out Ole Bull, leaning casually against the wall near the candle, arms folded across his chest in the posture of a skeptic, and an amused smile on his face. Other guests tittered nervously, and a few appeared genuinely fearful, although they held their ground.

Lola Montez rose in the dim light and peered about. "Frank? Ted Booth? Are you here?"

They weren't. "I'm so sorry," Miss Montez murmured to the guests. "We'll begin very soon. Oscar?" The hired piano boy stuck his head in the door. "Oscar, please go fetch Mr. Mayo and Mr. Booth, if you can find them, and anyone else who can still stand. I believe there's room for a few more souls in here."

This was doubtful, but Oscar took off running out the back of the house and up the hill. In the meantime, Miss Montez introduced the spiritualists, Mr. and Mrs. Pemberton. They were both garbed in black and were as odd-looking a pair as you might hope to find—she was tall and all angles, and he was short and stout, with a high, nasal voice. "Welcome, dear friends," Mr. Pemberton began. "The spirits we seek this evening visit us at great risk, sustained only by your faith. The lifeline to the other side is fragile. We beg of you your respect, and concentration--"

Loud footsteps and laughter rang down the hall. A voice I recognized as Mr. Booth's moaned a ghosty, "OOoooooooooo!!" as he and Mr. Mayo stumbled into the dining room, followed by a handful of other revelers.

"Shhh! Shhh!" Mrs. Pemberton scolded them. "This is a very sober occasion."

"Then perhaps we've come to the wrong place, madam," said Mr. Booth.

"We are somewhat lacking in sobriety, dear lady," Mr. Mayo hooted.

"Oh, Frank, shut up and behave yourself," said Lola Montez. "And you, too, Ted. My apologies, Mrs. Pemberton, they are very bad boys this evening. Come on, everyone," she said to the newcomers. "Come in. We'll make room."

Mr. Booth and Mr. Mayo pressed into the corner with Sophie, her blacksmith and me. I sniffed whiskey on them and the sweet, smoky smell from the hilltop. For a second, Mr. Booth's eyes flashed in the candlelight, his pupils larger and blacker than I had ever remembered them. The girl was not with him, which, I confess, gave me a tiny bit of relief.

Once everyone had settled down, the Pembertons went at it in earnest. The folks at the table joined hands. Mrs. Pemberton spoke a short prayer, that only spirits who came in love would visit us this night. Mr. Pemberton chanted away in some foreign tongue and hummed a few bars of an eerie little tune. Then there was a long silence, except for the rustling and shuffling of the nervous crowd. Finally, BANG!!, the table shook violently.

"Earthquake!!" Mr. Mayo guffawed, and then he exclaimed, "Ow! Damn!!" as someone poked him hard.

Miss Montez whispered to the Pembertons, "I am so sorry. Please go on."

"The spirits are preparing to come through the veil," said Mrs. Pemberton, stern as a schoolmistress. "Please, be attentive, everyone."

We waited some more. Mr. Booth teetered a bit—I felt him brush against me. Then, a child whimpered, "Papa!" Her voice was thin, and far away, and provoked gasps from half the gentlemen in the room. As she cried out again, I tried to place her—first she seemed to call from up in one corner, near the ceiling, then from another, and finally, most surprisingly of all, her tiny voice rose out of Mr. Pemberton's mouth.

"Who's your papa, dear?" asked Mrs. Pemberton.

"Papa, I can't find my china doll," the child wailed. "You sent her from San Francisco, but I've lost her!"

"Alice!" whispered Mr. Southwick. "Is that Alice?"

"A-L-I-C-E," the girl replied. "I can spell! But I can't find my doll."

"Alice, the doll is with your mother," said Mr. Southwick, "to remember you by."

"Mama cried," said Alice. "I was cold, and then I couldn't find anyone."

I began to feel cold myself, wondering if my dead brothers and sisters had ever been as desolate as Alice sounded.

"You must tell her what's in your heart, Mr. Southwick," said Mrs. Pemberton, her tone now very tender.

"I love you, Alice," said Mr. Southwick, tears glistening on his cheek. "Your mother and I miss you every day. Someday soon, we'll be with you, and you won't be alone."

The exchange was touching, but it was also a little odd to see Mr. Southwick professing eternal affection to the person of Mr. Pemberton, a stout gent with sidewhiskers. "When you come to me, Papa," lisped Mr. Pemberton. "Will you bring my doll?"

"Of course, honey. Don't you worry."

"I won't. Bye-bye, Papa." And little Alice's voice faded away.

"No, wait!!" called Mr. Southwick, but it was too late. The mine owner pulled out his silk handkerchief and wiped his eyes.

Mr. Pemberton slumped in his chair, lifeless save for a flutter of his lids. If the man was merely an actor, he was a damned good one. If not, if he was the real article, I prayed that he wouldn't conjure up Emmett. My meeting with my father's ghost in the quiet of Hamlin's bookstore had been a gift, just the two of us and the tabby cat. Emmett had chosen the time and the place to find his daughter. I couldn't imagine what he might have burst out with if he had been "summoned" into a crowded room. He never liked being told what to do, and being ordered to appear by a little fat man would have galled him past endurance. He'd have been forced to start that heavenly newspaper just so he could write a scathing editorial about presumptuous spiritualists.

Mrs. Pemberton gestured for the guests to once again join hands. Mr. Pemberton grimaced and squirmed, and the rest of us waited. Mrs. Pemberton finally said, "Please, we must be patient. A soul is struggling to reach us, but it is a trial for him. He is bound to the other side by much pain."

We waited minutes more, Mr. Pemberton frozen in his chair. Sophie squeezed in closer to her blacksmith. Suddenly the candle flame wavered, then sputtered out. The gasps of the guests woke the bird. She let out an unearthly squawk, terrifying the ladies into screams.

A match scratched and flared, illuminating Mr. Bull's elegant fingers. He grinned, touched the flame to the candlewick, and blew out the match. Tiny wisps of smoke rose about him. As the candle flame took tenuous hold, Mr. Pemberton moaned and in a deep, resonant voice cried out, " A cunning man did calculate me birth, and told me that by water I should die...."

Mrs. Pemberton shifted to the edge of her chair. "Yes?" she whispered.

"Poor soul. Did you drown, then?"

"In tears, madam, and in tempest. Far from home and tossed upon the waves."

"Folland?" called out Miss Montez. "Matt? Is that you?"

"Nay, dear lady, nay."

"Then whom might you have been in this life?" Mrs. Pemberton asked. "Have you a name, sir?"

"Who is it that can tell me who I am? You see me here, you gods, a poor old man, as full of grief as age, wretched in both!"

Mr. Frisbie leaned across the table and, in a low voice, exclaimed, "Mrs. Pemberton, that's King Lear! We booked that show only last season. You can't call him up. He's not real!"

"Shhhh!" hissed Mrs. Pemberton. "There are mysteries we must respect!"

"But Lear's a—"

"Shhh!!!!!!" Mrs. Pemberton tightened her grip on Mr. Pemberton's hand and once more addressed the spirit, fictitious or no. "Whom amongst us do you seek?"

"Me boy, me poor fool," wailed the spirit. "I loved him most, and sought to set my rest on his kind nursery. But he did not come to me!"

"He abandoned you?"

"How sharper than a serpent's tooth it is to have a thankless child!" the spirit roared. Beside me, Mr. Booth's hands were shaking. He gripped his arms across his chest to still them.

"May we be of help, spirit?" said Mrs. Pemberton.

"Send the boy to me," urged the spirit. "Let me see him in me touch."

Mrs. Pemberton gazed about the room. "Which of you is this boy?"

She was met with dead silence. No one was about to claim the old spook. But the spirit was persistent. "Come, boy," he beckoned, in his deep tones. "Come away, to the father who loved ye best! We two alone shall sing like birds in the cage—"

"Shut up!" exploded from the shadows. All eyes turned to Mr. Booth.

"Edwin!" cried the ghost. "So we'll live, and pray, and sing, and tell old tales—"

"Stop! Stop!" Mr. Booth pushed his way toward the table. "You fraud! You can't even speak for yourself, you have to hide behind another man's words—"

Lola Montez sat straight up, as if lightning had tickled her toes. "It's old Booth!" she exclaimed.

"It's a sideshow!" snarled Mr. Booth.

"Ted," said Miss Montez, "Speak to him—you can give him some peace—"

"I say, damn him, Lola, and damn you, too!"

Mr. Booth fought his way toward the door, but the room was so packed, and so dark, that we were hard put to make way for him. Mrs. Frisbie rose as he struggled to press through, but her chair remained wedged in his path. He hoisted it and tossed it behind him. It skidded across the tabletop and landed squarely upon Mr. Pemberton, whose cry was in his own high-pitched tones. Mr. Booth, Sr., had clearly vacated Mr. Pemberton's person and winged his way back to the spirit world without his "boy."

Blood spurted from the spiritualist's nose and drenched his ample waistcoat. The guests let out shrieks and curses, and the cockatoo flew, panicked, over our heads. Mr. Booth at last escaped into the hall, while Sophie wailed, "Poor Ted!" into my ear. Frank Mayo charged over to Lola Montez's side.

"Lola," Mr. Mayo demanded, "did you have anything to do with this?"

"No!" she replied. "No!" He glared at her. "Well, yes...but no!"

"Did you set this up?"

"No! The Pembertons asked for a list of souls we might wish to summon. But no one told them what to say!"

"And you put Ted's father on the list?"

"He's haunted by that old man. I thought it might help—"

"Help? That's the last thing Ted needs. You might as well have taken your horsewhip to him!"

Lola Montez sobbed. Mr. Bull put an arm about her shoulders. "You're his friend, Frank. Perhaps you could find him and see what you can do for him."

Frank Mayo glowered at Miss Montez, then turned and squeezed his way through the dining room door, but he had barely made it to the porch when we heard the sound of hoofbeats in the road. Mr. Booth and his pinto were heading out of town.

The party was over. Through her tears, Miss Montez saw to it that Mr. Pemberton had ice for his nose, and that such revelers as wished to were bedded down in the guest house and about the yard. I piled into the wagon with Sophie and her blacksmith. Sophie promptly fell asleep on his shoulder, and I must have dozed on hers, for all I remember of the journey back to Nevada is being deposited upon the theatre steps.

> Sunday, July 20. *Outside North San Juan. We are camped in a clearing. Evening, no performance. Two months ago today, Emmett and I celebrated my sixteenth birthday. Now, nothing of that life remains—*

Saturday morning, the morning after Lola's soiree, was slow and peaceful. I had time to enjoy the cornbread Buck gifted me with and to finish my journal entry. I even washed a few of the frills for the evening's *Richelieu*. The warm breeze from the west had them dry in minutes.

A few members of the company drifted in and out of the theatre, as leaves turn in a lazy creek eddy. About two-thirty, I headed up Coyote Street to the Frisbies' vacant lot, where most of the stock save for the team were kept, and I visited Lem Mule for a bit. As excited as he was for his oats, he nibbled them from my palm as delicately as a lady.

Mrs. Burnham had called the company for three-thirty to finally go over those musical numbers for the benefit, and by the time I got back to the theatre, a handful of folks were sprinkled about. Mr. Thayer and Ulysses were punctual, as always. Mr. Leach and the Blisses were already busy with scenery, and Mrs. Burnham had arrived from her hotel.

The breeze had strengthened and blown some of the lighter costume pieces from the line into the dust. As I scrambled after them, Harry Brown hastened into the lot. "Harry," I began, but he refused to turn my way, and it took the heart out of me. I stared at him, clutching my pile of pantaloons, as he hurried up the stairs.

Presently Sophie ambled in on the arm of Mr. Harvey. She wore a fresh frock, and her hair was neatly combed. She kissed her blacksmith farewell and skipped up into the theatre. Mr. Moone arrived five minutes later, and I was glad, for his sake, that Mr. Harvey had already made his exit.

Perhaps Sophie was the messenger of the outcome of Miss Montez's seance, for Mrs. Burnham and she spent considerable time inside the theatre before Mrs. Burnham came out onto the landing and nervously scanned the back lot. "Has anyone seen Ted Booth today?" she asked. We had not. She sent Buck Bliss on a run down to Mr. Booth's hotel.

About four o'clock, Frank Mayo appeared, tired and hung-over. Mrs.

Burnham was on him like a duck on a June bug. “Has Ted been with you, Frank?”

“No, ma’am.”

“Do you know where he might be?”

“No, I don’t.”

“I heard the party ended on a sour note.”

Frank shrugged. “The Prince of Denmark had some harsh words for the Countess of Landsfeldt, and he headed back over the hill before daylight.”

“He was upset?”

“I’d say so. He galloped that pinto hell-for-leather up Mill Street, and that was the last I saw of him.”

Buck Bliss returned from the hotel, shaking his head. “Nary a sign of Booth since yesterday afternoon.”

Mrs. Burnham’s countenance took on twenty years, but then she quickly donned a cheerful smile and said, “We don’t need him for the musical numbers, anyway. Let’s go in and get them sorted. Then we can all relax before the show.”

Sharp cries and shouts rang out from somewhere up Nevada’s hilly streets. A church bell pealed, the wild music of an alarm, and was answered by a second frantic bell, blocks away. We were blinded on all sides by the broad frame of the theatre and by the other buildings bordering the lot. Mrs. Burnham ran down the steps to Mr. Leach’s side. “What do you think it is, Jeriah?”

Mr. Leach sniffed, his bristly mustache aquiver, and uttered the words we all dreaded to hear, “I reckon it’s a fire.”

The west wind was now blowing smartly, bringing us proof of a conflagration that, seconds before, had offered up no sign. We stood aghast as smells of burning wood wrapped themselves about us and tendrils of smoke streaked the sky above our heads.

“Buck and Jimmy,” ordered Mr. Leach, “check out front!”

The Blisses raced toward Coyote Street, but before they could clear the lot, they were nearly run down by Mr. Burnham. He was mounted bareback on one of the wagon team’s lead horses, pulling the rest of the bays along at a furious trot. He slid to the ground.

“Grab those lines!” he shouted to the Bliss boys. “That whole block around Hamlin’s store is in flames, and it just jumped the street to the U.S. Hotel. Hitch up, and let’s get what we can into the wagon!”

"Is anyone trying to stop it?" cried Mrs. Burnham.

"Of course, they're trying," Mr. Burnham shot back, "but the wind has whipped it up. At first, it was only a couple of buildings by the blacksmith's, but, in minutes, it was a dozen." Fear gleamed in Mr. Burnham's blue eyes. "When the stableman ran for the livery, I ran after him and grabbed the team before he cut them loose with the rest of the stock. Hurry. Pack up what matters, and let's get the hell out of here."

Mr. Leach fought to keep a calm demeanor. "Ben, you and I can hitch the wagon. Let's send the boys up Coyote to round up the rest of the horses before someone decides to borrow them."

"All right," nodded Mr. Burnham, "but they need to be quick about it."

Mr. Leach loaded Buck and Jimmy with tack from the wagon, and they hastened off once more for Coyote Street. I ran after Buck, my heart in my throat. The only animal on that lot that didn't belong to Mr. Leach was my dear Lem.

"Please, "I said, "I know that mule of mine isn't one of your uncle's horses, but please, Buck, keep an eye out for Lem, too."

Buck smiled me a big bear smile and growled through his beard, "Don't you worry, Miss Emma. That mule's a good old critter. We'll have him ready for you." Then the Blisses hustled out into the commotion of the street.

Mr. Burnham and Mr. Leach hurried the team into harness, whilst the rest of us rushed in and out of the theatre, ants scrambling to save their young from a flooded anthill. Costumes were chucked into trunks and champagne baskets or thrown loose into the wagon, topped by swords, hand properties, makeup scooped off of tables—whatever we could grab. Every time I dashed out of the theatre with an armful, the sky was blacker, and the air was thicker with acrid smoke. Embers swirled on the wind. I pulled down the kerchiefs still clinging to the line, and we tied them over our noses and mouths. Even Harry Brown was not too proud to wear lace, although Tom Bell might have thought us a ridiculous bunch, rummaging the theatre in dainty linen masks.

"Burnham!" Mr. Frisbie came running toward us from the street, in his shirtsleeves and streaked with ash.

"What's it like out there?"

"Terrible. I've seen plenty of fires but never one that moved this fast." He gazed up at his theatre, grief on his countenance. "Can you believe it? I just put eight hundred seats into the damned place. Cushioned seats!"

"Where's Caroline?" worried Mrs. Burnham. "And the boy?"

"They'll be all right. Our building's a fireproof. I closed the shutters myself before I left."

"They're locked inside?"

"They're safe."

Mr. Leach frowned. "I wouldn't count on it, Frisbie."

Mr. Frisbie's eyes widened. "It's a fireproof, for God's sake. Anyway, I'm only here for the ledgers. I'm heading back over there in a minute."

"If you're going up to the office," Mr. Burnham cut in, "I need the cash box out of the safe."

Mr. Frisbie nodded, and Mr. Burnham and he galloped off into the theatre. Mr. Leach finished up with the harness and soothed the team.

Nevada was now ablaze as much with panic as with flames. What we could not see, we could hear—shouts and cries, frantic horses, barking dogs, the rattle of wagons and carts in the crowded streets, and, most fearful of all, the crackling of flames, and the whoosh of the infernal wind as it spewed sparks from rooftop to rooftop. I could barely believe my ears when I picked up a familiar wail floating above the cacophony. "Louise! Louise!" A minute later, Mrs. La Rue stumbled into the back lot. She was at loose ends, tear-stained and her hair falling down. "Have you seen Louise?"

Mrs. Burnham hurried to her side. "She hasn't been here, Clarissa."

"Oh, no!" Mrs. La Rue began to buckle at the knees.

Mrs. Burnham put her arms about her. "When did you last see her?"

"She was playing on the back steps of the rooming house on Nevada Street. She was supposed to stay there!"

"Have you seen Mr. Peele today?"

"No!" Mrs. La Rue began to wail again. "And he couldn't have seen her from the street. She was behind the house. Are you sure she didn't come this way, to find someone to play with?"

"We haven't seen her, Clarissa," said Mrs. Burnham, gently.

Mr. Thayer stepped in, "Maybe she's found some corner in the theatre for a hideout. Shall we take a look?"

"Oh, please!"

Mr. Thayer grasped Mrs. La Rue's hand, and they made haste into the building.

"Mrs. Burnham," I said, "I know a place where she might be, by the creek." This was Louise's secret spot that I'd come upon seeking water for Lem, a hideaway she'd made her own with flutter mills and a leafy bed.

"Can you spare me?"

"How quickly can you get there?"

"As fast as I can."

"If we're not here when you come back, or if you can't get to this spot, meet us up Coyote Street, where the horses are. We'll wait as long as the fire lets us."

"Yes, ma'am."

She suddenly reached out and hugged me. "You be careful, Emma Lightfoot."

"I will," I said, and I turned and ran.

I did not try to fight my way through the streets. Instead, I scrambled between buildings to the ravine Lem and I had found and made my way along the bank of Deer Creek. For all it was a woodsy spot, that creek bed was lively, filled with every sort of soul, some panicky, some very still. The hoofbeats of terrified horses pounded through the scrub as they stampeded from the smell of smoke. Jays dived about, screaming to the flames to steer clear of the tinder of their nests, while frantic rabbits zigzagged and grey squirrels darted through the trees. A black cat with moon eyes stared my way from a limb, witnessing the end of its world.

Shortly, I found a ruined flutter mill and the scattered branches of a small girl's bower. "Louise!" I shouted. "Louise!!!"

I started south along the bank. "Louise!"

I'd traveled about fifteen paces when I spied her, standing up to her ankles in the water, eyes wide and riveted to the smoke and flame up the hill. "Louise!" She did not move. A doe led two quivering fawns in leaps to the far side of the creek, a bare dozen feet from the girl, but still she did not stir. I waded over and took her hand. Only then did she glance my way. She was trembling. "Louise, are you all right? Your mother's about to split a gut, she's so worried about you."

The child did not reply.

"Louise, your shoes are soaked. You'll catch holy hell for it. Come on, we have to go." Instead of hastening my way, Louise turned and stared down the creek bed. I followed her gaze, and, through the willow scrub, caught a flash of black and white.

"Have you seen Mr. Booth today?" I asked.

"I saw him over there," she said, pointing downstream. "He's dead."

"Show me!"

We splashed our way to a spot where the creek widened into a deep pool. Near the bank stood the pinto, bedraggled, reins hanging loose in the water. Boulders were tumbled about the pool's rim, and nowhere could I spy Mr. Booth.

"Where is he, Louise?"

Swift as a lizard, she scrambled up over the rocks. I hauled myself after her. "He's right there."

Below us, wedged between the boulders belly-down, lay Mr. Booth. Only his head and shoulders were above the water line, resting on a tiny strip of sandy bank. "He won't talk," whispered Louise. "He's a ghost now."

"You stay here."

I edged my way down to him. His face was turned toward me. His skin was white from the cold water and his lips blue. I touched his forehead, and he was clammy as a corpse, but when I put my fingers before his mouth, I felt warm breath. I smelled it, too. "He's not a ghost, Louise," I announced. "He's intoxicated."

I shook him and called his name, but I could not rouse him. I grabbed him by the elbows and tried to drag him up the bank, but he was a dead weight, and a slippery one at that. "Louise, come help me!" I finally cried.

The child scampered down. She clasped one arm while I grabbed the other and the back of Mr. Booth's coat, and we hauled him up so that only his boots were still underwater. But how we were to lift him onto his horse was a mystery. As I pondered the dilemma, a voice called out, "Emma! Emma Lightfoot!"

I turned to the child. "Did you hear that?"

"It's Mr. Thayer."

We both put up a racket, hollering his name until he called back. Soon, Ulysses burst through the brush and rushed over to sniff Mr. Booth. When Mr. Thayer sighted us, he shouted, "Emma! Thank God! And Louise! Come here, child!" He put his arms about the girl. "We have to hurry, the wagon's about to pull out. Hop onto my back, Louise!" But Louise pointed down at Mr. Booth, still lying amongst the boulders.

"He won't wake up," she said.

"Oh, God, no," murmured Mr. Thayer.

"He's not dead," I said, "not yet. But we need help. His horse is just a piece down the creek."

"Run, then, Miss Lightfoot," said Mr. Thayer, "and bring it up to meet us."

He turned Mr. Booth over and dragged him further onto the sand.

"Louise, you stay by my side." Then he shook Mr. Booth and hollered, "Ted," but Mr. Booth slept on, his dark locks streaked across his brow.

I dashed off, praying that the horse was still there. The creek bed was becoming more crowded by the minute, and not merely with critters. I had to dodge a human family, the mother herding five weeping young to the safety of the stream, their shirt sleeves and pinafores pressed up over their mouths.

The pinto had drifted some, but I grabbed the reins and led him upstream. Mr. Thayer slung the limp Mr. Booth over the saddle and hoisted Louise onto his own back. Then we fought our way up the bank and toward the theatre.

In the short spell that we had been by the creek, all of Broad and Commercial Streets had exploded into flame. Even as we scurried up the ravine, the heat pressed upon us—my half-healed sunburn blazed afresh, and my cheeks burned like coals.

We squeezed into the back lot. The wooden buildings about us were already afire, and the roof of the theatre smoldered. The wagon still waited, the horses stamping and spooky. Mr. Thayer pulled the inert Mr. Booth from the saddle and laid him in the wagon bed atop a pile of costumes, then lifted Louise in beside him. "You stay by Mr. Booth," he ordered the child. "He needs you." Sophie planted herself beside Mr. Booth, too, and pulled my blanket over him.

As Mr. Thayer lashed the pinto's reins to the rear of the wagon, Mrs. La Rue gushed her thanks and pleaded, "Might you be going back to the house on Nevada Street? Some of our things are still there!"

Mr. Thayer shook his head. "Mrs. La Rue, the house won't even be there in a few minutes. Stay with the company. I intend to."

Mr. Burnham and Mr. Leach urged everyone to gather by the wagon and to flee from the lot before the buildings began to collapse about us. "That's it!" shouted Mr. Burnham. "Stick close to the team!" Still, a few of the company—Mr. Mayo, Mr. Moone, and Mrs. Burnham—continued pulling pieces out of the theatre. I was about to heed Mr. Burnham and climb into the wagon when I realized I had forgotten something dear to me—Miss Montez's gift, the pale blue party dress. I ran up into the dressing room and pulled it off its hook. I did not linger, as the smoke and the darkness were fearsome, but on my way out, I spied a champagne basket kicked into a corner of the men's dressing room. It was Mr. Booth's, filled with the beautiful costumes that had been his father's. I could not leave them for the flames to devour. I lifted the basket, and, choking, made my way to the door and downstairs to the wagon.

Mrs. Burnham was hurrying in my wake, rescuing goblets and paste crowns from their cabinet backstage. She hurled them down into the dust of the lot and raced back toward the theatre. Mr. Burnham dashed after her and gripped her by the arms. "That's it, Hattie. That's enough!"

Mrs. Burnham twisted about in his grip. "The thrones!" she screamed at him. "The thrones are still up there!"

"The hell with the thrones. Let them go!"

Mrs. Burnham stared at him as if he were a traitor who should be shot. "We need them!"

"No, Hattie, we need to get ourselves out of here. And everyone else, too. Now!"

Mrs. Burnham broke loose, and, an ashy madwoman, made for theatre again, but Mr. Burnham was taller and stronger. This time, he seized her entire person, lifted her from the dust, and threw her onto the wagon seat. "Jeriah," he ordered Mr. Leach, "keep her there."

"Indeed," Mr. Leach replied. He reached for Mrs. Burnham's arm. She thrust him away with a screech. "Hattie!!" he barked, his voice harsher than I had ever heard it before. They glared at each other, but she remained on the wagon.

Mr. Frisbie crossed to her, clutching his account books and begrimed with cinders. "In the end, Hattie," he sighed, "it's only a theatre," but the tears in his eyes belied the truth of his lines.

"Everyone accounted for?" demanded Mr. Burnham.

"I believe so!" replied Mr. Leach.

Mr. Burnham grasped the harness of the larger lead horse. "Then let's get the devil out of here!"

Mr. Leach shook the lines, and Mr. Burnham coaxed the horses forward along the narrow strip by the side of the theatre and out toward the chaos of Coyote Street. The scene before the theatre's vestibule was a terrible one, the street clogged with fugitives struggling toward the hills beyond town. Sheets of flame whipped about buildings on both sides of Coyote's cramped passage. As rooftops and walls fell in, the wind scattered fiery brands down upon the frightened townspeople and their panicked horses.

We were about to turn the wagon into the tide of traffic when one of Frisbie's stage hands, blackened with soot, came tearing after us. "Frisbie!

Frisbie!" he screamed. "Your family!"

Mr. Frisbie pressed his way over to the man. "What? What is it?"

"They're trapped up there! Up in your place! Fetch a ladder!"

Mr. Frisbie's ledgers crashed to the theatre steps, and he rushed back into the building. "Make it fast!" the man shouted after him. "The roof's ablaze!" He dashed off the way he'd come, disappearing into the smoke.

In seconds, Mr. Frisbie burst from the lobby, dragging a ladder. He hurried so, that he tripped and tumbled on the steps. In an instant, Mr. Moone was out of the wagon and at Mr. Frisbie's side. He helped the man to rise; then they each took an end of the ladder, and, fighting against the flow of refugees, headed for Main Street.

Harry Brown had kept close by the team, helping Mr. Burnham to calm the horses, but, as he saw Mr. Moone come to Frisbie's aid, he called out, "I'm going, too."

"We can't wait for you, Harry," warned Mr. Burnham. "It's too dangerous."

"I'll find you."

"Look for us up at the other lot, with the rest of the stock."

"Right." Harry nodded, and he took off, too.

Sophie peered after Mr. Moone, distress in her eyes. The windows in a shop across the street exploded, spewing shattered glass and flames into the road. "Sumner!!!!" she shrieked, and before I knew it, she had leapt out of the wagon and was racing after the men.

I'm not sure why—Sophie's terror, or the thought of Mrs. Frisbie's smile as she'd sent me off with that extra piece of pie—but my legs took over then, too, and, in a blink, I had abandoned the wagon and was chasing Sophie around the corner to the Frisbies' rooms in the "fireproof" building.

Every wooden structure at that end of Main was ablaze—my kerchief was now useless, and I covered my mouth with my work apron to keep the blasting heat from my lungs. The Frisbie's "fireproof" still stood, but it had become a monument to the folly of the term. The buildings on either side were engulfed in flames, collapsing into piles of glowing timbers that warmed the bricks of the "fireproof" as surely as coals might heat a brick oven, and which threatened to bake whatever had taken refuge within. The pine sash about the windows was already charred, and the wooden roof let loose billows of smoke and flashes of fire. The Frisbies' hope for an escape route, the entry on the side of the building, was lost to view, buried under the conflagration of what had once been the *Journal* office.

From the top story, behind the iron shutters, came pounding and muffled shouts and screams. Frisbie ran frantically back and forth in the street, from window to window, hollering, "The latches, open the latches," to no avail. Like my flatirons, the metal shutters had warmed and swelled, and it would have taken a fearsome strength to brave their heat and pull the latches free. Finally, Frisbie screamed, "The parlor! That latch is broken! Try the parlor!" The pounding ceased, and, for a moment, all we could hear were the terrible sounds of crackling and snapping. Then, from the window at the far end of the top floor, came the groan of metal. One of the shutters was flung wide, and then the other. Smoke poured out into the street, and the horrified face of Mrs. Frisbie stared down upon us.

Frisbie flung the ladder against the bricks and scrambled up its length, then moaned as he realized it had fallen a man's height short of the window. He began to shake from despair. Mr. Moone stood below him on the street. "Frisbie!" he shouted, "Come down, let me have a go!" Reluctantly, Mr. Frisbie abandoned the ladder, and, while Harry Brown and he clutched its base, Mr. Moone ascended. When he arrived at the top rung, he lightly, gracefully, leapt up and grabbed the window ledge. Sophie, who had run to my side and seized my hand, cried out, but Mr. Moone did not seem to hear. His grip was sure. He dug the toes of his boots into the crevices between the bricks and raised himself up enough to sling one leg over the window sill. Then, as Mrs. Frisbie hauled on his sleeves, he lifted himself into the dark and smoke of the parlor. Mrs. Frisbie disappeared and returned with her son in her arms.

"Harry, come on up to the top of the ladder," Mr. Moone called down, and, as Harry climbed, Mr. Moone lifted the frightened Lyman Austin onto the ledge.

The boy began to scream and cling to Mr. Moone like a terrified monkey. Mrs. Frisbie leaned over to him and whispered in his ear, and then Mr. Moone said, in a hearty voice, "Come on Lyman, we'll do what they do in the circus! Let me show you!" He gripped the boy's arms and coaxed Lyman to hold fast to his. Then, with a, "Close your eyes now, and don't fight Mr. Brown!" he lowered the child out of the window, where Lyman Austin hung suspended against the bricks until Harry could grab his legs and work him into his arms. Harry hurried the boy down to Mr. Frisbie and hastened once more up to the window. I rushed over and took Lyman Austin by the hand while his father turned back to the ladder. I held the child close.

"You see," I said. "You're all right. Now it's your mama's turn."

But Mrs. Frisbie was shaking her head and resisting Mr. Moone's efforts to lower her out of the window. She shouted, "Sarah! We have to find Sarah!" This was the Frisbies' Cornish girl, who'd served our dinner so industriously.

"Where?" Mr. Moone shouted back. "Where is she?"

"In the back room, hiding under the bed!" Mrs. Frisbie gasped. "I can't leave her!"

Flames rained down behind them as the ceiling began to fall. "Go!" commanded Mr. Moone. "Go now! I'll look for her. But GO!"

Mrs. Frisbie stepped to the window. She flung a leg over the sill and held tightly to Mr. Moone's arms as Lyman Austin had. Then she kicked her other leg out and dangled in the smoky air until Harry could fight his way around her skirts and petticoat, grasp her, and ease her onto the ladder. She clambered down and rushed over to Lyman Austin.

Mr. Moone paused long enough to see Mrs. Frisbie safely into Harry's embrace, and then he vanished. The lace curtains burst into delicate flame, waving toward us like golden banners. We could spy nothing through the window save fire, as the settee, the pianoforte, the toy locomotive, all, ignited into a blaze. Sophie squeezed my hand so hard the blood stopped flowing. Her eyes fixed upon the window, she cried, over and over, "Please, God, please God, please God!"

Minutes passed. At length, Mr. Moone stumbled into sight. He carried a limp and blackened Sarah. His red hair glowed more brightly than ever, like polished copper, and I realized that it was ablaze. His shirt and waistcoat were smoking.

Sarah was unconscious, and Mr. Moone struggled to press her dead weight through the window. Harry perched on his toes, on the top rung of the ladder. Mr. Moone edged the young woman, bit by bit, over the sill, until she swayed by a single arm over Harry's head. "Frisbie!" Mr. Moone screamed, "Climb up, and watch out for Brown!" Mr. Frisbie scrambled up the rungs, and I rushed to grip the ladder at the bottom. Mr. Moone's shirt dissolved into fingers of fire. "I have to drop her, Harry! Ready? One, two --"

Mr. Moone never made it to three. With a roar and an explosion of sparks and flame, the roof gave way, collapsing into the inferno of the parlor, and dragging the floor down into the hell of the basement. I caught a fleeting glimpse of Mr. Moone's face before he disappeared. He looked surprised. For a split-second, one blackened hand clutched the window sill; then he was gone.

Sarah plummeted hard onto Harry's head and shoulders. He managed to grasp her, but they would have tumbled to the ground had not Mr. Frisbie strained to steady them.

Behind me, Sophie shrieked, "No! No! Sumner, no!!" and collapsed into the ash and cinders of the street.

Harry cried out, too, "Moone!!" He thrust the senseless Sarah down to Mr. Frisbie and reached toward the empty shell of the window, clawing at the brick. Then he balanced himself on the tip of the ladder, about to imitate Mr. Moone's leap.

A voice screamed, "No, NO!"—and this time, it was mine.

Harry had lifted both arms, ready to spring, when a sheet of flame blasted out of the window. It threw him back, and he slid halfway down the ladder before he caught a rung. He crouched there, above the street, still howling, "Moone!"

Mrs. Frisbie put an arm about Sophie, but the girl's wails only grew more shrill.

Mr. Frisbie laid Sarah in the street and listened for breath. "She's alive," he said, "but she won't be for long if we don't get her to air. We have to go."

The wind was a cyclone, whipping down Main Street, lifting and spitting fire into every corner, but Harry Brown didn't budge from the ladder. "Harry," I pleaded, "listen to Mr. Frisbie. Come down. We have to go. "

"Moone is in there."

"It's too late," urged Mr. Frisbie. "We can't help him. But the women need you. Sarah can't move on her own, and Sophie can't even stand—"

"Harry," I begged, "please come down! Now!"

Harry lifted his sooty face. He was weeping. Until that moment, I'd never seen him do anything but laugh at the world.

"Please, Harry!"

He gazed at me for a second, then descended. I helped him pull Sophie to her feet and load her, sobbing, over his shoulder. Mr. Frisbie scooped up Sarah, while Mrs. Frisbie clutched Lyman Austin. The ladder burst into flames as swiftly as a toothpick thrown on the coals. We ran for our lives.

The streets had nearly emptied of fugitives. Here and there, we encountered another human, features obliterated by ash, a lump of coal more than a person, or we dodged a frantic horse, eyes wild, galloping in terror before the flames. Fear lent wings to our feet, despite our burdens, but as quickly as we fled, the fire pursued, a beast with hot breath and scorching arms. Our skins blistered, our hair singed, we ran the fiery gauntlet up what had once been Coyote Street. We passed the theatre, where tongues of flame shot into the sky, more brilliant than a hundred footlights. The Frisbies averted their eyes, but Lyman Austin stared in horror, mouth agape, at the bonfire that had been his family's fortune.

As we neared the upper end of the street, where the buildings were scattered amongst open plots, the fire abated. Still, the smoke hung about us, a thick and blinding fog. When we finally reached the Frisbies' empty lot, we could perceive no sign of the wagon nor of the Star Troupe's horses.

"It seems they've gone on," gasped Mr. Frisbie, as he gently lowered Sarah to the ground.

But from the far side of the lot came a long whistle, then another, and the cry, "Ulysses!"

I made out a tall man over by the pasture fence. "Mr. Thayer!" I called.

He turned and loped our way. "Emma Lightfoot?"

"Yes, sir."

"Thank heaven."

As he drew near, he spied the Frisbies crouched beside Sarah. "Frisbie! Is that your hired girl? Will she be all right?"

"I don't know, Gus," replied Mr. Frisbie. "It was terrible."

Sophie, cradled in Harry's arms, moaned.

Mr. Thayer quickly took in Sophie's swollen eyes and the grief on Harry's countenance. Frowning, he glanced down the road. "Where's Moone?"

Mr. Frisbie was the only one amongst us who could find his voice. As Mr. Thayer realized the dreadful news, he turned away and wiped his face on his sleeve.

Mrs. Frisbie stepped to him and murmured, "We owe Sumner Moone our lives, Gus. He was a very brave man."

Mr. Thayer nodded. "Absolutely." He crossed over to Sophie, brushed the hair from her tear-soaked cheek, and lifted her from Harry's arms into his own. "Come along, dear," he said. Only then did I notice that

Harry's hands were horribly burned--blistered and shiny against the blackened linen of his sleeves. He had said nothing. Perhaps the pain in his heart had overwhelmed the pain of his burns.

"The wagon headed up the hill, to Sugar Loaf," Mr. Thayer went on. "We can catch up with them there. Frisbie, are you and your folks coming with us?"

"Sarah needs a bed and a doctor, if we can find one," said Mrs. Frisbie.

"I reckon we'll rest here for a piece, and then head over to my brother's claim," Mr. Frisbie said. "He has a cabin across Deer Creek. Caroline?"

"That'll do for now." Mrs. Frisbie reached out, delivered me a hug, and then wrapped her arms about Harry, too. "Thank you," she said. "Thank you for my son's life." She stepped to Sophie and kissed her brow. "God be with you," she whispered to the girl, and then, "You be careful, Gus."

As we trudged out onto Coyote Street, I glanced over my shoulder and caught sight of Lyman Austin waving us a small, sorrowful goodbye. Then the Frisbies disappeared into the pall of smoke.

We labored along the road until it narrowed and began to climb the tall hillside to the north of town. There, we were not alone. Clusters of Nevada's citizens, breathless and exhausted, paused by the trail, too stunned by the calamity playing out below to take another step.

At long last, as my lungs were burning, and my legs were aching from the climb, Mr. Thayer exclaimed, "There they are! Beyond the brush!" The management had found a small, level spot off the trail and had squeezed horses, wagon, and company into it. We stumbled over to them as Frank Mayo shouted, "Hallelujah! They made it!" We were embraced and welcomed like long-lost children.

Buck Bliss stared at me and exclaimed, "Miss Emma, you're shaking like a leaf!" He took me by the hand and led me over to where he'd picketed Lem Mule. "Will this help?" Lem gently nudged me. I put my arms about the old boy's neck, and I did, indeed, feel more steady on my feet.

It took the rest of the company but a few seconds to sense Mr. Moone's absence. The cries of joy turned swiftly to silence, but for Sophie's sobs. Mr. Thayer lifted the girl into the wagon, and Harry and he took the others aside to deliver the terrible news.

I laid my face against Lem's shoulder and gazed out at the scene below. The city of Nevada, the Queen of the Northern Mines, was a sea of flames from one end to the other. Above it all hung an inky canopy, properly funereal. I spied the grand, new Court House blazing away, a beacon raging on the hill above Pine Street. The heat from its conflagration lifted countless bits of paper into the sky, all those writs and complaints now fodder for the wind.

Nevada must have had two dozen or more "fireproofs" sprinkled throughout her downtown. Their brick walls had held out longer, perhaps, than the wooden buildings, but now, they began to succumb to the heat lapping against their mortar. One by one, with great rumbles, they fell in upon themselves, tossing embers and dust hundreds of feet into the violent air. I had turned away and leaned once more toward Lem for comfort, when we were shaken by a fearsome blast from the city below. The mule flattened his ears and rolled his eyes. I have no doubt my calm companion would have fled had I not gripped his halter with all my strength. I thought perhaps a bolt of lightning had capped off the city's destruction, ripping a big "fireproof" in the center of town to flaming bits, but the only clouds hanging over the dreadful scene were clouds of smoke.

"Powder," muttered Buck Bliss, at my side.

Of course. Blasting powder is as common in a mining town as beans and hardtack. It is stored in basements and back rooms in all her corners. In the early minutes of the conflagration, as citizens scurried to cache their goods in the sturdiest of the brick buildings, those refuges had become huge powder kegs.

Now, having held out longest against the inferno, they had reached that searing point where fire and powder "kiss and then consume." In the next quarter hour, we witnessed the demise of half a dozen of these fine buildings, not crumbling into their own foundations but exploding in a flashing thunder of smoke, scattering burning brands and red-hot bricks as surely as they did their owners' hopes.

While most of us kept our eyes riveted on the spectacle below, Mr. Leach and Buck Bliss hustled about attending to those in the worst fixes. Mr. Booth had come back to the world of the living, as horrifying as it was, and leaned grimly under a pine, Frank Mayo at his side. Jimmy Bliss kept a deliberate distance from Mr. Booth, but Buck brought Mr. Booth water and insisted that he drink. Mr. Leach carved out a space for Sophie amongst the tumbled finery in the wagon, where he left the girl wrapped in a blanket and her grief. When he carried a tin of axle grease over to Harry, I delivered Lem Mule into Jimmy Bliss's care and rummaged the wagon for some loose muslin to rip into bandages. Mr. Leach tenderly dabbed Harry's blistered hands, and I wrapped them as gently as I could. Harry was stoic, although his hands bore the look of boiled ham. Mr. Thayer presently knelt down with his personal bottle of whiskey and encouraged Harry to sip—"It might take the edge off the pain, boy. It's better than nothing." Harry took him up on his offer and, as Mr. Thayer held the bottle to his lips, drank with determination.

The sun had almost set, a scarlet bullseye in a blackened sky, when the management gathered beside the wagon to make order out of scattered props and costumes and to confer about the company's next move. "I say we put as much distance between ourselves and Nevada as we can," declared Mr. Burnham. "Pack up the wagon and our 'Fiery Star' and head out. There should be moonlight tonight, and we'll be able to see the road."

Mr. Leach turned to him, a stack of rapiers in his arms. "Our next booking is Downieville, Ben. The Downieville road's way over on the west side of town. We'd have to pick our way around the fire in the dark."

"I know the road, Jeriah."

"It would behoove us to wait." Mr. Leach dropped the swords into their case. "We can start the minute the sun comes up. Besides, we have folks who are in no shape to travel."

"And we have Sumner Moone!" Harry Brown struggled over to them. "Are we going to go off and forget about him?"

Sophie must have been listening, because, out of the wagon, rose a tearful, "Noooo!"

"Moone is gone, Harry," said Mr. Burnham. "We have to look out for everyone else, now. Besides, it's a furnace down there. It might be days before we could reach Frisbie's place. And I doubt if we'd find much if we did."

"Still, it's wrong," said Harry, biting back tears.

Mr. Thayer hurried to Harry's side. "I'll tell you what—if we camp here tonight, and that blaze burns out enough, I'll work my way into town tomorrow at dawn and see what's up."

Mr. Burnham began to object, but Mr. Thayer cut him off. "We owe it to Moone, Ben. And we're all worn around the edges. Some of us are worse. Harry can't even hold a rein. A few hours' delay isn't going to make much difference."

"It's reckless to hang around here."

Mr. Thayer only shrugged.

Mrs. Burnham frowned and thrust the last of her precious crowns into its box. “Why don’t we put it to a vote, Ben? This affects everyone, not just you and me.”

“It’s madness to sit here—”

“We all cared for Sumner. You did, too, I know. And we should all have a choice about how we want to handle losing him.”

Mr. Burnham held out for a while, but by and by, the company, except for Ted Booth, gathered for a quick vote. Mr. Booth, blue circles about his eyes and despair within their depths, abstained. Everyone else but Mr. Burnham was for sticking it out on the hillside overnight, despite the nastiness of the air and the dark wraith of incendiarism hanging over us.

Later, I went to the wagon to dig out Lem’s bag of oats and turned up half a stale biscuit I’d stashed for myself. I determined to make it a treat for Ulysses, until it struck me that I hadn’t seen the dog since Deer Creek. Mr. Thayer had whistled for him in the Frisbies’ lot, but Ulysses had never come. We were missing not one, but two company members—the one who made us laugh, and the one who would have plopped down at my side and made the day’s nightmare more bearable. Mr. Thayer crouched on a boulder a few feet beyond the wagon, staring mournfully down at the remains of the city. I did not doubt his desire to look for Mr. Moone in the morning, but I realized that he would be searching for more than one brave soul.

As darkness descended upon us, the wind began to die. Now and again, a crimson tongue of flame shot upward into the night, but mostly, the fire settled into the blackened ruins of the city. The company, exhausted, found it a strain to do more than stare at the spectacle, though some of us managed to set up a bare bones camp. Mrs. Burnham and I tried to make room for sleepers in the wagon, and Sophie wound down her grieving from wails to whimpers.

Though night had fallen, the moonlight and the fire cast a glow upon the hillside, and it was clear that dozens, perhaps hundreds, of other refugees shared Sugar Loaf with the Star Troupe. Some clung to the company of those whom they knew, but others wandered by our spot, searching for family or friends, or simply too shocked by their fates to stick in any one place.

The smoky moon was high in the sky when two figures approached our camp. “Hattie Burnham?” called out one of the men. “Hattie?

Are you there?"

The other man had a twang in his voice. "Is this the Star Troupe?"

Masked in soot, the pair was almost unrecognizable. Mrs. Burnham poked her head out of the wagon and squinted, then exclaimed, "James Hamlin! You're safe and sound!" She hopped down and rushed to him, seizing his hands. "I am so happy to see you, James. Though I expect you've lost your store, and for that, I am sorry."

Mr. Hamlin smiled. "No need to be. We saved the store. We lost part of the roof, but most of the books made it. We even salvaged Isis."

"Isis?" I said.

Between the darkness and the coat of ash, it took Mr. Hamlin a second to place me. "Miss Lightfoot! Salutations! Isis is the tabby. Her whiskers melted, but the dear girl will grace our shelves for years to come. Providence was smiling upon her." Mr. Hamlin stopped himself. "I'm sorry," he said to the Burnhams. "I don't mean to appear jubilant." He removed his hat. "We ran into the Frisbies on the road. I am grieved beyond words at the loss of Moone."

"He was such a goddamned cheerful fellow," declared the other man. "I am sorry as the devil that he has crossed over!"

My ear told me this was Mr. Eben Card, Mr. Fletcher's cousin from Tennessee, and no longer the dandy we had met upon the road to Nevada. He was hatless and tieless, and whatever finery remained on his long bones was blackened and shredded by the fire. Mr. Hamlin put a hand on Mr. Card's shoulder. "Eben is searching for his cousin," he said.

Mr. Booth staggered to his feet. "Fletcher?"

Mr. Hamlin nodded. "If any of you see Mr. Fletcher, will you ask him to come by my store?"

Sophie was hit by another wave of sobs. Mr. Card turned a worried look toward the wagon. "Is that Miss Griffith?"

"Yes," said Mrs. Burnham. "She's grieving Mr. Moone."

"May I offer her my condolences?"

"You may try."

Mr. Card hurried over to the rear of the wagon and gently whispered into it. Out of earshot, Mr. Hamlin confided, "This is a wild goose chase, this search for Fletcher. He's lost, but Eben won't give him up, so I'm tagging along with him until he can."

"How do you know Fletcher didn't make it?" asked Mr. Booth, his beautiful voice hollow with fear for his friend.

"He was seen closing himself inside his law office, latching those infernal iron shutters. His building was that big "fireproof" at Broad and Pine. The first one to blow itself to bits."

"Oh, no. No. Not Fletcher, too." Mr. Booth sank into himself, collapsing onto his knees in the dirt. Mrs. Burnham's eyes glistened with tears, although she hastily wiped them as Mr. Card returned. Mr. Hamlin and I quickly urged Mr. Booth to his feet.

"Miss Griffith is a lovely lady," Eben Card said to Mrs. Burnham. "I wish I could say more that would be of comfort." Under his smears of soot, Mr. Card looked perhaps fourteen, too tender for tragedy. "Well, come along, Hamlin. Fletcher's probably found himself a bed somewhere, while we're traipsing about in the brush."

"Could be, Eben," said Mr. Hamlin. "Farewell, friends. And Godspeed to you." He touched his hat, Mr. Card gave a little bow, and they vanished through the smoke and scrub into the night.

Mr. Booth stumbled to his blanket and curled up as if he wished he could melt into the earth. No one else had the heart for conversation, so we sought our beds. Sophie and the La Rues claimed the wagon. I found a flat spot not far from Lem, and once I had kicked away the rocks and twigs, it was tolerable. I threw down my blanket and stared up at the grey moon, a moon that Mr. Fletcher, with his delight in the heavens, would still have found a reason to love. As worn as I was, sleep did not come until that moon was deep in the western sky. The last thing I remember was a soft whistle floating down from somewhere up the hill, as Mr. Thayer called through the darkness for Ulysses.

Come the pale light of dawn, we rose up out of our blankets as specters might float up from their graves—darkened with ash, grit in our teeth, a sober lot. The Blisses filled a tub with a few inches of water for washing faces and hands. Though the water was soon blackened, it was a blessing, and we all were a mite more human for it.

Mr. Thayer had already departed camp. As I was combing the cinders from my hair, the Blisses spotted him laboring back up the road. Mr. Leach hurried to his side. "Did you get down into town?" he asked. "Any word of Moone?"

Harry rushed over, still wrapped in his blanket. "Did you find him, Gus?"

By now, the Burnhams had gathered round, too, and Sophie peered out of the wagon. The girl's eyes were almost swollen shut.

"I found Frisbie," said Mr. Thayer. "The streets are a nightmare—you have to pick your way through bricks and timbers, and it's all still smoldering. Somehow, I got myself over to Frisbie's building, and, believe it or not, there was Frisbie himself, pacing up and down and going at the wreckage with a poker. But it's still ablaze in there."

Mr. Booth hastened to Harry's side. "Could Moone have survived somehow? Found a corner in the cellar?"

Mr. Thayer shook his head. The lines in his face, creased with soot, were sadder than ever. "A mouse couldn't have made it. Nothing could have."

For once, Sophie made no sound, although her mouth was open, fighting for breath.

"Frisbie will take care of him, if they find him," Mr. Thayer added. "They'll give him a hero's funeral. But they won't even be able to get in there for a day or so. Maybe more." He reached into his pocket. "Frisbie found this in the street." He brought out a stickpin, the gold filigree about its carnelian blackened and fused. "He thought it might have belonged to Moone." Mr. Thayer handed the pin to Sophie. "Do you think it's his?"

"Oh, yes!" Sophie grasped the battered bit of metal and held to her heart. "Oh, yes."

"You keep that, Sophie," said Mrs. Burnham, though no one could have pried the pin from Sophie's fingers anyway.

"All right," said Mr. Burnham. "Thank you, Gus. Now let's pack it up. Twenty minutes."

Harry didn't move. "Shouldn't we say some words for Moone?"

"A prayer meeting?" Mr. Burnham shook his head and made for the horses.

Mr. Leach stopped him. "No, a service. Even if it's a short one. To say farewell. It's the Christian thing to do."

"Jeriah, the man's not here," said Mr. Burnham. "There's not even a body to bury."

Mrs. La Rue spoke up, and, for the first time since the fire, her voice was steady. "When our baby died, there was hardly anything left of him. He was so tiny and lost in his box, Louise and I couldn't bear it. So, we put him to rest with his blanket and his little rag dog. Louise tucked in flowers and a sweet biscuit, and he wasn't so alone then. We sent him off to heaven with his treasures. Maybe we could leave a little box for Mr. Moone."

"Please, let's," said Sophie, and, so, it was decided. Mr. Burnham, Mr. Leach and the Blisses harnessed the horses, while Harry and Mr. Thayer sought out a spot for Mr. Moone's relics to rest. Buck Bliss cleared molasses bottles out of a sturdy wooden box. Sophie reached for my hand and begged, "Please help me, Emma!" Together, we went through Mr. Moone's champagne basket. Choosing the right bits to go into the ground wasn't easy. Sophie couldn't bear to part with his beaver hat or the concertina. But we managed to fill the box with treasures--Mr. Moone's worn copy of Shakespeare's plays, his bone-handled razor, a costume ring with a blue stone. Louise gathered a handful of purple flowers and placed them carefully into the box. Mr. Mayo encouraged Mr. Booth to carve Mr. Moone's name on the box's lid with his penknife, and he did so, beautifully. Then we carried the remnants of our friend up to the top of Sugar Loaf, where Mr. Thayer had dug a hole under a stately pine.

We set the box on the edge of the grave and circled around. We were a bedraggled group of mourners, but each of us tried, as best we knew, to send Mr. Moone's shade off with a blessing. The La Rues led us in a sweet "Amazing Grace," as the Blisses accompanied them on guitar and fiddle. Mr. Booth rendered the psalm, "The Lord is my Shepherd," his voice deep and sweet as the sea, and asked God to remember Mr. Fletcher, too. Sophie, clutching the beaver hat, tried to sing, but she barely got out a note before tears overwhelmed her. "Now, there's no one to love me," she whispered, and uttered nothing more.

Everyone else tried to pitch in a sentence or two. Mr. Leach prayed for comfort for Mr. Moone's soul, and Frank Mayo asked the Lord to make the departed's trip to the next world a quick one and to have a stiff whiskey waiting for the man. Even Mr. Burnham spoke—"He rose up to heaven in smoke, the Hindu way, but, Lord, don't hold that against him. He was a good man."

I was too sad to come up with much. "He was kind to me," I said. "He had heart and more grit than most."

Mr. Thayer lowered the box into its hole. All that remained of Sumner Moone, it was barely bigger than the box of the baby bird I had failed to save when I was small, tiny Wing.

In a trice, we covered it with earth and started back toward the wagon. The "service" had taken a mere ten minutes, and the sun was still low in the east. Mr. Burnham would have his early departure.

As Mrs. Burnham and I were seeing a weeping Sophie downhill,

Frank Mayo fell in by our side. "Hattie," he said, "I have to go."

"What?"

"I have to go back to Grass Valley. To Lola's."

We stopped, right there in the manzanita. "Frank, we're booked into Downieville. We can't wait for you to go to Grass Valley."

"Then don't wait. But I have to find Lola and let her know I'm all right."

"We can send her word."

Mr. Mayo shook his head. "No, I have to be there. You know she'll throw her doors open to anyone who's lost a home in the fire. That's Lola. She'll need me."

"Frank," Mrs. Burnham pleaded, "we've just lost Sumner. It'll be hard enough to cover his roles. We can't afford to lose you, too."

"You can do *The Iron Chest* and *Shrew*."

I feared Mrs. Burnham might weep along with Sophie. "Frank—"

"Look," Mr. Mayo said, "if it turns out that Lola can spare me, I'll catch up with you in Downieville. Is that fair?"

Mrs. Burnham sighed, "No. Although I don't suppose I have a choice. Go. Tell Lola about Sumner, and let her know that the rest of us are amongst the living. Give her my best."

"Thank you," Mr. Mayo grinned. "I will." Then he bounded off through the brush.

Back at the campsite, the company gathered blankets and gear and stowed them in the wagon. As we made a last check of the place, Buck Bliss shouted out, "Ha! Anyone missing an old black dog?"

Mr. Thayer ran to Buck's side and peered down the road. The dog was limping, singed and sooty, but as soon as Mr. Thayer whistled, he lifted his head and picked up his gait. "Ulysses!"

Mr. Thayer hied down the hill, scooped the animal into his arms, and carried him back to the wagon. Tears welled in his eyes, although he was laughing and ruffling Ulysses's blackened fur until it gave off clouds of ash. "I'd say that's a dog of a different color!" he joked. Then, he caught Sophie staring at him, and the laughter died. "I'm sorry, Sophie," he said. "I'm just so glad he found us."

"I know," said Sophie, and she patted the dog on the head.

In truth, after so much horror, the sight of Ulysses's return from the underworld cheered us all. He was exhausted and thirsty, and his paws were badly blistered, but he had made it home. Mr. Thayer wrapped him in a blanket and laid him gently over his horse's back, just before the saddle.

Mrs. Burnham's dappled grey was tied next to Lem. As Mrs. Burnham gathered the reins and mounted up, Ted Booth stepped to her side.

"Maybe I should leave, too, Hattie," he said.

"What the hell—?"

He pushed up his hat brim. The circles about his eyes were even darker than they'd been last night. "You'd be better off without me."

"What are you talking about? If you leave, too, we might as well give up the ghost. Call it quits. We can't replace you."

"You may find yourself wishing you had."

"Ted, I can't have this conversation now. I can't do it. Get on your horse. We'll talk about it later."

She tried to back the grey away, but Mr. Booth put a hand on its bridle. "Hattie—"

"Please," Mrs. Burnham said.

They stared at each other until, at last, Mr. Booth turned on his heel and mounted the pinto. In silence, the riders and wagon fell into line and started toward the road. Behind us, I caught a last glimpse of the tall pine on the hilltop and sent up a good wish for Sumner Moone.

MONDAY, JULY 21. *Camptonville. Evening—*

Mr. Burnham steered the team deftly down Sugar Loaf and across the scorched fringes of Nevada. He skirted, as best he could, the town's hot spots, where sooty citizens scrabbled through beds of ash, and he finally turned us onto the rutted trail of Hoyt's Road.

Mr. Burnham and Mr. Leach had stripped off the wagon canvas, with its bright lettering advertising the Star Troupe, and folded it into the wagon bed. Little else would have pegged us as a company of actors. The flash and flamboyance had vanished. We were a somber bunch.

The road twisted along the edge of a ravine, then into a broad meadow. Those of us who were mounted spread out, single file. There was no chatter, no singing or games. Fear had shaken us into silence. My companion on the trail was the memory of my dearest friend Evangeline, as she giggled at our jokes, her little dog Sparky at her side. I deeply regretted not having made it to the Red House to save my friend from the Placerville fire, and I could not comfort myself with the hope that

Miss Alice had hastened Evie and the rest of her "girls" out of the way of danger. I have fretted ever since for what Evangeline may have suffered, but I could not have imagined what that terror truly was until I had seen it with my own eyes on the fiery streets of Nevada.

At the rear of our caravan, the Bliss brothers led a string of unsaddled horses—Sophie's dainty sorrel and Harry's big black, as well as Mr. Burnham's steed and Mr. Moone's riderless roan. The wagon bed was crowded. Louise had protested that she wished to ride with Mr. Thayer, but she had been gently denied—Ulysses had claimed that honor. Sophie was burrowed into a blanket between a couple of trunks, where she clutched an ashy handkerchief, soggy with tears. I longed to knock the girl upside the head and shout, "If you'd been kinder to Moone in the first place, you wouldn't be so miserable now!" But she had such a pathetic air about her that I chastised myself. Maybe she truly had loved Mr. Moone, but simply couldn't see it until he'd been burnt to a crisp.

Harry Brown had found a corner of the wagon where he could lean against a champagne basket, eyes closed, his bandaged hands upon his lap. He occasionally winced, but he said nothing. For several miles, the only voice to be heard was Mr. Thayer's, softly speaking encouragements to Ulysses.

As we rode through the mournful pines above the Yuba canyon, Ted Booth kept his pinto to the rear of the caravan. I feared I'd look back and find that he'd disappeared into the trees.

Before we descended to the river, the Burnhams declared a break by the trickle of a stream. I let Lem loose in the grass nigh the bank and sought what I longed for most, to pull off my boots, soak my toes, and splash coolness on my face.

I was crouched by the stream's edge when I spied Mrs. Burnham leading her grey mare to water. She had a grim set to her jaw; her hair was still flecked with ash and falling about her face. It seemed disrespectful to intrude upon her mood, and I pulled back into the foliage to don my boots.

I doubted that she saw me, burdened as she was by her troubles. She pulled a cigar and a match from her saddlebag, lit up, and, as the mare drank, nervously stalked the water's edge. Finally, she settled on a fallen log and took a long drag.

"Hattie?" I spied Mr. Booth's slouch hat coming through the leaves.

Mrs. Burnham groaned. "Ted, no, not now."

I debated leaving as quietly as I could, but I was only half-shod.

Mr. Booth strode over to the log and claimed a spot beside Mrs. Burnham. "I'm an idiot to follow in the company's dust, when I should turn tail and head out."

Mrs. Burnham threw down her cigar and stamped on it. "Damn it, Ted!"

"It should have been me instead of Moone or Fletcher. I would have traded places with them in a heartbeat."

I spied Lem grazing serenely off in the trees, but it was too late for me to bolt. I pulled my knees up to my chest and became a fly on the wall.

"I don't know why you want to keep me on, Hattie."

"Because I'm selfish," snapped Mrs. Burnham. "Ben and I have put everything into this tour, and you're our star. We're not playing to full houses because the Burnhams are on the bill."

"Between the fires and the press, I might drive your patrons right out the theatre door."

"I can't even let myself think that thought." Mrs. Burnham paced the bank, then cast a worried glance at Mr. Booth. "And how the hell would we replace you, Ted, now that we're out on the road? I don't know how we'll cover for Sumner." Her voice caught in her throat; she brought her hand up to her mouth.

Mr. Booth gave a sorrowful nod. "Moone will be a hard act to follow."

"Yes, he will. And you would be, too."

Mr. Booth turned away and kicked gravel into the stream. "I've proven Leach right. I'm not to be trusted. I need a spy on my tail as much as the old man did."

Mrs. Burnham delivered him a hard look. "And what does that mean?"

Mr. Booth was silent.

"All right, Ted," she said, "you level with me. Where were you before those fires? If you have an alibi, for God's sake, give it to me."

Mr. Booth shook his head. "I can't remember a blessed thing, Hattie. I fight off the bottle every day, you know that, but when I'm sad, or scared, I thirst for it. And when it dulls the world enough, I don't remember things. I don't know how I got into that creek bed yesterday, I don't know anything."

"That's unfortunate."

"When the old man was in a lunatic spell, there was no telling the damage he could do. It would seem I truly am his son." Mr. Booth sank down on the log and dropped his face into his hands.

Mrs. Burnham stood over him. "You bow to that so easily, Ted. 'The sins of the fathers' and all the rest of it. Fight it, for God's sake." She perched by him on the log and met his eye. "Do you really think you're insane enough to incinerate a town? To kill?"

Mr. Booth was silent for a moment. I held my breath for fear of his reply.

"I hope not," he finally whispered, so softly I could barely hear. "I don't think I have the cruelty in me to ruin all those lives."

Mrs. Burnham nodded. "Then what shall we do?"

"I have no right to lay down terms. If you want me out, I'll go, gladly. And if you want me to stay, I will."

"There's not another Hamlet for a hundred miles. We need you, and that's that."

"All right."

"And, for what it's worth," Mrs. Burnham added, laying her hand on his, "I don't believe you have the cruelty in you, either."

I wanted to shout my agreement on the subject, but I bit my tongue. Mrs. Burnham's mare was wandering my way up the creek, and I prayed she wouldn't sniff me out. I was saved by Mrs. Burnham's whistle—the horse turned and ambled back the way she'd come. Mrs. Burnham took the reins and led the grey toward the wagon. Mr. Booth kicked one more stone in the water and quickly followed.

As we journeyed into the steep Yuba canyon, a small drama unfolded in the wagon bed. Shortly after we'd left Nevada, Sophie had tossed open Sumner Moone's carpet bag, rummaged frantically through his clean shirts, and hauled out a whiskey bottle. By the time we reached the canyon rim, it was half-empty, and Sophie was sloppy drunk, dripping tears into her sodden hankie. Harry tried more than once to dissuade her from the whiskey, but she would holler, "Don't you dare!" and other words I cannot repeat, and clutch the bottle closer to her chest. Clarissa La Rue glared at her, stiff with disapproval. When Sophie's language turned especially ripe, Mrs. La Rue clapped her hands over Louise's ears and squeezed her daughter as far away from Sophie as the wagon would allow. Finally, she could tolerate no more and exploded, "Shut up, you stupid girl!" Sophie's reply was to take a long swig.

At the bottom of the canyon, we paused to gather our riders before crossing Hoyt's Bridge. Mrs. La Rue stood up in the wagon and shouted at Mr. Burnham, "She's intoxicated! She's pouring hard liquor down her throat in front of my daughter! It's intolerable!"

By then, Sophie had hit a quiet patch, eyes closed, her cheek leaning innocently against Harry's shoulder.

"Harry," whispered Mrs. Burnham, "can you talk that bottle away from her?"

Harry shook his head. "I've been trying to for the last hour."

"Is she asleep?"

"Maybe."

"Gus," pleaded Mrs. Burnham, "you have a good reach. Can you slip it out of her hand?"

Mr. Thayer nodded and stealthily climbed into the wagon, but he had no sooner eased his fingers around the neck of the bottle when Sophie jerked herself up and seized it back with a "NO!!!" For a second, it appeared she might bring it right down on Mr. Thayer's head.

Mrs. Burnham threw up her hands. "Let her be."

"You can't!" screeched Mrs. La Rue. "Louise and I won't ride another mile with her."

"Then come on down," demanded Mr. Burnham. "We've plenty of extra horses. Buck, saddle up the sorrel."

Mrs. La Rue stared at him as if he'd dropped from the moon. "I don't ride!"

"I do!" piped up Louise.

"You do not!" said her mother. "If anyone should ride, it's Miss Griffith."

"Miss Griffith couldn't ride a rocking horse right now," said Mr. Burnham. "If you have a problem with the lady's grief, you can either shut up or mount up. What'll it be?"

Mrs. La Rue gasped like a fish out of water.

"We'll get you the sidesaddle, Clarissa," said Mrs. Burnham, as one might cajole a balky child. "And the sorrel is a sweet little mare. I'll lead her for you. Jeriah, can you take Louise?"

"My pleasure," said the stage manager.

"It's not right," said Mrs. La Rue, tears in her eyes.

"No," sighed Mrs. Burnham. "Not much is right just now, but let's do the best we can and get across this river. Shall Jeriah take Louise?"

Mrs. La Rue nodded, reluctantly. Louise smiled as Mr. Leach lifted her up before his saddle. After more than her fair share of fretting, Mrs. La Rue was boosted onto the sorrel, where she clung, white-knuckled, to the horse's mane. Soon, we were filing across the wooden bridge above the lovely Yuba and turning onto the trail beyond the rocky shore.

Sophie, now quite awake, turned once more to the whiskey bottle. It loosened her grief and lubricated her regrets. The shade of Sumner Moone settled into the wagon. Sophie crooned endearments to the ghost; her sobs soared to the treetops.

In the end, the road brought this tragic scene to a quick conclusion. Our ascent out of the canyon was rougher than the trip down had been, and Sophie's stomach proved no match for the double poison of alcohol and rude jolts. Harry, despite his wounded hands, held the girl's head over the wagon's side as her heaves stifled the opera of her woe.

The sun was deep in the west when we arrived on the main street of North San Juan. A few of the company had held out hopes for a hot bath and a clean bed, but the tents and wagons scattered about bespoke an overflow of refugees from Nevada, and the "Full Up" signs were already posted in the windows of the camp's hotels. In the middle of town stood a neat little theatre, directly under the gigantic flume that divides North San Juan in two—a flume that arches over the streets like a monstrous bridge to nowhere, dripping down on the passersby below and encouraging clusters of wildflowers in its damp shadow.

A bill by the theatre's door proclaimed that it was booked for the evening by a husband-and-wife team. I got a gander at the details:

GRAND MAGIC PERFORMANCE

FOR ONE NIGHT ONLY

FIRST APPEARANCE OF THE GREAT EUROPEAN WIZARD

DELPHINO!

ASSISTED BY

MADAME DELPHINO

WHO WILL PERFORM THE GREAT FEAT OF

SLEEPING IN THE AIR!

The bill boasted a picture of the beautiful Madame Delphino in an elegant turban. She floated dreamily above a magical platform, an angel on an invisible cloud!

Mrs. Burnham had hoped to find the theatre vacant and to provide some sort of small show, but most of us were relieved it was booked. We moved on across town, and, a quarter mile past city limits, Mr. Burnham spied a quiet glade. It was a sweet spot, empty of refugees, with plenty of grass for the stock, and, best of all, a little pond! We hurried to pitch tents about the clearing and then, exhausted as we were, found the enthusiasm to shed some of our soot in the pond. Ladies dipped first, whilst the gentlemen tactfully turned their backs to us; then the men went in, and finally even the grateful stock were given a scrubbing. I waded into the water with Lem Mule and, with the help of a comb and a pail, went to work on the old boy, from long ears to tail. He thanked me by loosing a happy bray that lifted the local birds out of the trees.

The Blisses rustled up a quick supper of hot cakes, bacon and dried apples. As the company dined by the wagon, Mrs. Burnham tapped a spoon on a tin plate and commenced one of her "stump speeches."

"Mr. Burnham, Mr. Leach and I know how hard the last days have been on all of you," she said, "and we are proud of your sand. We know, with your help, we can carry on."

"Without Moone?" asked Buck Bliss.

"We'll miss Sumner. Deeply. But I hope we can cover his roles. With luck, we'll get Frank Mayo back, and he can step into *Shrew* and *Iron Chest*. And if we can find an empty stage along the road, we can improvise a little entertainment. Sing for our suppers. What do you say?"

The company was too thrashed for enthusiasm, but, at last, Mr. Thayer spoke up. "I'm with you, Hattie. The show goes on."

Mr. Booth added a grim, "I'm with you, too."

Jimmy Bliss glared at Mr. Booth. "And if there's another fire? What do we do then?"

Mr. Booth bit back his reply and simply stared down at the dust. It took Mrs. Burnham an instant to find her voice. "There won't be another fire, Jimmy. And we can't give in to fear. Now, what about the rest of you? Shall we give Downieville our best shot?"

In the end, everyone delivered a subdued acquiescence, and most of the company retired to their tents. The La Rues claimed the wagon, so Buck and Jimmy spread their beds over by Mr. Leach's tent on the far side of the clearing. I decided a spot beside the wagon would do for me.

Tired as I was, I was not wound down enough for sleep. At dusk, I went over to Harry's tent with a tin of grease and a roll of clean muslin for his hands, but he was nowhere to be found. I made a round of the other tents, softly calling, "Harry?" to no avail, until I heard a faint, "Emma, here," from the direction of the water. I nearly stepped on the boy before I saw him. He was lying on his belly in the mud, his seared hands plunged into the cold water of the pond. "It's the only way I can get relief," he sighed.

"I brought you some more grease," I said.

"That stuff just holds in the heat. Sorry, but this is better."

I knelt beside him. "Have you been here long?"

"I don't know. Since before supper was laid out."

"Did you eat anything?"

"I'm not hungry. That whiskey Gus gave me last night left me with a nasty stomach."

"What can I do to help?" I asked.

"Nothing," Harry replied. "Sit with me, maybe."

And so I did, not saying much. A few stars brightened above us. By and by, Mr. Thayer, laying out a blanket for Ulysses, spotted me from his tent. "Emma Lightfoot, is that you over there by the pond?"

"Yes, sir. And Harry."

"Harry? Where?" He hurried over and discovered Harry sprawled in the muddy reeds.

"Is he all right?" Mr. Thayer inquired.

"Not too good," I said.

"Harry," said Mr. Thayer, crouching, "why don't we get you to bed? You'll be more comfortable."

"No."

"You'll add mosquitos to your miseries if you stay by the water."

"I don't care, Gus. If I have to lie here all night, like a pig in a wallow, I will. The cold leaches out the fire so I can bear it."

Mr. Thayer stood. "Emma," he said, "can you keep him company a mite longer?"

"Of course."

"Good. I'll be back as soon as I can."

Mr. Thayer hastened toward the road. He returned in a mere twenty minutes, despite the darkness that had settled in.

"Emma?" he called.

"Right here."

"Good." He toted a bucket in each hand. "Ice," he said, "from one of the saloons. Emma, help me get Harry to his tent, and then go fetch a couple of big bowls from the wagon. The ones Buck uses for biscuit dough. And a spoon."

Harry protested, but once Mr. Thayer had slipped a few chips of ice into his hands, he let himself be persuaded back to his bed. We tucked him in, a sizable sack of flour at his back to prop him up, and a bowl of ice on either side. He sank his blistered hands into the coolness, leaned back, and let out a breath.

Mr. Thayer reached into his coat pocket and pulled out a small blue bottle. "Take a few drops of this, too," he said.

"If it's whiskey, Gus, no thanks."

"It's laudanum. It'll help. Just a small bit--half a spoonful--every few hours."

Mr. Thayer popped the bottle's cork, measured the medicine into the spoon, and delivered Harry a dose. Then he lifted one of the buckets, a bit of ice still rattling in the bottom. "I have a canine patient who can use a little nursing, too," he smiled. "Call me if you need me, Harry. Goodnight." He set the bottle and the spoon by Harry's side and ducked out of the tent.

"I could fetch a candle and read to you," I offered.

"Thank you, but no."

"Shall I leave?"

"No. Don't."

Harry was barely visible in the darkness, but I knew his eyes were upon me. I took a breath and said, "I am deeply sorry, Harry, for pitching that rock at your head. It wasn't my shining moment. Can you forgive me?"

He snorted. "Cinder-Emma, I grew up the babe at the end of a string of sisters. I had every object known to woman tossed at me—hairbrushes, shoes, even the family Bible. Of course, I forgive you. Besides, you missed me by a mile."

"Did not."

"Did, too. I'm an expert at dodging implements of feminine revenge, very quick on my feet. That's why I'm such a delightful dance partner."

He gave a little laugh. Perhaps it was the laudanum, perhaps it was in some small way my company, but it was heartening to hear.

"Emma," he said, "can you reach my carpetbag, over in the corner there? There's a paper sack in it."

I fished it out.

"Thank you," he said. "Sorry I'm so useless."

"I'm just sorry that you were burned," I said.

He grinned. "At least it wasn't my gorgeous profile. My face is my fortune, you know." He turned his head and struck a tragic pose. I giggled, but a moment later, he pressed back against the flour sack, fighting the pain.

I sniffed the paper bag. "Peppermints. Of course."

"Booth brought them to me earlier. He picked them up in town somewhere."

"Then open your mouth," I said, and I placed a peppermint between his lips. "Good for the digestion," I added. "Or so I've been told."

"Good for whatever ails you," said Harry. "I'd better have another."

A skirt rustled in the grass outside the tent flap. "Harry?" murmured Mrs. Burnham. "Are you awake?"

"Yes, ma'am," said Harry.

"May I come in?"

"You may. Join the party."

Mrs. Burnham peered in, a lantern in her hand. "Miss Lightfoot! Am I interrupting?"

"Not at all."

"I wanted to see how you were doing, Harry."

"Tolerable."

"Do you have a minute?" Mrs. Burnham asked.

This was my cue to depart. "Goodnight, Harry."

"Don't go yet."

"Oh, I must. Get some rest, if you can, and I'll see you in the morning. Mrs. Burnham," I said, handing her the bag, "there is medicine in that paper sack, and I reckon it's up to you to deliver the patient his next dose."

On my way to the wagon, I passed Sophie's tent. A high-pitched snore whistled through the canvas. The girl had found some peace in slumber, brief as that mercy might be.

Wrapped in my blanket, I found I still could not sleep. My blisters stung, and my brain jumped about. I gathered my candle stubs and began to record the events of the fire in my journal. As I wrote, Mrs. Burnham's lantern shone through the darkness. After five minutes, she left Harry's bedside and made a round of the other tents, until she had checked on all of us. Then she returned to her own quarters, spoke a few words to Mr. Burnham, and blew the lantern out.

OBITUARIES

MR. SUMNER MOONE
MR. S.W. FLETCHER, ESQ.

I do not know the details of their lives, where they were born or who their parents were. I simply know that they perished in the conflagration of Nevada, and that they were both fine men, who lived with passion and made our lives the richer for it. Where have they gone? Saturday morning, they awoke with the rest of us, and now they have vanished, leaving only an empty beaver hat and memories behind.

As I lay in my blanket last night, staring up at the countless stars beyond the pines, I took heart in the ones that streaked, brilliant fire, across the sky. Mr. Moone longed to be a "star," and Mr. Fletcher to fly amongst them. I hope they are up there now, bright and beautiful.

—Emma Lightfoot

I awoke this morning to Buck's skillet grating on the coals. I sniffed bacon and, when I peered under the wagon to the other side, spotted several pairs of boots around the fire pit. Mr. Leach and both Blisses were there, and the Burnhams. Mr. Thayer passed by me with a cup of coffee and disappeared into Harry's tent. I pulled my blanket about my shoulders and wandered over to the fire. Buck offered me a couple of slices of bacon and then passed a plate to Louise in the wagon.

"If we're going to make it to Goodyear's Bar, we should move soon," said Mr. Burnham.

"Anyone seen Booth yet?" inquired Mr. Leach. "He won't be able to keep gentleman's hours today."

"He's around," said Buck. "He showed up for coffee as soon as the pot boiled and then took off for town for tobacco. He'll be back."

Mrs. Burnham spread a map on the little property table and studied it intently as she nibbled a bit of Buck's johnnycake. She looked up just long enough to wish me a "Good morning, Miss Lightfoot."

"Morning," I said.

"We're hoping for an early start, so make ready as soon as you can."

"Yes, ma'am." I snagged one more piece of bacon and started off to check on Lem.

"Oh, Miss Lightfoot," Mrs. Burnham called after me, "I expect Miss Griffith is still sleeping it off, but would you please give her a call as you pass by?"

"Yes, I will." I tossed my blanket into the wagon, slipped on my boots, and hastened over to Sophie's tent.

I leaned down at the flap. "Sophie? Are you awake?" The snoring had ceased, but she didn't stir. "Sophie? You need to wake up. We have to get ready. Are you all right?" I peeked in. Her blanket lay there and her hankie. Her skirt and blouse were tossed into a corner, and her shoes stood empty by the tent door. But Sophie was nowhere to be found.

I hurried back to the breakfast fire. "Sophie's not there," I blurted.

"Well, where is she?" demanded Mr. Burnham.

"I don't know."

"Could she have gone with Ted, Buck?" asked Mrs. Burnham.

"If she did, she went without her clothes," I said.

Mrs. Burnham ran over to Harry's tent. "Gus? Is Sophie in there with you two?"

Mr. Thayer stepped outside. "No. I haven't seen her. What's wrong?"

"She's missing." Mrs. Burnham hurried to Sophie's tent, Mr. Thayer on her heels, and peered in. "Where could she have gone without her shoes?"

At the same moment, they both looked over to the pond. Mrs. Burnham dashed to the water's edge, tore off her boots and skirt, and waded in until only her head was above water. Then she began to dive. Mr. Thayer called, "Buck, Jimmy, Ben! Help!" and he followed Mrs. Burnham into the pond. Soon they were all bobbing under the surface and up again like strange ducks, frantically seeking Sophie.

Harry Brown dragged himself out of his tent. He was pale, his hair tousled. It was clear he'd had a sleepless night, laudanum or no. His hands were without bandages--they were purple and swollen, more painful-looking than they'd been the day before. "What's going on?"

"Sophie's missing," I said. "She might be in the pond."

He started for the water, but I caught his arm. "Harry, don't jump into a rescue with your hands all raw. Please, stay here. I'm going to take a look around. If the Burnhams finish with that pond before I get back, tell them I won't be long."

"Where will you be?"

"Following my nose. Now get back into your tent, all right?"

"I should look for Sophie."

"Harry, you've already been a hero ten times over. I'll go look for the both of us, and you go lie down now. Please."

He finally nodded. I glimpsed relief in his eyes as he disappeared into his tent.

I ran across the clearing to Lem, loosed him from the picket line, and swung up onto his bare back. We started in a circle around the glade, spiraling out with each turn. The mule picked his way along, as I hollered, "Sooo-phie!!" through the woodland. But Sophie did not reply.

I was about to concede that the girl was, indeed, deep in pond mud, when the mule stopped in his tracks and pricked his ears. At first, I heard nothing. Then, from far off, came a tearful soprano, barely more than a whistle on the wind. I gave Lem his head, only halting to pick up the thread of the voice as it rose and fell. It led us, in the end, to a lone buckeye in a field.

The grass about us was knee-high, deep enough to hide most anything. We followed a plaintive rendition of "Blue-Tailed Fly" over to the buckeye, and might have planted a hoof right on the girl had not Lem, with his mule sense, stopped a breath shy of the Songbird of the West.

She lay on her back, her shift spread out on the grass. It rippled in the morning breeze--she seemed to float there, a fallen angel, except that her feet, bloodied from the scrub, were anything but divine. She stared up at the sky and shifted her tune to a mournful snatch of, "A buckwheat cake was in her mouth, a tear was in her eye."

"Sophie," I said, "you have to get up. Let's go."

"No."

"Everyone's looking for you. You can ride Lem back."

She ignored me and sang on, "Don't you cry for me...."

The look in her eye wasn't quite right, but I couldn't leave her lying on the ground for the coyotes. I slipped off Lem and pleaded, "Sophie, come on back now, it'll be all right." I reached for her hand.

The minute my fingers touched hers, she shrieked, "No!" Then she flew up and bounded across the field to a sizable oak. She scrambled up the tree, torn feet or no, and clung to a limb. "I'm not going! I can't, and you can't make me!"

She was right—I couldn't. I could only hope she'd stick up there while Lem and I dashed back to camp. As we came loping into the glade, the last of the searchers, Buck and Jimmy, were straggling up the bank of the pond. The other rescuers stood in the clearing, dripping and distressed, except for Mr. Booth, who had just returned from town.

"I've found her!" I exclaimed.

"Is she all right?" asked Mr. Leach.

"That's debatable," I replied, "but follow me."

A few souls would have sufficed, but Mrs. Burnham and all the men, including poor Harry, rushed after Lem and me. We found Sophie still in her tree. As the sodden company spread out about the trunk, she shouted at us, "Go away! Leave me be!"

"Sophie," replied Mrs. Burnham, "we've been worried to death for you. Please come down."

Sophie scrambled to a higher branch.

"Sophie," said Mr. Burnham, "we're heading out of town in a few minutes. I doubt you'll want to be left behind, hanging in a tree in your underthings. Get down. Pronto!"

Sophie scowled at him, furious. "I'm not going!"

Mrs. Burnham fought to keep cool. "We have a booking in Downieville, Sophie, and we need you—"

"I don't care!!! I can't bear it. I want to go home."

"Ohio?"

"No!" Sophie howled. "Sacramento. I have friends in Sacramento."

"We'll see your friends on the way south—"

"No!"

"Sophie, Sumner would say, 'Go on, there's a show to do—'"

"Sumner's not here!!!" the girl sobbed, and she gripped the tree limb tighter.

Sophie's words hit Mrs. Burnham like a blow. She folded her arms across her chest, holding her heart in. "No, he's not. He's not here," she said.

Mr. Booth stepped through the tall grass and stood beneath Sophie's limb. "Sophie?" he called. She stared down at him through her tears, and he smiled at her, sweetly. "But soft, what light through yonder window breaks?" Sophie didn't exactly smile back, but she didn't shriek at him, either. He moved swiftly to the tree trunk, and, smooth as a cat, made his way up to her side. For a moment, he simply kept her company, a road-weary Romeo playing to a Juliet in a tattered shift. Then he whispered to her, "We're all grieved for Sumner, Sophie. And grieved for you, too. We are so sorry." At last, she lifted grateful eyes to his. "If you would just come back to camp, where it's safe, I'm sure that we could figure out how to get you home." He put a hand out to the girl, and she grasped it, clinging to him. "Here. Let me help you down."

In a trice, Mr. Booth guided Sophie to the ground. Rather than setting her on the mule, he lifted her and carried her like a child all the way back to camp. She wrapped her arms about his neck and buried her head against his shoulder. When he set her carefully down in the wagon bed, he climbed in beside her and kept vigil. The Burnhams and Mr. Leach gathered round the property table and sought to come up with a plan.

"We have to let her go," said Mr. Leach.

"Agreed," said Mr. Burnham. "We can't be talking her out of trees for the rest of the tour."

"Maybe she'll snap out of it," said Mrs. Burnham. "She's a trouper."

Mr. Leach shook his head. "She's done in."

"How would we even get her to Sacramento?" Mrs. Burnham went on. "The coaches won't be running through Nevada."

"No," said Mr. Burnham. "But the Downieville stage comes through here and then heads on to Marysville. She can catch a steamer downriver from there."

"Oh, God," wailed Mrs. Burnham. "What will we do without her?" She crumpled into a prop chair and covered her face with her hands.

Mr. Thayer stepped forward. "Hattie, we'll do what we always do. We'll sing for our suppers. We'll manage."

Mrs. Burnham stared at the others, unwilling to give it up. At last, she sighed, "All right, all right, let her go. We'll pack her things and get her dressed. Ben, can you send someone to find out when the stage leaves?"

Mr. Thayer spoke again, "Hattie, I know you don't want to hear this, but it's a long trip, and Sophie's in bad shape. We can't simply turn her loose alone in the wilderness."

"Gus, we can't even spare the dog at this point."

"No, he's right," said Mr. Leach. "She shouldn't travel by herself. I could talk to Jimmy. He could at least see her to Marysville."

"No," said Mr. Thayer. "Send Harry."

I was helping the Blisses clear up breakfast, but I stopped, a skillet still in my hands.

"We can't do without Harry!" exclaimed Mrs. Burnham. "After we've lost Moone and Frank—"

"Harry's of no use to you," said Mr. Thayer. His voice, usually so calm, was forceful. "He can't hold a sword or a script, he can't ride, and if it wasn't for ice and laudanum, he wouldn't have made it this far. He needs a doctor."

"There must be a doctor in Downieville," said Mrs. Burnham.

"Maybe. But he needs one now, not after two more days of rattling through canyons in a wagon. If we can get him on the coach this morning, he can be in Marysville before evening."

"Gus, I talked to him last night, and he thought he'd be all right."

"He was on laudanum. And he won't complain--he doesn't want to disappoint you."

I knew Mr. Thayer was right, but it didn't cheer me.

Harry had slipped back into his tent on Sophie's return. Mrs. Burnham hastened over to the flap. "Harry," she called, "are you able to come out and talk?"

"Yes." Harry emerged slowly, peaked and without a trace of his usual cheer. Mrs. Burnham softened at the sight of him.

"Harry, Gus thinks we should send you down to Marysville, where you can find a doctor. I hate to admit it, but from the look of you, he may be right."

"Can you spare me?" Harry asked.

"If Frank catches up with us, maybe. And Sophie could use your company. She's going home. Do you want to go with her?"

Harry hesitated, then said, "Yes, ma'am. I'm sorry to say it, but I do. I'll look out for her." He cracked the tiniest of smiles. "She can lift all the heavy baggage."

We bustled about, making ready. Jimmy Bliss was sent into town for news of the stage. Then we helped our invalids spruce for their journey. I washed Sophie's wounded feet and gently slipped fresh hose over them. Mr. Thayer buttoned Harry into his best shirt and gave him a quick shave. Louise handed each of the travelers a prized button from the stash in her tin box as a goodbye gift.

I determined that Harry should have fresh bandages to protect his hands on the long trip. I was gathering muslin strips in the wagon when I heard Mrs. Burnham demand, "You saved the cash box, didn't you?"

"You saw me, yourself," snapped Mr. Burnham.

"Then give them their salaries!"

"Payday's not until Thursday."

"Ben, they need the cash for the road. For the stage fare. Just pay them, for God's sake! Pay them for the part of the week that they did work—"

"We don't have it," said Mr. Burnham.

There was a heavy silence. I could barely breathe, myself, so painful was the thought of losing payday.

Finally Mrs. Burnham spoke, her voice edged like a knife, "We played to full houses in Nevada. Where did all that money go?"

"I banked it. At Wells Fargo. How could I know the damned place would go up in smoke?"

"You banked everything?"

"Everything but spare change, just enough to get us to Downieville. It seemed like a good idea, what with fires and outlaws about."

"Why didn't you tell me?"

Mr. Leach was bringing the team up to the wagon. Mrs. Burnham rushed over to his side. "Jeriah, did Ben mention to you that our funds were incinerated in Nevada?"

"He did not," bristled Mr. Leach. "I would appreciate the details, Burnham."

Mr. Burnham filled him in.

"Do you at least have the receipt?" Mr. Leach demanded.

"Of course I have the receipt. I'm not an idiot."

"Is there a Wells Fargo office in Downieville?"

"Yes," said Mrs. Burnham. "Right near the bridge."

"Then, when we arrive, we'll march on over there and see they make good," said Mr. Leach.

"They will," said Mr. Burnham. "There's no point in having a fit over it."

"We still have to come up with something for Harry and Sophie," said Mrs. Burnham. "There must be enough in the cash box to help them out."

"Not if we want to pay tolls, tend the stock, get our bills posted—"

"All right, all right. Then what have you got on you, Ben?" said Mrs. Burnham.

I peered out of the wagon as Mr. Burnham emptied his pockets onto the little table, while Mr. Leach dug down deep into his. Mrs. Burnham rummaged her reticule until, between them, they'd come up with close to fifteen dollars.

"Better than nothing," said Mrs. Burnham.

The funds were divided between Harry and Sophie, with a solemn promise from Mr. Burnham that he would send the rest of their salaries to the Wells Fargo account of Mr. Booth's brother June in Sacramento. June Booth was one of the Star Troupe's backers, and, with luck, their money would be waiting for them when their boat docked.

Harry took the news of this wrinkle with good grace. Sophie was so desperate to go "home," she would have left on any terms. Nevertheless, before I wrapped Harry's hands, I dug in my bedroll for my old sock and fished the twenty-dollar gold piece Mr. Booth had lent me out of it. After I'd done my nursing duty, I pulled the coin from my apron pocket and laid it before my patient. Harry's eyes widened. "Cinder-Emma, did you rob a bank?"

I laughed. "No. Not yet. I have it on loan from a guardian angel, who would be most pleased if I loaned it to you. Take it, to make your trip safe and comfortable."

"If I do, I shall have to see you again, to repay the debt."

"I'm not very sure these days where I'll turn up next."

"Then you must find me," said Harry. "Why don't I give you my family's address in San Francisco? My parents are so stodgy, Emma—so pleasingly stodgy—that they'll be in that house until Doomsday, I promise you! Fetch that journal of yours, and write it down for me."

"All right."

I started for the wagon, but Harry called out, "Emma? If you have my address, might I expect a letter from you from time to time?"

"I reckon."

He smiled at me, downright cheerful for the first time in days. "You're a good friend, Emma Lightfoot, and it would grieve me to lose you."

I don't know if I blushed, then, or if I just felt the heat from my blistered cheeks, but it warmed me to know that I had earned a place in Harry Brown's affection.

Shortly, Jimmy Bliss returned with the dire news that the stage had already left North San Juan, departing shortly after dawn. Sophie began once more to weep. Mr. Thayer took one look at the situation, mounted his horse, and trotted off toward town. He was gone for a very long hour, but he returned with a brightly painted wagon, drawn by a pure white steed. The wagon canvas read, "The Great Delphino!" in bold black and gilt letters. Mr. Thayer introduced the couple in the wagon to the company. Mr. Delphino was darkly handsome, Madame Delphino, fair and petite—so delicate, it was easy to imagine her floating in the ether. "These are my dear friends from circus days," Mr. Thayer said. "Magicians extraordinaire! They have completed their engagement in North San Juan--save for their disappearing act--and have graciously offered to give our invalids a lift down into the valley."

The company broke into applause and cheers for the generous couple. It was a shame we were not to spend more time with them, but the magicians had to reach their next destination before nightfall, and they could not transport themselves with an "Abracadabra!" Sophie and Harry were loaded into the rear of the wagon between a "magic cabinet," decorated with gaudy flowers and vines, and an ornate cage of white doves, who cooed pleasantly at the newcomers. Mr. Delphino gave the lines a shake, and we followed the wagon to the road, shouting "Goodbye!" and "Thank you!" as the travelers hastened away to the west. Sophie was lost to sight in the wagon bed, but Harry remained by the opening in the canvas. He managed a jaunty smile and waved a bandaged hand in my direction. Then they vanished around a bend in the road.

Because of the morning's difficulties, it was nearly noon before the Star Troupe began the trip east toward Downieville. We never made it as far as Goodyear's Bar but stopped, instead, to spend the night on the outskirts of Camptonville. Camptonville is an unearthly place--the hillsides about it are scarred by "hydraulic mining," where the soil is blasted away from the rock by huge nozzles of water. Part of the main street perches precariously on the edge of a hydraulic abyss. I tried not to look down as we passed by, fighting back the thought that the rumbling of wagon wheels on the road might, at any second, yield to the sound of the earth tumbling out from under us.

TUESDAY, JULY 22. *Goodyear's Bar, quite late. Our camp by the river—*

Last night's "entertainment" in Camptonville was short and sweet—most of the company was back at camp by nine. Our site was congenial enough, an abandoned claim with a crumbling shanty. No one was inclined to sleep in the shanty itself—Mrs. La Rue pronounced it "disgusting" for the spiders and bedbugs residing there, although the insects found it paradise. The true luxury of the claim was its well, offering good water for horses and humans alike.

The La Rues once again staked out the wagon for sleeping quarters, and I laid my blanket on the ground nigh it. Mr. Burnham promptly changed out of his theatre clothes and headed back into town. The rest of us stuck close by. Buck Bliss built a fire, and, for a while, the actors kept company, but soon, most headed for bed. I stayed up to write in this journal, on my promise to Mr. Leach that I would douse the flames before I turned in.

One by one, the lanterns and candles in the tents were snuffed out. Mrs. Burnham's lantern burned later than the rest. I was deep into my scribblings when I heard, "Miss Lightfoot?" at my shoulder. Mrs. Burnham stood there, a couple of books in her hands. I closed my journal.

"Miss Lightfoot, these are my copies of *Taming of the Shrew* and *The Iron Chest*. I was wondering if you would look them over, especially the parts of Blanche and Bianca. We might be able to work you into the performances in Downieville."

"Thank you!" Those were Sophie's roles, much larger than the Player Queen. My heart did a flip-flop. "I hope I can handle it."

"I believe you can. You've surprised me from the day we met. Besides, audiences are forgiving this far into the hills. You could probably still hold the book, and all would be well."

"Triple salary?" I asked.

"Triple salary."

She handed me the two small, worn volumes, one so thumbed that the pages were loose. With them, she handed me a dose of stage fright and a helping of something finer--the dear privilege of a role!

I thanked her again, and she wished me goodnight. Then I skimmed through the dog-eared pages. More fascinating than the text itself were Mrs. Burnham's notes, flooding the margins and the end-papers of each play. Some were simple hieroglyphics, like "X DL" or "Exit UR," that I guessed might be for moves. But others told the stories of the characters. "Enter with bravado," she marked for Katherine. "Let Petruchio know who's boss!" Or for Lady Helen, "Play with deep fear for Mortimer, and *love*!" I realized that there, in her penciled scrawls, was the magic that lifted the words from the page and brought them to life. She crafted her roles, just as my father Emmett had sweated over the exact turn of phrase in his editorials.

As I pored over the scripts, the fire burned low. I rose to toss another chunk of wood on the coals, when I heard an odd, hollow sound. Perhaps an animal, far off? Certainly not Louise's night terrors, and not a snore, either. I stood, absolutely still, and caught it again. It came from Mrs. Burnham's tent, where the lantern still shone.

I told myself to mind my own business. But the small sound went on, and, after several minutes, I tiptoed to the open door of her tent. Mrs. Burnham sat at her makeshift vanity. Her hair was undone, and her cheeks glistened in the lantern light. She clutched a silver picture frame to her breast, the one I had witnessed while fetching her laundry. It enclosed the daguerrotype of her bright-eyed babe Henry, and she swayed back and forth with it, as if she could rock Henry's image to sleep. Her grief was too private for me to intrude upon, and I quietly backed away.

Shortly after I returned to the fire, Mrs. Burnham stepped out into the night and drifted off on one of her solitary strolls. I went about stowing her books and readying my blanket. I was just about to douse the coals, when my eye was caught by the flare of a match, struck behind the canvas of the Burnham's tent. I knew Mrs. Burnham was nowhere about. When I heard a childish giggle, I sneaked over to the tent once more and peeked in.

Louise had tossed Mrs. Burnham's best shawl about her shoulders and slipped into the woman's place before the vanity. I almost laughed out loud, she looked so like a miniature Hattie Burnham, tilting her head just so. She had stolen one of Mrs. Burnham's thin cigars out of its silver box and was delicately blowing smoke rings into the air. It shocked me to see the child puffing away, although, I confess, the sight was so amusing, I let her go on.

Louise hummed, and posed in the mirror. Then she took a long drag on the cigar until the end burned hot and bright. She held out the fringe of the shawl and deliberately, precisely, laid the cigar to it. I thought perhaps she was only playing, pretending to come so close to the silk. When the shawl's embroidered roses glowed redder, I speculated they had simply caught the lantern light. But when the flame jumped to the lace on the sleeve of the girl's night gown, I hissed, "Louise!!!" She turned to me, ablaze, her blue eyes cool as ice. I tore Mrs. Burnham's blanket from the cot and threw it about the child, then rolled her, a smoldering bundle, across the earthen floor of the tent. She fought me like a wildcat, but, in the end, I pinned her and forced her to face me. "Louise, what in hell are you doing? WHY?"

Mrs. Burnham hurried through tent flap and stopped, appalled, as she spotted me straddling Louise. "What's going on in here?"

"Louise has tried to incinerate herself," I replied.

Mrs. Burnham stared down at the child, swaddled in the blanket. "Louise, what happened?"

The girl stared right back at her, a piglet in a poke.

"She set herself ablaze," I said, and pointed to the cigar still smoking on the tent floor. Mrs. Burnham rushed over and stamped it out.

"Is that true, Louise?" demanded Mrs. Burnham. "Why?"

Louise remained silent.

I supplied Mrs. Burnham with the details. When I arrived at the part about Louise's sleeve catching fire, the child finally stated, matter-of-factly, "My arm hurts." We unwrapped her then, and as the charred shawl and the singed lace peeled away, no more words were necessary. Mrs. Burnham sat back on her heels, horrified.

"I don't see as she's badly hurt," I said. "Mostly just red, maybe a few blisters."

Mrs. Burnham placed her hand on Louise's cheek and gazed straight into her eyes. "What have you done, Louise? What have you done?"

Louise blinked her long lashes and murmured, "Nothing."

"Why did you start a fire?"

"I don't know."

"Have you done this before?"

The child simply closed her lids, blotting Mrs. Burnham out.

Mrs. Burnham studied the girl's silence, then said, "There's some of Lola's lotion on the vanity, Emma. Rosewater and glycerine. Maybe you could spread it on Louise's arm. Would you like that Louise?"

"Yes."

Mrs. Burnham's voice was beginning to shake. "There are handkerchiefs in my trunk. You can pick out a couple for bandages." She turned to me. "Emma, I'm going out for a while. Will you watch Louise? Stay in the tent, and don't take your eyes off of her. Not for a minute."

"Yes, ma'am."

"And please, not a word of this. Not to anyone."

"Shouldn't Mr. Booth know? Or Mr. Thayer?"

"Not now."

"But we should--"

"Please, Miss Lightfoot. Promise me."

Her eyes were desperate. "I promise," I said.

Mrs. Burnham lit a lantern and left the tent. She climbed into the wagon, then woke Mrs. La Rue. Mrs. Burnham spoke softly at first, but Mrs. La Rue's replies were sleepy and unhappy, and Mrs. Burnham quickly took on a firmer tone. Soon, the two women left the wagon and hastened away into the woods.

I opened the jar of lotion and went about dressing Louise's burns. Every so often, voices drifted back our way, faint as night birds. Their words were lost, but once I caught a burst of shouting from Mrs. La Rue that soon shifted to the high notes of a wail.

Louise was mute as we wrapped the linen kerchiefs about her arm. She was listening, too, and I spied a flicker of fear on her countenance.

"I'm sorry I had to toss you about, Louise," I said, but she only shrugged. "Can you tell me why you burned that shawl?"

The life went from her eyes, as if a veil had dropped, and she turned away—the only answer I would get. I took a lace from my boot, and we played cat's cradle until Mrs. Burnham and Mrs. La Rue returned to the tent. Mrs. La Rue's eyes were swollen, and her cheeks red. She went to Louise and stroked the child's brow. "We'll need stage fare," she muttered. "We spent every penny you gave us last week just to get ourselves this far."

"Mr. Burnham's not here," Mrs. Burnham replied. "He has the key to the cash box."

Mrs. La Rue was immovable. "We are without funds."

Mrs. Burnham lifted a small, carved box from her vanity and pulled out a necklace and a bracelet. "Here, these are gold. They're worth much more than the stage fare."

Mrs. La Rue grasped them without even a "thank you." Perhaps she had no words left. As mean as she'd been to me, I felt for her. I wouldn't have stood in her shoes for the world.

"We have to get you packed and into town," said Mrs. Burnham. "The stage comes through a little after dawn." She turned to me. "Emma, please go wake Mr. Thayer. Quietly. Tell him I'll explain when he gets over here."

Mr. Thayer woke with a grumble, but he pulled his trousers over his long johns and tailed me to Mrs. Burnham's tent. He was taken aback to find the La Rues there. Mrs. Burnham wasted no time. "Louise was playing," she said, "and she fell into the fire. She's not badly hurt, but her mother has decided that this tour is too dangerous for a child. They're leaving on the morning stage. We don't need to wake the rest of the company, but we could use your help."

"I don't see Ben about."

"No. You don't."

"What can I do?"

"For openers, you can lend us twenty dollars, if you have it. For their expenses. I can't get into the cash box."

Mr. Thayer lifted an eyebrow, but he replied, "I reckon."

"Thank you. And we need to get their baggage into town."

"All right." Mr. Thayer turned to the La Rues. "I'm truly sorry to see you go," he said.

"I'm grateful," Mrs. La Rue replied, in a small voice, while Louise said, simply, "Goodbye."

Mrs. Burnham accompanied the La Rues to the wagon to help them dress and pack and to keep a vigilant eye on Louise. Mr. Thayer and I went in search of Lem and lashed the La Rues' champagne baskets onto the old boy's back. Soon, we all trudged through what was left of the night into Camptonville, Mr. Thayer toting Louise upon his shoulders, and me leading Lem. We unloaded at the stage stop before the Western Hotel, where Mrs. Burnham remained with the La Rues to see them onto the coach. As Mr. Thayer and I departed town in the grey light of dawn, Louise and Clarissa La Rue sat stiffly on the bench before the hotel. Brushed, and washed, and in their best clothes, they bore the somber aspect of the banished.

I feared for what might become of them.

When we returned to camp, Mr. Thayer picketed Lem for me. I was exhausted from the night's doings. The sunrise, pale as it was, stabbed at my eyes. I grabbed my blanket, made myself a nest in the wagon, and promptly slipped into oblivion.

It seemed I had only been asleep for seconds when I was brought back to the surface by the clinking of the coffee pot. Mr. Leach and the Blisses were up and about, and soon, Mr. Booth and Mrs. Burnham joined them at the breakfast table. I decided to ignore them and had almost sunk back into my dreams, when I heard mention of the La Rues, followed by Mrs. Burnham's announcement that they had left the company because of Mrs. La Rue's worry for Louise's "safety." Folks were surprised at the news, though not deeply disappointed—Clarissa La Rue had been a burr under the saddle for most of the company. Only Mr. Booth sounded a note of sorrow, "I shan't be able to wish Louise farewell."

Soon, Buck Bliss was growling a sweet, "Rise and shine, Miss Lightfoot," at the wagon's tailgate, proffering a cup of coffee in his big paw. The coffee's warmth was a comfort, and I surrendered to the notion that I must, indeed, rise, even if it was impossible to shine.

I had made my way to the table and claimed a biscuit when I caught sight of Ben Burnham heading for his tent. He was rumpled and bleary-eyed, as if he, too, had been up all night. When Mrs. Burnham spotted him, she demanded, "Where have you been? We could have used you last night."

"That's a change of tune."

"Where were you?"

"Enriching our coffers, sweetheart."

"At cards?"

"You've been on my back about payroll—"

"You promised you'd stay away from the poker table. How much did you lose?"

Her words sounded an alarm to Mr. Leach. He hastened out of his tent, scowling.

"You're so quick to judge, Hattie," snapped Mr. Burnham.

"Don't tell me. You used last night's cash as a stake. Is there anything left?"

"We're up by a couple hundred dollars. More."

Mr. Burnham marched into their tent and hauled out the cash box. With great show, he pulled a sizable poke from his pocket and tossed it, clinking, into the box. He locked it up with a flourish and dumped the whole thing in Hattie Burnham's arms. "Happy?"

"It's not worth the risk, Ben."

"Well, there we are. Damned if I do, and damned if I don't." He spied Mr. Leach frowning his way. "Good morning, Jeriah. I expect you have an opinion, too."

"I expect I do," replied Mr. Leach. He delivered Mr. Burnham a black look and turned away to strike his tent.

Once more upon the road, we headed east into the Sierra Nevada. The trail led us along a wide ridge between forks of the Yuba River. The bowl of the sky was closer, and I knew we were leaving the foothills for the granite heights of the mountains.

The road was lively—we met with wagons and coaches, and, especially, big pack teams of hardy mules. Lem was cheered by the sight of his brethren. He nickered and brayed and no doubt gloated to them, "I'm on light duty boys! No loads of beans and ore for me! Just a skinny girl to spoil me!" When the road looked to be even for a piece, I gave him his head, pulled one of Mrs. Burnham's scripts out of my saddlebag, and went to work learning the words.

My concentration, though, was not the best—I was often pulled from the text, not by sounds, but by silence. I missed Harry's laugh bursting forth from along our line, and the cheer of Mr. Moone's voice ringing out in song. When I lost Emmett, his absence walked about with me—it still does. Losing so many of our theatre "family" leaves the same sort of hole. Even the air feels empty.

Mr. Booth rode his pinto up abreast of Lem, and his smile rescued me from my thoughts. "Hard at work, I see."

"I'm doing my best."

"What roles do you have there?"

"Blanche and Bianca."

"Lovely. Although that Bianca is a silly simp. You'll have to bring your acting skills to the fore with that one. Let me know if you need help."

"Can you provide me with simp lessons, Mr. Booth?"

He chuckled. "One of my specialties, Miss Lightfoot," he said, his voice suddenly feminine and lisping. Even when he played the fool, he was handsome—maybe more than ever. "You know," he went on, "the smaller this company gets, the more ridiculous it is to stand on ceremony. Please call me Ted."

"Oh, I tried to a while back, Mr. B—Ted. But I found it difficult."

"Why? Do I still frighten you? That time on the river—"

"Oh, no, no." I hesitated. I had to search for the words, to find a way to say it without blushing. "It's because I admire your acting so." And then I blushed, anyway.

"Thank you, Emma," he nodded, and, for a while, we rode along in comfortable silence—the journey was a little less lonely.

Finally, Ted spoke. "Do you know, Emma, that this trail goes all the way over the mountains? If we keep riding, we'll reach the desert on the far side and join up with the main road that leads back to Missouri. From there, you can catch a steamer up the Ohio to the Erie Canal, and then go on to New York City."

"Just by following this mule trail?"

"Umm-hmm. Or you could turn a little south and wind up at my home. At my mother's house in Maryland."

This was a surprise. I had heard so much talk of Ted's father, I hadn't stopped to think of his mother.

"Is your mother still alive, Mr.—Ted?"

"Yes, I'm blessed there. I still have my mother, very sweet, very beautiful. I've not seen her for four years now. When I return east, the first thing I shall do is hold her in my arms."

I could only imagine the joy of such a reunion.

"I miss my brothers and sisters, too," he added.

"Are they grown?"

"Mostly. My sisters are young ladies. The boys are boys. Joey's the baby. Johnny's a hellion, but we have hopes for him." Ted turned to me, a twinkle in his eye. "What do you say? Shall we break away from this bunch and gallop our steeds over the mountains to Maryland?"

As outrageous as the idea was, I was tempted to shout, "Yes!" Instead, I came back with, "And pass up the chance to play a silly simp?"

"Ah. Spoken like a true Thespian," laughed Ted.

We passed the time pleasantly for a stretch, although, in the back of my heart, I felt a twinge for my own lost family. Perhaps Ted sensed where my mood had led, for he brought up his own sorrow for our missing companions. He asked about Louise, about whether I might have seen her before the La Rues took their leave. Had she been upset at their departure? Had her father made more threats?

I longed to spill the truth to him, but the weight of my promise to Mrs. Burnham stopped my voice in my throat. I could simply utter that I had seen her for a few minutes and she had been fine.

Even with Ted's companionship, our day's trip was a lengthy one, ending with a wicked descent down into the canyon of the North Fork of the Yuba. The sun had already slipped behind the mountains when, at last, we rode into Goodyear's Bar, one of those camps strung along a skinny strip of riverbank. As we journeyed down the main street, the Burnhams kept their eyes open for a venue to stage an entertainment. The sole prospect was a small Masonic Hall. There were no bills by the door announcing rival companies for the night. Mr. Burnham halted the team, while Mrs. Burnham went in search of the building's management, but she returned in short order. "They said no. They've no bookings, but the membership has a meeting tonight. So, that's that. There aren't any other spaces sizable enough. We could try to play a saloon, but I'm in no mood to dodge drunks and cheap whiskey. What do you think, Jeriah?"

"Agreed," said Mr. Leach.

"Ben?"

"Whatever. But we should find a spot to camp near the river, so we can water the horses."

"I'm hankering to sleep under a roof, tonight, Burnham," said Ted. "A real bed and a bath that's more than pond water. I reckon I'll go investigate the hotels."

"I second that," said Mr. Thayer, with a grin.

Ted and Mr. Thayer stuck with the company until we'd found a decent spot upriver, and then they departed into town with the promise they'd return after supper to read through *Taming of the Shrew*. Most of us were taking on new roles, and several scenes were being cut, so I, at least, welcomed the idea of a rehearsal.

The Blisses built a campfire, and with the glow of lanterns, we found enough illumination to gather in a circle by the river and rehearse. Sitting on the sand in the flickering light, listening to the rushing of the river and the sounds of Shakespeare's words spoken by the likes of Ted and Mrs. Burnham, I was more than content, despite all our hardships. I was, for the moment, downright happy.

WEDNESDAY, JULY 23. *By a small stream high on the ridge, late afternoon. It's chilly and damp—*

After our rehearsal last night, the company went off to their beds. I reclaimed my old haunt, the wagon, set out the last of my candle stubs, and, wrapped in my blanket, wrote in this journal for a long while, only turning in when the letters on the page blurred before my eyes.

Sometime deep in the night, I was awakened by Mrs. Burnham. "Ben?" she called, softly, and then, a more insistent, "Ben!"

I peered out into the darkness. By the light of the moon, I made out Mr. Burnham striding across the camp, and, over by their tent, the pale outline of Mrs. Burnham, in her shift. Her voice was still fuzzy from sleep.

"Ben, where are you off to?"

"Get back to bed."

"Don't go into town."

"I'll go where I damn well please."

"Did you take that poke? With the Camptonville cash?"

Mr. Burnham whirled about. "That's all you care about--the money and the troupe. If you want to keep me in your bed, Hattie, make me feel welcome. I don't hanker to spend my nights with the debt-collector."

"Do you have that poke?"

"Go back to bed!" Mr. Burnham started off again, but Hattie Burnham was right on his tail.

"We have tolls to pay tomorrow. We can't even cross the river without cash—"

The Bliss brothers stirred over by Mr. Leach's tent.

"We'll have it!" said Mr. Burnham. "Now leave me be!"

"No!" Mrs. Burnham grabbed at her husband's coat pockets.

"Damn it, stop!!!" Mr. Burnham seized her arms and shoved her hard. She stumbled back and sprawled into the dirt.

"Ben!" Mr. Leach rushed over in his long johns, the Blisses at his back. Buck and Jimmy lifted Mrs. Burnham to her feet. Something dark poured from her nose, glistening in the moonlight.

"What's going on?" Mr. Leach demanded.

"A disagreement," Burnham snarled, "between a man and his wife. Butt out, Leach!"

"He has our cash!" Mrs. Burnham wiped at her nose with her hand, but the blood only smeared across her face. "He was sneaking off into town."

"The company's funds are my business, too, Burnham," said Mr. Leach.

"I handle the money! If I want to build on our assets, I'll do it."

Mr. Leach gave him a look of disgust. "Where's the cash?"

Mr. Burnham was silent.

"Hattie," Mr. Leach went on, "is the cash box in your tent? Would you fetch it, please?"

Mrs. Burnham hurried into the tent and returned with the iron box. She set it in the table.

"Unlock it, Burnham," demanded Mr. Leach. "I'd like to know exactly what we have on hand."

Mr. Burnham pulled the poke from his pocket. "It's all right here. Every penny of it."

"You'd be wise to return it," said Mr. Leach.

"Fine," said Mr. Burnham. He pulled out the key and threw open the box.

Mr. Leach peered inside. "The damn thing's empty."

"Not any more." Mr. Burnham tossed in the poke and turned the lock.

Mr. Leach was not impressed. "Where's that Wells Fargo receipt? I'd like to see it, if it exists. Now."

"It's safe."

"WHERE?"

"That's for me to know, Leach."

"You've been playing us for fools, Burnham. For weeks, now, stupid fools!"

"You're a liar—"

"And you're a godforsaken thief!"

At that, Mr. Burnham hauled back and punched Mr. Leach right in his otter mustache. The blow dropped the stage manager, but before Burnham could do more damage, he was stopped dead by the cold click of a rifle. Buck Bliss had seized the weapon from behind the wagon seat and aimed it squarely at Mr. Burnham's head. "I could lay you out right here," Buck growled.

Jimmy Bliss gave a hand as Mr. Leach struggled to stand, his long johns streaked with dust. "No, Buck," Mr. Leach spat, "he's not worth it." But Buck kept Mr. Burnham in his sights. "I'll take the cash box for now," Mr. Leach went on, "and you damned well better come up with that receipt by morning. Wells Fargo is our first stop."

Mr. Burnham said nothing, only glared at Mr. Leach and the Blisses, who glared right back. In the end, Mrs. Burnham stepped forward. Her bloody nose had left an ugly stain on her shift. She pleaded, "Go to bed now, Ben." Mr. Burnham thrust the cash box at Mr. Leach, and Buck Bliss lowered the rifle.

Mr. Burnham brushed past his wife and stormed into their tent, ransacking it for his gear. Then he took off upriver, where he could be heard tossing his blanket and truck to the ground. Hattie Burnham disappeared into the tent, and Mr. Leach and the boys headed back to their own quarters. As they passed the wagon, Mr. Leach called in a low voice, "Good night, Miss Lightfoot."

I stirred a few times in the night—even with my blanket, my feet were cold. I woke a little after dawn to raindrops tapping on the wagon's canvas and the rumble of thunder echoing off the canyon walls. A few days ago, we would have welcomed a turn in the weather, to purge the ash from the air, but this morning, it brought a gloom that only deepened the dark mood hanging over us from last night's brawl.

Buck Bliss divided up a tin of leftover biscuits, as Mr. Leach pulled India rubber coats from a box in the wagon. The stage manager's lip was split and swollen. Mrs. Burnham had washed the blood from her face, but her humiliation shadowed her still.

Despite the damp, Buck Bliss got a fire going and brewed a pot of coffee. As Mr. Leach handed Mrs. Burnham a tin cup, he muttered, "Where's Ben?"

"I don't know, Jeriah. Still sleeping?"

"Jimmy," said Mr. Leach, "go rustle up Burnham. We should move before this weather worsens."

Jimmy's silence shouted that he'd rather take a quick jaunt into hell.

"I'll go," said Mrs. Burnham. "I expect he's just up the bank a piece."

It was a good ten minutes before she returned, struggling through the brush and breathing hard. "He's not there," she said. "I made out the spot where he'd spread his blanket, but that's it."

A check of the horses proved that Burnham's buckskin was missing. "Could he have gone ahead to Downieville to post our bills, Jeriah?" asked Mrs. Burnham. "Had you two talked about who'd be advance man?"

"We might have, Hattie." Mr. Leach's bruised lip thickened his speech, and he sounded worn. "It's possible."

"Then we'll catch up with him in town." She hurried toward her tent, to pack up.

Mr. Leach hastened after her. "I'll tell you what, Hattie, I'll go ahead myself. I'll help him out if I find him, and I'll check out the theatre. Buck can drive for you. It's only four miles. Just don't let anyone tumble into the river, all right?"

Mrs. Burnham managed a tiny smile. "You have my word."

In a trice, Mr. Leach mounted up and was on his way. A few minutes later, Ted and Mr. Thayer arrived in camp, bathed and shaved, but scratching from the vermin who had shared their rustic hotel. "Adios, Goodyear's bugs!" said Ted, as we headed for the trail.

The route to Downieville was by way of a toll road, a narrow trace that wound between the river rushing over its bed of grey boulders and the shadowy, blue-green pines marching up the canyon walls. The rain, which would have laid the dust on a more even road, turned the rocky passage slick. Buck was slow and steady with the team, and Jimmy rode, a patient sentinel, at the rear of the string of riderless horses. Mist lifted from the water to dissolve into clouds masking the mountain peaks.

Because the way was rugged, and our progress halting, it was late morning by the time we approached Downieville. The road climbed the side of the canyon for a spell before it descended into town, and from that rise we sighted the city that had made so many rich.

It lay in a valley, surrounded by majestic heights and crosscut by two rivers. On a sunny day, before the trees had been hewn from the hillsides, it might have been a sweet sight, but today, the dark skies and the drizzle lent it a damp and somber tone, and the mountains looked down with disdain upon the town's flimsy efforts at habitation. Laid out on twisted streets, buildings clung like water plants to the riverbanks. A good flood would have washed them all downstream like tailings—indeed, the waterways were littered with the dead wood of abandoned flumes and miners' flotsam.

For Mrs. Burnham, though, Downieville was Eureka. On the rise, she squeezed her grey mare past the wagon to triumph in the view. "There she is, boys!" she called out. "There's a fine little stage and a tidy hotel waiting for us!" She urged her horse to a trot, despite the rough trail, and hastened us into town.

In a blink, we found ourselves on Downieville's narrow main street. Ahead of us, between a muddy plaza and one of the town's bridges, we spied four riders, spread out across the road. "I believe that's Jeriah!" exclaimed Mrs. Burnham. "And a welcoming committee!" I squinted through my specs and made out Mr. Leach, although Mr. Burnham was nowhere in sight. As we rode closer, the men flanking Mr. Leach bore little resemblance to our usual, cheerful fans of the Thespian art. One was a big man, in a long, black raincoat; the other two were grim and scruffy types. They had rifles slung across their saddles.

Mrs. Burnham led us forward and greeted Mr. Leach with a bright, "Hello, Jeriah!"

"Hello," said Mr. Leach, gloomy as a pallbearer.

"Have you found Ben, yet?"

"No, Hattie, I haven't."

"Did you check the hotel?"

"Yes. Ben's not in Downieville, I'm sorry to say. These gentlemen can vouch for that, they've helped me look."

"He might show up."

"He won't." The stage manager's bluntness surprised Mrs. Burnham into silence. “He’s gone,” Mr. Leach went on. “And it won’t do any good to lie to yourself about him, Hattie.”

Mrs. Burnham frowned, then sat up very straight in the saddle. “Fine. We’ll do tonight’s show without him. He can never remember his damned lines, anyway. Buck, the theatre’s at the back of the plaza. Let’s get the wagon on over there.”

“No, Buck,” said Mr. Leach. “Drive the team up the street, behind us. Jimmy, move those horses across, too, and tie them by the wagon.”

The Bliss brothers did as they were told, while Mrs. Burnham stared in astonishment. “What’s this about?”

Mr. Leach nodded to the big man in the raincoat. As the gentleman reached into his coat pocket, a badge gleamed on his chest. He pulled out a folded paper, rode over to Mrs. Burnham, and laid it in her hand.

“It’s a Writ of Attachment, Hattie,” said Mr. Leach. “I’m sorry. But I don’t have a choice.”

“What does it mean?”

“It means I’m taking possession. Ben has left a string of bad debts all up and down the trail. Livery stables, hotels, printers. I’ve staved off a few of those creditors out of my own pocket, and the fires have distracted God knows how many more, but the Star Troupe owes unpaid bills from here until Doomsday.”

“Jeriah—I didn’t know,” stammered Mrs. Burnham.

“Truly? Too bad, because you’re as liable for those debts as Ben is.”

“But all that money from Nevada, there’s more than enough to pay what we owe. All we need is the receipt—”

“You really think there’s a receipt, Hattie?”

Mrs. Burnham paled.

Mr. Leach went on. “Whatever happened to that money—up in smoke, the card table, Lord knows—you and I are not going to see a cent of it. All I can do is to protect what’s mine. If I don’t attach it now, someone else will, and I could lose everything.”

Mrs. Burnham urged her grey to Mr. Leach’s side. “Jeriah, please—”

“The wagon, the tack and the horses already belong to me, Hattie. And Ben owed the boys and me salaries and rent—”

“You were paid—”

“Our pittance as actors, yes, but not what’s due Buck and Jimmy as grooms and stagehands, or what I’m owed for the wagon and team, or my investment—”

"Then let us perform. Tonight will be your benefit, Jeriah. I'll turn over every penny—"

"Hattie," sighed Mr. Leach, his voice heavy, "The show is over. Time to pack it up and go home."

"But Downieville has always liked us. And we haven't even started for the southern camps. Give me a chance to make things right—"

"No. It grieves me, but this is business—"

"Please, Jeriah—"

"No!!!" hollered Mr. Leach, "It's too damned late!!!"

Mrs. Burnham shot the stage manager a wild look, then wheeled her mare and took off. The shorter of the scruffy types spurred his horse after her and seized the grey's bridle. "Leave me be!" shouted Mrs. Burnham. The mare, spooked by the furor and the man's harsh touch, reared and spilled Mrs. Burnham into the muck of the plaza.

Ted and Mr. Thayer leapt out of their saddles and hurried to her side, lifting her, muddied and shaken, to her feet. "Are you all right?" said Mr. Thayer. The scruffy man grabbed the mare's reins and handed her off to Jimmy.

"We have to get to the theatre," gasped Mrs. Burnham. "I need to speak to the manager!"

The constable in the raincoat brought up his rifle. "No, ma'am, you don't." His two cohorts lifted their own weapons and drew beads on us. My knees shook against Lem's sides. "Who's Booth?"

Ted stepped boldly forward. "I am."

The constable scowled—this young man in his rain-soaked serape hardly resembled a famous star—but he went on, "We have a pleasant and a prosperous city here, and we're going to keep it that way. We don't need a crazy actor setting it ablaze. Once we sort out what's owed, you and your friends can turn about and hightail it out of town. Understand?"

Mrs. Burnham glared at the big man. "Ted Booth is no incendiary!"

"Can you prove that, ma'am?" said the constable. "How do you know he won't strike a spark in the night just to see this city light up like Nevada?"

"He had nothing to do with Nevada!" cried Mrs. Burnham.

I could no longer bear my silence. "Mr. Booth is no firebug!"

"Well, now," said the constable, "that's very touching, you ladies having such faith in the man, but my job is to keep this city safe. And I will. Booth, if you stay in Downieville, I promise you a quick trip to the bridge."

My stomach twisted in a knot. Not long ago, the Mexican woman, Josepha, had swung from a Downieville bridge, for no better reason than that she was a Mexican and a woman. The smaller deputy lifted his coil of rope and flaunted the noose dangling from its end.

Mr. Thayer ignored him and strode over to Mr. Leach. "Jeriah, do you believe this nonsense?"

"I don't know, Thayer. I'm simply here to take care of business."

"Jimmy?" said Mr. Thayer, but Jimmy shuffled and stared at the ground.

Ted had stood somberly before the constable, but now he set his gaze on Buck Bliss. "Et tu, Buck? Do you believe I'm a killer?"

Buck met his eye. "No, Ted. I believe you've been my friend."

The constable snorted. "Lovely, all this dainty baring of our souls, but it does not fill the city coffers. Let's divvy up these goods, and if you ladies and gentlemen cooperate, we'll let you vacate the city limits without stretching anyone's neck. Where do we begin, Leach?"

"With the horses and tack. They're all mine."

"Then hand them over!" shouted the constable.

"How are the women supposed to get out of here on foot?" Mr. Thayer demanded. "Have a little compassion, Leach, and at least spare them something to ride!"

"I can do better," said Mr. Leach. "The boys and I are leaving town this afternoon. Miss Lightfoot, you're welcome to travel with us. And you, too, Hattie, if you wish."

Mrs. Burnham turned on the stage manager, eyes blazing. "Over my dead body!" she hissed.

"Suit yourself," replied Mr. Leach. "What about you, Thayer? I have no beef with you—"

"No thank you," said Mr. Thayer, with royal disdain.

"Miss Emma?"

A part of me yearned to say, "Yes," to surrender to the comfort of Buck Bliss's biscuits and the safe haven of the wagon bed, but I could not utter the word. The three people at my side had offered me trust and kindness, and I could not turn my back upon them. "I don't believe I can accept your offer," I said.

"I'm sorry to hear that."

Mr. Leach nodded to the constable, and the big man hollered, "Let's have those horses, now!"

Mr. Booth and Mr. Thayer yielded their mounts, and Jimmy led the animals over to the other stock. But when the taller of the deputies made a grab for Lem, I shouted, "Keep your hands off this mule! He's mine!"

"Not any more, girlie," the man smirked, and tried to pull me down.

"You son of a bitch!" growled a voice nigh my saddle, and, quick as a snake, Buck Bliss seized the man by the collar and tossed him aside. "This here mule belongs to Miss Lightfoot, and no one else," Buck roared. "The saddle and the bridle, too. And if you do her harm over that critter, I'll break you like a match stick!"

The deputies glared at us, a pair of nasty hyenas, but Mr. Leach called to them, "The mule is the girl's, so leave her be," and they backed off a piece. Then he turned their attention to the goods in the wagon. "The scenery and those baskets of costumes can stay right where they are. They're going with us."

"Hold on, Leach," Mr. Thayer cut in, "some of those costumes are private property. They're not yours to take. Though how the hell Ted and I are going to pack ours out without horses is a mystery to me."

Mr. Leach scowled. "All right, Thayer. We'll transport them for you. Write to me in Sacramento when you're ready for them. And Hattie, I'll hold your property for thirty days, until you can make good on what you owe. After that, it goes up for auction. You know where to find me."

"I'm afraid I do," Mrs. Burnham muttered.

By now, the bridge and the plaza had filled with onlookers, an audience to the Star Troupe's humiliation. A few were shopkeepers—a grocer in his apron, a baker with flour upon his sleeves—but most were rough sorts who had naught to do but amuse themselves with the sideshow before them. "Deadbeat actors," they rumbled, "skipping out on what's owed." Worse, I heard the name "Booth" tied to the words "flames," and "the damned 'Burnham Down' Company." Mr. Leach took in the crowd, too, and hurried about his business, handing our carpetbags and other possessions to the constable, who piled them in the street. Ted, Mr. Thayer and I would be allowed to claim what was ours, but Mrs. Burnham's bag and her big trunk were rummaged for valuables. Although the luggage held no cash, her elegant cigar box, her fine brush and comb, and a few bits of jewelry were tossed into a canvas sack.

The shorter deputy upended her carpetbag and gave it a shake. A small silver frame, enclosing a daguerrotype, spilled into the road. The deputy snatched it, gave the frame a quick polish on his grimy sleeve, and slipped it into his pocket. "No!" shrieked Mrs. Burnham. "No! You can't have that! That's Henry!!!"

Mr. Thayer turned on Mr. Leach. "For God's sake, man! That's all she has of the boy!"

"Leave it!!" Mr. Leach barked. The deputy snarled an obscenity, then reluctantly tossed Henry's picture into the street. Mrs. Burnham dived for the daguerrotype and tucked the treasure into her pocket.

The constable was losing patience. "Damn it, Leach! Generosity's fine for the collection plate, but all you've done is pare away at our cut. If you can't make it worth the city's while, you're on your own."

The crowd took up the constable's sentiment and grumbled, "Pay up! Pay up!!"

Mr. Leach turned to Mrs. Burnham. "Is that all, Hattie? Anything else you have tucked away there?"

Mrs. Burnham threw back her shoulders. "Yes!" She pulled her gold wedding band from her finger and hurled it at Mr. Leach. "You're welcome to it, Jeriah. May it bring you the same luck it brought me."

The deputies still had a hungry look about them. The short man spied Ulysses, who had taken up his spot under the wagon. "What about this dog?" he speculated. "Is he worth a red cent?" The deputy reached a hand for Ulysses's collar, and the dog, bless him, let out a nasty growl. The man jerked back.

"Ulysses!" Mr. Thayer commanded. Ulysses trotted docilely over to his master and sat at his heel, his tongue lolling. Laughter rippled through the plaza. Mr. Leach eyed the crowd once more. Better to leave them laughing than to let them flare into something worse.

"We're finished here," he announced.

The constable handed us a nasty look. "Then take that mangy dog and get the hell out of town. Now!"

We scrambled to scoop what was left to us from the ransacked pile in the road. I brushed the mud off the rim of Emmett's hat and donned it. Through the back of the wagon canvas, I could spy my beautiful gown from Lola Montez, tumbled amongst the champagne baskets. There was no way to pack it out. I bid it adieu and took comfort in the weight of my journals and the other little volumes nestled in my bag.

We hustled out of Downieville and toward the Yuba canyon. The constable and his deputies, on horseback, nipped at our heels. The crowd tossed trash and rocks and filled the air with catcalls as they swarmed along beside us. I had the safety of Lem beneath me, but my companions were on foot and vulnerable. Ted kept his eyes front and his chin up, despite a whiskey bottle whizzing perilously close to the crown of his head.

By the time we reached the canyon road and the tollkeeper's station, most of the riffraff had grown bored and fallen away. Ted and Mr. Thayer scrounged in their pockets for the toll, and we bid the constabulary a not-very-fond adieu.

We hastened up the road, barely speaking and not looking back. Mrs. Burnham limped from her fall. She kept apace for the first mile or so, but then she began to lag. Mr. Thayer, Ted and I halted, so she might catch up. "Mrs. Burnham," I offered, "please take Lem."

"Thank you," she replied, "but I can't say as I'd be any more comfortable in the saddle."

"He's a smooth ride," I said.

She shook her head. "My backside is deeply compromised at the moment. But we could move more quickly if we packed Lem with our bags and such. Can we figure a way to lash them on, Gus?"

"Absolutely."

We piled our burdens in the road while Ted and Mr. Thayer rigged our blankets into slings. They had no sooner begun to knot them to Lem's saddle, when hoofbeats pounded up the trail. The two unwashed deputies appeared around a bend. We were sitting ducks there on the road, with naught but the river below us and the canyon walls above. They trotted up to us, rifles drawn, and pointed them at Ted and Mr. Thayer.

"Hold it right there!" ordered the big deputy. "You fellows have been holding out on us. You had plenty for the tollkeeper."

"Barely," replied Mr. Thayer. "Besides, Mrs. Burnham has already settled up as best she can. The rest of us don't owe you anything. You have no right."

"I figure rights depend on the company you keep," said the bigger deputy.

"It's firebugs don't have no rights," sneered the littler man.

"Where's the constable?" demanded Ted.

"Having lunch and a whiskey at the Excelsior," said the big fellow. "As if it was your business to know. Now, empty your pockets, gentlemen."

The deputies dismounted and held out a battered hat, while Ted and Mr. Thayer handed over the few dollars they still possessed. I was decked in Emmett's clothes, and I turned out my pockets, too, but they were empty even of cornbread crumbs. I must have appeared a poor prospect, for the deputies stopped short of uncovering the five dollars and sixty-one cents and my ring hidden in the sock pinned inside my trouser leg. They moved on instead to the carpet and saddle bags, ripping through them as vultures might strip the bones of a carcass. There was little of value, but for Mr. Thayer's watch fob and both men's razors. I sent up a small thought of thanks as my journals and other books were tossed aside, but the slim pickings turned the deputies more sour by the minute. They pocketed what little they'd stolen and made for Lem. The tall deputy seized his reins and commenced to tug at him.

Lem has no liking for bottom-feeders. He flattened his ears and dug in his heels. "Giddup, damn you!" shouted the deputy, and he delivered Lem a blow right above the crescent scar on his forehead. Lem let out a ferocious bray.

"No!" I screamed. The mule was of the same opinion. He whirled about, sending the blankets flying. Then he kicked out with his rear legs, landing a hoof squarely upon his kidnapper's jaw and laying the man out flat. I was impressed.

The smaller deputy ran to his cohort's side. "He ain't dead, but he ain't going to rise up any time soon, neither," he muttered, before he emptied the other man's pockets into his own. He turned to Mrs. Burnham. "I believe you have something of mine," he said. "Something small and silver. Hand it over."

"That's her son's picture," protested Mr. Thayer.

"It's all right, Gus," said Mrs. Burnham. "It's in here." She reached calmly into her pocket, and, quick as lightning, did indeed whip out something small and silver. Her derringer flashed like a little fish as she aimed it directly between the scruffy man's eyes. "I would dearly love to squeeze this trigger," she said, ice in her voice. The man shifted his gaze in terror to where his rifle lay abandoned by his partner's side. "Don't even try it. Gus? Ted?" Mr. Thayer and Mr. Booth quickly claimed the rifles. "Now, get the hell out of here." But the man only stared, stuck in his tracks. "Move!" Mrs. Burnham fired, and the echo of the shot crackled up and down the canyon, spooking the deputies' horses and sending them dancing away down the trail. The man reached in horror up to his ear, where the bullet had drawn blood. Mrs. Burnham seized a rifle from Ted and shoved the barrel against the man's chest. "There's a second shot here, and your name's on it, I promise you. Now, git!" she snarled. The deputy stumbled back and, despite his wobbly legs, began to run. "I've never shot a man in the back before," hollered Mrs. Burnham, "but there's always a first time!" The man bounded off like a jackrabbit. Ulysses barked after him in triumph.

"Let's head out!" said Mr. Thayer. We tossed our possessions into the bags, made fast the slings, and loaded Lem up.

"Should we take the rifles?" Ted wondered.

"I expect we've paid for them out of what they've stolen," said Mr. Thayer. "I say, pack 'em along."

"Done," Ted replied. "Thank God at least one of us knows how to use them."

Mrs. Burnham never registered his compliment. She hied up the trail, the rest of us at her heels. Fear and shock drove us on, despite the roughness of the road. When we reached Goodyear's Bar, we hastened around the fringes of town until we picked up the trail that led us out of the canyon. The ascent made Ulysses pant and put fire into my legs and lungs. We didn't slow until we reached the ridge top, where we turned into a pine grove to breathe. Mrs. Burnham stumbled and sank onto the forest floor. Her shoulders trembled.

"Hattie?" Ted called to her, but she did not reply.

Mr. Thayer knelt by her. "Ted, hand me a blanket."

Ted hurried to loose one of Lem's slings, and Mr. Thayer draped the blanket about Mrs. Burnham's shoulders, then took her hand. "Hattie, are you all right?"

She shook her head and tried to speak, but her teeth were chattering. At last, she spit out, "It's all ashes, Gus. We're busted. 'In disgrace with fortune....'"

"Maybe. Maybe not. We'll manage, somehow. "

"Think so?" she said, without conviction.

Mr. Thayer nodded. "It's been a particularly bad day, that's all."

"Bad? Hell, we've been cleaned out, worse than Tom Bell could ever have imagined. And by our friends and relations. At least Bell's honest about being a thief."

She had a point. Mr. Thayer didn't even try to argue her out of it, just put an arm about her and soothed her until the trembling eased a bit.

Ted crouched close by, near tears. "I'm so sorry, Hattie," he said. "This is my fault, too. I've been a curse to you. I wish I knew how to make it better—"

"Why don't you find us some water, Ted?" suggested Mr. Thayer. "I expect Hattie's done in for the afternoon. Maybe you could scout the road a piece and turn up a spot to camp. Miss Lightfoot could help you out."

"Yes, I could," I said.

So, Ted and I headed up the trail and, before long, came upon a trace of a brook. We followed it until the pines opened out onto a level spot, far enough from the road that we might escape the eyes of other travelers. "This will do, Chicken," said Ted, though his voice was heavy with discouragement. He was so distressed, I could hardly mind being once more referred to as poultry.

As we trudged back to the others, I said, "Ted, you are not a curse. You mustn't think that way. Please believe me."

"I believe your sincerity. You were brave to stick up for me before the constable, and I'm deeply grateful. But I have put us all in peril."

I was mightily tempted to spill the truth about Louise and her love of flames, but I bit the words back. I had promised Mrs. Burnham my silence, despite the burden of such a secret. Perhaps she had already told Ted about the girl. Or perhaps she had good reason to keep him in the dark and would enlighten him as soon as she could. I changed the subject to what a fine mule we had in our company, with his long-eared courage and his glorious aim, and I managed to bring a faint smile to Ted's countenance.

THURSDAY, JULY 24. *Somewhere west of Camptonville. Evening. I write by firelight—*

I dreamt of wolves, growling, and snapping, and harrying us up a trail. One bared his teeth and lunged at me. I cried out and woke. In the dawn's light, all was peaceful, my companions still in slumber, even Ulysses, curled up beside Mr. Thayer. The wolves' growl rumbled again, and I realized I was being pursued by my own empty belly.

I stretched and sought the stream to pacify my appetite with a drink. When I returned, Mr. Thayer and Mrs. Burnham were coming to. Soon Ted had joined us, more or less—his eyes were still heavy with sleep. As we shook our blankets, Mr. Thayer said, "Friends, we have been turned out upon the heath. However, we still have our skins, and I expect we need a plan to keep them. Where shall we go from here?"

"Where can we go?" wondered Mrs. Burnham. "There's a trail of ashes to our south—no point in backtracking that direction. Do you think the Downieville law will still come after us?"

Mr. Thayer shrugged. "There'd be no justice in it, though some fool might want to get even with us for yesterday. I expect we should get ourselves back to a place where we have friends, as quickly as we can. Sacramento, I reckon. Does anyone have funds left upon them?"

Mrs. Burnham shook her head.

"I have nothing, either," said Ted. "But, Emma, might you have hung onto that gold piece I lent you?"

"No, it's gone," I replied, and I told of how I'd sent it off with Harry Brown.

"Well, we can't begrudge him," said Ted. "You did the right thing, Emma."

"Thank you," I said. "And I'm not flat broke. I still have five dollars and sixty-one cents hidden upon my person. I put it at the company's disposal!"

"Then that shall buy us breakfast," smiled Ted.

"Thank you from our hearts, Miss Lightfoot," said Mr. Thayer.

"Indeed," added Mrs. Burnham.

"Ted," said Mr. Thayer, "you've walked out of these hills before, haven't you?"

"Yes," replied Ted, with a solemn nod. "When I got news of my father's death, we were playing Nevada. Or we'd tried to—the snow was so deep that winter, it nearly buried the theatre. No stages were running, but I couldn't wait for a thaw, so I started on foot for Marysville. I had to fight through drifts instead of ashes, but I made it."

"Is it worth heading that way, then?" asked Mr. Thayer. "We haven't stage fare, but if we can walk as far as Marysville, maybe we can scrape up cash for the steamer to Sacramento. Hattie?"

"I suppose. But we should lay low as much as we can, until we reach the flatland."

"Agreed," said Mr. Thayer. "Let's put some quick distance between us and Downieville." We loaded up and began our journey. We followed the road as best we could, but we avoided the stage coach and the pack teams, ducking off into the brush when they overtook us, as rabbits flee coyotes. At first, I found myself grateful for Emmett's boots. They saved my feet from the rocks in the roadbed, but, by midday, they had begun to chafe and rub blisters into my toes and heels. Mrs. Burnham's feet were just as bad--her riding boots were for riding, not for an overland trek--and she was still limping from her fall. Mr. Thayer suggested she climb onto Lem for a bit.

"Today, my feet are far more tender than my posterior," she admitted, and with a little rearrangement of our baggage, she mounted up. Later, I spelled her in the saddle, much to the relief of my toes.

Still, Lem could not assuage our stomachs. In the late afternoon, we came upon one of the stage stops along the trail, and Mr. Thayer said, "Miss Lightfoot, if you can spare your cash, I'll see what I can rustle up for our dinner."

We stripped the baggage from Lem's back. Mr. Thayer shed his grey coat, rolled up his shirt sleeves, and donned Emmett's hat. He swung himself up into Lem's saddle. "What do you think?" he said with a grin. "Will I pass for an old mucker?"

"You were born for the role," said Mrs. Burnham. And, indeed, with his salt-and-pepper beard coming in and the grime of the trail upon him, Mr. Thayer might have been out on some hardscrabble claim for weeks.

"That old mule's a nice touch, too," added Ted.

"I appreciate a good supporting cast," said Mr. Thayer. "Wish me well!"

Mr. Thayer returned in half an hour with a small bundle. "It's not much," he said, as he slipped off Lem. "Highway prices. Still, thanks to you, Miss Lightfoot, we shall not starve."

We doled out our dinner--a decent amount of hardtack, a small round of cheese sliced into quarters, and a handful of raisins apiece. It was pheasant and champagne to us and gone in minutes. Mr. Thayer, of course, thin as the man already is, shared his ration with a delighted Ulysses.

"Did you pick up any news, Gus?" asked Mrs. Burnham.

"No, the place was nigh empty. Nor did I see a newspaper about. But I do believe we should press on." He handed me Emmett's hat. "Shall we hit the trail, Miss Lightfoot?"

We did and kept a good pace. By a little before sunset, we had skirted Camptonville. A wind was coming up, and the clouds of a quick mountain storm were once again gathering. Mrs. Burnham suggested we keep an eye out for an abandoned shanty to shelter in. At length, Ted spotted a path worn in the grass between scattered oaks and pines. We followed it until it spilled into a clearing by the side of a creek. There stood a neat little habitation—a log cabin, a small stable, and a garden patch with a few rows of corn and beans. We paused to sense if its owner was about. The place was silent, save for the wind in the trees and bird calls—no clucks of chickens, no horse or mule in sight. The corn was wilting, in desperate need of water.

"Perhaps he's by the creek," said Ted. "Wait here, and I'll see what I can find."

He made his way quietly past the side of the cabin to the center of the clearing, then disappeared down toward the creek. He returned in a few minutes, shaking his head. He glanced into the stable, turned again toward the cabin, and stopped in his tracks.

"Ted?" Mr. Thayer hurried to his side and followed Ted's gaze. " I believe you ladies should stay where you are," he said.

Of course, we didn't. As we hastened around the cabin's corner and faced the door, we saw him—a young man in miner's garb, sprawled on the front porch beside his three-legged stool. A pistol lay by his hand, and a letter was pinned to his shirt. Dried blood stained the rough planks under his head. I could not bring myself to look closely at his face, but I shall always remember the sight of his boots, hanging over the porch step. His feet were smallish for a man's, like Emmett's.

For a heartbeat or two, we simply stood there, as if we'd intruded upon someone's most private moment. A dust devil swept through the yard, and the envelope on the man's chest fluttered.

"There's no stock, not even a mule," said Ted. "He must have sold them or turned them loose." He stepped onto the porch beside the man, knelt, and unpinned the letter from his shirt. He handed it to Mr. Thayer, then went into the cabin and fetched a blanket. He draped the blanket gently over the body, as if tucking the man in.

"Is there an address, Gus?" asked Mrs. Burnham.

"Yes. Mrs. Homer Abell, Appleton, Wisconsin."

"Open it. He wouldn't have left it so if he hadn't meant for us to read it," said Mrs. Burnham.

Mr. Thayer drew a small sheet of foolscap from the envelope and silently looked it over, then handed it to Mrs. Burnham. She read it quickly, passed it to me, and turned away. It went something like this:

My deerest Hannah

If you receev this letter you will know that I no longer toil in this vale of tears. I pray God will fergive me and I pray you will too. I had hopes for us of the golden kind but all is terned to sand. I have failed sweet Hannah and I despare of showing my face befor you. Sech a failure does not deserve your faith. I am comferted that you are in the care of your parents and I hope sum day you may find a man who truly merits your affeckshuns. My last thots shall be of you and of our boys.

With deep and abyding love

Homer

Ted finished covering the corpse, and I offered him the letter. He hesitated but then perused it, and his eyes filled with tears.

"I'll post it for him when I can," said Mr. Thayer. "I can do that much."

"We should bury him," said Ted, "before the animals go to work on him. He must have a shovel here, somewhere."

"Maybe so," said Mr. Thayer.

Mrs. Burnham made her way back to the porch. "It's late," she said. "The sun's almost set. And Mr. Abell isn't Sumner's little box. It'll take hours to dig a decent grave in this red clay and rock. You'll never finish before midnight."

"We can't just leave him," said Ted.

"I don't feel right staying here for the night," replied Mrs. Burnham. "This is his place, not ours, and it's so melancholy, it makes me want to lie down and die, too. We should move on."

Mr. Thayer ruminated on this and then suggested, "Ted, perhaps we could lay him out in the cabin, where he'll be safe from critters. It's likely his neighbors will come by in the next few days looking for him, and they can give him a proper service. Can you live with that?"

Ted frowned. "It's better than nothing."

"Miss Lightfoot?"

I agreed to the plan, though, deep down, I doubted that Homer Abell had neighbors who cared about his fate. It might have been sheer loneliness that had brought the man so low.

Ted and Mr. Thayer went into the cabin to prepare a spot for Homer on the bed, then they lifted him inside, laid him carefully on the blankets, and covered him up. They left his pistol by his hand, so those as found him might know what his fate had been. Ted stood beside the bed and recited "The Lord's Prayer" in his deep, musical tones. Mrs. Burnham and I found a few yellow buttercups near the creek. We set them in a jar and left them on the stool by the door.

As Ted and Mr. Thayer came out onto the porch, Mr. Thayer said, "Hold on a minute." He ducked back inside and returned with an armful of pots and pans, a carving knife, a bag of cornmeal, and a small slab of bacon.

Ted was shocked. "Grave robbing, Gus?"

"He won't need it now," said Mr. Thayer, "If he was alive, he'd probably be happy to sit us down to supper. It's a shame we couldn't have stopped by a few days ago."

"It is."

"If we leave the food, it'll just draw varmints to the cabin, and we need it worse than they do. Come on, Ted, help me load it up."

Ted reluctantly took the bacon and found a home for it in his saddlebag. Soon, we had Lem packed. Ted and Mr. Thayer made sure the cabin window was shuttered and the door tightly latched. By now, dusk was closing in, and the birds had ceased their chorus. Homer Abell's resting place lay hushed and shadowy—save for the rustle of the wind and the buttercups glowing softly on the three-legged stool.

As we made our way back to the road, the skies opened up and did their best to drown us. There was no chance of finding a shanty. We squeezed under a ledge by the side of the trail and waited out the downpour, but it left us seeking shelter in the dark. We picked our way along until Mr. Thayer made out a clearing off the south side of the road. We stumbled across it for a piece and settled for a spot where the meadow met the trees. We scavenged enough wood for a fire and held our blankets before the flames to dry them as best we could.

Mr. Thayer fried up some of the bacon. Ulysses was thrilled by the prospect of bacon for supper, but the rest of us lacked enthusiasm. The rain had dampened our bodies, and Homer Abell had dampened our spirits. Mrs. Burnham and Mr. Booth were very quiet and soon turned in. Mr. Thayer stuck it out a while longer, tending the flames. I tried, by firelight, to write in my journal, but my mind kept straying to Homer's boots and the paper flapping on his chest as the dust devil cut through the yard.

"Are you all right, Miss Lightfoot?" inquired Mr. Thayer.

"I reckon. I'm just sad for that man. It was a lonely thing to find him like that."

"Yes."

"I know I lack years," I said, "and I haven't seen that much of the world, but I don't understand how Homer Abell could give it up so easily. He was young—his fortune could have turned around tomorrow, and, now, he won't be there to see it."

"I don't know as we can always understand someone else's despair," said Mr. Thayer. He poked the fire with a stick. "Some can take it, and some can't, Emma."

"He said he'd failed Hannah. But Hannah might not see it that way at all. She might love him and grieve that she's lost him. Then he's only made things worse than he could imagine."

"Yes. But when you feel as godforsaken as he did, you don't think straight. All he could see was that he'd failed. That's a painful place for a man to be. I know."

"You do?"

"Yes. When my wife took my daughters and left me, I could hardly get out of bed in the morning."

I had no idea Mr. Thayer had had a family, let alone lost them. I closed up my journal. "Why would she do such a thing?"

"Well, in her eyes, I was a failure, as a husband, anyway. In the beginning, she thought loving an actor was romantic. She didn't understand that theatre's about low pay and being on the road half your life. One spring, when I was touring Tennessee, she packed up and went to live with her sister. She found herself a grocer with a financial future and a prominent place in the Baptist Church."

"And you missed her?"

"Oh, Emma, she broke my heart."

"Did you think of ending your life?"

"For a short piece. Then I got an offer to play Iago in Cleveland." He chuckled. "And I got myself a dog."

Soon Mr. Thayer and the dog were curled up in a blanket, snoring in harmony. Ulysses sounded the treble notes and Mr. Thayer the bass. I threw another piece of wood on the fire and went back to my journal, but, by and by, I surrendered to darkness and sought my bed. I vowed to think pleasant thoughts to soothe myself to sleep. What should they be? Memories of sugar plums with my best friend, Evie? Of champagne on the banks of the American River? No—I chose to conjure Emmett, humming off-key as he readied the press, in the lamp-lit office of *The Placerville Rattler.*

FRIDAY, JULY 25. *Just off the Marysville Road—*

We are a bedraggled bunch. We had hoped to reach a traveler's rest called Oregon House this afternoon, but we have fallen short. Bleeding feet have slowed us, and the rigors of the trail. I long for Professor Wilson and his magnificent hot air balloon, the Glory. When first I witnessed them in Placerville, in the wake of Emmett's death, I found the courage to rise above my troubles. Though the skies that crown this trail are ruthlessly empty, I catch myself glancing upward in hope of that golden orb. Oh, for the Glory, to lift us into the heavens and waft us to Sacramento!

Ted is deathly quiet, a weight upon his heart. Mrs. Burnham, too, has lost spirit, grieving for her dreams. Mr. Thayer remains stoic, making sure we all put one foot in front of the other. And Ulysses is paw-sore, but he's the only soul—save Lem—who has found enjoyment in this day. As long as he's with Mr. Thayer, he's happy. This argues a great deal in favor of a dog's disposition.

We must be making progress. As we've journeyed west, the dense pines have thinned. Steep canyons have yielded to rolling hills. Our campsite, on the shore of a small lake, would be considered pleasant, were we not worn to the bone.

As the sun set, and the sky turned inky, Mr. Thayer went about clearing up our supper and stowing the remnants of our supplies. I brought my journal to the fireside, and Ted took himself off to a boulder by the water's edge. He remained there, starlight on his shoulders, deep into the night. I longed to go speak cheerful words to him, but the stillness of his silhouette kept me at a distance. Indeed, Ulysses went tail-wagging over to his feet, and, although Ted absently patted his head, the animal soon returned to the fire. He slumped down with sorrowful dog eyes, as if he knew he'd intruded on some dark hole in Ted's soul.

Mrs. Burnham was silent, too, staring into the flames. At last, she rose, spread her blanket, and settled down into it.

"Ow!" she yelped. "God damn!" Mr. Thayer hurried over. "This is what it's come to, Gus. Blisters on my feet and thorns in my ass. Just when I think it can't get any worse, it's time for another indignity. Ow."

She was near tears.

Mr. Thayer and I helped her shake the offending thorns from the blanket's folds and move it to a more congenial spot. She sat herself gingerly down. Mr. Thayer crouched beside her.

"Any better?" he asked.

"I suppose. I'm getting too old for this, Gus. I don't have the strength. Not for thorns, not for picking up the pieces. I'm finished."

"We've all been down before, Hattie. And we've come back."

She shook her head. "No, the troupe is beyond resurrection, and, unlike gents, who can play leading men until they drop, I am of a 'certain age' where I won't be able to pull it off much longer. I reckon it's time for that boarding house."

Mr. Thayer settled on the blanket at her side. "You'd never be happy in a place like that."

"I might be. I'd take in a theatre clientele—ladies and gentlemen of the profession. I'd have a parlor, with a gilt copy of Shakespeare's works on a shelf, right by the Bible. And I'd bake perfect apple pies for our suppers. God, a slice of apple pie would hit the spot right now."

"And, of course," said Mr. Thayer, "your clientele would always pay their rent promptly and in cash."

"Of course. Oh, hell, maybe it's only a pipe dream to run to when prospects are bleak, but it'd be better than the mess we're in now."

"I'm sorry about Ben."

"I'm not."

"The man robbed you blind, Hattie. You, and June Booth, and the rest of us."

"True, and I'm regretful for his thievery. I'll never be able to make it right with everyone. But I'm not sorry about his departure. I don't miss the man." She hugged her knees and stared into the fire. "Although, I confess, Gus, I do have a pain in my heart."

"Yes?"

"Yes. Now that he's gone, I miss Tench and Henry more than I ever did. All the way from Downieville, their ghosts have kept me company, just out of reach. I long for them, and I don't know how to make it stop. Perhaps I never will."

"You need to let them go, Hattie. Not banish them—they'll always be in your heart--but give them a little room. Room for you to breathe, maybe room for them, too. I can't believe they'd want you to suffer so."

"I don't let go easily," said Mrs. Burnham. "I think you know that."

"Oh, I do. I saw you charge across that plaza in Downieville. And I admire your sand no end. But this is different. Letting go isn't always failure. Or lack of love."

Mrs. Burnham studied Mr. Thayer, as if she were taking him in for the first time. Then she gave his hand a squeeze. "Thank you, Gus. I'll give it consideration."

They sat together in silence, until their gaze fell upon Ted, down by the water. "Do you think he's talking to his ghosts?" wondered Mrs. Burnham.

"No doubt about it," replied Mr. Thayer. "Though your ghosts are a much more benign lot than his are."

"Yes," murmured Mrs. Burnham. "Sweet ghosts."

Presently, they turned in. I continued with my journal for a spell longer, then called it a night, too. I was dozing off to the thought of my own sweet ghosts, when a cold, wet nose nuzzled my cheek. Ulysses plopped himself at my side. He snuggled in close, and we dropped down swiftly into our dreams.

SATURDAY, JULY 26. *Between Oregon House and Brown's Valley. An abandoned claim. Evening—*

We made better time today, despite sizzling heat and the dust of the road. We reached Oregon House by midmorning. Mr. Thayer hunted up a storekeeper who took the better of the rifles in trade. Ulysses went along on this expedition. The two of them found an audience amongst the loafers on the store's front porch, and, soon, dollars dropped into Emmett's upturned hat. Mr. Thayer returned with a loaf of real bread, a sizable chunk of ham, and a tiny sliver of cake. We ate as if that dinner might be our last. Which it still may turn out to be.

He also brought back the news that Marysville had burned a few days before Nevada had exploded into flames. Ted was stunned.

"What?" he exclaimed. "A fire I didn't set?"

No one replied to Ted's remark, but Mr. Thayer uttered what we all were thinking—that perhaps we should skirt the city limits of Marysville, too. "We'll have to play it by ear," he said. "One day at a time."

By late afternoon, we were once more seeking a spot for the night. It was Mrs. Burnham who spied an overgrown path, too deep for a deer trail but too narrow for a wagon. It followed a dry stream bed up to a patch of woodland, nestled at the foot of gentle hills. From a distance, we could make out a board shanty with the roof half stove in. As we hastened into the shanty's yard, we were startled by a flutter. Quick as quail, two small figures darted into the brush above the claim. They left the yard empty, save for a well with a rude winch, and a tiny, brown creature sitting in the dust. The creature rolled about and took us in with wide eyes. It decided it didn't much like the view and set up a wail.

"Good God," exclaimed Mrs. Burnham, "it's a baby!" She hastened over to the child and scooped it into her arms, whilst the rest of us stared. It was a skinny little thing with a swollen belly and matchstick arms, garbed only in a necklace of tiny shells. "What could have happened to its mother?"

"Those were children who ran from us," said Ted.

Mr. Thayer nodded. "Not much bigger than this one."

"Were you left behind, sweet thing?" cooed Mrs. Burnham. "Hush, baby, hush. We won't hurt you." She held the little fellow against her chest and began to gently sway with him, crooning, "Way up yonder, above the moon, a bluejay lived in a silver spoon...." She cradled that baby so tenderly, you never would have known that she had shot a man in the ear a few days before. The child was calmed by her touch—the wail became a whimper and then a snuffle. He laid his cheek against her shoulder.

"He's not even old enough to walk," she said.

"What are we going to do with a baby?" said Ted.

"We could wet some of that bread and see if he'd eat it."

"Hattie, he's an Indian baby," said Mr. Thayer. "Probably a Maidu. He has people out there somewhere. If we leave him where we found him, they'll come back for him."

"He's too little to just leave," replied Mrs. Burnham. "A coyote could swallow him whole."

Mr. Thayer crossed quietly over to the shanty and peered in through the open door. "They're not using the place for shelter. No one's been in there for months." He gazed about. "I don't know how safe this spot is. Ted, why don't we look around a bit?"

While they checked the premises, I went to the well to see if I could draw some water for Lem. I cranked the winch and lifted, not a wooden bucket, but a basket. It was so finely woven that it held water. "Look at this," I called to Mrs. Burnham.

"It's Indian," she said. "That's why they were here. The stream's gone dry, and they came for the well."

She beckoned Ted and Mr. Thayer from their search. We gathered about the basket, with it's beautiful patterns, but before we could speculate upon it, we were startled by a crackle in the brush. It could have been a doe, tiptoeing about. We stared toward the far side of the yard, but we could make out nothing. Then a tiny rustle pulled our attention to a buckeye tree. There stood an Indian woman. She was small, and thin, and clutched a rabbit pelt.

"She looks younger than Miss Lightfoot," said Mrs. Burnham.

The woman began to tremble.

"She's afraid of us," I said.

"She has a right to be," said Mr. Thayer. "The state of California would pay us twenty-five dollars for her scalp."

The woman began to speak in a passionate tongue I'd never heard, and to gesture from the pelt to us and from the baby to herself.

"I believe we've found the mother," said Ted.

"She wants to trade," said Mr. Thayer. "That pelt is likely all she has, but she'll give it for the baby. I reckon she's worried we'll steal him."

"We wouldn't steal a baby," I said.

"No, but plenty would. They'd kill the mother and take the child to sell. He'd be an orphan, after all, and the state would smile upon it."

Mrs. Burnham's eyes flashed. "No mother should lose her baby," she said. She stepped carefully toward the Indian woman. The woman nervously thrust the pelt at Mrs. Burnham, but Mrs. Burnham shook her head at it and held out the little boy. He smiled at his mother and reached for her. Swiftly, the woman seized the child and vanished into the undergrowth.

"Do you think we should move on?" asked Ted. "They seem more frightened of us than we are of them."

"Yes. Hardly a war party," replied Mr. Thayer. "Hattie?"

Mrs. Burnham had tears in her eyes. She wiped them with her hand. "If the woman had a husband or other men with her, wouldn't they have come for the child instead? She might be alone with those kids. She'll not harm us."

"You may be right," said Mr. Thayer. "I reckon we should stay put. It's late in the day, and at least there's water here. And there are still bunks in that shanty. You ladies could sleep in there if we cleaned it out a bit."

We chased the mice and spiders from the shanty, laid fresh grass on the boards of the bunks, and spread our blankets. Mr. Thayer and Ted built a fire in the yard and picketed Lem for me. We even managed a wash at the well. Afterwards, Ted and I sought out flat stones for our supper plates, while Mr. Thayer and Mrs. Burnham sliced bread and ham and set the meat to frying in the pan. Soon, the rough clearing smelled like Sunday dinner.

We gathered about the fire and had barely begun to dig in, when Ted stopped and gazed toward the brush on the distant side of the clearing. "I believe we have an audience," he whispered. Two small faces were peering out at us from the leafy scrub. "Are those the ones from this afternoon?"

"Looks like it," I said. "Girls, I think."

Ted slowly stood and held his stone out to them. The girls stared at it longingly, but they didn't budge from their cover. "Emma," he said, "You might scare them less than I do. Can you take this over there?"

I stepped softly and slowly toward the brush. The faces quickly disappeared into the leaves, but I set the stone down anyway, at the very edge of their hiding place, and returned to the fire. We went about our supper as if those children weren't there at all, but, soon, out of the corner of my eye, I spied a couple of small hands reaching out and stripping that flat rock clean. Ted smiled.

Just then, the Indian mother slipped into view by the buckeye, clutching the baby. She called out to the girls in the unhappy tone of a mother who'd been disobeyed. The girls skittered to her, but before they could all disappear, I hastened her way with my own "plate." She clung to her baby tightly, her fierce look declaring that she'd never trade the boy for a slice of ham, but I went ahead and placed the stone as close to her feet as I dared. Then, I hied back to the fire. She watched me, surprised. When I was at a safe distance, she squatted, and, sharing bits with her children, devoured what was before her.

Mrs. Burnham handed me a slice of her own ham. "Well done, Miss Lightfoot," she said.

Before the Indian woman could vanish back into the trees, Ted called out, "Do you speak English?"

The woman had no reply.

"Habla espanol?"

"Si," she whispered. "Poco."

"Bueno."

"Gracias por la comida."

"De nada."

I don't know much more Spanish than that, but Ted went on with the mother for quite a spell as her girls clung tightly to her legs. Sometimes they had to repeat themselves and speak with their hands, and Ted was careful to keep his distance. I managed to pick up a few more words, as Ted asked, "Donde esta su esposo?" The woman hung her head and replied with a phrase we all knew too well, "Muerto. Esta muerto."

At length, Ted gestured to her to wait and retrieved his carpetbag. He threw it open and pulled out his coat and extra shirts. He piled them together, set his tobacco pouch and pipe on the top, and said, "Emma, please take these to her." I did, and laid them at a safe distance from her spot. "Por ustedes," said Ted. Then he pulled his handkerchief from his pocket, swiftly tied it into the shape of that famous rabbit, Sir Hare-old, and began to fool with it. This time, instead of a British bent, the silly hare spoke Spanish. He flailed at imaginary enemies with sticks and pebbles, and he finally drew smiles and even a giggle or two from the little ones before he collapsed into a ridiculous heap in the dust. He, too, was added to the pile of treasures and soon was in the arms of the little girls.

Not to be outdone, Mr. Thayer said, "I believe this is Ulysses's cue!" At first, the Indian family was wary of the dog, but Ulysses soon won them over with a rainbow of tricks. The children were especially taken with his flips, which drew small gasps, and his comic death, that, I confess, outdid Sir Hare-old's.

The mother and children never left the safety of their cover on the fringe of the shanty yard, and we never tried to come too close, but my companions and I did attempt to give them what little we had. Perhaps we looked foolish to them, especially when our offerings were performances. After Ulysses had taken his bow, Mr. Thayer pulled out his mouth organ, and we sang camp tunes and lullabies. The notes of the mouth organ startled the little ones, but they did not flee from us. They huddled in their places, rapt, until the last song was sung. Then, the mother gathered Ted's gifts, and, along with the daylight, they disappeared into the woods.

Perhaps the family gifted us, too. They were an audience for my companions and brought them out of last night's dreadful gloom.

I cannot help but worry for the mother and her little ones. I know, now, what it is to be an outcast, living in flight. But my fellow travelers and I have hope of reaching friends and safety. Where can this family go but deeper into the brush? And, though we were chased from Downieville by the threat of a rope with Ted's name on it, no one dares to claim twenty-five dollars for our scalps.

SUNDAY, JULY 27. *South of Marysville, a farm on the shore of the Feather River—*

This morning, we half-expected the Indians to visit us for breakfast, but when Ted went to the well and found an empty rope on the winch, we knew that someone had carefully untied the water basket in the night. On the earth nearby was set a smaller, lovely basket, with the rabbit pelt folded neatly inside. The Maidu family had bid us farewell.

Today, we were determined, come hell or high water, to reach Marysville and the Feather River. The road was carrying more traffic, and we were cautious, although, by now, even our best friends may not have known us. The men were bearded. Mr. Thayer had shed his formal grey coat days ago and had become more and more a grizzled miner. Mrs. Burnham was thin and tanned, the lines about her eyes and mouth deeper than before. Minus her costumes and jewelry, she could have passed for any gold camp wife. I didn't wish to think of my own appearance. My hands were dry and cracked. More freckles had appeared upon my arms, and no doubt, all about my face. In Emmett's clothes, with my hair up under my hat, I must have resembled a scruffy boy.

Ted Booth, on the other hand, had only become more handsome. With his serape and wide hat, his dark eyes and skin browned by the sun, he was born to play the Spaniard. This day, he was an especially melancholy Spaniard. As I rode nearby on Lem, I studied him out of the corner of my eye to calculate why his sorrow only made him more attractive.

Presently, I offered Mrs. Burnham a turn on Lem and trudged along beside Ted. "What did you find out about the Maidu family?" I asked. "Did the woman say her husband was dead?"

"I'm afraid so," Ted replied. "He died of a fever. They have no man to hunt for them, so they're doing the best they can on acorns and berries, and snaring a few rabbits."

"Then I'm glad we shared our food," I said. "And I expect they can use your clothes."

"Maybe. If they can't wear them, they can trade them, or she can cut them up for the children."

Mr. Thayer had picked up the end of our conversation. "That was a fine coat, though, Ted."

Ted shrugged. "It doesn't matter. I won't be needing it."

We made few stops along the road. In the morning, Mrs. Burnham had torn strips from her extra linen blouse and passed them out to us to bind the blisters on our feet, although the bandages created their own raw spots. Nonetheless, no one was willing to pause long enough to give in to the irritation. With or without bandages, we were doomed to sore feet, and we simply moved forward.

At length, in the midafternoon, we reached the eastern outskirts of Marysville, where it sprawled across a point of land carved out by the union of the Yuba and the Feather Rivers.

A freight wagon rumbled up behind us on the road. Mr. Thayer took himself over to the driver and conversed a bit. When he hied himself back our way, he announced, "If we're going to Sacramento, we'll have to get ourselves past those rivers somehow. The only bridge without a toll is on the far side of the city."

"What about the steamboats?" asked Mrs. Burnham. "My feet are hash. Maybe we could trade that last rifle for the fare."

The remaining rifle was an old, rusty thing, as ugly as its previous owner. "I don't know, Hattie," said Mr. Thayer. "We can check the fares at the steamship office and go from there."

As large a town as Marysville was, we crossed to her western shore in half an hour. The smell of smoke still clung to the city, and the ring of hammers signified new structures rising up over the ashes of the old ones. As we neared the free bridge, we spied the office of the California Steam Navigation Company. Their steamship schedules were posted in the window.

"Look!" exclaimed Mrs. Burnham, "The 'Cleopatra' leaves in the morning!"

"Yes," said Mr. Thayer, "but take a gander at the fares. Seven dollars apiece to Sacramento, and God knows how much in freight for the mule. It might as well be seven hundred dollars. And that old rifle is hardly worth two bits."

"We could have done it," I admitted, "but that I gave Ted's gold piece to Harry Brown. Though I don't regret it."

"No, and you shouldn't," said Mr. Thayer. "Let's get ourselves over the river, for now. Maybe we can hitch a ride downstream on a flatboat or some such."

We hastened across the bridge and onto a road that followed the river south toward Sacramento. We were no longer in the world of mountain rivers cutting through deep canyons. The Feather was a valley river, broad, smooth, and lined with sand and willows.

There was traffic upon the Feather's glassy surface, but much of it was small craft, suitable for a Sunday. Mr. Thayer's hoped-for flatboat did not appear. The sun was sinking, along with our spirits, when a farm wagon rattled by us. The driver, a fellow with whiskers and a ready smile, handed us a wave. Mr. Thayer took heart and called after him. The driver halted his team.

"Howdy," said Mr. Thayer, cheerful as a cricket. "My family and I are footsore and weary. May we trouble you for a lift?"

"Where are you folks headed?"

"Back east. We have 'seen the elephant,' as they say in the camps. But, for now, we're headed wherever you are."

The driver grinned. "You're in luck then. I left my load at the market in the plaza yesterday. Climb on up!" Mr. Thayer boosted Mrs. Burnham and me into the wagon bed, set Ulysses between us, and joined the driver on the forward seat. Ted followed behind on Lem. "The name's Gabriel," offered the driver, an Irish lilt in his voice. "And who might you be?"

"Thoreau," said Mr. Thayer. "Henry Thoreau."

Mrs. Burnham rolled her eyes. "Dear God," she whispered to me. "He must be brain-weary."

"Pleased to make your acquaintance, Mr. Thorough!" said the Irishman.

"Likewise. And that's my wife, Kate, in the back there, and my daughter, Ella."

"Oh," said Mr. Gabriel, glancing over his shoulder at me. "That's a girl, then!" I smiled at him with as much feminine charm as I could muster under the circumstances.

"Yes, indeed, a father's joy," said Mr. Thayer. "Now, on the mule, there, is my claim partner, Edgardo Baca. And last, but not least, the family dog, Rex."

Even Mr. Booth, still in his dark mood, had to fight back the glimmer of a smile.

Mr. Gabriel was the talkative sort, full of questions and quips, and Mr.

Thayer did his best to keep the man entertained as we journeyed along the riverbank. By the time we'd covered a half-dozen miles, they were the best of companions.

By now, the sun had set, leaving a glow in the west and touching the river with silver. We passed fat cattle grazing in wide fields, and, in the last of the light, orchards with golden peaches hanging heavy on the boughs. My stomach rumbled at the thought of a juicy peach fresh from the tree.

Mr. Gabriel pulled up his team before an elegant gate. "This is as far as I go, folks." Mr. Thayer, Mrs. Burnham and I hopped out of the wagon. Through the iron work of the gate, I spied a fine mansion, its graceful porches silhouetted against the shining river. Lamps were being lit in the windows. The mansion was surrounded by lush gardens and rows of tall pecan trees. In the distance, a grassy bank sloped down to a landing on the water. "Have we just stumbled into heaven?" I murmured to Mrs. Burnham.

Mr. Thayer thanked Mr. Gabriel for his help and his company, and then wondered, "What is this place, Gabriel?"

"Hock Farm, they call it."

Mrs. Burnham stepped quickly to the driver's side. "Mr. Gabriel, as you can tell, we've had a long journey, and we're losing the light. Might we camp by the river here?"

Mr. Gabriel hesitated.

"My daughter and I would feel much safer on your farm, Mr. Gabriel, than we would on the open road."

"If it was just me, Mrs. Thorough, you'd be welcome. But Captain Sutter is wary of strangers these days."

"Captain Sutter?"

"Yes, ma'am. I'm sure you can understand. The Captain gave the shirt off his back to the miners in forty-nine, and they overran his Sacramento lands, destroyed his home there. Hock Farm is all he has left."

"But we've quit the mining business," said Mr. Thayer.

"And you're nice folks, too," Mr. Gabriel replied. "But the Captain has a rule here—none but his own workers and family may come and go on Hock Farm."

A cold clang sounded in my heart. The gate of heaven had just swung shut.

Mr. Thayer wasn't ready to give up, and he kept on for a while with Mr.

Gabriel. I took this time to flop on the grass and pull off my offending boots. If we were going to march in the dark, I was going to tend to my feet first. Blood had seeped through my stockings and bandages and had left stains at the ankles and toes. I began to unwind the linen strips and, when I caught Mr. Gabriel's eye, made no attempt to hide the wreckage of my feet. Mr. Thayer spied it, too, and made a last plea. "My daughter and wife are in a bad way, Gabriel."

Mr. Gabriel frowned. "Wait here. Captain Sutter has taken his family to San Francisco to dodge the valley heat. Woodward is his caretaker, and he's a square enough fellow. Let me see what I can do, Thorough."

Mr. Gabriel drove the wagon through the gate and closed the iron lattice behind him. We waited. Stars began to burn in the wide sky. I was ready to nap right there in the grass, to the lullaby of the river, when Mr. Gabriel returned with a tall gentleman decked in fine boots and sporting a trim mustache.

"I'm Woodward," he announced. "I understand you're friends of Gabriel and you're in a fix."

"Yes, sir," replied Mr. Thayer. "All we ask is a spot to throw down our blankets. We'd be no trouble."

"We can't have folks camping on the farm, I'm afraid. It encourages squatters. But Gabriel has persuaded me to invite you in for the night as his guests--provided you're on your way in the morning. He'll show you to the kitchen and then to your lodgings." Lodgings! What a sweet word!

We thanked Woodward and Gabriel up one side and down the other. Then Mr. Gabriel led us to the adobe bunkhouses where the hands slept. We were offered bunks with fresh ticks and clean blankets. O, paradise!

After we had stowed our baggage, Ted and I followed Gabriel to the horse barn, where Lem was presented with his own fine accommodation—a stall with straw upon the floor and hay in the manger. I patted him as he settled in, and he nickered contentedly. As Ted and I departed, I could hear my dear mule munching away in the barn's soft shadows.

Before Gabriel took his leave, he directed us all to the farm's kitchen. Though supper had already been cleared, the cook, Elisabeta, cheerfully set us plates of tender beef, spicy beans, and cornbread, and laid a bowl of scraps on the earthen floor for a grateful Ulysses. At the end of our meal, Mrs. Burnham begged an old wooden tub and a kettle of warm water from the cook, and we carried them back to the bunkhouse, where we each took a turn at a foot bath. Her feet were worse off than mine, a spot on the back of her ankle beginning to fester. After the comfort of the warm water, she curled up in her bunk, her head cradled upon a pillow. As weary as I was, I needed a few moments to attend to this journal. I sat and wrote by quiet candlelight; then I followed her into sweet repose.

MONDAY, JULY 28. *Not far from the bank of the Feather River, camped amongst cottonwoods—*

I have lost my dear Lem Mule. My heart has not been so desolate since Emmett passed, and Evie fled Placerville's flames.

Mrs. Burnham and I rose at dawn this morning, along with the help. We found Mr. "Thoreau" and "Edgardo Baca" at one of the wide tables on the kitchen patio. We indulged ourselves in a breakfast of porridge and eggs, and peaches piled into a big blue bowl. I confess, I tucked a couple of those peaches into my pockets for later—one for me and one for Lem.

As we'd promised Woodward an early departure, Mr. Thayer, Ulysses and I went to the barn to saddle the mule and load him up with our baggage. But, before we fetched Ted and Mrs. Burnham, Mr. Thayer suggested we stroll down to the landing. We spied Mr. Woodward, seeing to barrels of beef. Mr. Thayer hailed him, "Good morning, sir!"

"Thorough!" Woodward replied. "Sleep well?"

"Indeed. What a pleasure to pass the night on soft ticks instead of hard earth. We thank you!"

"I'm glad we could oblige."

"Now, if we could only pass the day upon the water, instead of the rough road, we should soon be delivered of our trials."

"We'll be sending a cattle boat downstream next week," suggested Mr. Woodward. "You and Mr. Baca could earn your family's passage by helping with the stock."

"That's most generous," said Mr. Thayer. He was eyeing the motley craft scattered about the landing. His glance fell upon an old rowboat, leaning up against a shed. "Does that skiff belong to the farm, Woodward?"

"It does. Captain Sutter and his children used to take it out to fish and explore the river. But that was long ago—the young ones are grown now, and the Captain's getting on. I'm surprised it's still here."

"Does it float?" wondered Mr. Thayer.

"Last time I looked."

"Might you consider a trade, Mr. Woodward?"

Mr. Woodward folded his arms across his chest. "I might."

My heart sank. That skiff would comfortably hold the human remnants of the Star Troupe, but it would never fit Lem. Nor could the old boy be expected to swim behind us all the way to Sacramento. Perhaps Mr. Thayer wasn't thinking that far ahead, but I quickly determined that if my companions finished their journey in a rowboat, it would be without me. I would travel on alone with my mule.

Mr. Thayer stepped over to Lem and untied the rifle from his saddle, but Mr. Woodward was no fool. He gave it a scornful look. "I believe this last saw action at the Alamo, Thorough. It should be put out of its misery before it blows up in someone's face."

Mr. Thayer replaced the rifle and pulled his mouth organ from his bag. "Are you a music lover, sir?" He riffled through a lovely set of chords, but Ulysses was the only one to greet them with enthusiasm, wagging his tail and singing along.

"Wouldn't be much use to me," said Woodward. "Not without the musician thrown into the deal. I have a tin ear, myself."

"I see," said Mr. Thayer. "Well, that's about all the earthly goods we possess, save a pelt, a pot and a skillet. I don't suppose you'd care to stock your kitchen?"

"No," said Mr. Woodward. "But I might consider that mule. He's as ugly as homemade sin, but he's steady. We can always use an extra mule on the farm."

Mr. Thayer was silent for a moment. I was so angry at the thought of bargaining Lem away that my hands began to shake. To his credit, Mr. Thayer said, "I'm afraid that mule's not mine to trade. He's my daughter's beast, and she's dearly fond of him."

Woodward turned to me. "What about it, young lady? Will you trade your mule? Yea or nay?"

"Nay," I replied, straight from my heart.

"Suit yourself."

"We appreciate the offer, Woodward," said Mr. Thayer, "but I expect the boat was a foolish idea, anyway." Mr. Thayer offered his hand to the caretaker. "We'll say farewell, then."

"God speed, Thorough," said Mr. Woodward.

I gripped Lem's reins and hurried him up the slope from the river. Mr. Thayer rushed after me. "I didn't mean to put you in a bad spot, Miss Lightfoot," he said. "I didn't know it would come down to the mule."

"I can't part from Lem, Mr. Thayer. He's been a salvation, for every one of us."

"You're right. He's a fine old creature, and I can't imagine you without him. We've walked this far, we can walk a bit more."

"How many miles is it to Sacramento?" I asked.

"About thirty-five."

Thirty-five miles seemed an infinity.

We started back toward the bunkhouses. "Miss Emma," said Mr. Thayer, "I know you are a resourceful young person, but have you thought of how you'll keep Lem once we get to Sacramento? It's a big city, and you can't simply put a mule out to graze. You'll have to board him. I'll help you, if I can, but I don't think any of us knows what awaits us, just yet."

"I'll manage," I said.

"I'm sure you will," nodded Mr. Thayer.

But, in truth, his question was an astute one, for I had no plan. I'd been so set on reaching the Promised Land of Sacramento that I hadn't thought of what I'd do when we finally arrived. I had no money, no prospects, and no way to keep my Lem Mule. I should just have to hope that Providence would smile on us in the days to come and help us stave off starvation.

As we neared the women's adobe, I spied Mrs. Burnham limping our way, favoring the foot with the festered ankle. "Any possibilities?" she asked Mr. Thayer.

"They might send a cattle boat down next week, if we want to work our passages on it."

"Next week? Oh, God, Gus, I don't know if we'll last another week."

"Then we'll just head on down the road. Something might turn up. Where's Edgardo?"

"Staring into a well over by the men's quarters. We need to get that boy moving."

We made our way across the farm toward the bunkhouse, past the bountiful summer gardens and corrals of well-tended animals. Captain Sutter's carriage horses gleamed; a pair of mules grazed happily over by the barn. I fought to stifle the thought that kept forcing its way into my brain—that perhaps Providence was already smiling on Lem. He would be better cared for on Hock Farm than I could ever manage on my own.

I thrust his reins into Mr. Thayer's hand and hastened back down to the landing. Mr. Woodward was still there, clearing up the little pier. I ran to him. "Mr. Woodward," I blurted, "if I trade you my mule, will you be good to him?"

He turned to me, surprised. "Of course, young lady," he said.

"He won't disappoint you," I replied. "I simply want kindness for him, that's all. And please don't think me a lunatic, but if I ever pass this way again, may I come through that gate and pay him a visit?"

Mr. Woodward smiled at me. "Of course, Miss Thorough. You just announce yourself as The Girl With The Mule, and the gate will swing open."

"Thank you, sir." I realized I should not draw this conversation out, or I would burst into tears. "His name is Lem," I said. "Where shall I put him?"

"Back in the barn, for now." Woodward offered me his hand. "It's a pleasure doing business with you, Miss Thorough."

I shook on the deal and hastened away as quickly as my sore feet could carry me.

By the time I caught up with Mr. Thayer and Mrs. Burnham, they'd been joined by Ted and were bidding Gabriel goodbye. "I've traded Lem for the boat," I announced.

My companions were taken aback, and Ted was angry, too. "Emma, that mule is dear to you. You shouldn't give him up for our sakes."

"I didn't do it for us," I said, and I meant it. "I did it for Lem. So, let's get this load off him."

Mr. Gabriel and I led Lem back to his stall and unsaddled him. There was no point in dragging his tack along with us—I traded it for food from the kitchen, salve for our feet, and a few dollars to stake myself in Sacramento. Given how worn the saddle was, Mr. Gabriel was generous in his terms, especially in my last request. "Will you think of him once in a while, Mr. Gabriel?" I asked. "Slip him some oats? Tell him he's not ugly?"

"Of course, Miss Thorough," he said. "He'll be part of the family."

Mr. Gabriel headed off for the landing, while I lingered with Lem. I pulled the peach from my pocket. He nibbled it with delight, and I hugged his neck. "Be happy here, old boy. If I'm lucky, I'll come back for you someday. And if I'm not, you have a good life." Lem nudged me with his big head and leaned against my shoulder. My throat tightened, and the tears pressed against my lids. I had to go, or I should perish there, on the spot. "Goodbye, good friend," I whispered, and hurried away toward the river.

The skiff was already in the water, loaded with our baggage and food from the kitchen. In minutes, we were on board, Mr. Thayer at the oars. As Gabriel waved us farewell from the pier, we made our way out into the river, caught the current, and floated swiftly downstream toward Sacramento.

The river was a pleasant highway, placid and gleaming in the sunshine. Its banks were fringed with soft grass and cottonwoods. But Mrs. Burnham, raised on a river, warned us to keep an eye out. "It's summer, and she's running low. There could be snags and rocks just below the surface. It won't hurt to be wary."

At first glance, all was well in our skiff, too. A sweet breeze rose off the water. In an act of confidence, Mr. Thayer donned his familiar grey coat. Mrs. Burnham and I stripped off our boots, draped our sad feet over the boat's side, and soothed them in the cool ripples. A bounty of bread and fruit awaited us in the canvas bag Elisabeta had provided from Hock Farm's kitchen. Best of all, we made good time, much better than we ever could have made on land. Soon, promised Mr. Thayer, the Feather would carry us right into the fabled Sacramento River.

But, under the surface, our souls were troubled with snags and wreckage of their own sort. As the hours slipped by, and we drifted closer to our destination, Mrs. Burnham grew increasingly anxious and worn. I silently grieved for Lem. And Ted sank deeper into his dark mood, staring off across the water and refusing to speak. Mr. Thayer was determined to cheer us, though he was playing to a tough audience. He finally turned the talk to our arrival in Sacramento, and the prospect of a bed in a fine establishment, with a hot bath and a tasty meal. "What do you say, Ted?" he asked, with a jovial grin. "Should it be the Union Hotel or the Palace?"

Ted looked right past him. Then he stood, muttered, "Not to be," and, as calmly as strolling into a parlor, stepped over the boat's rim and into the river. His rainbow serape sank out of sight. The slouch hat bobbed up and drifted with the current. For a second, we could only gasp; then Mrs. Burnham leapt over the boat's edge and followed him down. It seemed a century before she fought her way back to the skiff's side, struggling for breath and clutching Ted, who promptly twisted free and headed back under. Mrs. Burnham cursed and disappeared after him. Mr. Thayer ordered me to grip the oars, and he, too, dived in, coat and all. Ulysses commenced a frantic bark.

The river rolled on, smooth and glossy, revealing nothing of the battle roiling her depths. At long last, Mrs. Burnham and Mr. Thayer hauled Ted to the surface, though, by then, they were yards from the boat. Mrs. Burnham and Mr. Thayer are the stronger swimmers, but Ted thrashed like a catfish on a line. Between mouthfuls of water, Mrs. Burnham screamed, "Damn you, damn you!" and Mr. Thayer shouted, "You idiot! You'll finish us all!" But Ted broke loose and, instead of heading back down, struck out across the river.

It was then that I committed my father's fatal mistake—inattention to detail. I was so drawn to the struggle that I took my eyes off the river. When the bow of the skiff slammed into a snag, I flopped about and bounced right into the water. The ice of it sliced into me. I thought, "This is it. Death has caught up with the last of the Lightfoots. He's tapped me on the shoulder." But as I scraped the rocky bottom, a voice in my head shouted, "Up, up! Go up!" and I kicked through the green water toward the sunbeams high above. When I broke the surface, I found no one save Ulysses, the only pilot in the boat. He yapped at me and paced, distraught, from stem to stern. Then he leapt over the boat's rail, as neatly as sailing through a hoop, and landed in the river beside me. I gagged on the splash, but, next thing I knew, I had my arms around wet dog. His coat prickled, and his dog paddle beat a rhythm on my ribs, but he was there. Not Death, but Ulysses. He guided me to the boat. I gripped its rim with one hand and my savior with the other.

I could not see my companions at first. From the shouting, it appeared they were working their way toward shore, and I finally caught a glimpse of them dragging Ted up onto the bank. I cried out, long and loud, and, at last, Mr. Thayer turned his eyes toward me. He plunged back into the river and swam swiftly toward us, although the current pulled us away downstream, and I despaired of his ever coming close enough. At last, he grasped the rail of the skiff, breathing hard, so pale that the veins on his temples pulsed purple. He put an arm around me—"Emma, push up now!"—and boosted me out of the water high enough that I could drag myself over the rim of the boat. Next, Ulysses came struggling over the side and shook a spray of river water in every direction. Then I reached out, and by some grace of God, helped Mr. Thayer climb on board without capsizing the lot of us. He seized the oars and turned us toward shore. As he rowed, straining against the current, Ulysses collapsed at my side, panting. I drew a hand across my brow to wipe the soggy locks from my eyes. My spectacles had vanished, to shine forever on the river bottom like a bit of fool's gold.

As we pulled into shallow water, Mrs. Burnham and Ted were still wrestling on the bank. Even with my spectacles, it would have been hard to recognize them, dripping as they were, and caked with sand and river mud. Mr. Thayer beached the boat and hastened over. Mrs. Burnham and Ted flailed about, hollering at each other, while Mr. Thayer, in his soaked grey coat, tried to get a grip on one or the other of them. But they were slippery as fishes. Ted shouted, "Let me go!" and took off for the water one last time. Mrs. Burnham tackled him, brought him down, and straddled him, pinning him to the ground. She shrieked, "Stop it! Stop it! You will not die, damn you!"

Ted shrieked back, "I'm already damned! Leave me be!"

Mr. Thayer crouched by his head. "You fool! This is no stage play with grand exits!"

And Mrs. Burnham shouted, "You're not Hamlet, for Christ's sake!"

Ted glared. "'I could accuse me of such things, that it were better my mother had never borne me!'"

"Shut up!" Mrs. Burnham yelled.

"With more offenses at my beck, than I have thoughts—"

"What? What *offenses*?"

Ted roared in her face, "A drunkard! A madman! A firebug! I've burned down half the state!"

Mrs. Burnham grew suddenly quiet. "You're not a firebug," she said, solemn as a judge.

"No? How do we know? Those fellows with the ropes seemed pretty sure. And if I *am*, I should swing—"

"You're not—"

"Fletcher and Moone might disagree—"

"Stop it!"

"Add murder to my sins—"

"Stop it! Stop it!! It wasn't you! It wasn't!!!" Mrs. Burnham declared this with such force that Ted finally did shut up. He stared at her.

Mr. Thayer leaned forward. "Hattie, what do you know?"

Mrs. Burnham slid off of Ted and leaned back in the muck of the bank. "I believe it was our own little Louise."

Mr. Thayer gaped at her in disbelief. Ted pulled himself up on his elbows.

"Louise? How?" said Mr. Thayer. "She's just a child."

And, then, at last, Mrs. Burnham spilled what she'd held in for days—how I'd come upon Louise in the Burnham's tent, how the girl had touched the glowing cigar to the shawl until it blazed. When she finished, Ted leapt to Louise's defense.

"She's an innocent," he argued. "Do you have proof? Did you see her start the other fires?"

Mrs. Burnham shook her head. "I pray to God she didn't. She denied it. Though the girl had a way of disappearing at the wrong moments."

"Anything can set those camps afire," Mr. Thayer insisted. "They're tinderboxes."

Mrs. Burnham sighed. "True. But Louise had her secrets. And for all the arguments I've made in my head to defend her, my heart is fearful for the child. She set herself afire without a blink."

The horror of this struck us all silent for a moment. Then Ted gazed at Mrs. Burnham, his eyes dark with sorrow. "Why didn't you say something sooner?"

"Ted, I've tried to defend you, to absolve you—"

"You've known since Camptonville."

"God help me, I didn't know what to do. Louise is a child. What do you do with a seven-year-old? Hang her? Ship her off to San Quentin? I was terrified of what would happen if word got out, not only to Louise, but to the whole company. Judging from our welcome in Downieville, I had a right to be."

Ted leaned in toward her. "I had a right to know."

"Yes. You did. But I had to get the girl as far away from the foothills as I could. Clarissa would only go if I agreed to keep what we'd seen a secret and buy them some time to get east to her family. It's a bargain I never should have made, and, Miss Lightfoot, I put you in a poor position, too. I made you promise you'd keep things to yourself, and I knew you didn't stomach the falsehood of it."

"No, I didn't," I replied. "I'm sorry, Ted."

"I'm sorry to everyone," said Mrs. Burnham. "I did not handle this well. In truth, there are very few things that I have done well on this journey."

"'All is turned to sand. I have failed,'" muttered Ted. He began to shiver. Perhaps the cold of the river was finally getting to him. My own teeth were chattering.

"I sure as hell have," said Mrs. Burnham.

"No, Hattie," said Ted, "that's my line. I have disappointed everyone, especially Louise. I should have helped her more. I failed the company, I even failed June. He doesn't like me, but he put his trust in me. And his money. I can't bear the thought of turning up again in Sacramento as a wastrel. I'd rather end up on the river bottom."

Mr. Thayer spoke, "Give June some credit, Ted."

"He never put much stock in me, Gus."

"I don't reckon he wants to dredge the river for you. He's your brother. He's a good man."

"And I am not." Ted wobbled to his feet, distraught. Mr. Thayer quickly stepped to his side and cut him off from the water.

I could no longer remain still. "But you *are* a good man, Ted," I stammered. "You are generous, and kind, and a fine actor—"

Ted shot me a pained look. "I'm a fraud. And a drunkard. And fires or no, half mad."

Mrs. Burnham jumped in. "You may be a crazy son of a bitch, but you're no worse than the rest of us. And when you choose to be, you're truly a great actor. Now, you *are* one hell of a drunk. You should work on that one."

Ted gazed out over the current. "I come by it honestly."

"Well, cast it out. Be the kind of actor the old man would be proud of."

Ted turned on her in fury. "Damn you! I am bedeviled by that old man's ghost! I'm sick to death of standing in his shadow!"

"He loved you, Ted," said Mr. Thayer.

"He terrified me! His binges and his rages and his tears! I was supposed to be his keeper, and he'd give me the slip time after time! I was horrified he'd end up dead on my watch. And he bloody well did."

"Ted, he was halfway across the country," said Mrs. Burnham. "There wasn't a thing you could have—"

"I should have been there! I stayed behind in California because I wanted to be free of him. Of craziness and shame. But he's still with me, I hear him in my brain and my heart, and he'll surely drive me mad! I was supposed to save him from himself." The tears began to roll down Ted's face, streaking the mud. "Well, I didn't save him. I didn't save him."

Mrs. Burnham came up behind him as he trembled there and wrapped her arms around his shoulders. "His death was his own, Ted. Not yours, his. No one could have saved him. And whatever you think your sins are, you know that he forgives you. He forgives you. May they all forgive us."

Ted fought against her grip for a moment, and then he broke and turned into her arms. She pulled him down on the sand and hugged him to her breast the way she had hugged her little daguerrotype of Henry, only this time, she held a living, breathing Ted instead of the sharp corners of a silver frame. "Shh, shh, all is forgiven," she whispered.

The séance at Lola's was smoke and skullduggery, a good show, nothing more. But here, on the banks of the bright river, the ghosts poured out of Ted and Mrs. Burnham and rose up through the willows to only God knows where. Maybe for a brief sojourn. Maybe for good.

In the midst of this scene, I confess to a less than noble thought. I envied the sanctuary Ted had found. While he had taken refuge in Mrs. Burnham's arms, I stood solitary, drenched and shivering, abandoned even by Ulysses, who had gone to Mr. Thayer's side. I stumbled over to the boat, in the hope of finding a blanket to throw over myself.

TUESDAY, JULY 29. *A ranch north of Sacramento—*

For a long while, we lingered in silence on the muddy bank, exhausted river rats. The sun began to sink behind the far shore, casting a glow on the water. It came to me that we had crossed the Feather and wound up on the opposite side from Hock Farm.

At length, Mr. Thayer went to Mrs. Burnham, where she cradled Ted, and gently tapped her on the shoulder. "Hattie?"

"Yes?"

"I reckon we should find ourselves a spot to camp. Maybe someplace away from the water. I'll take a look around. Will you be all right here for a piece?"

"I expect so."

Mr. Thayer wasn't gone long. When he returned, we pulled what we needed from the skiff, and he hid the boat in a patch of scrub along the shore. Then we trekked a few hundred feet inland to a sandy spot amongst a clump of cottonwoods. The river was out of sight, if not out of hearing. Ted still had a few lucifer matches in his bag. It took most of our energy to build a fire and change from our wet clothes into whatever we could find that was dry. We nibbled cold food from Elisabeta's sack, and, within minutes, Ted and Mrs. Burnham laid out their beds and fell into a quick slumber. They slept like babes. I know, because I did not.

I was still cold to the bone from my soaking, and stood, turning first one side and then the other to the fire. I tried writing in my journal, grateful that it hadn't gone to the bottom with my spectacles. Finally, I wrapped myself in my blanket and settled down on the sand, but my mind raced on with worries and regrets. I hoped that Evie was safe and that Lem Mule slept, content, in his new stall. For a moment, I thought I heard Harry Brown's laughter in the distance, and my heart brightened—I sat up and stared into the darkness, hoping he might appear. Then I realized I had only heard the rippling of the river.

Sometime, very late into the night, I dozed, leaving Mr. Thayer as lone sentinel. When I finally awoke, I discovered a bunch of wild roses and a handful of sweet blackberries carefully laid by my blanket. Mrs. Burnham opened her eyes to the same gift. Ted, usually the slugabed, was up and about, helping Mr. Thayer cook us breakfast.

I don't know if Mr. Thayer ever truly slept. By the time I awoke, he had already sought out the lay of the land. After breakfast, as Ted folded up his blanket, Mr. Thayer took Mrs. Burnham and me aside. "The main road to Sacramento is only a stone's throw from us," he confided. "It's much more traveled than the road on the west side, and we could easily catch a ride. Maybe we should keep the boy off the water for now."

"Maybe. But the boat is so much quicker, Gus," Mrs. Burnham replied.

"Do you think he'll stay in it?"

"I believe he will. I know he will."

"All right," said Mr. Thayer, though worry still furrowed his countenance. "Then we'd best push off. Miss Lightfoot, will you help me with these bags?"

Mr. Thayer and I hefted carpet bags and blankets and toted them down to the bank. He dragged the skiff from its hiding place, but before we could begin to load up, he stopped, and gazed across the river to the far shore. "What the hell is that?" he wondered.

I followed his look, but without my specs I couldn't make out much. "What?"

"Some critter is kicking up the water over there and shaking the scrub."

I shaded my eyes and peered. "A deer?"

"Nope. Too big for a deer. A horse, maybe. It's running up and down the bank."

My heart began to race. "Can you spy its ears?"

"No, I'm afraid it's too far. It could be a—"

But Mr. Thayer never finished his thought, for, at that moment, the critter loosed a call out over the water like a rusty iron door dragging open. Spectacles or no, I knew the sender of that greeting.

"Lem!" I shouted. "It's Lem!" I ran out into the water and waved my arms like a lunatic. "Lem! Lem!"

My mule let out one more bray, long and joyous, then plunged into the river and began to swim our way.

"I'll be damned," chuckled Mr. Thayer. "Look at him go!"

I squinted until my eyes ached and finally made out Lem's fine old head and long ears just above the water. We cried out encouragements to him, and he paddled his way toward us with all his heart. But when he reached the middle of the river, where it ran deep and strong, he began to drift downstream. "Lem, Lem!" I screamed. "Over here, boy!" But, despite our calls and a ferocious struggle, he was dragged away by the current and disappeared from sight. "Oh, no, where did he go?" I wailed to Mr. Thayer. "Can you see him at all?"

"I believe so. Come on, Miss Lightfoot! Quickly!" He pulled the skiff out into the water, and I scrambled in. Mr. Thayer pointed us downstream and began furiously to row. For minutes, all I could hear was his labored breathing and my own voice ringing in my ears, hollering "Lem!" At last, Mr. Thayer rested the oars and glanced downriver.

"There he is! Can you make him out? He's tired, but he knows we're here. Keep calling, MIss Lightfoot!"

I did. Lem's face came into focus, his eyes rolling, and his huge ears flattened back. Mr. Thayer delicately rowed us to within feet of the mule. I'm sure, if he could have, Lem would have climbed right into that boat beside us. A sodden halter was draped about his big head, and a length of broken lead line floated out beside him. "Miss Lightfoot, see if you can grab that line," Mr. Thayer said. "Careful, though, the last thing you need is another dunking."

While Mr. Thayer eased us just downstream of Lem, I gripped the skiff's rail and reached as far as I dared. My fingers closed on the wet line. I held on for dear life.

"Got it!" I hollered, as I slid back into the bottom of the boat.

"Good!" cheered Mr. Thayer. "Now, let's deliver him over to the bank, all right? But, for God's sake, don't let him pull you over the side. I'll go slow and easy."

Mr. Thayer rowed us downstream, and, bit by bit, closer to the river's edge. Lem puffed and snorted like some fantastical sea serpent, until, at last, his hooves struck against the river bottom. As he fought his way up the bank, I leapt out of the boat and hurried to my friend's side. There he stood, my soggy, splendid old mule. He had chosen us over Paradise.

Can a mule smile? I would swear that Lem Mule had a big grin on his face as he shook the river off his hide. I expect I did, too. I hugged his neck, and I might have hung there for most of the morning had not Mr. Thayer said, "I imagine Hattie and Ted might be wondering where we disappeared to, Miss Lightfoot. Perhaps we should hasten upriver."

"I reckon so. Lem looks beautiful though, doesn't he?"

"Absolutely. He's the best-looking, wet old mule I've seen of late."

Mr. Thayer pushed the skiff back out into the shallow water by the bank and rowed north, as Lem and I walked the shore nearby. We hadn't gone half a mile, when we heard hollering. "Emmmmm-a! Thaaa-yer!" We hallooed back and shortly came upon Ted and Mrs. Burnham pacing the muddy stretch where we had washed up the day before. The baggage that Mr. Thayer and I had tossed aside was still strewn across the sand.

Mrs. Burnham spotted Mr. Thayer first, as he beached the skiff. "Gus! What happened? You disappeared!"

"Good news!" replied Mr. Thayer. "Look behind you!" Mrs. Burnham and Ted turned just as I led Lem out of the willows and over to the water's edge. Ted beamed. "You found your mule!"

"More like he found us!"

"Thank God! It was a dreadful sight, I tell you, to come upon the bags tossed about and no sign of you and Thayer. We feared you'd been washed away."

"How did you come across Lem, Miss Lightfoot?" wondered Mrs. Burnham.

I hastily recounted how we'd spotted him across the river, how he'd charged into the water, and how Mr. Thayer and I had helped him safely ashore. "Lem knew where he wanted to be," I added. "And, of course, I can't leave him now, not after all he went through. So, if the rest of you need to take the skiff to Sacramento without us, I expect we'll manage. There'll be no hard feelings."

Ted hurried over and wrapped me in his arms. "Emma Lightfoot," he said, "there's no way I would send you down the road alone. You're a fine friend, and that mule has earned our company and more. I'm sticking with you, whether by land or by sea."

"I second that," said Mr. Thayer. "Hattie, how are your blisters today?"

"Better."

"Can you ride bareback?" I asked.

"Most certainly," she replied. "I always wanted to play a frontier girl, bareback on my pony. I believe I should seize the opportunity!"

And so, we made ready to travel by land. Mr. Thayer and Ted concealed the boat once more. ("For safekeeping," said Mr. Thayer. "You never know.") Without a saddle to rig, we carried most of the baggage and our bedrolls on our backs. Ted boosted Mrs. Burnham onto Lem, and I walked by the mule's head. Soon, we departed the bank of the Feather River and turned onto the Sacramento Road. I could not stop smiling. Providence had delivered me my mule, and Ted Booth had hugged me.

For the first time in days, we were a cheerful lot. Ted and Mrs. Burnham both carried themselves lightly this morning, eased at least for now of the darkest of their burdens. Mrs. Burnham began to sing as we made our way down the road, and soon we all joined in on choruses of "Nelly Bly" and "Bound for the Promised Land." Even Lem, the music-lover, found a spring in his step.

We had traveled only a short piece when a figure dashed past us with a boy on its back. At first, I took it to be a tall, skinny man with a waddle, but, at second glance, I made out a long neck and feathers. It was Othello, the Rowe Circus's errant ostrich! The boy had a familiar look about him, too. "Jake!" I called out. "Jake Barry!"

The boy deftly turned the ostrich and trotted him back our way. I recognized the outlaw glint in the bird's eye. He was bridled and sported a red leather saddle.

"Do you remember me, Jake? One of the girls from the Star Troupe? I'm Emma Lightfoot. We visited your circus in Auburn."

Jake handed me a quizzical look. "I do remember you," he said. "But, my, you've changed."

"We've had a rough week, I'm afraid."

"I don't reckon I've met your friends."

"No. This is Mrs. Burnham, this is Mr. Thayer, and this here is Mr. Booth."

Jake's mouth dropped. "Oh. Mr. Booth. Folks are looking for you."

Mrs. Burnham frowned. "What sort of folks?"

"Friends, I think. A fellow named Frank, and another Mr. Booth from Sacramento."

"Frank Mayo?" asked Ted.

"Maybe," replied Jake. "I don't know that much about it, but if you take a mind to wait, Rowe's Circus is only five minutes behind you."

Othello was getting restless, shaking his reins and dancing from side to side. "I believe this bird needs to move," said Jake. "But I'll take word back to the wagons."

"Please do," said Mr. Thayer.

Jake gave a cluck, and Othello bounded away. "Goodbye, Miss Lightfoooooot!!" the boy called, as they galloped off the way they'd come.

"The circus," sighed Mrs. Burnham.

"And a good thing, too, Hattie," replied Mr. Thayer. "Thank God it's the circus. The Rowes are decent folk. We need friends right now."

Ted nodded. "Maybe our fortunes have turned, Hattie. Perhaps there's a little serendipity waiting in the wings."

There was. Soon, we spied dust up the trail; then the gilded circus wagons and the graceful horsemen and women came into view. They were led by Mr. Rowe on Adonis and Mrs. Rowe on a milk-white mare--the circus owners who had so kindly invited some of us theatre folks backstage when our paths had crossed back in Auburn. Although the circus company and its accoutrements were a mite worn from their travels, they were nonetheless a celestial sight. The Rowes hastened toward us, and Mr. Thayer dashed over to greet them. "Joe! Eliza!"

"Gus Thayer!" declared Mr. Rowe. "You're a sight for sore eyes!"

"I could say the same, Joe!" grinned Mr. Thayer.

Mr. Rowe tipped his hat to Hattie and me and gave Ted a nod. "Delighted to see you folks, too, especially to find you safe and sound. There have been some worried parties scouring the foothills for you."

"Miss Lightfoot!" said Mrs. Rowe, in her silvery voice. "Jake mentioned that you were here. So lovely to see you again." She brought her elegant mare over to my rawboned mule and offered me her hand. Even though my own hand was cracked and rough, she clasped it as if we were dear friends.

"Joe," said Mrs. Burnham, "the boy on the bird mentioned you'd run across a gentleman named Frank. Might that have been Frank Mayo?"

"Yes, indeed. We ran into him in North San Juan. He'd ridden up to Downieville to meet you and missed you by a day."

"Lucky for him," said Mrs. Burnham.

"So I understand. He'd gone to the theatre, found out from the manager about the goings-on, and slipped back out of town as quickly as he could. He'd searched for you, but he hadn't turned up a trace—he was in a state when we came across him."

"We did our best to lay low," said Mr. Thayer. "Maybe we laid a little too low."

"Where's Frank now, Joe?" wondered Mrs. Burnham.

"He said he was headed for Sacramento, to Mr. Booth's brother, to give him the news. I expect he made it, because we came across a search party on the Downieville Road a couple of days back. But they must have missed you by miles, if you were already down here on the Feather."

Ted hurried to Rowe's side. "Was my brother with them?"

"He was, yes," said Rowe. "And worried to death. He'll be happy to see you—to see all of you. Please, travel with us. We have extra horses and room in the wagons."

"We'll be passing the night at a ranch, just north of Sacramento," said Mrs. Rowe. "It's a sweet place, along the river. Please, be our guests. You can rest up and then head into Sacramento with us in the morning, if you like."

I wanted to shout, "Oh, yes, yes, we like!!!!" Fortunately, I bit my tongue until Mr. Thayer and Ted had accepted the invitation in a more genteel fashion, and even Mrs. Burnham had come up with a sincere, "Thank you!"

I can now boast that I have joined the circus, if only for a day. Mrs. Burnham was offered a seat in a wagon, and I hopped on Lem's back. As I rode, one or another of the circus company fell in beside me, with a "Welcome" and pleasant small talk. I did not feel a stranger.

Much of the time, too, Ted Booth was my companion. When he is not wrapped in his own tragedy, he is delightful and amusing, and today he was at his best. Sometimes I was so charmed, I felt the familiar blush start to rise in my cheeks, and I fought to keep from turning beet-red under my sunburn.

Midday, we climbed a gentle rise. Ted led me off the road, out of the traffic, and pointed. "There it is, Emma! The Sacramento River."

I squinted to the west, where the Feather mingled her waters with the storied Sacramento, the wide, shining river that ran through the heart of California. I knew, from maps and tales, that the Sacramento was the lifeblood of the city of that name, flowing from its waterfront all the way to San Francisco and out into the immense Pacific Ocean. I knew that Ted would soon be following the river's course to the sea. Then he would traverse through the jungles of Panama and, at last, return to the eastern shores. I was saddened to think of his departure, and I envied him the adventure of it.

Near sundown, we arrived at the ranch that Eliza Rowe had spoken of. The loveliness of its setting gave Hock Farm a run for the money. Pale yellow fields, dotted with oaks, rolled down to the riverbank.

The wagons were circled, the stock was fed and watered, and the remnants of the Star Troupe were showered with small kindnesses by the members of Rowe's company. Not a single disparagement of the circus escaped Mrs. Burnham's lips.

As darkness fell, rough planks were set on barrels by the Rowes' wagon and dressed up with a linen cloth and silver. Lanterns were hung and candles lit, as the stars twinkled above and the river sang in the distance. The circus cook did his best to keep our plates and glasses filled. My heart was full, too, with gratitude for our good fortune—first, to have fallen into the gracious company of our hosts, and then, doubly fortunate that they, like my companions, were "show-people." They knew, without being told, of the hardships we had seen.

The supper conversation was jovial, a swapping of old theatre and circus stories, that sometimes made me laugh so I could barely chew my food. But, once the plates were cleared and the sherry poured, the talk turned serious.

"I'm sorry we missed your *Hamlet*, Mr. Booth," said Mr. Rowe. "I heard it was very fine."

Ted smiled, a shy smile. "Thank you. And it was Miss Lightfoot's debut." He raised his glass to me, and I could not help but smile, too.

"We'd hoped to catch it when our paths crossed yours," said Mr. Rowe, "but our schedule has been tossed into the air so many times, we hardly knew if we were coming or going."

"It's been a tough summer," said Mrs. Burnham.

Mrs. Rowe delicately sipped her sherry. "We were supposed to be playing Downieville tonight, but when we heard from Mr. Mayo what happened there, we turned ourselves around and headed south for Sacramento."

"The whole business had a nasty feel to it," said Mr. Rowe. "Now, we're just hoping for better luck in the southern mines."

"How have your houses been?" asked Mrs. Burnham.

"Uneven. We're barely keeping our heads above water. And the fires have played havoc with our bookings."

Mrs. Burnham pushed her coffee away. "Yes, we know about the fires."

"I'm so sorry," said Mr. Rowe. "I didn't mean to—"

"It's all right, Joe, it's all right. But did you hear any talk about us on the road? Rumors?"

"No, nothing until the Downieville incident."

Mrs. Rowe shook her head. "That was frightening, Hattie."

"It certainly was," said Mrs. Burnham. "I suspect the Star Troupe will be known as the Donner Party of this year's theatrical season."

"You won't find that to be the opinion of other show-folk, Hattie," said Mr. Rowe. "We all know that it could have been any of us. As you said, it's been a tough summer."

"The whole state is hurting," said Mrs. Rowe. "Look at the Vigilance Committees."

Mr. Rowe frowned. "You can tell people are in trouble when they take the law into their own hands. They can't control their lives, so they find a scapegoat, and take charge by handing out quick 'justice.'"

"It may have been quick, Joe," said Mr. Thayer, "but, in Downieville, it was definitely not justice."

"No. To be honest, Gus, I think show-people are sometimes more vulnerable than a grocer or a blacksmith might be." Mr. Rowe rubbed his beard thoughtfully. "We stand out from the crowd. We come and we go, and it's easier to sacrifice an outsider than one of your own citizens."

Ted took this conversation in quietly, but, when he finally spoke, all he said was, "My brother was truly worried about me?"

Mrs. Rowe laid a gentle hand on his. "Yes, Mr. Booth. Deeply worried. Mr. Rowe and I have sent a rider into Sacramento tonight, to assure him that you're safe. It would be cruel to keep him in despair for another night."

Ted clasped Mrs. Rowe's fingers. "I'm grateful."

Wednesday, July 30. *Evening. Ebner's elegant Hotel, Sacramento—*

The circus folk rose early on this bright morning, and so did we. The stock was tended, the company breakfasted, and the wagons swiftly loaded. A gentle breeze from the river promised fair travel, and, before the sun had cleared the treetops, we were on our way.

We were not long into the morning's journey when Ted suddenly halted his mount and stared ahead. A carriage and team were dashing our way, kicking up a cloud. Ted's shoulders tensed. "I believe that's June."

The driver rattled up to the front of the circus caravan. He was a distinguished-looking man with a remarkable resemblance to Ted, except that he was older and bore the aspect of a businessman rather than an actor. He leapt down from the carriage, greeted the Rowes enthusiastically, and spilled out, "Where's Ted?" Before the Rowes could reply, Ted urged his horse forward, and June ran to his side. "Ted! Thank God!" He clasped Ted's hand. Ted finally relaxed into a smile, then lowered himself from the saddle. June delivered him a huge bear hug, and Ted hugged him back.

Mr. Thayer grinned. "I do love a good resurrection."

"Thayer!" June Booth threw an arm over Mr. Thayer's shoulder. "Welcome back from the wilderness! And Hattie! When Rowe's man galloped in last night, we were so relieved!" Ulysses trotted over to June and extended a paw. June laughed and shook it. "Even the dog has lived to tell the tale! Hallelujah!"

Mr. Thayer nodded my way. "June, I'd like you to meet Miss Emma Lightfoot and her miraculous mule, Lem. She is a fine actress and a nimble wardrobe mistress. She has also saved our bacon on more than one occasion. Miss Lightfoot, Mr. June Booth."

Mr. June Booth touched his hat. "Delighted, Miss Lightfoot!" His eyes were kind. I liked him right off.

June Booth wished us to ride into Sacramento with him. The carriage was a double-seater, with plenty of room for my companions and our bags. Lem and I could trot along beside it. "We'll go to the Forrest," Mr. June Booth said. "We're rehearsing *A New Way to Pay Old Debts* there, and the cast would like to welcome you back."

We thanked the Rowes and our other circus friends from the bottoms of our hearts, tossed what we had into the carriage, and hurried off toward Sacramento.

On the outskirts of the city, we hastened past a ruin, a jumble of twisted beams and ravaged walls. I stared at it, wondering what kind of warfare could have brought it down, until I realized it was the remnants of Sutter's Fort. I had seen it before, when Emmett and I had first come west. Then, we had found it to be an oasis after the terrible journey across deserts and treacherous peaks. It's fields and orchards spread green across the valley floor; its wide, adobe entrance welcomed us, a gateway to the

Promised Land of California. For the first time in months, I remember feeling safe.

Gazing at the fort's shell, I knew it wasn't warfare that had delivered such destruction. Progress had stolen its bricks and overrun its gardens. No wonder Captain Sutter had retreated to Hock Farm.

Still, as we turned west and made our way toward the waterfront, I could not help but be entranced by the city of Sacramento. It is the biggest and the busiest city I have ever seen! Its streets are bustling, lined with countless buildings of brick and iron, two and three stories high! Beyond the rooftops, where the Sacramento River laps at the city's doorstep, floats a forest of masts, and shouts and steamboat whistles signify the comings and goings of the city's fortune-seekers.

Mr. June Booth guided the carriage down "K" Street, adroitly weaving around coaches and freight wagons. It was soon clear that he was a popular gentleman in Sacramento—folks on the street called out enthusiastic salutations as we passed, and he cheerfully returned them. My companions were greeted familiarly, too. The first time Ted heard his name sung out, he winced, but when it was followed by, "Bless you, you made it, young man!" and he realized that the portly speaker was offering her good wishes rather than a noose, he smiled, waved, and relaxed back into the carriage seat. Even though no one hollered out, "Emma Lightfoot, so happy to see you!" I was warmed by this bubbling forth of affection for my friends.

Soon, Mr. June Booth pulled the team up before a grand, imposing building. This was the new Forrest Theatre. The front steps were crowded with actors. Before the carriage had even come to a halt, we were surrounded by them and showered with welcomes and embraces. In a trice, we were shepherded into the theatre, past the bust of the actor Edwin Forrest and backstage to the Green Room. The Green Room! In the theatres of the mining camps, an actor was lucky to have some cramped cubby to dress in, but here was a whole room filled with soft chairs, just for the performers to take their ease backstage. In the midst of this Green Room, spread upon a wide table, was a feast to celebrate the safe return of the survivors of the Star Troupe—fruit and cake, cider and champagne. We had finally come home.

For the next half-hour, the Green Room crackled with laughter and good wishes. Mr. Thayer kept us in stitches with his wit, and Ulysses yipped in delight. The room became even livelier when Frank Mayo burst in. He delivered us huge hugs and lifted Ted Booth right into the air, shouting, "We few, we happy few, we band of brothers!" Ted then groaned, "Gracias!" as they pummeled each other. I was glad that Frank's horseplay included only fists, not foils, as there was a wealth of glassware and china in the room.

When the last bottle was drained, and the cake was naught but crumbs, the cast was called back to work, but June Booth, a friend of his named Mr. Butler, and Frank Mayo lingered with us in the comfort of the Green Room. "I can barely drag myself out of this chair," said Mrs. Burnham. "I believe I have gone to heaven."

Mr. Thayer grinned. "It certainly beats a thorn bush."

"So that's where you were," said Frank Mayo. "Hiding in the thorn thickets like jackrabbits."

"Nigh to it," replied Mrs. Burnham. "We were keeping a low profile."

"I don't blame you," said Frank. "Once I found out what had happened, I couldn't get out of Downieville fast enough. I was looking over my shoulder for days."

"We scoured the sticks for you," said Mr. June Booth, "and the longer we went without a sign, the more terrible the possibilities became. So, tell us, truly, where were you?"

We spilled out the story of our misadventures, save for the details of Louise's departure. Perhaps my companions felt those sorrowful events were best shared in private. As our tale unfurled, June Booth took in every word. He was sympathetic, and his countenance darkened only at the mention of Ben Burnham's duplicity and Mr. Leach's turning us out into the street. "You don't treat partners that way," he fumed. "He could have wired me, and we could have come to some kind of agreement. The man is clearly not of the theatre."

"I'm to blame, too, June," said Ted. This was hard for him, confessing to his brother. "I screwed up, and I cost you a bundle. I'll do everything I can to pay you back, I swear."

"I accept that offer," said June Booth. "You can pay me back by honoring your bookings on the East Coast. Show them what you can do."

"June, I haven't a penny. I can't even get to San Francisco, let alone to New York."

"You don't have your costumes, either," said Mrs. Burnham. "Leach is holding them for ransom."

"He has Hattie's trunk, too," said Mr. Thayer, "and mine, and Brown's—

most all of them, I'd guess."

"Leach has communicated with me," said June Booth. "A terse communication. He's putting the Star Troupe's costumes and properties up for auction on the twelfth of next month. If you want to buy them back before then, you're welcome to. Gus, I think he's only put a "transport charge" on your things, but Ted and Hattie will have to come up with his full price."

"A *what* charge?" said Mr. Thayer. "The man must be seriously put out."

"Ben should never have punched him," said Mrs. Burnham. "That was the beginning of the end."

"Ben punched him?" grinned Frank.

"That's water under the bridge, now," said June Booth. "The bottom line is, you need funds, all of you. And Butler and I have an idea, at least for the short term."

I hadn't paid much attention to Mr. Butler. He was a well-dressed fellow, maybe thirty.

"Butler, here, truly is a man of the theatre, although he masquerades as an architect. But he has a business sense extraordinaire, and he'd like to help us put together a benefit. Butler?"

Mr. Butler stood, a tall, shy man, with tanned cheeks and the most pleasant smile. He quickly laid out the plan: the Forrest Theatre was available a week from Saturday, many of the local actors wanted to support Ted, Mrs. Burnham and the rest of the Troupe, and he knew he could get word out and bring in a full house.

Ted gave Butler a worried glance. "No one's spooked that I'll burn the Forrest down?"

"No! The community is in sympathy with you, I promise."

"You saw your welcome, Ted," added June. "What we need to do now is get you back on the stage. Butler and I suggest *Richard III*. It wasn't in your rep in the mines, but this'll give you a chance to dust it off before New York. What do you say?"

Ted accepted with gratitude and hope. June and Mr. Butler vowed they'd go to work on the plan that very afternoon. "Now, about accommodations," said June Booth. "Ted, you're welcome to stay with the Mrs. and myself. How are the rest of you fixed? Thayer?"

Mr. Thayer had friends to bunk with out on "L" Street. They were fond of canines and understanding of pecuniary shortcomings. He reckoned he'd head that way.

"Hattie," said Frank, "I have a room in a sweet little boardinghouse by the river; the rent's cheap and the food isn't bad. I think they might have a place for you over there."

"Thanks but no thanks, Frank," replied Mrs. Burnham. "I'm on my way to that new hotel, Ebner's, down the street."

"It's expensive," warned June.

"I don't give a damn," said Mrs. Burnham. "I deserve it, at least for a night or two. It's swank and clean, and I can get a hot bath."

Then, all eyes turned to me. "Emma?" said Ted, "where shall you roost?"

I felt a lump in my throat. This could be our moment of parting. "I'll find something," I replied.

"She's coming with me," said Mrs. Burnham.

My heart lifted, and then, just as quickly, fell. "Thank you, ma'am," I said, "but you can't sneak a mule into a swank hotel."

Mr. Thayer jumped in. "Miss Lightfoot, I've been pondering this since we pulled that mule from the river. My friends are out past the fort, on a few acres. There's even a shed behind the house. Would you trust me with Lem for a couple of days, until you get your plans in order? You'd be doing me a favor. I could ride that old boy out there and save my feet the trouble."

I couldn't imagine anyone better suited to tend my mule. "Oh thank you!" I said. I suddenly felt the need to hug Mr. Thayer, and I did so, right before everyone.

Soon we parted, all of us in our separate directions. I felt strangely lonely, although I still had Mrs. Burnham's company. "Leave your things right here, Miss Lightfoot," she said. "We have a couple of stops to make before we grace the Ebner with our presence."

We marched out of the theatre and a short distance toward the river, where Mrs. Burnham led us into a bank building, with mahogany counters and fancy ironwork. She stepped right up to one of the mustachioed managers and asked for her "box." He fetched a metal container from the bank safe and left us in privacy. "Miss Lightfoot," said Mrs. Burnham, "this is a lesson for you, especially if you pursue a life in the theatre. Think like a squirrel. Stash a few extra nuts about town for emergencies." She opened the box and held up a necklace with flashing stones. "Burnham gave me this when he proposed. It's worth more than the marriage ever was." She tucked the necklace into her reticule and snapped the box's lid shut. "All right, Miss Lightfoot," she said, "let's be on our way."

We headed over to "J" Street where Mrs. Burnham stopped before a brick building with three golden balls hung over the door. As we entered, the pawnbroker, a man in shirtsleeves and a green vest, sang out, "Hattie Burnham! I heard you were back in town! Anything good for me today?"

"Just the usual, Zeke," she smiled, and spread her necklace on the counter.

"Those stones are glass, you know," said the pawnbroker.

"Yes, I know. But the gold is real, and you know that, too."

While they haggled, I looked about at the stickpins and tortoiseshell combs, the silver and china, the statue of a lamb, and the banjo hanging on the wall. Some of those items would be reclaimed. Most of them wouldn't. Precious objects, all, that had been brought around the Horn or over the prairie, along with dreams that had since gone bust. They made me sad. They made me think of Emmett's printing press.

Mrs. Burnham, however, was not the least bit sentimental. She was practiced at this routine and as charming as she was tough. She did not relent until she had dazzled that pawnbroker and struck her deal. Then, with a little wave to the smitten Zeke, she led me out the door, smiling.

We hastened to Ebner's Hotel. A "suite" was available, and we checked ourselves in to an evening of good food, warm baths, and sweet, clean sheets.

FRIDAY, AUGUST 1. *Evening. Ebner's. At the desk in our room—*

Yesterday morning, Mrs. Burnham and I treated ourselves to a late breakfast in the hotel dining room. As she buttered her toast, she announced, "Miss Lightfoot, you and I are going on a shopping expedition. We resemble ragpickers, and it simply will not do."

She was right. I was surprised that they had let us into such a swank establishment in our tattered state. Still, I hesitated. "Mrs. Burnham, I can't afford shopping. I can't even pay you back for the marmalade on my biscuits here."

Mrs. Burnham frowned at me. "Emma Lightfoot, listen up. The food and accommodations are on me. They're the least I can do. If you feel obliged to pay me back for the clothes, we can talk about that later, after you get your share from the benefit, though, truly, you needn't worry about it. I know a shop where we can get them on credit." She lifted the coffee pot and topped off both our cups.

"I didn't know I was part of the benefit," I said.

"Of course you are. I wouldn't do it if you weren't given a share, nor would Ted, nor Gus."

"No one said anything yesterday."

"I suppose we just assumed you understood. I'll speak to June and Butler today, if you'd like, and make sure they know you're on board. You'd be perfect as Clarence's daughter. Does that suit you?"

"Of course it does!"

"Excellent. Then let's go buy something smart, something we can actually be seen in on the streets of Sacramento!"

Presently, we arrived at the dress shop Mrs. Burnham had spoken of. The owner, Miss Adele, was a good-humored woman who sewed costumes for the theatre, as well as the street wear on her store's racks. She and Mrs. Burnham went on like old friends and had the best of times suggesting items for me.

"This skirt will match your eyes, young lady," said Adele, draping its folds over her arm.

"And the blouse frames your face in the loveliest way," said Mrs. Burnham. "Can you see that, Miss Lightfoot?"

I thought I might. It was a bit strange to get these feminine opinions of my appearance. As I was growing up, Emmett never paid much attention to drawing out the color of my eyes. If I was clean, and not too raggedy, he was happy, however hit-and-miss my wardrobe.

Still, as I looked in the mirror, I liked what I saw. The clothes were simple but expertly made, and the person who stared back at me was, well, a young woman, someone quite different from the skinny girl on muleback. I smiled at my reflection.

"Are you pleased?" asked Mrs. Burnham.

"She should be," said a voice from the doorway.

I whirled about in surprise, to be greeted with a familiar laugh. "Hello, Cinder-Emma!"

"Harry Brown!" Mrs. Burnham and I exclaimed, both in the same breath, and we burst into a flurry of questions. "How are you?" "Why are you in Sacramento?" "How did you find us, Harry?"

"June told me where you were staying. After that, I followed my hunches, and I asked every storekeeper on "K" Street if two lovely ladies had passed their way. I've been five minutes behind you for the last half hour!"

Mrs. Burnham chuckled. "Well, we weren't too lovely until now. But I'd say, with Adele's help, we've definitely improved upon our images."

"You both look splendid."

"What brings you to town, Harry?" inquired Mrs. Burnham.

"Oh, June Booth wired me as soon as he'd heard from Rowe that you were safe. I took the steamboat up from San Francisco yesterday. I'm staying over with Frank, along the river. And I expect I'll be here for a while—June and Butler asked me to do the benefit next week."

What a delightful turn of events!

"How are your hands, Harry?" asked Mrs. Burnham. One of them was still wrapped in gauze.

"Much better, thank you."

"And how did you and Sophie manage on your journey back?" I asked.

"The Delphinos were guardian angels. They brought me to a doctor and shipped Sophie off to her friends. I can tell you all about it if you have a little time this afternoon."

I looked to Mrs. Burnham. "I'd love to Harry, but I'm not exactly sure—"

"Oh, of course she has the time, Harry," said Mrs. Burnham. "Wear what you have on, Miss Lightfoot, and I'll have the rest of our packages sent to the hotel. You two deserve a little respite after all the misery we've seen."

"I know a good cafe, Emma—" said Harry.

"Oh, Harry, I don't have much in the way of funds—"

"Well, I do," replied Harry, with a grin. "My father is a dear man. When I departed yesterday, and he offered me a generous pouch of spending money, I did not refuse. I know he would be disappointed if I didn't put it to good use."

"For heaven's sake, go, Emma! Have fun! Goodbye!" laughed Mrs. Burnham. Harry offered me his arm, and Mrs. Burnham and Miss Adele shooed us cheerfully out of the store.

SOCIETY NEWS.—**Friday last, Miss Emma Lightfoot, actress and journalist, was sighted in the company of Mr. Harry Brown, rising young Thespian. The pair was**

observed enjoying a spirited excursion of the city of Sacramento. They took a jaunt along Front Street, admiring the steamboats and sailing ships and greeting the arrival of the new "R" Street locomotive, the view of which was a first for Miss Lightfoot They dined at the city's best ice cream parlors and candy stores.

Miss Lightfoot was fashionably garbed in a skirt of pale green, a blouse of fine linen, and a silk shawl. Mr. Brown was dapper, as always. The pair will soon grace the stage of the Forrest Theatre in what is hoped will be a high point of the theatrical season, **Richard III**, starring the Young American Tragedian, Mr. Edwin Booth.

The afternoon's adventure was highlighted by a spin via cabriolet to the neighborhood of Sutter's old fort to pay a call on Miss Lightfoot's dear and loyal friend, Mr. Lem Mule.

—E. R. Lightfoot, Society Ed.

Monday, August 4. *Late afternoon. The Green Room of the Forrest Theatre—*

This is a most congenial spot. We've been rehearsing *Richard III*. The cast is sizable, so actors are always passing through the Green Room between scenes, and I've made some delightful new friends.

Earlier, Mr. Butler and June Booth gathered the actors here. Mr. Butler stood before us, a twinkle in his eye. "I have persuaded some of our patrons, twisted the arms of others, and have gathered enough cash to make loans to the Star Troupe survivors! These funds will get you through the week and allow you to buy back your costumes from Mr. Leach in time for the benefit."

Cries of "Thank heaven!" and "Hallelujah!" rang through the Green Room.

"However," Mr. Butler went on, "I have done the Star Troupe's arithmetic, and the calculations are sobering. *Richard* will surely sell out, but it will bring us only enough to pay off some of the company's debts. Ted shall still have to swim to New York. And so, June, Ted and I propose"—and Mr. Butler paused here to build the suspense—'Edwin Booth's Farewell to the West,' an entire week of performances to take place near the end of the month. Ted shall star in *Hamlet*, and *Richelieu*, *Brutus*, *Macbeth* and a second performance of *Richard III*. It shall be a tour de force—a great tragic role every night!"

"Butler's already at work on this," added June Booth, "and the buzz shall be heard all over Sacramento!"

The excitement at this proposal has lingered in the Green Room through the afternoon. Of course, the true "man of the hour" is Ted Booth. All eyes are upon him. These performances are his chance, not only to bring in cash at the box office, but to make good for the sake of those who have had faith in him—June Booth and Mr. Butler, Mr. Thayer and Mrs. Burnham, and many more of us. It's also his moment to believe in himself. If he feels the weight of these expectations, he has not run from them. At least, not yet. He has carried his burdens with grace and good humor. Most important, he has remained sober. We are all holding our breaths for him, and, so far, so good.

Not long ago, Ted came to Mrs. Burnham and me to offer us our roles in his "Farewell" week. He spoke to me as if I was doing him the favor, instead of the reverse. "Miss Lightfoot, I cannot imagine anyone else as the Player Queen. Please, will you take her on again?"

Of course, I accepted! My roles will be thankfully small, but I shall be in every play but *Brutus*!

Mrs. Burnham was grateful, too, but she held back, asking Ted for time to ponder the engagement. "I want to help, Ted," she said, "but the signs are all about. Maybe I should listen to them--retire and go into a steadier line of work."

"The boardinghouse?"

"Possibly."

Ted shook his head. "I can't see it, Hattie. But it's your choice. Think about it. We can keep your roles open for a few days."

"Thank you, dear Ted," said Mrs. Burnham.

It seemed foolish to me, the idea of turning Ted down, but I tried not to judge Mrs. Burnham. I haven't stood in her shoes, and I'm grateful for it.

I have written once more to my friend Evie, care of Captain Smith in Placerville, as there was no hope of receiving a letter from her in

Downieville. I shall keep my fingers crossed for a happy outcome.

Wednesday, August 6. *Evening. Spencer's Boardinghouse, by the river—*

Last night, Mrs. Burnham and I chose to spend a quiet evening in our accommodations at Ebner's. She was writing letters at the desk in the sitting room, and I had headed for the bedroom to fetch my journal, when there was a rap on the door. "Yes?" called Mrs. Burnham.

"Delivery," announced a muffled voice.

Mrs. Burnham frowned, and cautiously stepped to the door. "I'm not expecting a delivery."

"I'd say it's worth a look."

"Ben Burnham," hissed Mrs. Burnham, "I know that's you, and there is no way in hell that I am opening this door for you. Go away."

"I don't think so. Open up, Hattie."

"No."

"Open up, damn it."

Mrs. Burnham strode calmly over to the desk and resumed her writing. I stood by the bed, clutching my journal and holding my breath for Burnham's next move. For a few seconds, all was silent. Then Mr. Burnham shouted, "I said open up!" He pounded on the door.

Mrs. Burnham took as much of his racket as she could bear, then hollered, "Stop it, Ben!"

He pounded harder.

"You'll wake up the whole hotel!"

"Good!! Now open this door, before I tear it off the hinges!" The banging grew fiercer.

"All right! Just stop. Stop!!" She loosened the bolt and opened the door a crack. "You certainly know how to charm a lady."

"Let me in."

"That's a bad idea, Ben. I have nothing to say to you."

He shoved the door wide, nearly flinging Mrs. Burnham off her feet, and stomped into the room. I retreated into the shadows behind the bed. I could just catch a glimpse of Burnham. "Nice diggins," he growled.

"I want you to go, Ben."

He planted himself on the settee and threw his boots up onto the cushioned brocade. "That's no way to welcome your husband, Hattie. Not when you can afford rooms at Ebner's. You must have turned up a little gold mine to have landed in such luxury."

"I'm living on pawn tickets—you saw to that."

"You're booked at the Forrest. That's the best house in town."

"Ben, if you're here for money, forget it. You can't squeeze blood from a stone."

He shrugged. "All right. I didn't come here to argue. But I reckon I can use a good night's sleep on fancy sheets. I believe I'll share in some of this bounty, sweetheart." He rose, shut the door, and threw the bolt. My heart sank at the sound.

"Get out!"

"Hattie—"

"If it's fancy sheets you want, go find your own. Buy them with what you stole from the rest of us!"

"I didn't steal anything. I protected it."

"You what?"

"Invested it. To keep it out of Leach's hands."

"Where is it?"

Mr. Burnham was silent.

"Where is it, Ben? We could surely use it."

"I don't have it on me."

"Then fetch it tomorrow morning, and we'll straighten everything out with our creditors. Where's it stashed?"

"I'm not telling you."

"Because you don't have it. You don't have it at all. You spent it on cards and whores. That money was our hope—for the company, for a chance to get back east, for *us*—and you threw it away with both hands." Mrs. Burnham's voice crackled with hell fire. It's a wonder Ben Burnham didn't melt and sizzle on the floor. "I don't know why in God's name I ever hitched myself to you, you deceitful son of a bitch!"

Burnham rushed at her and thrust himself right in her face. "You needed me. You needed a driver to drag your damned frills and scenery from one godforsaken hole to another. A wagon and a driver and some muscle to back it up."

"I should have hired it, not married it, for Chrissake."

"Damn right, Hattie. It would have been less of a lie."

"I loved you."

"You never loved me. I was useful for a while, and you wrote yourself the lines to dress it up as something better than it was, but you never loved me the way you loved that milksop Fairchild."

Mrs. Burnham gasped as if she'd been struck in the belly, and then, in a small voice, she pleaded, "He's gone, Ben. He's dead. Leave him be."

"Hell, no. He's been a permanent lodger with us from the day we said, 'I do.' His goddamn ghost slipped in between our sheets every night. Sat there at the breakfast table and sniffed the bacon before it hit my plate. You cheated me, Hattie."

"Go away. I'm tired. Please."

"You owe me."

"What? An apology? Fine. I'm sorry. I didn't love you enough. Now, please go."

"I don't think so. It should be my turn, for once. I'm sick of being your bit player. I want the lead."

"Get away from me. You stink of whiskey."

"I'm your husband, darlin'."

"Don't touch me!"

They struggled—a chair tipped and crashed to the floor. I had few choices—I could rush in and try to take on Burnham myself, which seemed foolish just then; I could dive under the bed, which seemed highly undignified; or I could duck into the wardrobe. I chose the last, squeezing in amongst our new clothes and leaving the door ajar just a crack. The protests and grunts from the sitting room went on until I heard Burnham's boots beating a path into the bedroom and Mrs. Burnham shrieking, "Put me down! Put me down!" He threw her on the bed.

"Stop! Please!" she gasped. "I have money."

He stood over her. "Where?"

"I'll get it. Only, please, back off." He took a step away. She rolled herself off the bed and staggered to the nightstand, facing away from Burnham. She opened the drawer—silver flashed in her hand. Through the crack, I saw her turn and heard the click of the derringer's hammer. "Now, get the hell out of here." She had the same wild look in her eye that she'd had in Downieville.

Mr. Burnham was silent. At last, sweet as honey, he said, "I'm sorry, Hattie. I didn't mean to upset you."

"Well, Ben, you did. I'm very upset."

"I can see that. Suppose I just leave?"

"Suppose you do."

He nodded and headed toward the door. Then, quick as snake, he whirled back and slammed Mrs. Burnham with his fist. She flew against the bedstead as the derringer skittered across the floor toward the wardrobe. Burnham grabbed her, lifted her up, and shook her. She yelped and tried to twist loose.

My moment had come. Without a thought, I stepped out of the wardrobe, seized the gun, and aimed it at Burnham. "I would dearly love to squeeze this trigger," I said, ice in my voice.

Burnham dropped Mrs. Burnham and stared at me, stunned. "What the—?" He looked to Mrs. Burnham and back to me. "Are you hiding understudies in the wardrobe, Hattie?" He took a step my way.

"Don't even try it," I said.

Mrs. Burnham struggled to her feet. "I'd listen if I were you, Ben. She shot a man's ear off outside of Downieville."

He glared at me. I did my best to glare right back. "Like Mrs. Burnham said, get the hell out of here. Move!"

He moved, sure enough, but he moved right at me. He was quick and terribly strong, and he grabbed my hand and squeezed it until I thought the bones would turn to jelly. All I could think was, "Do not let go, *do not*!" And I didn't. I wrestled him like Jacob with the angel. Mrs. Burnham seized a stool and tried to beat him off me. As I feared I might drop to my knees, the derringer exploded in my hand.

There was silence. I looked down, and for all that the room was shadowy, there was clearly a new hole in Mr. Burnham's boot.

"You shot me in the foot," he screeched, as he fell upon the bed. "She shot me!"

Mrs. Burnham dragged herself to my side. "You shot your own damn self," she replied. "If you'd had some manners, you could have saved yourself the trouble."

A fist thundered on the door. "Open up!" a man shouted. "It's the management!" Mrs. Burnham nodded to me, and I hurried to loosen the bolt. The Ebner's desk clerk stood there, a shotgun in his hands. I invited him in, forthwith. "What's going on here?" he demanded.

Mrs. Burnham stepped into the bedroom doorway. "We ladies have been assaulted by a drunkard," she said.

From the room behind her, Ben Burnham wailed out, "That's a lie! They assaulted me! I've been wounded!"

The desk clerk hurried into the bedroom to find Burnham still sprawled upon the bed, hugging his boot. Mrs. Burnham and I followed. "He forced his way in here. He disturbed the peace, he brutalized both of us women, and he damaged hotel property," said Mrs. Burnham.

"I have a right to be here. I'm her husband!" Burnham shouted.

"He's not my husband," I said.

Burnham delivered me the evil eye. "That's the little she-wolf that fired on me."

"I beg to differ," said Mrs. Burnham, cool as steel. "I'm a witness. Mr. Burnham had his hands about the weapon when it fired. He was about to turn it on us when he got his own just desert."

The manager picked up the derringer from the floor. "*This* is the weapon? This toy?" He dismissed Burnham with a snort. Then he turned to me. "Are you all right, young lady?"

"I hope so," I said, trying my best not to sound like a she-wolf. I held out my arm and pulled the sleeve back from my hand and wrist. The skin was already purple from Burnham's grip. "He is not a gentleman," I said.

"I can see that," replied the desk clerk. He looked to Mrs. Burnham's torn clothing and the trickle of blood at the corner of her mouth. Then he shook his head at Burnham and muttered, "You reek like a still." He pointed the shotgun at Burnham's chest. Burnham's eyes widened. "Do you ladies want to press charges? Shall I fetch the sheriff?"

"Not me," said Mrs. Burnham. "I'd like to keep this very quiet, if you don't mind. But I don't know about Miss Lightfoot."

"I can live with that," I said. "For now."

"But I want him out of here," said Mrs. Burnham, with a set to her jaw that brooked no argument.

"We're in agreement," nodded the clerk. "Get up!"

"I'm shot in the damned foot!" Burnham hollered.

"That's a shame," said the clerk. He jabbed at Burnham with the gun barrel. "Now, move!"

Mr. Burnham wisely obliged, though he made it a point to groan all the way to the door and down the hall. Mrs. Burnham slid the bolt and sank onto the settee. "Oh, dear God," she whispered. I made my way to her side. "That was lively."

We sat for a moment, finding our breaths.

"I shot him in the foot," I said, in disbelief.

"Absolutely not," said Mrs. Burnham. " It was his own fault. He's lucky it wasn't worse. Someday, someone will come after him whose aim is true, and the target won't be his foot."

"I still feel awful," I sighed.

"Are you truly all right?" asked Mrs. Burnham.

"I don't know."

"Let me see your hand."

I laid the hand in my lap. Despite its ugly hue, I could still move all my fingers.

"Thank God you were here," said Mrs. Burnham. She put a gentle arm about my shoulders. I felt that too-familiar stinging at the back of my eyes. "My brave Emma," she said.

I was no longer inclined to be brave. I had worn that one out. I surrendered to the tears that I had held back since Emmett's death and I wept, from the deepest corners of my heart. I wept for Mr. Moone and Homer Abell, Mr. Fletcher and the tiny bird, Wing. I wept for Mrs. Burnham's baby Henry and little Zachary Taylor. I sobbed for Emmett and Evangeline. Most of all, I grieved for the comfort of my long-lost mama, for her arms about me, and for their promise that the world could do me no harm.

THURSDAY, AUGUST 8. *Late in the evening. Spencer's parlor—*

Yesterday, the morning after Mr. Burnham's unwelcome visit, Mrs. Burnham awoke at sunrise, a woman with a mission. Before breakfast, she took paper from the little desk and wrote to Ted, June and Mr. Butler, graciously accepting all the roles that she had been offered for Ted's benefit week. Then she urged me to pack up. We stopped at the hotel desk long enough to post the letters and to check out. Though he'd been our ally the night before, the weary desk clerk was relieved to see us go. "Good luck, now, ladies," he nodded. We stepped out onto the street and made our way to the boardinghouse by the river.

When we arrived, Harry Brown and Frank Mayo were in the dining room, still polishing off their toast. When they heard Mrs. Burnham speaking to the landlady, they dashed into the hall, happy as pups to welcome us. They helped us carry our things to our room, a comfortable spot with a wide window and lace curtains. Mrs. Burnham was critical of the dust and the condition of the carpet, but I found the place to be thoroughly pleasant. "It's about time you two started slumming with the rest of us starving actors," said Harry, his mouth still full of toast.

Frank laughed. "They couldn't pass us up any longer! Isn't that true, ladies? You checked in for our superb company."

"In a way, that is true, Frank," said Mrs. Burnham, and she filled them in on the barest details of Mr. Burnham's late-night visit. Frank and Harry were outraged at Burnham and swore to be our guardians and escort us safely to and from the theatre. Mrs. Burnham gave them each a peck on the cheek. "Thank you, boys," she said, "and Frank, I'll take you up on your offer right now. I have an errand to run. Can you come along, while Harry keeps Miss Lightfoot company?"

"I surely can," said Frank. "Where to?"

"To an attorney," said Mrs. Burnham. "I am filing for divorce!"

By the time we convened for rehearsal, word of our adventure had spread through the company. Ted arrived with a bouquet of white roses and, to my surprise, laid them in my arms. "I heard you were a heroine last night, Emma," he said. "How's your hand?"

I held it out. "Not bad. The swelling's already disappearing."

He lifted the hand and gently kissed it. "That's to make it better," he said. It was almost worth the injury to receive the cure!

Today was our dress rehearsal for *Richard III*. Ted was at the mirror in his dressing room, waiting to start Act I, when June Booth stepped behind him, lifted a crown, and set it on his brow. "This is yours now, Ted," he said. "You've earned it." It was their father's *Richard III* crown, which the old actor had given to June, as his eldest son. At first, Ted could not speak. Then he rose, embraced the smiling June, and whispered, "Thank you, brother." During the rehearsal, I watched from the wings the scene where Richard is offered England's crown. Though it is a stage property of gilt and paste jewels, Ted grasped the diadem as if it was the dearest thing on earth.

While we women were dressing, I turned to Hattie Burnham for her opinion on how to braid my hair. "Mrs. B—" I began,

She cut me right off. "Stop, stop. Emma Lightfoot, this is the last time you will call me 'Mrs.' I have no right to that title from you—I am no longer your employer, nor your superior in any way. I am your elder, yes, but that is one fact I do not need to be reminded of. And, as for Burnham, I'm through with that appellation. I'm re-baptizing myself Carpenter this very minute. Harriet Carpenter. Hattie, to you. May I call you Emma? In moments of other than extreme crisis?"

"Of course!" I replied, "Of course you may—Hattie." For the rest of the rehearsal, though we were performing the bloodiest of tragedies, I found myself smiling in the wings.

SATURDAY, AUGUST 9. *By the window of our room at Spencer's. Early afternoon.* Richard III *opens tonight!—*

I can now pen this memorial:

THE LIGHTFOOT FAMILY

Hattie assured Ted, as she embraced him on the muddy riverbank, that their ghosts would forgive them. But I have found it a trial to forgive my ghosts—Emmett, for exiting this world so carelessly; my sweet mother, for "losing" herself; and all those little brothers and sisters for vanishing under the earth before I even had the chance to know them. Perhaps they have also found it hard to forgive me. I have cheated Death and refused to journey with them into darkness.

I have struggled to write my family a proper obituary because I could not salvage the memories to paint their pictures clearly. Yet I could not have wept for them so deeply if I did not know them in my heart. Emmett promised on his deathbed, "I will always be with you," and so he is. So are they all. They're in my blood and my bones, in my hands and the color of my eyes. They're in the way I admire a deep blue sky streaked with high clouds. I must trust that I am not solitary, that my family's love floats along with me as I step through life. And I must believe in this simple truth—that they did the best they could. We all did the best we could. I couldn't save Emmett, and my parents couldn't save themselves for my sake. But it wasn't for lack of trying, or for lack of love.

If I cannot honor my family in the words of an obituary, I can do so in the way I live from day to day. This is easier said than done—life is not for the faint of heart—but it is the best I can offer. And I can take the affection that they would have hoped to give to me and pass it on to others who, whether blood family or not, yearn for love. One needn't be kin to be family. Perhaps some of my "new" family are already in this world, only waiting to be found. Perhaps I can even allow myself the tiny hope of a "posterity!" You never know. "Chase your dreams!" said C. E. Lightfoot, and sometimes he was on the money.

—Emma Lightfoot

Sunday, August 10. *About 10 p.m. In our room—*

We opened *Richard III* last night. It was what they call a "resounding success!" Sacramento was Edwin Booth's friend, and he deserved its friendship. Backstage, he had been nervous, pacing and trying to breathe, but once before the footlights, he never faltered. He had new confidence and caught effortlessly (or so it seemed!) all the shades of a man possessed by power. I reckon he had a right to Richard's crown.

Of course, Hattie was beautifully tragic, and Mr. Thayer is a man of many faces, able to play almost any role. And Harry, and Frank—well, I could go on and on. As for me, I remembered my words and did not fall down upon my entrance. I am making progress!

Before the play, as I made up at the mirror, a musical voice called out to me, "Emma, dear!" There, in the doorway, stood Sophie Griffith. She was pale, and thinner, but full of genuine good wishes. She was still staying with her friends and was taking a little "vacation" from the stage. By her side was another young man—not her usual burly flirtation, but a sober fellow with spectacles and good manners. Sophie pressed a gift wrapped with a lavender ribbon into my hand—a tortoiseshell comb, it turned out—before they went off into the house to claim their seats.

Tom Bell was not in the auditorium this night—I actually listened for his lunatic hoot and was grateful for its absence. After the play, as we were shedding our costumes, I said to Hattie, half-joking, "No pink roses tonight!"

"No," she said, staring solemnly into her mirror. "There won't be any more pink roses."

"Are you sure?"

"Quite. I had a letter from Frisbie yesterday. A Vigilance Committee caught up with Tom Bell, right outside of Nevada."

"Oh," was all I could reply, although I should have been glad. He was an outlaw.

"Tom stepped over the line," Hattie went on. "He and his gang killed a woman and two men in a robbery. Frisbie said the sheriff arrived to find Tom dangling from a tree. He was still decked in his boiler plate."

"Then we've heard the last of that crazy laugh," I said. "Are you relieved?"

"I suppose so.... He was a sweet young man, once—but that was a lifetime ago."

This morning, those of us residing at Spencer's slept in, and then we celebrated with a scrumptious dinner in the afternoon. Mrs. Spencer, it seems, once "trod the boards" herself and is pleased to have theatre folk about. So, a number of the cast members gathered in her dining room to feast on chicken pot pie and apple fritters and laugh at the funny stories that flew about the table.

Just before dusk, Mr. Thayer and Hattie departed for a walk along the river. He had had a new grey coat tailored, and she wore one of Adele's gowns. As they strolled off, arm in arm, they made a handsome couple. Ulysses, freshly bathed and proudly sporting a new collar, trotted happily behind them.

Presently, some of the other cast members headed off for their lodgings, but Ted, Harry and Frank determined they would go out on the town. "Come along with us, Emma," they tempted me. "It's a nice night. No time to sit in your room, scribbling in that opus of yours." In the end, I could not resist them. I was, I confess, a bit worried about what they might get us into, as all three had been "bad boys" on occasion. But I needn't have fretted. All of them were gentlemen—albeit lively, funny, gentlemen—and the wickedest thing that crossed anyone's lips that evening was lemon phosphate. The sunset was glorious, the stars a sparkling canopy, and the breeze off the water made one grateful to be alive. As we ambled the streets of the city, people stared my way, and I realized, with some amazement, that I was escorted by three of the handsomest men in Sacramento. Who could have ever imagined?

THURSDAY, AUGUST 14. *9 p.m. Our room—*

Earlier this evening, I was relaxing in the parlor with a copy of the *San Francisco Call*, skimming the advertisements in the back pages, when my eye was caught by a small column of out-of-state news. A few sentences told of a theatre accident in Klamath Falls, up Oregon way. A fairy star was "lost in flames" after her hem was set ablaze by the footlights. Her name was Laura Larson, and she was memorialized for "a sweetness of voice" and "eyes of the deepest blue."

There are dozens, perhaps hundreds, of fairy stars about with pleasing voices and blue eyes. Louise may already be safely in the East, nestled in the arms of watchful relatives. I hope so with all my heart. But if Laura Larson was our La Petite, she was truly "lost" long ago.

I shall keep this to myself for now. I cannot see how it would help Ted or Hattie or any of the others to contemplate it.

Saturday, August 16. *After rehearsal. The writing table in our room—*

At long last, I have received a letter from Captain Avery Smith in Placerville. I copy some of it here:

> *I regret that I did not respond to you sooner, Miss Emma. As the Post Office burned in the recent fire, it took some time for your letters to find me. Once they did, I confess, I set them aside, as I was without a roof over my head. But now, a new stable has arisen from the rubble, and life has commenced once more.*
>
> *I was pleased to hear of your adventures, and that your old Lem has served you well. On occasion, stories have happy endings, even for ancient mules.*
>
> *I wish I could write of a joyful conclusion for Evangeline. Neither she nor her Sparky have been seen since the conflagration. The Red House was back in business within a day of its demise, but Miss Alice reports that she has not laid eyes on Evie since she and the girls dashed away from the flames. Evangeline and her little dog have vanished.*
>
> *I shall keep your letters to her, in case she appears again in these parts. Mrs. Gee sends her affection but reminds you to "Get cash*

up front!" with theatre people. I send my own good wishes as well, Miss Emma.

With best regards,
Capt. Avery Smith

I grieve that Evie is nowhere to be found. Yet, I choose to hope that she is not lost, but is simply on her own journey, as I have been. When the time is right, we shall find each other. Someday, on some street, somewhere, a thin girl with brown curls and a little dog tucked under her arm will come my way. We'll catch each other's eyes, and there shall be a sweet reunion.

WEDNESDAY, AUGUST 20. *The small hours of the morning. The parlor at Spencer's—*

I cannot sleep. My mind is spinning.

We opened Hamlet tonight, the first of Mr. Booth's five "farewell" performances leading up to his benefit. Right before the curtain rose, excitement sparked about the theatre! I watched as much of the performance as I could from the wings. Ted Booth was so fine, he inspired everyone else to go beyond their best. The audience applauded throughout the performance—we had to hold our lines until the thunder had passed, simply to be heard.

Before my first entrance, I passed Ted in the hall backstage. "Emma!" he whispered, and then he delivered a kiss to my forehead! My heart raced, and my cheeks began to burn with delight. "Break a leg," he said.

I could manage only a breathy, "Thank you. The same to you!" before he hurried off into the wings.

Ted's Hamlet is so handsome and soulful that a part of me wishes I was Ophelia lying in her grave, just so he would leap in there and swear he loved me.

When the curtain fell on the last scene, the cast scrambled in the darkness to find the entrances for our bows. I ran through the wings so I would not be late, but I was as blind as a bat without my specs. As I rounded a painted flat, I collided smack into one of the actors. He put his arms about me and kissed me, right on the lips! It was a real kiss, and a lovely one! All I could think was, "Ted!"—first with delight and then, suddenly, with fear, the kind that strikes quickly and leaves you shivering.

I needn't have worried. I stepped back, and it was not Ted who smiled at me. It was Harry Brown. A very handsome, very happy Harry Brown. I kissed him right back, and the second kiss was even sweeter than the first.

In the end, love is a mystery. I wish that I had Evie by my side to help me unravel the tangle of my heart. Sometimes I can hardly stand in the same room as Ted Booth without my pulse racing, while I am as comfortable as a cat with Harry. Are my feelings for Ted infatuation? And for Harry, affection?

Perhaps I love Ted for the magic he can work on the stage. I love the actor. Not that Ted isn't a good, kind man, but there's a dark place in his soul that can eddy down like a whirlpool and take a girl that loves him with it—or, at least, make her shiver at the thought.

Harry Brown is a fine actor, too, and he knows what suffering is. But there is a sunshine in Harry's nature that buoys me up in my own black moments, and helps us both to rise above the bumpiest parts of life's road. Not to mention that, when he kissed me, I felt beautiful—and I still do, hours later, even if I cannot sleep.

Sunday, August 24. *Early afternoon. The bench on Spencer's porch—*

My companions and I have been speculating on where to cast our lots once Ted has finished his "farewell." Mr. Thayer says he's comfortable staying with his friends out by the fort, although, when he glances Hattie's way, he's quick to add that he'd be game for any opportunity, anywhere. Frank Mayo flirts with the idea of following Lola Montez east, although Hattie tries to dissuade him and keep him safely in California. And Hattie seems to have abandoned her boardinghouse plans, at least for the time being, for she speaks of acting jobs in one town or another.

As for me, Harry Brown has invited me to go to San Francisco with him. I hesitated, at first, because of Lem. Fortunately, Harry took no umbrage at being denied for the sake of a mule. He understood, and he reminded me that mules can take passage on steamboats just as humans can. He swears his father would be as pleased to buy a ticket for our "friend" Lem, as he would be to book passage for us.

So—perhaps I shall go to San Francisco and see the Pacific Ocean! I would be a guest in Harry's parents' house and meet all six of his sisters. Harry promises that they will coo over me as a bevy of quail might coo over a chick. I'm not sure that I wish to be thought of once again as poultry, but, if his sisters are as lively and smart as Harry, their company would be a delight.

I now have enough change in my pocket to purchase new spectacles, so, wherever I wind up, I shall be able to see the leaves on the trees and the stars in the sky. Huzzah!

Ted Booth's week of "farewell" performances has been the talk of the town. He has been disciplined, and unflagging, and sober, and deservedly built the audience's excitement to last night's Richelieu, his benefit performance. The house was overflowing, and the applause as Ted took his bow boomed like the sea. One of the city's leading citizens ran up onto the stage and delivered Ted Sacramento's gift—a gold pin in the shape of a hand, clasping a diamond between the thumb and forefinger.

I was saddened when the curtain dropped last night, partly because it meant Ted would soon depart. However, the unsinkable Mr. Butler has announced one more benefit performance—a final, final farewell!—for Monday next. Mr. Booth shall play Iago in Othello! Miss Lightfoot shall play a lady-in-waiting! And the rest of my companions shall fill Spencer's with cheer for a few days more.

In The Union's "Amusements" section this morning was another happy announcement—Professor Wilson is in Sacramento! The Glory has been resurrected and will soon grace our skies!

TUESDAY, SEPTEMBER 2. *Spencer's. Just before sunset—*

I have packed most of my things in my new valise for the morning's departure, but I must write before I tuck my journal away. I HAVE ASCENDED! No—even better—WE have ascended!

Othello played last night, and Ted was a splendid Iago. Once again, the house was packed to the rafters with well-wishers, and this time, as he took his bow, his admirers handed him an elegant, gilt-and-leather bound volume of Shakespeare's works—just the sort that Hattie had imagined adorning her boardinghouse parlor.

This morning, early, some of us took Ted to breakfast to bid him farewell face to face and to celebrate the success we hope awaits him. He accepted our good wishes with shy pleasure, although he finally begged, "Stop, now, stop. Please, or I shall cry into my coffee!"

After breakfast, we walked him to the waterfront, where a smart little steamboat puffed away at the dock. Every actor in Sacramento turned out, and a multitude of fans—the blushing girls who crowd the stage door, the leading citizens, the grocers and blacksmiths who simply enjoy a good show. The theatre musicians played merrily, accompanied by shouted felicitations. Ted turned to us and gave each of us our final goodbye. As he hugged Hattie and me, he murmured, "Sweet ladies, you have given me life and living!"

The steamboat whistle sounded, and, from the rail, the captain gestured Ted to come aboard. Ted frowned. "June," he said, "have you seen Butler this morning?"

June Booth shook his head. "He should have been here ages ago."

"He has the proceeds from last night's benefit. He promised to bring them by before the boat left."

"I can send someone to his house, but it's a far piece from here."

"Maybe the captain will stand by for a few minutes." Ted ran up the gangplank and, quickly, was in earnest conversation with the man. The captain appeared sympathetic, but, in the end, he shook his head.

"Damn," muttered June.

Ted threw his hands into the air and was about to disembark, when we heard shouts of, "Wait! Wait! Hold that boat!"

It was Butler, fighting his way through the crowd. He was panting, his face red as an apple. He nigh unto fell into June's arms, as a messenger in a play might collapse after dashing through the enemy lines.

"What happened to you?" said June.

"I couldn't get a cab! They're all here! Every cab in the city was commandeered by Ted's admirers!" Butler gasped. "I had to run all the way across town!"

"Well, don't stop now," said June. He took Butler by the arm and hustled him up the gangplank.

"Butler!" Ted exclaimed. Butler stumbled over and handed Ted the pouch of cash. Ted threw an arm about his shoulders. They turned to face the throng on the wharf and took a laughing bow, as the crowd went crazy. Then the boat's whistle blew, Butler hastily descended, and, waving to us all, Ted made his exit from Sacramento. Harry and I watched the steamboat glide downriver, until the last puff of her chimneys had vanished from view. Pieces of our hearts journeyed with her.

Harry offered me his arm, and we started off along the river front. "Where to?"

"Back to Spencer's," I replied. "First."

"First?"

"Umm-hmm. I have plans for the rest of the morning."

"Oh," said Harry. The bounce went out of his step. "All right. I guess I'll see you later, then."

"All right," I said. "Unless you want to be included."

"Of course!"

"Good! Then we need to hurry. Professor Wilson's casting off at ten a.m. sharp! We'll have to take Lem—Mr. Thayer left him hitched behind the house."

Harry stopped and frowned. "Emma—"

"Umm-hmm?"

"Do you plan to cheer Wilson on from down below, or to—"

"Ascend?"

"Yes."

"Ascend, of course. I was hoping you might be game, too."

"Oh, God. Aren't you afraid we'll wind up in the river?"

"A little. But I'm more afraid that I'll never get the chance to fly. Besides, I can't believe fate would dump us into the Sacramento after everything else we've been through."

"Fate does anything it damn well pleases."

I took his hand, the one that was most healed. "Listen, Harry, just come along with me, and stay on the ground. I'll be so much braver if you're there to send me off."

"Emma, I can't let you go up there alone."

"Sure you can. I can take care of myself."

"You think I'm afraid."

"No. I know you're a hero."

"I'm simply being sensible—"

"Oh, me, too. You know me, Harry, I'm a very sensible girl. But this is one time when it's worth it to take the risk, don't you see?"

He shook his head, but he was smiling. "I see that I'm about to fly. It's unnatural, and it's lunatic, and I'm about to launch myself into the heavens."

"Thank you!" I pulled a cardboard stub from my reticule.

"Here's your ticket!"

"You already have tickets?"

"One. I knew if I waited until the last minute, we'd never get on board, so I bought a ticket yesterday."

"Only one?"

"Of course. Remember? Ladies are free!"

The ascension was to take place south of town, in an open field. Harry and I squeezed the both of us onto Lem, and we hastened away. We arrived in the nick of time. Beyond Professor Wilson's bright banner hovered the Glory, straining at her ropes. The field swarmed with spectators, and a crowd of hopeful passengers pressed about the balloon. Harry and I tied Lem in the shade of an oak, and, grasping our ticket, hurried to the front of the line.

"Hello, young lady!" exclaimed Professor Wilson. "You made it! Come aboard!"

We climbed up into the big basket, joining a handful of other intrepid souls. Soon, all was ready. Professor Wilson delivered his speech to the crowd. As applause rang through the field, he hustled into the basket and secured its wicker gate.

His assistants loosed the ropes, and the Glory sprang free of the earth, shooting upward. My stomach flipped, and I laughed, "Jehosaphat's cat!" I peered down over the edge of the basket, and there was Lem, grazing in the shade and growing tinier by the second. A flock of birds darted beneath us, then veered away, spooked by this huge creature that loosed "ooh's" and "ah's" into their sky.

To the north of us lay the city, the ribbon of her waterfront bustling with miniature wagons and toy ships. "Harry!" I said, "There's the Forrest!"

"Could be," he replied. "And maybe Spencer's, way over there by the water. And, look, Emma—can you make it out? The fort!"

As we lifted higher, we spied the gleaming curves of the American River, where it finished its long journey from the mountains and poured itself into the Sacramento. And below this confluence, the broad Sacramento flowed, glistening, past the city, then wound toward the sea. It was dotted with water craft. In particular, one minuscule ship caught my eye. "Harry," I cried, "look—that boat with the steam trailing from the chimney, downriver there! Is that Ted's ship?"

"Maybe!"

"Hey, Ted!" I waved, and Harry joined in. "Howdy, Ted, howdy!" we yelled, like a couple of crazy people, until the other passengers joined in the fun, too. Maybe it was the thin atmosphere up there that made us all so silly.

Suddenly, we hit a bumpy patch of air. "Hold on, ladies and gents!" hollered Professor Wilson. I pitched about, but I quickly gripped the nearest rope. Harry wound his arm securely about my waist.

"I don't want you flying away from me yet, Cinder-Emma," he smiled.

"No," I replied, and I leaned in toward him. I fit perfectly under his arm.

Far to the east, we could see the Sierras, snow still clinging to their highest peaks. To the west, lay a gentler range of hills. "Over there, Emma," said Harry, "beyond that low spot in the mountains, is the bay, and then, across that, San Francisco, and then—the ocean itself!"

By now, the wind had calmed, and the Glory's ride had become as smooth as silk. We floated up there in the heavens, a pair of angels. "I believe I shall go with you, Harry," I said. "I would love to see the ocean."

"Truly?" said Harry, and then he shouted, "Hurrah!" He turned about. "She's going with me!" he exclaimed to Professor Wilson and the other passengers. "To San Francisco! Hallelujah!"

The passengers cheered, and Professor Wilson gave us a wide smile—although I expect he's accustomed to happiness erupting at the higher elevations.

Harry stepped to my side, wrapped both arms about me, and delivered me one of his lovely kisses. The wind gently wafted the balloon away from the city and out over golden fields and woodlands. The world, for this moment, was ours. There it lay before us, shining and glorious, only waiting for our next adventure to begin. Who could hope for more?

—Emma Rose Lightfoot

ACKNOWLEDGMENTS

Every bit of art is an act of faith. My deep thanks to those who offered hands and hearts as I journeyed to bring FIERY STAR to the page:

Kelley Weir, Charmaine Fujioka, Karen Lewis, Virginia Drake and Michael Wells-Oakes, dear friends and theatre buddies, who were the wind beneath my wings from FIERY STAR'S beginnings.

The Sierra Muses, especially Jenifer Bliss, Mila Johansen and Shirley DicKard, angels of encouragement.

Sands Hall and Tanya Egan Gibson, most insightful editors.

Those who so generously shared with me their own experiences as writers and independent publishers: Jack Saunders, Maria Brower, Kevin McKeon, Patricia Dove Miller, and Betsy Graziani Fasbinder .

Kim Culbertson, an inspiration.

Joyce Keating of JRK Literary for her belief in FIERY STAR.

Julie Valin, with her creativity, perseverance. and good cheer.

My theatre family, with their comradeship and great stories.

My aunt, Helene Rivers, a pioneering San Francisco newspaperwoman, who welcomed me to the "Chron" as a child, to a world where copy flew overhead through pneumatic tubes, and my name magically appeared printed backward on a bit of lead.

Professor Robi Sarlos, who decades ago suggested, "Why don't you write that paper about the frontier theatre?" He piled some books into my arms and sent me off to do research that I'm still wrapping up.

The Rivers family. Like the Lightfoots, we all did the best we could.

ABOUT THE AUTHOR

LESLIE RIVERS is a writer, actress, director, and teacher, and she thinks herself lucky to have made her life in the theatre. When she was in her teens, she acted in a production of *Bus Stop*, staged in an old, 19th century hall. Beyond the rear of the building was the American River, smelling sweetly of sand and willow and a stone's throw from the spot where the California Gold Rush began—a cradle for what would one day be her novel, *Fiery Star*.

Leslie went on to earn her B.A. in Dramatic Art at UC, Davis, and her M.F.A. in Acting from Stanford. After graduation, she waved her family farewell, traveled to the Midwest to perform in summer stock, and then journeyed on to New York City, where she was based for the next five years, acting in Manhattan and regional theatres. At last, she began to long for California. Like Dorothy in the Emerald City, she clicked her ruby slippers and headed home. While continuing to act, direct and write for the professional theatre, she also became a university professor in the Los Angeles area, where amongst her students she found wonderful future directors, teachers and actors, including Academy Award winners.

Leslie now resides in the foothills of California's Sierra Nevada Mountains, where she and her daughter enjoy the wild turkeys and deer who amble through their yard.

For more, visit *www.leslieannrivers.com.*

Made in the USA
San Bernardino, CA
25 November 2018